Emile Zola

THE CONQUEST OF PLASSANS

Translation and introduction:
Ernest Alfred Vizetelly

Mondial

Mondial
New York · Berlin

Emile Zola: The Conquest of Plassans
(French original title: "La Conquête de Plassans")

Translation, introduction:
Ernest Alfred Vizetelly

ISBN 1-59569-048-4
ISBN 978-1-59569-048-7

Library of Congress Control Number: 2005936824

Cover painting: Uday K. Dhar

www.mondialbooks.com

Emile Zola

The Conquest of Plassans

French Literature
published by Mondial:

Emile Zola: The Fortune of the Rougons
(ISBN 1-59569-010-7 / 978-1-59569-10-4)

Emile Zola: A Love Episode
(ISBN 1-59569-027-1 / ISBN 978-1-59569-027-2)

Emile Zola: The Fat and the Thin
(a.k.a. The Belly of Paris)
(ISBN 1-59569-052-2 / ISBN 978-1-59569-052-4)

Emile Zola: Abbé Mouret's Transgression
(a.k.a. The Sin of the Abbé Mouret)
(ISBN 1-59569-050-6 / ISBN 978-1-59569-050-0)

Emile Zola: The Dream
(ISBN 1-59569-049-2 / ISBN 978-1-59569-049-4)

Emile Zola: Doctor Pascal
(ISBN 1-59569-051-4 / ISBN 978-1-59569-051-7)

Emile Zola: Fruitfulness
(ISBN 1-59569-018-2 / 978-1-59569-018-0)

Victor Hugo: The Man Who Laughs
(a.k.a. By Order of the King)
(ISBN 1-59569-013-1 / 978-1-59569-013-5)

Victor Hugo: History of a Crime
(ISBN 1-59569-020-4 / 978-1-59569-020-3)

Honoré de Balzac: Maître Cornelius
(ISBN 1-59569-017-4 / 978-1-59569-017-3)

Anatole France: Penguin Island
(ISBN 1-59569-029-8 / 978-1-59569-029-6)

INTRODUCTION

With the end of the century there has come in France a great revival of the struggle between religion and free thought which has so long been waged there; and the stupendous effort put forth by the Roman Catholic Church to annihilate the Third Republic has placed the country in a condition of unrest such as it has only known on the eve of its chief Revolutions. Behind the notorious Dreyfus case, behind the shouts of 'Long live the army!' and 'Death to the Jews!' behind all the so-called Nationalism and Militarism, the Church has been steadily, incessantly working, ever fanning the flames of discord, ever promoting and fostering coalitions of malcontents, by whose help it hopes to recover its old-time paramountcy. Time alone can reveal the outcome of this great effort, this 'forlorn hope' assault upon institutions which have hitherto kept Catholicism in check and tended so largely to the diffusion of free thought; but personally I am inclined to think, with all due allowance for partial successes achieved here and there, that this Clerical movement, however skillfully engineered under the cloak of patriotism, and however lavishly financed by the bulk of the money derived from the Lourdes 'miracles,' over which the Assumptionist Fathers preside, and the offerings of zealots throughout the country, will ultimately result in failure, for France is not at heart a religious country, and when faith, has departed from a nation can it be restored?

The meaning of the Clerical movement to which I have referred is twofold. In the first place there is the perfectly natural and legitimate desire of the French Catholics to recover lost ascendency; and in the second place there is the conviction of the Vatican and the French episcopate generally that France is the only country which under favourable circumstances might be in a position to restore the temporal power of the Holy See. In that respect the Pope can hope for nothing from Spain or Austria or the Catholic States of Germany. In France rests the sole hope of the Papacy; and thus on political as well as religious grounds the establishment of a Catholic *régime* in place of the present-day free-thought Republic is the one great dream of those who direct the fortunes of the Holy Roman and Apostolic Church.

All who know anything of modern history are aware that in 1849 a French army overthrew the Roman Republic and reinstated Pius IX. in possession of the so-called patrimony of St. Peter, and that in after years, until France indeed was vanquished at Sedan, the presence of

French forces alone enabled the Pope to continue in the exercise of his territorial sway. Both the Royalist reactionaries who sat in the National Assembly of the Second Republic, and the Prince-President of that time, afterwards Napoleon III., lent support to Pius IX., and in return expected to receive the countenance and help of the French clergy in their various designs upon France. But the clergy always seeks its own ends, and more than once its policy varied, now being in favour of the Royalists and now in favour of Louis Napoleon, according as it seemed likely to secure greater benefits from one or the other.

Even when the contest for supremacy was over, when the Republic had been murdered at the Coup d'Etat, and the hopes of the Count de Chambord had been destroyed by the triumph of Napoleon the Little, the clergy did not give unqualified support to the new government. True, on the 1st of January, 1852, Monseigneur Sibour, Archbishop of Paris, officiated at a solemn 'Te Deum' at Notre Dame in honour of the triumph of a bribed and drunken soldiery over the defenders of the Constitution; but Louis Napoleon had scarcely become Emperor before a large section of the clergy began to protest that the new *régime* was by no means sufficiently Clerical. The course adopted in these circumstances was very characteristic and significant. An education law had been passed in 1850, giving many privileges and advantages to the clergy, such indeed as they had not possessed since the downfall of Charles X. But comparative liberty in educational matters was more than the French episcopate, eager for domination as the price of its adhesion to imperialism, could willingly allow, and before long a celebrated and remarkably well written newspaper, 'L'Univers,' initiated a campaign against the Empire, taking as its standpoint that the Pope was the virtual sovereign of the world, and that everything must be subservient to the interests of the Roman Church. Half the French episcopate actively supported the view which followed, i.e. that the education of the young ought to be entirely under priestly control, the priests being the vicars of the Pope, even as he (the Pope) was the vicar of the Deity. There were some curious and even amusing incidents in the course of that now forgotten campaign. For instance, it was actually proposed to abolish the study of the Greek and Latin classics in France, a suggestion which many of the Bishops vigorously upheld, though others of a scholarly turn pleaded plaintively in favour of Horace and a few others, whose writings, if edited in a Christian spirit, might yet, they thought, be allowed among young men of proved morality!

With the educational controversy many political matters soon became blended. The Italian revolutionaries were at that time doing their utmost to frighten Napoleon III. into fulfilment of his early promises respecting the liberation of Italy; and the Vatican, anxious for the maintenance of the old order of things, since any change must help on its own fall, made desperate efforts to prevent the interference of France in Italian affairs, unless indeed it were for the consolidation of the Papal power. Even as in recent times the Assumptionist Fathers have intrigued for the overthrow of the Third Republic, so did the Société de St. Vincent de Paul—which nominally was a mere charitable organisation—seek to turn the Empire into a priestly *régime,* or in default thereof to overthrow it. The position of Napoleon III. was the more difficult since his own wife, the Empress Eugénie, acted as the Vatican's spy and agent. Matters at last reached such a pass that the Emperor's Minister, Billault, had on the one hand to prohibit political allusions in sermons, under pain of fine and imprisonment, and on the other to break up and scatter the intriguing religious societies. Nevertheless the Empire's position remained a difficult one to the very last, and Napoleon III. was often sorely puzzled how to steer a safe course between the claims of the Pope and the clergy and the aspirations of Italy and its well-wishers; to say nothing of the views of all those who, thinking of France alone, by no means approved of priestly power in politics.

It is on the state of affairs to which I have alluded, the hostility of a part of the French clergy to the Empire in its earlier years, that M. Zola has based his novel, ' The Conquest of Plassans.' The priests, subservient to the Vatican, lead the town into a course of opposition against imperial institu-tions, and the Government then despatches thither an impe-cunious and unscrupulous priest, one Abbé Faujas, for the purpose of winning it back again. Such tactics were not infrequently employed at that time. Whilst a part of the clergy simply followed its own inclinations, others venally took pay from the Empire to do its dirty work. As often as not they subsequently betrayed their paymaster, using the positions into which they were thrust for the satisfaction of their personal ambition. Still, for a while these needy hangers-on at the Ministry of Public Worship proved useful allies, and the Empire was only too ready to employ them. It will be seen, then, that the theme chosen by M. Zola rests upon historical fact, and it may be taken that his story embodies incidents which actually occurred under such conditions as those that I have described.

The 'Conquest of Plassans' may well be read in conjunction with 'The Fortune of the Rougons,' M. Zola's earlier work, as the scene in both instances is the same, and certain personages, such as Félicité Rougon and Antoine Macquart, figure largely in both books. In the earlier volume we see the effect of the Coup d'Etat in the provinces, almost every incident being based upon historical fact. For instance, Miette, the heroine of 'The Fortune of the Rougons,' had a counterpart in Madame Ferrier, that being the real name of the young woman who, carrying the insurgents' blood-red banner, was hailed by them as the 'Goddess of Liberty' on their dramatic march. And in like way the tragic death of Silvère, linked to another hapless prisoner, was founded by M. Zola on an incident that followed the rising, as recorded by an eyewitness.[1] Amidst all the bloodshed, the Rougons, in M. Zola's narrative, rise to fortune and power, and Plassans (really Aix-en-Provence) bows down before them. But time passes, the revolt of the clergy supervenes, by their influence the town chooses a Royalist Marquis as deputy, and it becomes necessary to conquer it once again.

Abbé Faujas, by whom this conquest is achieved on behalf of the Empire, is, I think, a strongly conceived character, perhaps the most real of all the priests that are scattered through M. Zola's books. I do not say this because he happens to be anything but a good man. M. Zola has sketched more than one good priest in his novels, as, for instance, Abbé Rose in 'Paris;' but in this one, Faujas, there is more genuine flesh and blood than in all the others. True, his colleagues, Bourrette and Fenil, are admirably suggested; the Bishop, too, an indolent prelate who surrenders the government of his diocese to his vicar-general, and spends his time in translating Horace (for he is one of the few who favour the classics), leaves on one an impression of reality; yet no other priestly creation of M. Zola's pen can to my thinking vie with the stern, chaste, authoritative, ambitious Faujas, the man who subdues Plassans, and who wrecks the home of the Mouret family, with whom he lives.

Leading parts in the story are assigned to Mouret and his wife Marthe, both of whom are extremely interesting figures. The genesis of the former's career and fate is contained in one of M. Zola's short stories, 'Histoire d'un Fou,' which he contributed to the Paris 'Evène-

[1] See Eugène Tenot's 'La Province en Décembre 1851,' Paris, 1865 (pp. 206 et seq., and 260 et seq.). Also Maquan's 'L'Insurrection du Var,' p. 127.

ment' before he took to book writing. The idea, so skillfully worked out, is that of a man who, although perfectly sane, is generally believed to be mad, and who by force of being thus regarded does ultimately lose his wits. In Marthe, his wife, the grand-daughter of a mad woman, we find the hereditary flaw turning to hysteria, in a measure of a religious character, such as subsequently becomes manifest in her son Serge, the chief character of 'Abbé Mouret's Transgression,' which work proceeds directly from 'The Conquest of Plassans.'

In the latter book, as in 'The Fortune of the Rougons,' M. Zola skillfully depicts all the life of a French provincial town such as it was half a century or so ago, and in this respect he has simply drawn upon his own recollections of Aix, where he spent so many years of his boyhood. Much that he records might be applied to such towns even nowadays, for electric lighting, and tramcars, and motor-cars, and increased railway facilities, have made little change in provincial society. There are still rival *salons* and *coteries* and petty jealousies and vanities all at work; and if new parties have succeeded old ones, their intrigues have remained of much the same description as formerly. The many provincials who in M. Zola's narrative gravitate around the chief characters are pleasantly and skillfully diversified, and seem very life-like with their foibles and ' fads ' and rivalries and ambitions. Possibly the most interesting are the Paloques, husband and wife, whom envy, hatred and all uncharitableness incessantly consume. Again, Madame Faujas, the priest's mother, is a finely-drawn character, but perhaps the failings of her daughter Olympe, and of Trouche, Olympe's husband, verge slightly upon caricature. As for old Rose, the Mourets' servant, though her ways are very amusing, and the part she plays in the persecution of her master renders her an indispensable personage in the narrative, it may be pointed out that she is virtually the same woman who has done duty half a dozen times in M. Zola's books—for instance, as Martine in 'Dr. Pascal,' as Véronique in 'The Joy of Life,' and so forth. It is rather curious, indeed, that M. Zola, so skilful in portraying diversity of character and disposition among his other personages, should have clung so pertinaciously to one sole type of an old servant-woman.

It is not my purpose here to analyse in detail the plot of 'The Conquest of Plassans,' but, having dealt at some length with the historical incidents on which the work is based, it is as well that I should point out that politics are not obtruded upon the reader in M. Zola's pages. Indeed, the book largely deals with quite another matter, that of 'the priest in the house,' showing as it does how the Mourets' home was wrecked by the combined action of the Faujases and the Trouches. In this connection the dolorous career of the unhappy Marthe is very vividly pictured. A fairly contented wife and mother at the outset of the story, she is won over to religion by Faujas, whose purpose is to utilise her as an instrument for the furtherance of his political and social schemes. But religion for her becomes a mysticism full of unrealisable yearnings, for she expects to taste the joys of Heaven even upon earth. Carried away by her religious fervour, she soon neglects her home; and her husband, it must be admitted, takes anything but the right course to win her back. She begins to loathe him and to indulge in an insane passion for the priest by whom she is spurned. Then hysteria masters her and consumption sets in; and between them those fell diseases bring her to an early grave. There are some finely conceived scenes between Marthe and Faujas; but the climax only comes towards the end of the volume, when Mouret, the husband who has been driven mad and shut up in a lunatic asylum, returns home and wreaks the most terrible vengeance upon those who have wronged him.

The pages which deal with the madman's escape and his horrible revenge are certainly among the most powerful that M. Zola has ever written, and have been commended for their effectiveness by several of his leading critics.

E. A. V.
MERTON, SURREY: Sept. 1900.

THE CONQUEST OF PLASSANS

I

Désirée clapped her hands. She was fourteen years old and big and strong for her age, but she laughed like a little girl of five.

'Mother! mother!' she cried, 'look at my doll!'

She showed her mother a strip of rag out of which she had been trying for the last quarter of an hour to manufacture a doll by rolling it and tying it at one end with a piece of string. Marthe raised her eyes from the stockings that she was darning with as much delicacy of work as though she were embroidering, and smiled at Désirée.

'Oh! but that's only a baby,' she said; 'you must make a grown-up doll and it must have a dress, you know, like a lady.'

She gave the child some clippings of print stuff which she found in her work-table, and then again devoted all her attention to her stockings. They were both sitting at one end of the narrow terrace, the girl on a stool at her mother's feet. The setting sun of a still warm September evening cast its calm peaceful rays around them; and the garden below, which was already growing grey and shadowy, was wrapped in perfect silence. Outside, not a sound could be heard in that quiet corner of the town.

They both worked on for ten long minutes without speaking. Désirée was taking immense pains to make a dress for her doll. Every few moments Marthe raised her head and glanced at the child with an expression in which sadness was mingled with affection. Seeing that the girl's task seemed too much for her, she at last said:

'Give it to me; I will put in the sleeves for you.'

As she took up the doll, two big lads of seventeen and eighteen came down the steps. They ran to Marthe and kissed her.

'Don't scold us, mother!' cried Octave gaily. 'I took Serge to listen to the band. There was such a crowd on the Cours Sauvaire!'

'I thought you had been kept in at college,' his mother said, 'or I should have felt very uneasy.'

Désirée, now altogether indifferent to her doll, had thrown her arms round Serge's neck, saying to him:

'One of my birds has flown away! The blue one, the one you gave me!'

She was on the point of crying. Her mother, who had imagined this trouble to be forgotten, vainly tried to divert her thoughts by showing her the doll. The girl still clung to her brother's arm and dragged him away with her, while repeating:

'Come and let us look for it.'

Serge followed her with kindly complaisance and tried to console her. She led him to a little conservatory, in front of which there was a cage placed on a stand; and here she told him how the bird had escaped just as she was opening the door to prevent it from fighting with a companion.

'Well, there's nothing very surprising in that!' cried Octave, who had seated himself on the balustrade of the terrace. 'She is always interfering with them, trying to find out how they are made and what it is they have in their throats that makes them sing. The other day she was carrying them about in her pockets the whole afternoon to keep them warm.'

'Octave!' said Marthe, in a tone of reproach; 'don't tease the poor child.'

But Désirée had not heard him; she was explaining to Serge with much detail how the bird had flown away.

'It just slipped out, you see, like that, and then it flew over yonder and lighted on Monsieur Rastoil's big pear-tree. Next it flew off to the plum-tree at the bottom, came back again and went right over my head into the big trees belonging to the Sub-Prefecture, and I've never seen it since; no, never since.'

Her eyes filled with tears.

'Perhaps it will come back again,' Serge ventured to say.

'Oh! do you think so? I think I will put the others into a box, and leave the door of the cage open all night.'

Octave could not restrain his laughter, but Marthe called to Désirée:

'Come and look here! come and look here!'

Then she gave her the doll. It was a magnificent one now. It had a stiff dress, a head made of a pad of calico, and arms of list sewn on at the shoulders. Désirée's eyes lighted up with sudden joy. She sat down again upon the stool, and, forgetting all about the bird, began to kiss the doll and dandle it in her arms with childish delight.

Serge had gone to lean upon the balustrade near his brother, and Marthe had resumed her darning.

'And so the band has been playing, has it?' she asked.

'It plays every Thursday,' Octave replied. 'You ought to have come to hear it, mother. All the town was there; the Rastoil girls,

Madame de Condamin, Monsieur Paloque, the mayor's wife and daughter—why didn't you come too?'

Marthe did not raise her eyes, but softly replied as she finished darning a hole:

'You know very well, my dears, that I don't care about going out. I am quite contented here; and then it is necessary that someone should stay with Désirée.'

Octave opened his lips to reply, but he glanced at his sister and kept silent. He remained where he was, whistling softly and raising his eyes now towards the trees of the Sub-Prefecture, noisy with the twittering of the sparrows which were preparing to retire for the night—and now towards Monsieur Rastoil's pear-trees behind which the sun was setting. Serge had taken a book out of his pocket and was reading it attentively. Soft silence brooded over the terrace as it lay there in the yellow light that was gradually growing fainter. Marthe continued darning, ever and anon glancing at her three children in the peaceful quiet of the evening.

'Everyone seems to be late to-day,' she said after a time. 'It is nearly six o'clock, and your father hasn't come home yet. I think he must have gone to Les Tulettes.'

'Oh! then, no wonder he's late!' exclaimed Octave. 'The peasants at Les Tulettes are never in a hurry to let him go when once they get hold of him. Has he gone there to buy some wine?'

'I don't know,' Marthe replied. 'He isn't fond, you know, of talking to me about his business.'

Then there was another interval of silence. In the dining-room, the window of which opened on to the terrace, old Rose had just begun to lay the table with much angry clattering of crockery and plate. She seemed to be in a very bad temper, and banged the chairs about while breaking into snatches of grumbling and growling. At last she went to the street door, and, craning out her head, reconnoitred the square in front of the Sub-Prefecture. After some minutes' waiting, she came to the terrace-steps and cried:

'Monsieur Mouret isn't coming home to dinner, then?'

'Yes, Rose, wait a little longer,' Marthe replied quietly.

'Everything is getting burned to cinders! There's no sense in it all. When master goes off on those rounds he ought to give us notice! Well, it's all the same to me; but your dinner will be quite uneatable.'

'Ah! do you really think so, Rose?' asked a quiet voice just behind her. 'We will eat it, notwithstanding.'

It was Mouret who had just arrived.[1] Rose turned round, looked her master in the face, and seemed on the point of breaking into some angry exclamation; but at the sight of his unruffled countenance, in which twinkled an expression of merry banter, she could not find a word to say, and so she retired. Mouret made his way to the terrace, where he paced about without sitting down. He just tapped Désirée lightly on the cheek with the tips of his fingers, and the girl greeted him with a responsive smile. Marthe raised her eyes, and when she had glanced at her husband she began to fold up her work.

'Aren't you tired?' asked Octave, looking at his father's boots, which were white with dust.

'Yes, indeed, a little,' Mouret replied, without, however, saying anything more about the long journey which he had just made on foot.

Then in the middle of the garden he caught sight of a spade and a rake, which the children had forgotten there. 'Why are the tools not put away?' he cried. 'I have spoken about it a hundred times. If it should come on to rain they would be completely rusted and spoilt.'

He said no more on the subject, but stepped down into the garden, picked up the spade and rake himself, and put them carefully away inside the little conservatory. As he came up to the terrace again his eyes searched every comer of the walks to see if things were tidy there.

'Are you learning your lessons?' he asked, as he passed Serge, who was still poring over his book.

'No, father,' the boy replied; 'this is a book that Abbé Bourrette has lent me. It is an account of the missions in China.'

Mouret stopped short in front of his wife.

'By the way,' said he, 'has anyone been here?'

'No, no one, my dear,' replied Marthe with an appearance of surprise.

He seemed on the point of saying something further, but appeared to change his mind, and continued pacing up and down in silence. Then, going to the steps, he cried out:

'Well, Rose, what about this dinner of yours which is getting burnt to cinders?'

'Oh, indeed! there is nothing ready for you now!' shouted the cook in an angry voice from the other end of the passage. 'Everything is cold. You will have to wait, sir.'

[1]A glimpse of François Mouret, and Marthe, his wife, is given in 'The Fortune of the Rougons,'—Ed.

Mouret smiled in silence and winked with his left eye, as he glanced at his wife and children. He seemed to be very much amused by Rose's anger. Then he occupied himself in examining his neighbour's fruit-trees.

'It is surprising what splendid pears Monsieur Rastoil has got this year,' he remarked.

Marthe, who had appeared a little uneasy for the last few minutes, seemed as though she wanted to say something. At last she made up her mind to speak, and timidly inquired,

'Were you expecting someone to-day, my dear?'

'Yes and no,' he replied, beginning to pace the terrace again.

'Perhaps you have let the second floor?'

'Yes, indeed, I have let it.'

Then, as the silence became a little embarrassing, he added, in his quiet way, 'This morning, before starting for Les Tulettes, I went up to see Abbé Bourrette. He was very pressing, and so I agreed to his proposal. I know it won't please you; but, if you will only think the matter over for a little, you will see that you are wrong, my dear. The second floor was of no use to us, and it was only going to ruin. The fruit that we store in the rooms there brings on dampness which makes the paper fall from the walls. By the way, now that I think of it, don't forget to remove the fruit the first thing to-morrow. Our tenant may arrive at any moment.'

'We were so free and comfortable, all alone in our own house,' Marthe ventured to say, in a low tone.

'Oh, well!' replied Mouret, 'we shan't find a priest in our way. He will keep to himself, and we shall keep to ourselves. Those black-gowned gentlemen hide themselves when they want to swallow even a glass of water. You know that I'm not very partial to them myself. A set of lazybones for the most part! And yet what chiefly decided me to let the floor was that I had found a priest for a tenant. One is quite sure of one's money with them, and they are so quiet that one can't even hear them go in and out.'

Marthe still appeared distressed. She looked round her at the happy home basking in the sun's farewell, at the garden which was now growing greyer with shadows, and at her three children. And she thought of all the happiness which this little spot held for her.

'And do you know anything about this priest?' she asked.

'No; but Abbé Bourrette has taken the floor in his own name, and that is quite sufficient. Abbé Bourrette is an honourable man. I know that our tenant is called Faujas, Abbé Faujas, and that he comes from the diocese of Besançon. He didn't get on very well with his vicar there, and so he has been appointed curate here at Saint-Saturnin's. Perhaps he knows our bishop, Monseigneur Rousselot. But all this is no business of ours, you know; and it is to Abbé Bourrette that I am trusting in the whole matter.'

Marthe, however, did not seem to share her husband's confidence, but continued to stand out against him, a thing which seldom happened.

'You are right,' she said, after a moment's silence, 'Abbé Bourrette is a worthy man. But I recollect that when he came to look at the rooms he told me that he did not know the name of the person on whose behalf he was commissioned to rent them. It was one of those commissions which are undertaken by priests in one town for those in another. I really think that you ought to write to Besançon and make some inquiries as to what sort of a person it is that you are about to introduce into your house.'

Mouret was anxious to avoid losing his temper; he smiled complacently.

'Well, it isn't the devil, anyhow. Why, you're trembling all over! I didn't think you were so superstitious. You surely don't believe that priests bring ill luck, as folks say. Neither, of course, do they bring good luck. They are just like other men. But, when we get this Abbé here, you'll see if I'm afraid of his cassock!'

'No, I'm not superstitious; you know that quite well,' replied Marthe. 'I only feel unhappy about it, that's all.'

He took his stand in front of her, and interrupted her with a sharp motion of his hand.

'There! there! that will do,' said he. 'I have let the rooms; don't let us say anything more about the matter.'

Then, in the bantering tones of a *bourgeois* who thinks he has done a good stroke of business, he added:

'At any rate one thing is certain, and that is that I am to get a hundred and fifty francs rent; and we shall have those additional hundred and fifty francs to spend on the house every year.'

Marthe bent her head and made no further protestations except by vaguely swinging her hands and gently closing her eyes as though to prevent the escape of the tears which were already swelling beneath her eyelids. Then she cast a furtive glance at her children, who had not appeared to hear anything of her discussion with their father. They were, indeed, accustomed to scenes of this sort in which Mouret, with his bantering nature, delighted to indulge.

'You can come in now, if you would like something to eat,' said Rose in her crabby voice, as she came to the steps.

'Ah, that's right! Come along, children, to your soup!' cried Mouret gaily, without appearing to retain any trace of temper.

The whole family rose. But Désirée's grief seemed to revive at the sight of everyone stirring. She threw her arms round her father's neck and stammered:

'Oh, papa, one of my birds has flown away!'

'One of your birds, my dear? Well, we'll catch it again.'

Then he began to caress and fondle her, but she insisted that he, also, should go and look at the cage. When he brought her back again Marthe and her two sons were already in the dining-room. The rays of the setting sun, streaming in through the window, lighted up the porcelain plates, the children's plated mugs, and the white cloth. The room was warm and peaceful with its green background of garden.

But just as Marthe, upon whom the tranquillity of the scene had had a soothing effect, was smilingly removing the cover from the soup-tureen, a noise was heard in the passage.

Then Rose rushed into the room with a scared look and stammered:

'Monsieur l'Abbé Faujas has come!'

II

An expression of annoyance passed over Mouret's face. He had not expected his tenant till the following morning at the earliest. He was just rising hastily from his seat when Abbé Faujas himself appeared at the door. He was a tall big man, with a square face, broad features, and a cadaverous complexion. Behind him, in the shadow, stood an elderly woman, who bore an astonishing resemblance to him, only that she was of smaller build and wore a less refined expression. When they saw the table laid for a meal, they both hesitated and stepped back discreetly, though without going away. The priest's tall black figure contrasted mournfully with the cheerfulness of the whitewashed walls.

'We must ask your pardon for disturbing you,' he said to Mouret. 'We have just left Abbé Bourrette's; he, no doubt, gave you notice of our coming!'

'Not at all!' Mouret exclaimed. 'The Abbé never behaves like other people. He always seems as though he had just come down from paradise. Only this morning, sir, he told me that you would not be here for another couple of days. Well, we must put you in possession of your rooms all the same.'

Abbé Faujas apologised. He spoke in a deep voice which fell very softly at the end of each sentence. He was extremely distressed, said he, to have arrived at such a moment. And when he had expressed his regret in a very few well-chosen words, he turned round to pay the porter who had brought his trunk. His large well-shaped hands drew from the folds of his cassock a purse of which only the steel rings could be seen. Keeping his head bent, he cautiously fumbled in it for a moment. Then, without anyone having seen the piece of money which he had received, the porter went away, and the priest resumed in his refined way:

'I beg you, sir, sit down again. Your servant will show us the rooms, and will help me to carry this.'

As he spoke, he stooped to grasp one of the handles of his trunk. It was a small wooden trunk, bound at the edges with iron bands, and one of its sides seemed to have been repaired with a cross-piece of deal. Mouret looked surprised, and his eyes wandered off in search of other luggage, but he could see nothing excepting a big basket, which the elderly lady carried with both hands, holding it in front of her, and despite her fatigue obstinately determined not to put it down. From underneath the lid, which was a little raised, there peeped, amongst some bundles of linen, the end of a comb wrapped in paper and the neck of a clumsily corked bottle.

'Oh! don't trouble yourself with that,' said Mouret, just touching the trunk with his foot; 'it can't be very heavy, and Rose will be able to carry it up by herself.'

He was quite unconscious of the secret contempt which oozed out from his words. The elderly lady gave him a keen glance with her black eyes, and then let her gaze again fall upon the dining-room and the table, which she had been examining ever since her arrival. She kept her lips tightly compressed, while her eyes strayed from one object to another. She had not uttered a single word. Abbé Faujas consented to leave his trunk where it was. In the yellow rays of the sunlight which streamed in from the garden, his threadbare cassock looked quite ruddy; it was darned at the edges; and, though it was scrupulously clean, it seemed so sadly thin and wretched that Marthe, who had hitherto remained seated with a sort of uneasy reserve, now in her turn rose from her seat. The Abbé, who had merely cast a rapid glance at her, and had then quickly turned his eyes elsewhere, saw her leave her chair, although he did not appear to be watching her.

'I beg you,' he repeated, 'do not disturb yourselves. We should be extremely distressed to interfere with your dinner.'

'Very well,' said Mouret, who was hungry, 'Rose shall show you up. Tell her to get you anything you want, and make yourselves at home.'

Abbé Faujas bowed and was making his way to the staircase, when Marthe stepped up to her husband and whispered:

'But, my dear, you have forgotten—'

'What? what?' he asked, seeing her hesitate.

'There is the fruit, you know.'

'Oh! bother it all, so there is!' he exclaimed with an expression of annoyance.

And as Abbé Faujas stepped back and glanced at him questioningly, he added:

'I am extremely vexed, sir. Father Bourrette is a very worthy man, but it is a little unfortunate that you commissioned him to attend to your business. He hasn't got the least bit of a head. If we had only known of your coming, we should have had everything ready; but, as it is, we shall have to clear the whole place out for you. We have been using the rooms, you see; we have stowed all our crop of fruit, figs, apples and raisins, away on the floors upstairs.'

The priest listened with a surprise which all his politeness did not enable him to hide.

'But it won't take us long,' Mouret continued. 'If you don't mind waiting for ten minutes, Rose will get the rooms cleared for you.'

An anxious expression appeared on the priest's cadaverous face.

'The rooms are furnished, are they not?' he asked.

'Not at all; there isn't a bit of furniture in them. We have never occupied them.'

Thereupon the Abbé lost his self-control, and his grey eyes flashed as he exclaimed with suppressed indignation:

'But I gave distinct instructions in my letter that furnished rooms were to be taken. I could scarcely bring my furniture along with me in my trunk.'

'Well, that just fits in with what I have been saying!' cried Mouret, in a louder voice. 'The way that Bourrette goes on is quite incredible. He certainly saw the apples when he came to look at the rooms, sir, for he took up one of them and remarked that he had rarely seen such fine fruit. He said that everything seemed quite suitable, that the rooms were all that was necessary, and he took them.'

Abbé Faujas was no longer listening to Mouret; his cheeks were flushed with anger. He turned round and stammered in a broken voice:

'Do you hear, mother? There is no furniture.'

The old lady, with her thin black shawl drawn tightly round her, had just been inspecting the ground-floor, stepping furtively hither and thither, but without once putting down her basket. She had gone to the door of the kitchen and had scrutinised the four walls there, and then, standing on the steps that overlooked the terrace, she had taken in all the garden at one long, searching glance. But it was the dining-room that seemed more especially to interest her, and she was now again standing in front of the table laid for dinner, watching the steam of the soup rise, when her son repeated:

'Do you hear, mother? We shall have to go to the hotel.'

She raised her head without making any reply; but the expression of her whole face seemed to indicate a settled determination to remain in that house, with whose every corner she had already made herself acquainted. She shrugged her shoulders almost imperceptibly, and again her wandering eyes strayed from the kitchen to the garden and then from the garden to the dining-room.

Mouret, however, was growing impatient. As he saw that neither the mother nor her son seemed to make up their minds to leave the place, he said:

'We have no beds, unfortunately. True, there is, in the loft, a folding-bedstead, which perhaps, at a pinch, madame might make do until to-morrow. But I really don't know how Monsieur l'Abbé is to manage to sleep.'

Then at last Madame Faujas opened her lips. She spoke in a curt and somewhat hoarse voice:

'My son will take the folding-bedstead. A mattress on the floor, in a corner, will be quite sufficient for me.'

The Abbé signified his approval of this arrangement by a nod. Mouret was going to protest and try to think of some other plan, but, seeing the satisfied appearance of his new tenants, he kept silence and merely exchanged a glance of astonishment with his wife.

'To-morrow it will be light,' he said, with his touch of *bourgeois* banter, 'and you will be able to furnish as you like. Rose will go up and clear away the fruit and make the beds. Will you wait for a few minutes on the terrace? Come, children, take a couple of chairs out.'

Since the arrival of the priest and his mother, the young people had remained quietly seated at the table, curiously scrutinising the new-comers. The Abbé had not appeared to notice them, but Madame Faujas had stopped for a moment before each of them and stared them keenly in the face as though she were trying to pry into their young heads. As they heard their father, they all three hastily rose and took some chairs out.

The old lady did not sit down; and when Mouret, losing sight of her, turned round to find out what had become of her, he saw her standing before a window of the drawing-room which was ajar. She craned out her neck and completed her inspection with all the calm deliberation of a person who is examining some property for sale. Just as Rose took up the little trunk, however, she went back into the passage, and said quietly:

'I will go up and help you.'

Then she went upstairs after the servant. The priest did not even turn his head; he was smiling at the three young people who still stood in front of him. In spite of the hardness of his brow and the stern lines about his mouth, his face was capable of expressing great gentleness, when such was his desire.

'Is this the whole of your family, madame?' he asked Marthe, who had just come up to him.

'Yes, sir,' she replied, feeling a little confused beneath the clear gaze which he turned upon her.

Looking again at her children, he continued:

'You've got two big lads there, who will soon be men— Have you finished your studies yet, my boy?'

It was to Serge that he addressed this question. Mouret interrupted the lad as he was going to reply.

'Yes, he has finished,' said the father; 'though he is the younger of the two. When I say that he has finished, I mean that he has taken his bachelor's degree, for he is staying on at college for another year to go through a course of philosophy. He is the clever one of the family. His brother, the elder, that great booby there, isn't up to much. He has been plucked twice already, but he still goes on idling his time away and larking about.'

Octave listened to his father's reproaches with a smile, while Serge bent his head beneath his praises. Faujas seemed to be studying them for a moment in silence, and then, going up to Désirée and putting on an expression of gentle tenderness, he said to her:

'Will you allow me, mademoiselle, to be your friend?' She made no reply but, half afraid, hastened to hide her face against her mother's shoulder. The latter, instead of making her turn round again, pressed her more closely to her, clasping an arm around her waist.

'Excuse her,' she said with a touch of sadness, 'she hasn't a strong head, she has remained quite childish. She is an "innocent," we do not trouble her by attempting to teach her. She is fourteen years old now, and as yet she has only learned to love animals.'

Désirée's confidence returned to her with her mother's caresses, and she lifted up her head and smiled. Then she boldly said to the priest:

'I should like you very much to be my friend; but you must promise me that you will never hurt the flies. Will you?'

And then, as every one about her began to smile, she added gravely:

'Octave crushes them, the poor flies! It is very wicked of him.'

Abbé Faujas sat down. He seemed very much tired. He yielded for a moment or two to the cool quietness of the terrace, glancing slowly over the garden and the neighbouring.

The perfect calmness and solitude of this quiet corner of the little town seemed somewhat to surprise him.

'It is very pleasant here,' he murmured.

Then he relapsed into silence, and seemed lost in reverie. He started slightly as Mouret said to him with a laugh:

'If you will allow us, sir, we will now go back to our dinner.'

And then, catching a glance from his wife, Mouret added:

'You must sit down with us and have a plate of soup. It will save you the trouble of having to go to the hotel to dine. Don't make any difficulty, I beg.'

'I am extremely obliged to you, but we really don't require anything,' the Abbé replied in tones of extreme politeness, which allowed of no repetition of the invitation.

The Mourets then returned to the dining-room and seated themselves round the table. Marthe served the soup and there was soon a cheerful clatter of spoons. The young people chattered merrily, and Désirée broke into a peal of ringing laughter as she listened to a story which her father, who was now in high glee at having at last got to his dinner, was telling. In the meantime, Abbé Faujas, whom they had quite forgotten, remained motionless upon the terrace, facing the setting sun. He did not even turn his head, he seemed to hear nothing of what was going on behind him. Just as the sun was disappearing he took off his hat as if overcome by the heat. Marthe, who was sitting with her face to the window, could see his big bare head with its short hair that was already silvering about the temples. A last red ray lighting up that stern soldier-like head, on which the tonsure lay like a cicatrised wound from the blow of a club; then the ray faded away and the priest, now wrapped in shadow, seemed nothing more than a black silhouette against the ashy grey of the gloaming.

Not wishing to summon Rose, Marthe herself went to get a lamp and brought in the first dish. As she was returning from the kitchen, she met, at the foot of the staircase, a woman whom she did not at first recognise. It was Madame Faujas. She had put on a cotton cap and looked like a servant in her common print gown, with a yellow kerchief crossed over her breast and knotted behind her waist. Her wrists were bare, she was quite out of breath with the work she had been doing, and her heavy laced boots clattered on the flooring of the passage.

'Ah! you've got all put right now, have you, madame?' Marthe asked with a smile.

'Oh, yes! it was a mere trifle and was done directly,' Madame Faujas replied.

She went down the steps that led to the terrace, and called in a gentler tone:

'Ovide, my child, will you come upstairs now? Everything is quite ready.'

She was obliged to go and lay her hand upon her son's shoulder to awaken him from his reverie. The air was growing cool, and the Abbé shivered as he got up and followed his mother in silence. As he passed before the door of the dining-room which was all bright with the cheerful glow of the lamp and merry with the chatter of the young folks, he peeped in and said in his flexible voice:

'Let me thank you again, and beg you to excuse us for having so disturbed you. We are very sorry—'

'No! no!' cried Mouret, 'it is we who are sorry and distressed at not being able to offer you better accommodation for the night.'

The priest bowed, and Marthe again met that clear gaze of his, that eagle glance which had affected her before. In the depths of his eyes, which were generally of a melancholy grey, flames seemed to gleam at times like lamps earned behind the windows of slumbering houses.

'The priest's not at all shamefaced,' Mouret remarked jestingly, when the mother and son had retired.

'I don't think they are very well off,' Marthe replied.

'Well, at any rate, he isn't carrying Peru about with him in that box of his,' Mouret exclaimed. 'And it's light enough! Why, I could have raised it with the tip of my little finger!'

But he was interrupted in his flow of chatter by Rose, who had just come running down the stairs to relate the extraordinary things she had witnessed.

'Well, she is a wonderful creature, indeed!' she cried, posting herself in front of the table at which the family were eating. 'She's sixty-five at least, but she doesn't show it at all, and she bustles about, and works like a horse!'

'Did she help you to remove the fruit?' Mouret asked, with some curiosity.

'Yes, indeed, she did, sir! She carried it away in her apron, in loads heavy enough to burst it. I kept saying to myself, "The apron will certainly go this time," but it didn't. It is made of good strong material, the same kind of material as I wear myself. We made at least ten journeys backwards and forwards, and I felt as though my arms would fall off, but she only grumbled, and complained that we were getting on very slowly. I really believe, begging your pardon for mentioning it, that I heard her swear.'

Mouret appeared to be greatly amused.

'And the beds?' he asked.

'The beds, she made them too. It was quite a sight to see her turn the mattress over. It seemed to weigh nothing, I can tell you; she just took hold of it at one end and tossed it into the air as though it had been a feather. And yet she was very careful and particular with it all. She tucked in the folding-bed as carefully as though she were preparing a baby's cradle. She couldn't have laid the sheets with greater devotion if the Infant Jesus Himself had been going to sleep there. She put three out of the four blankets upon the folding-bed. And it was just the same with the pillows; she kept none for herself, but gave both to her son.'

'She is going to sleep on the floor, then?'

'In a corner, just like a dog! She threw a mattress on the floor of the other room and said that she'd sleep there more soundly than if she were in paradise. I couldn't persuade her to do anything to make herself more comfortable.

She says that she is never cold, and that her head is much too hard to make her at all afraid of lying on the floor. I have taken them some sugar and some water, as madame told me. Oh! they really are the strangest people!'

Then Rose brought in the remainder of the dinner. That evening the Mourets lingered over their meal. They discussed the new tenants at great length. In their life, which went on with all the even regularity of clock-work, the arrival of these two strangers was a very exciting event. They talked about it as they would have done of some catastrophe in the neighbourhood, going into all that minuteness of detail which helps one to while away long nights in the country. Mouret was especially fond of the chattering gossip of a little provincial town. During dessert, as he rested his elbows on the table in the cool dining-room, he repeated for the tenth time with the self-satisfied air of a happy man:

'It certainly isn't a very handsome present that Besançon has made to Plassans! Did you notice the back of his cassock when he turned round? I shall be very much surprised if he is much run after by the pious folks here. He is too seedy and threadbare; and the pious folks like nice-looking priests.'

'He has a very gentle voice,' said Marthe, indulgently.

'Not when he is angry, at any rate,' Mouret replied.'Didn't you hear him when he burst out on finding that the rooms were not furnished? He's a stern man, I'll be bound; not one of the sort, I should think, to go lounging in confessional-boxes. I shall be very curious to see how he sets about his furnishing to-morrow. But as long as he pays me, I don't much mind anything else. If he doesn't, I shall apply to Abbé Bourrette. It was with him that I made the bargain.'

The Mourets were not a devout family. The children themselves made fun of the Abbé and his mother. Octave burlesqued the old lady's way of craning out her neck to see to the end of the rooms, a performance which made Désirée laugh. After a time, however, Serge, who was of a more serious turn of mind, stood up for 'those poor people.'

As a rule, precisely at ten o'clock, if he was not playing at piquet, Mouret took up his candlestick and went off to bed, but that evening, when eleven o'clock struck, he was not yet feeling drowsy. Désirée had fallen asleep, with her head lying on Marthe's knees. The two lads had gone up to their room; and Mouret, left alone with his wife, still went on chattering.

'How old do you suppose he is?' he suddenly asked.

'Who?' replied Marthe, who was now beginning to feel very sleepy.

'Who? Why, the Abbé, of course! Between forty and forty-five, eh? He's a fine strapping fellow. It's a pity for him to wear a cassock! He would have made a splendid carbineer.'

Then, after an interval of silence, he vented aloud the reflections which were exercising his mind:

'They, arrived by the quarter to seven train. They can only have just had time to call on Abbé Bourrette before coming here. I'll wager that they haven't dined! That is quite clear. We should certainly have seen them if they had gone out to the hotel. Ah, now I should very much like to know where they can have had anything to eat.'

Rose had been lingering about the dining-room for the last few moments, waiting for her master and mistress to go to bed in order that she might be at liberty to fasten the doors and windows.

'I know where they had something to eat,' she said. And as Mouret turned briskly towards her, she added: 'Yes, I had gone upstairs again to see if there was anything they wanted. As I heard no sound, I didn't venture to knock at the door, but I looked through the keyhole.'

'Why, that was very improper of you, very improper,' Marthe interrupted, severely. 'You know very well, Rose, that I don't approve of anything of that kind.'

'Leave her alone and let her go on!' cried Mouret, who, under other circumstances, would have been very angry with the inquisitive woman. 'You peeped through the keyhole, did you?'

'Yes, sir; I thought it was the best plan.'

'Clearly so. What were they doing?'

'Well, sir, they were eating. I saw them sitting on one corner of the folding-bedstead and eating. The old lady had spread out a napkin. Every time that they helped themselves to some wine, they corked the bottle again and laid it down against the pillow.'

'But what were they eating?'

'I couldn't quite tell, sir. It seemed to me like the remains of some pastry wrapped up in a newspaper. They had some apples as well—little apples that looked good for nothing.'

'They were talking, I suppose? Did you hear what they said?'

'No, sir, they were not talking. I stayed for a good quarter of an hour watching them, but they never said anything. They were much too busy eating!'

Marthe now rose, woke Désirée, and made as though she were going off to bed. Her husband's curiosity vexed her. He, too, at last made up his mind to go off upstairs, while old Rose, who was a pious creature, went on in a lower tone:

'The poor, dear man must have been frightfully hungry. His mother handed him the biggest pieces and watched him swallow them with delight. And now he'll sleep in some nice white sheets; unless, indeed, the smell of the fruit keeps him awake. It isn't a pleasant smell to have in one's bedroom, that sour odour of apples and pears. And there isn't a bit of furniture in the whole room, nothing but the bed in the corner! If I were he, I should feel quite frightened, and I should keep the light burning all night.'

Mouret had taken up his candlestick. He stood for a moment in front of Rose, and summed up the events of the evening like a genuine *bourgeois* who has met with something unusual: 'It is extraordinary!'

Then he joined his wife at the foot of the staircase. She got into bed and fell asleep, while he still continued listening to the slightest sounds that proceeded from the upper floor. The Abbe's room was immediately over his own. He heard the window of it being gently opened, and this greatly excited his curiosity. He raised his head from his pillow, and strenuously struggled against his increasing drowsiness in his anxiety to find out how long the Abbé would remain at the window. But sleep was too strong for him, and he was snoring noisily before he had been able to detect the grating sound which the window-fastening made when it was closed.

Up above, Abbé Faujas was gazing, bare-headed, out of his window into the black night. He lingered there for a long time, glad to find himself at last alone, absorbed in those thoughts which gave his brow such an expression of sternness. Underneath him, he was conscious of the tranquil slumber of the family whose home he had been sharing for the last few hours; the calm, easy breathing of the children and their mother Marthe, and the heavy, regular respiration of Mouret.

There was a touch of scorn in the way in which the priest stretched out his muscular neck, as he raised his head to gaze upon the town that lay slumbering in the distance. The tall trees in the garden of the Sub-Prefecture formed a mass of gloomy darkness, and Monsieur

Rastoil's pear-trees thrust up scraggy, twisted branches, while, further away, there was but a sea of black shadow, a blank nothingness, whence not a sound proceeded. The town lay as tranquilly asleep as an infant in its cradle.

Abbé Faujas stretched out his arms with an air of ironic defiance, as though he would have liked to circle them round Plassans, and squeeze the life out of it by crushing it against his brawny chest. And he murmured to himself:

'Ah! to think that the imbeciles laughed at me this evening, as they saw me going through their streets!'

III

Mouret spent the whole of the next morning in playing the spy on his new tenant. This espionage would now enable him to fill up the idle hours which he had hitherto spent in pottering about the house, in putting back into their proper places any articles which he happened to find lying about, and in picking quarrels with his wife and children. Henceforth he would have an occupation, an amusement which would relieve the monotony of his everyday life. As he had often said, he was not partial to priests, and yet Abbé Faujas, the first one who had entered into his existence, excited in him an extraordinary amount of interest. This priest brought with him a touch of mystery and secresy that was almost disquieting. Although Mouret was a strong-minded man and professed himself to be a follower of Voltaire, yet in the Abbé's presence he felt the astonishment and uneasiness of a common *bourgeois*.

Not a sound came from the second floor. Mouret stood on the staircase and listened eagerly; he even ventured to go to the loft. As he hushed his steps while passing along the passage, a pattering of slippers behind the door filled him with emotion. But he did not succeed in making any new discovery, so he went down into the garden and strolled into the arbour at the end of it, there raising his eyes and trying to look through the windows in order to find out what might be going on in the rooms. But he could not see even the Abbe's shadow. Madame Faujas, in the absence of curtains, had, as a makeshift, fastened some sheets behind the windows.

At lunch Mouret seemed quite vexed.

'Are they dead upstairs?' he said, as he cut the children's bread. 'Have you heard them move, Marthe?'

'No, my dear; but I haven't been listening.'

Rose thereupon cried out from the kitchen: 'They've been gone ever so long. They must be far enough away now if they've kept on at the same pace.'

Mouret summoned the cook and questioned her minutely.

'They went out, sir: first the mother, and then the priest. They walked so softly that I should never have known anything about it if their shadows had not fallen across the kitchen floor when they opened the street door. I looked out into the street to see where they were going, but they had vanished. They must have gone off in a fine hurry.'

'It is very surprising. But where was I at the time?'

'I think you were in the garden, sir, looking at the grapes in the arbour.'

This put Mouret into a very bad temper. He began to inveigh against priests. They were a set of mystery-mongers, a parcel of underhand schemers, with whom the devil himself would be at a loss. They affected such ridiculous prudery that no one had ever seen a priest wash his face. And then he wound up by expressing his sorrow that he had ever let his rooms to this Abbé, about whom he knew nothing at all.

'It is all your fault!' he exclaimed to his wife, as he got up from table.

Marthe was about to protest and remind him of their discussion on the previous day, but she raised her eyes and simply looked at him, saying nothing. Mouret, contrary to his usual custom, resolved to remain at home. He pottered up and down between the dining-room and the garden, poking about everywhere, pretending that nothing was in its place and that the house simply invited thieves. Then he got indignant with Serge and Octave, who had set off for the college, he said, quite half an hour too soon.

'Isn't father going out?' Désirée whispered in her mother's ear, 'He will worry us to death if he stays at home.'

Marthe hushed her. At last Mouret began to speak of a piece of business which he declared he must finish off during the day. And then he complained that he had never a moment to himself, and could never get a day's rest at home when he felt he wanted it. Finally he went away, quite distressed that he could not remain and see what happened.

When he returned in the evening he was all on fire with curiosity.

'Well, what about the Abbé?' he asked, without even giving himself time to take off his hat.

Marthe was working in her usual place on the terrace.

'The Abbé!' she repeated, with an appearance of surprise. 'Oh, yes! the Abbé—I've really seen nothing of him, but I believe he has got settled down now. Rose told me that some furniture had come.'

'That's just what I was afraid of!' exclaimed Mouret. 'I wanted to be here when it came; for, you see, the furniture is my security. I knew very well that you would never think of stirring from your chair. You haven't much of a head, my dear—Rose! Rose!'

The cook appeared in answer to his summons, and he forthwith asked her: 'There's some furniture come for the people on the second floor?'

'Yes, sir; it came in a little covered cart. I recognised it as Bergasse's, the second-hand dealer's. It wasn't a big load.' Madame Faujas came on behind it. I dare say she had been giving the man who pushed it along a helping hand up the Rue Balande.'

'At any rate, you saw the furniture, I suppose? Did you notice what there was?'

'Certainly, sir. I had posted myself by the door, and it all went past me, which didn't seem to please Madame Faujas very much. Wait a moment and I'll tell you everything there was. First of all they brought up an iron bedstead, then a chest of drawers, then two tables and four chairs; and that was the whole lot of it. And it wasn't new either. I wouldn't have given thirty crowns for the whole collection.'

'But you should have told madame; we cannot let the rooms under such conditions. I shall go at once to talk to Abbé Bourrette about the matter.'

He was fuming with irritation, and was just setting off, Marthe brought him to a sudden halt by saying:

'Oh! I had forgotten to tell you. They have paid me six months' rent in advance.'

'What! They have paid you?' he stammered out, almost in a tone of annoyance.

'Yes, the old lady came down and gave me this.'

She put her hand into her work-bag, and gave her husband seventy-five francs in hundred-sou-pieces, neatly wrapt up in a piece of newspaper. Mouret counted the money, and muttered:

'As long as they pay, they are free to stop. But they are strange folks, all the same. Everyone can't be rich, of course, but that is no reason why one should behave in this suspicious manner, when one's poor.'

'There is something else I have to tell you,' Marthe continued, as she saw him calm down. 'The old lady asked me if we were disposed to part with the folding-bed to her. I told her that we made no use of it, and that she was welcome to keep it as long as she liked.'

'You did quite right. We must do what we can to oblige them. As I told you before, what bothers me about these confounded priests is that one never can tell what they are thinking about, or what they are up to. Apart from that, you will often find very honourable men amongst them.'

The money seemed to have consoled him. He joked and teased Serge about his book on the Chinese missions, which the boy happened to be reading just then. During dinner he affected to feel no further curiosity about the tenants of the second floor; but, when Octave mentioned that he had seen Abbé Faujas leaving the Bishop's residence, he could not restrain himself. Directly the dessert was placed on the table he resumed his chatter of the previous evening, though after a time he began to feel a little ashamed of himself. His commercial pursuits had made him stolid and heavy, but he really had a keen mind; he was possessed of no little common sense and accuracy of judgment which often enabled him to pick out the truth from the midst of all the gossip of the neighbourhood.

'After all,' he said, as he went off to bed, 'one has no business to go prying into other people's affairs. The Abbé is quite at liberty to do as he pleases. It is getting wearisome to be always talking about these people, and I, for my part, shall say nothing more about them.'

A week passed away. Mouret had resumed his habitual life. He prowled about the house, lectured his children, and spent his afternoons away from home, amusing himself by transacting various bits of business, of which he never spoke; and he ate and slept like a man for whom life is an easy downhill journey, without any jolts or surprises of any kind. The whole place sank back into all its old monotony. Marthe occupied her accustomed seat on the terrace, with her little work-table in front of her. Désirée played by her side. The two lads came home at the usual time, and were as noisy as ever; and Rose, the cook, grumbled and growled at everyone, while the garden and the dining-room retained all their wonted sleepy calm.

'You see now,' Mouret often repeated to his wife, 'you were quite mistaken in thinking that our comfort would be interfered with, by our letting the second-floor. We are as quiet and happy as ever we were, and the house seems smaller and cosier.'

He occasionally raised his eyes towards the second-floor windows, which Madame Faujas had hung with thick cotton curtains, on the day after her arrival. These curtains were never drawn aside. There was a conventual look about their stern, cold folds, and they seemed to tell of deep, unbroken silence, cloistral stillness lurking behind them. At distant intervals the windows were set ajar, and allowed the high, shadowy ceilings to be seen between the snowy whiteness of the curtains. But it was all to no purpose that Mouret kept on the watch, he could never catch sight of the hand which opened or closed them, and he never even heard the grating of the window fastening. Never did a sound of human life come down from the second floor.

The first week was at an end and Mouret had not yet had another glimpse of Abbé Faujas. That man who was living in his house, without he ever being able to catch sight even of his shadow, began to affect him with a kind of nervous uneasiness. In spite of all the efforts he made to appear indifferent, he relapsed into his old questionings, and started an inquiry.

'Have you seen anything of him?' he asked his wife.

'I fancy I caught a glimpse of him yesterday, as he was coming in, but I am not sure. His mother always wears a black dress, and it might have been she that I saw.'

And as he continued to press her with questions, Marthe told him all she knew.

'Rose says that he goes out every day, and stays away a long time. As for his mother, she is as regular as a clock. She comes down at seven o'clock in the morning to go out and do her marketing. She has a big basket, which is always closed, and in which she must bring everything back with her, coal, bread, wine and provisions, for no tradesman ever calls with anything for them. They are very courteous and polite; and Rose says that they always bow to her when they meet her. But as a rule she does not even hear them come down the stairs.'

'They must go in for a funny sort of cooking up there,' said Mouret, to whom all these details conveyed none of the information he wanted.

On another evening, when Octave mentioned that he had seen Abbé Faujas entering Saint-Saturnin's, his father asked him about the priest's appearance, what effect he had made upon the passers-by, and what he could be going to do in the church.

'Ah! you are really much too curious!' cried the young man, with a laugh. 'He didn't look very fine in the sunshine with his rusty cassock, I can vouch for that much. I noticed, too, that, as he walked along, he kept in the shadow of the houses, which made his cassock look a little blacker. He didn't seem at all proud of himself, but hurried along with his head bent down. Two girls began to laugh as he crossed the Place. The Abbé raised his head and looked at them with an expression of great softness—didn't he, Serge?'

Thereupon Serge related how on several occasions, as he was returning from the college, he had at a distance followed the Abbé, who was on his way back from Saint-Saturnin's. He passed through the streets without speaking to anyone; he seemed to know nobody and to be rather hurt by the suppressed titters and jeers which he heard around him.

'Do they talk of him, then, in the town?' asked Mouret, whose interest was greatly aroused.

'No one has ever spoken to me about him,' Octave replied.

'Yes,' said Serge, 'they do talk of him. Abbé Bourrette's nephew told me that he wasn't a favourite at the church. They are not fond of these priests who come from a distance; and besides he has such a miserable appearance. When people get accustomed to him, they will leave the poor man alone, but just at first it is only natural that he should attract notice.'

Marthe thereupon advised the two young fellows not to gratify any outsider's curiosity about the Abbé.

'Oh, yes! they may answer any questions,' Mouret exclaimed. 'Certainly nothing that we know of him could be likely to compromise him in any way.'

From that time forward, with the best faith in the world and without meaning the least harm, Mouret turned his sons into a couple of spies. He told Octave and Serge that they must repeat to him all that was said about the priest in the town, and he even instructed them to follow him whenever they came across him. But the information that was to be derived from such sources was quickly exhausted. The talk occasioned by the arrival of a strange curate in the diocese died away; the town seemed to have extended its pardon to the 'poor fellow,' who glided about in the shade in such a rusty old cassock, and its only apparent feeling for him now was one of disdain. The priest, on the other hand, always went straight to the cathedral and so returned from it, invariably passing through the same streets. Octave said, laughingly, that he was sure he counted the paving-stones.

Then Mouret bethought himself of enlisting the help of Désirée in the task of collecting information. In the evening he took her to the bottom of the garden and listened to her chatter about what she had done and what she had seen during the day, and he always tried to lead her on to the subject of the tenants of the second floor.

'Now, just listen to what I tell you,' he said to her one day. 'To-morrow, when the window is open, just throw your ball into the room, and then go up and ask for it.'

The next day the girl threw her ball into the room, but she had scarcely reached the steps of the house before the ball, returned by an invisible hand, bounced up from the terrace. Her father, who had reckoned on the child's taking ways leading to a renewal of the inter-course which had been interrupted since the day of the priest's arrival, now lost all hope. It was quite clear that the Abbé had made up his mind to keep to himself. This rebuff, however, only made Mouret's curiosity all the keener. He even condescended to go gossiping in corners with the cook, to the great displeasure of Marthe, who re-proached him for his want of self-respect; but at this he became angry with her and defended himself by lies. However, as he felt that he was in the wrong, it was only in secret that he henceforth talked to Rose about the Faujases.

One morning she beckoned to him to follow her into the kitchen.

'Oh, sir!' she said, as she shut the door, 'I have been watching for you to come down from your room for more than an hour.'

'Have you found out something then?'

'Well, you shall hear. Yesterday evening I was chatting with Ma-dame Faujas for more than an hour!'

Mouret felt a thrill of joy. He sat down on an old tattered rush-bot-tom chair, in the midst of the dirty cloths and vegetable parings left from the previous day, and exclaimed:

'Go along! make haste!'

'Well,' continued the cook, 'I was at the street-door saying good-night to Monsieur Rastoil's servant, when Madame Faujas came downstairs to empty a pail of dirty water in the gutter. Instead of immediately going back again, without even turning her head, as she generally does, she stopped there for a moment to look at me. Then it struck me that she wanted to speak to me, and I said to her that it had been a beautiful day, and that it would be good for the grapes. She said, "Yes, yes," in an unconcerned sort of way, just like a woman who has no land and has no interest in such matters. But she put down her pail and made no attempt to go away; she even came and leant against the wall beside me—'

'Well! well! what did she say to you?' cried Mouret, tortured by his impatience.

'Well, of course, you understand I wasn't silly enough to begin to question her. She would have gone straight off if I had. Without seeming to intend anything, I suggested things to her which I thought might set her talking. The Curé[1] of Saint-Saturnin's, that worthy Monsieur Compan, happened to pass by, and I told her he was very ill and wasn't long for this world, and that there would be great difficulty in filling his place at the cathedral. She was all ears at once, I can tell you. She even asked me what was the matter with Monsieur Compan. Then, going on from one thing to another, I gradually got talking about our bishop. Monseigneur Rousselot was a most excellent and worthy man, I told her. She did not know his age, so I told her that he was sixty, very delicate also, and that he let himself be led by the nose. There is a good deal of talk about the vicar-general, Monsieur Fenil, who is all powerful with the bishop. The old lady was quite interested in that, and she would have stayed out in the street all night, listening.'

An expression of desperation passed over Mouret's face. 'But what you're telling me is what you said yourself,' he cried. 'What was it that she said? That's what I want to hear.'

'Wait a little and let me finish,' Rose replied very calmly.

'I was gradually gaining my purpose. To win her confidence, I ended by talking to her about ourselves. I told her that you were Monsieur François Mouret, a retired merchant from Marseilles, and that you had managed in fifteen years to make a fortune out of wines and oils and almonds. I added that you had preferred to come and settle down and live on your means in Plassans, a quiet town, where your wife's relations lived. I even contrived to let her know, too, that madame was your cousin, that you were forty years old and that she was thirty-seven, and that you lived very happily together; in fact, I told her all about you. She seemed to be very much interested, and kept saying, "Yes, yes," in her deliberate way; and, when I stopped for a moment, she nodded her head as though to tell me she was listening and that I might go on. So we went on talking in this way, with our backs against the wall, like a couple of old friends, till it was quite dark.'

Mouret bounced from his chair in angry indignation.

'What!' he cried,' is that all? She led you on to gossip to her for an hour, and she herself told you nothing!'

---

[1]Parish priest.

'When it got dark, she said to me: "The air is becoming quite chilly." And then she took up her pail and went back upstairs.'

'You are nothing but an idiot! That old woman up there is more than a match for half a score such as you.

Ah! they'll be laughing finely now that they have wormed out of you all that they wanted to know about us. Do you hear me, Rose? I tell you that you are nothing but an idiot!'

The old cook waxed very indignant, and began to bounce excitedly up and down the kitchen, knocking the pots and pans about noisily, and crumpling up the dusters and flinging them down.

'It was scarcely worth your while, sir,' she hissed, 'to come into my kitchen to call me insulting names. You had better take yourself off. What I did, I did to please you. If madame finds us here together talking about those people, she will be angry with me, and quite rightly, because it is wrong for us to be doing so. And after all, I couldn't drag words from the old lady's lips if she wasn't willing to talk. I did as any one else would have done under the same circumstances. I talked and told her about your affairs, and it was no fault of mine that she didn't tell me about hers. Go and ask her about them yourself, since you are anxious to know about them. Perhaps you won't make such an idiot of yourself as I have done.'

She had raised her voice, and was talking so loudly that Mouret thought it would be more prudent to retire, and he did so, closing the kitchen door after him, in order to prevent his wife from hearing the servant. But Rose immediately pulled it open again, and cried after him down the passage:

'I shall bother myself about it no longer; do you hear? You may get somebody else to do your underhand business for you!'

Mouret was quite vanquished. He showed some irritation at his defeat, and tried to console himself by saying, that those second-floor tenants of his were mere nobodies. Gradually he succeeded in making this opinion of his that of his acquaintances, and then that of the whole town. Abbé Faujas came to be looked upon as a priest without means and without ambition, who was completely outside the pale of the intrigues of the diocese. People imagined that he was ashamed of his poverty, that he was glad to perform any unpleasant duties in connection with the cathedral, and tried to keep himself in obscurity as much as possible. There was only one matter of curiosity left in connection with him, and that was the reason of his having come to Plassans from Besançon. Queer stories were circulated about him, but they all seemed very improbable. Mouret himself, who had played the spy over his tenants simply for amusement and in order to pass the time, just as he would have played a game at cards or bowls, was even beginning to forget that he had a priest living in his house, when an incident occurred which revived all his curiosity.

One afternoon as he was returning home, he saw Abbé Faujas going up the Rue Balande in front of him. Mouret slackened his pace and examined the priest at his leisure.

Although Abbé Faujas had been lodging in his house for a month, this was the first time that he had thus seen him in broad daylight. The Abbé still wore his old cassock, and he walked slowly, with his hat in his hand and his head bare in spite of the chilly air. The street, which was a very steep one, with the shutters of its big, bare houses always closed, was quite deserted. Mouret, who quickened his pace, was at last obliged to walk on tip-toes for fear lest the priest should hear him and make his escape. But as they neared Monsieur Rastoil's house, a group of people turning out of the Place of the Sub-Prefecture entered it. Abbé Faujas made a slight détour to avoid these persons. He watched the door close, and then, suddenly stopping, he turned round towards his landlord, who was now close up to him.

'I am very glad to have met you,' said he, with all his wonted politeness, 'otherwise I should have ventured to disturb you this evening. The last time it rained, the wet came through the ceiling of my room, and I should much like to show it you.'

Mouret remained standing in front of him, and stammered in confusion that he was entirely at the Abbé's service. Then, as they went indoors together, he asked him at what time he should go to look at the ceiling.

'Well, I should like you to come at once,' the Abbé replied, 'if it wouldn't be troubling you too much.'

Mouret went up the stairs after him so excited that he almost choked, while Rose followed them with her eyes from the kitchen doorway quite dazed with astonishment.

IV

When Mouret reached the second floor he was more perturbed than a youth at his first assignation. The unexpected satisfaction of his long thwarted desires, and the hope of seeing something quite extraordinary, almost prevented him from breathing. Abbé Faujas slipped the key which he carried, and which he quite concealed in his big fingers, into the lock without making the faintest noise, and the door opened as silently as if it had been hung upon velvet hinges. Then the Abbé, stepping back, mutely motioned to Mouret to enter.

The cotton curtains at the two windows were so thick that the room lay in a pale, chalky dimness like the half-light of a convent cell. It was a very large room, with a lofty ceiling, and a quiet, neat wall-paper of a faded yellow. Mouret ventured forward, advancing with short steps over the tiled floor, which was as smooth and shiny as a mirror, and so cold that he seemed to feel a chill through the soles of his boots. He glanced furtively around him and examined the curtainless iron bedstead, the sheets of which were so straightly stretched that it looked like a block of white stone lying in the corner. The chest of drawers, stowed away at the other end of the room, a little table in the middle, and two chairs, one before each window, completed the furniture. There was not a single paper on the table, not an article of any kind on the chest of drawers, not a garment hanging against the walls. Everything was perfectly bare except that over the chest of drawers there was suspended a big black wooden crucifix, looking like a dark splotch amidst the bare greyness of the room.

'Come this way, sir, will you?' said the Abbé. 'It is in this corner that the ceiling is stained.'

But Mouret did not hurry, he was enjoying himself. Although he saw none of the extraordinary things that he had vaguely expected to see, there seemed to him to be a peculiar odour about the room. It smelt of a priest, he thought; of a man with different ways from other men. But it vexed him that he could see nothing on which he might base some hypothesis carelessly left on any of the pieces of furniture or in any corner of the apartment. The room was just like its provoking occupant, silent, cold, and inscrutable. He was extremely surprised, too, not to find any appearance of poverty as he had expected. On the contrary, the room produced upon him much the same impression as he had felt when he had once entered the richly furnished drawing-room of the prefect of Marseilles. The big crucifix seemed to fill it with its black arms.

Mouret felt, however, that he must go and look at the corner which Abbé Faujas was inviting him to inspect.

'You see the stain, don't you?' asked the priest. 'It has faded a little since yesterday.'

Mouret rose upon tip-toes and strained his eyes, but at first he could see nothing. When the Abbé had drawn back the curtains, he was able to distinguish a slight damp-stain.

'It's nothing very serious,' he said.

'Oh, no! but I thought it would be better to tell you of it. The wet must have soaked through near the edge of the roof.'

'Yes, you are right; near the edge of the roof.'

Mouret made no further remark; he was again examining the room, now clear and distinct in the full daylight. It looked less solemn than before, but it remained as taciturn as ever. There was not even a speck of dust lying about to tell aught of the Abbé's life.

'Perhaps,' continued the priest, 'we may be able to discover the place from the window. Just wait a moment.'

He proceeded to open the window, but Mouret protested against him troubling himself any further, saying that the workmen would easily be able to find the leak.

'It is no trouble at all, I assure you,' replied the Abbé with polite insistence. 'I know that landlords like to know how matters are going on. Inspect everything, I beg of you. The house is yours.'

As he spoke these last words he smiled, a thing he did but rarely; and then as Mouret and himself leaned over the rail that crossed the window, and turned their eyes towards the guttering, he launched out into various technical details, trying to account for the appearance of the stain.

'I think there has been a slight depression of the tiles, perhaps even a breakage; unless, indeed, that crack which you can see up there in the cornice extends into the retaining-wall.'

'Yes, yes, that is very possible,' Mouret replied; 'but I must confess, Monsieur l'Abbé, that I really don't understand anything about these matters. However, the masons will see to it.'

The priest said nothing further on the subject, but quietly remained where he was, gazing out upon the garden beneath him. Mouret, who was leaning by his side, thought it would be impolite to hurry away. He was quite won over when his tenant, after an interval of silence, said to him in his soft voice:

'You have a very pretty garden, sir.'

'Oh! it's nothing out of the common,' replied Mouret. 'There used to be some fine trees which I was obliged to cut down, for nothing would grow in their shade, and we have to pay attention to utility, you know. This plot is quite large enough for us and keeps us in vegetables all through the season.'

The Abbé seemed surprised, and asked Mouret for details. The garden was an old-fashioned country garden, surrounded with arbours, and divided into four regular square plots by tall borders of box. In the middle was a shallow basin, but there was no fountain. Only one of the squares was devoted to flowers. In the other three, which were planted at their edges with fruit-trees, one saw some magnificent cabbages, lettuces, and other vegetables. The paths of yellow gravel were kept extremely neat.

'It is a little paradise,' said Abbé Faujas.

'There are several disadvantages, all the same,' replied Mouret, who felt extremely delighted at hearing his ground so highly praised. 'You will have noticed, for instance, that we are on a slope, and that the gardens hereabouts are on different levels. Monsieur Rastoil's is lower than mine, which, again, is lower than that of the Sub-Prefecture. The consequence is that the rain often does a great deal of damage. Then, too, a still greater disadvantage is that the people in the Sub-Prefecture overlook me, and the more so now that they have made that terrace which commands my wall. It is true that I overlook Monsieur Rastoil's garden, but that is very poor compensation I can assure you, for a man who never troubles himself about his neighbour's doings.'

The priest seemed to be listening out of mere complaisance, just nodding his head occasionally but making no remarks. He followed with his eyes the motions of his landlord's hand.

'And there is still another inconvenience,' continued Mouret, pointing to a path that skirted the bottom of the garden. 'You see that little lane between the two walls? It is called the Impasse des Chevilottes, and leads to a cart-entrance to the grounds of the Sub-Prefecture. Well, all the neighbouring properties have little doors giving access to the lane, and there are all sorts of mysterious comings and goings. For my part, being a family man with children, I fastened my door up with a couple of stout nails.'

He looked at the Abbé and winked, hoping that the priest would question him about the mysterious comings and goings to which he had just alluded. But Abbé Faujas seemed quite unconcerned; he merely glanced at the alley without showing any curiosity on the subject. Then he again gazed placidly upon the Mourets' garden. Marthe was in her customary place near the edge of the terrace, hemming napkins. She had raised her head on first hearing voices, and then had resumed her work again, full of surprise at seeing her husband at one of the second-floor windows in the company of the priest. She now appeared to be quite unconscious of their presence. Mouret, however, had raised his voice from a sort of instinctive braggartism, proud of being able to show his wife that he had at last made his way into that room which had so persistently been kept private. The Abbé, on his side, every now and then let his calm eyes rest upon the woman, though all that he could see of her was the back of her bent neck and her black coil of hair.

They were both silent again, and Abbé Faujas still seemed disinclined to leave the window. He now appeared to be examining their neighbour's flower-beds. Monsieur Rastoil's garden was arranged in the English fashion, with little walks and grass plots broken by small flower-beds. At the bottom there was a circular cluster of trees, underneath which a table and some rustic chairs were set.

'Monsieur Rastoil is very wealthy,' resumed Mouret, who had followed the direction of the Abbe's eyes. 'His garden costs him a large sum of money. The waterfall—you can't see it from here, it is behind those trees—ran away with more than three hundred francs. There isn't a vegetable, about the place, nothing but flowers. At one time the ladies even talked of cutting down the fruit-trees; but that would have really been wicked, for the pear-trees are magnificent specimens. Well, I suppose a man has a right to lay out his ground so as to please his own fancy, if he can afford to do so.'

Then, as the Abbé still continued silent, he continued:

'You know Monsieur Rastoil, don't you? Every morning, from eight o'clock till nine, he walks about under his trees. He is a heavy man, rather short, bald, and clean shaven, with a head as round as a ball. He completed his sixtieth year at the beginning of last August, I believe. He has been president of our civil tribunal for nearly twenty years. Folks say he is a very good fellow, but I see very little of him. "Good-morning," and "Good-evening," that's about all that ever passes between us.'

He stopped speaking as he saw several people coming down the steps of the neighbouring house and making their way towards the clump of trees.

'Ah, yes!' he resumed, lowering his voice, 'to-day's Tuesday. There is a dinner party at the Rastoils'.'

The Abbé had not been able to restrain a slight start, and had then bent forward to see better. Two priests who were walking beside a couple of tall girls seemed particularly to interest him.

'Do you know who those gentlemen are?' Mouret inquired.

And, when the priest only replied by a vague gesture, he added:

'They were crossing the Rue Balande just as we met each other. The taller and younger one, the one who is walking between Monsieur Rastoil's two daughters, is Abbé Surin, our bishop's secretary. He is said to be a very amiable young man. The old one, who is walking a little behind, is one of our grand-vicars, Abbé Fenil. He is at the head of the seminary. He is a terrible man, flat and sharp, like a sabre. I wish he would turn round so that you might see his eyes. I am quite surprised that you don't know those gentlemen.'

'I go out very little,' said the Abbé, 'and there is no house in the town that I visit.'

'Ah! that isn't right. You must often feel very dull. To do you justice, Monsieur l'Abbé, you are certainly not of an inquisitive disposition. Just fancy! you've been here a month now, and you didn't even know that Monsieur Rastoil had a dinner-party every Tuesday! Why, it's right before your eyes there from this window!'

Mouret laughed slightly. He was forming a rather contemptuous opinion of the Abbé. Then in confidential tones he went on:

'You see that tall old man who is with Madame Rastoil— the thin one I mean, with broad brims to his hat? Well, that is Monsieur de Bourdeu, the former prefect of the Drôme, a prefect who was turned out of office by the revolution of 1848. He's another one that you don't know, I'll be bound. But Monsieur Maffre there, the justice of the peace, that white-headed old gentleman who is coming last, with Monsieur Rastoil, don't you know him? Well, that is really inexcusable. He is an honorary canon of Saint-Saturnin's! Between ourselves, he is accused of having killed his wife by his harshness and miserliness.'

Mouret stopped short, looked the Abbé in the face and said abruptly, with a smile:

'I beg your pardon, but I am not a very devout person, you know.'

The Abbé again waved his hand with that vague gesture which did duty as an answer and saved him the necessity of making a more explicit reply.

'No, I am not a very devout person,' Mouret repeated smilingly. 'But everyone should be left free, is it not so? The Rastoils, now, are a religious family. You must have seen the mother and daughters at Saint-Saturnin's. They are parishioners of yours. Ah! those poor girls!

The elder, Angéline, is fully twenty-six years old, and the other, Aurélie, is getting on for twenty-four.' And they're no beauties either, quite yellow and shrewish-looking. The parents won't let the younger one marry before her sister; but I dare say they'll both end by finding husbands somewhere, if only for the sake of their dowries. Their mother there, that fat little woman who looks as innocent and mild as a sheep, has given poor Rastoil some pretty experiences.'

He winked his left eye, a common habit of his whenever he indulged in any pleasantry approaching broadness. The Abbé lowered his eyes, as if waiting for Mouret to go on, but, as the latter remained silent, he raised them again and watched the people in the garden as they seated themselves round the table under the trees.

At last Mouret resumed his explanatory remarks. 'They will stay out there, enjoying the fresh air, till dinner-time,' said he. 'It is just the same every Tuesday. That Abbé Surin is a great favourite. Look how he is laughing there with Mademoiselle Aurélie. Ah! Abbé Fenil has observed us. What eyes he has! He isn't very fond of me, you know, as I've had a dispute with a relation of his. But where has Abbé Bourrette got to? We haven't seen anything of him, have we? It is very extraordinary. He never misses Monsieur Rastoil's Tuesdays. He must be ill. You know him, don't you? What a worthy man he is! A most devoted servant of God!'

Abbé Faujas was no longer listening. His eyes were constantly meeting those of Abbé Fenil, whose scrutiny he bore with perfect calmness, never once diverting his glance. He was even leaning more fully against the iron rail, and his eyes seemed to have grown bigger.

'Ah! here come the young people!' resumed Mouret as three young men arrived on the scene. 'The oldest one is Rastoil's son; he has just been called to the Bar. The two others are the sons of Monsieur Maffre; they are still at college. By-the-by, I wonder why those young scamps of mine haven't come back yet.'

At that very moment Octave and Serge made their appearance on the terrace. Leaning against the balustrade they began to tease Désirée, who had just sat down by her mother's side. However, when the young folks caught sight of their father at the second-floor window, they lowered their voices and quietly laughed.

'There you see all my little family!' said Mouret complacently. 'We stay at home, we do; and we have no visitors. Our garden is a closed paradise, which the devil can't enter to tempt us.'

He smiled as he spoke, for he was really amusing himself at the

Abbe's expense. The latter had slowly brought his eyes to bear upon the group formed by his landlord's family under the window. He gazed down there for a moment; then looked round upon the old-fashioned garden with its beds of vegetables edged with borders of box; then again turned his eyes towards Monsieur Rastoil's pretentious grounds; and last of all, as though he wanted to get the plan of the whole surroundings into his head, directed his attention to the garden of the Sub-Prefecture. There was nothing to be seen here but a large central lawn, a gently undulating carpet of grass, with clusters of evergreen shrubs, and some tall thickly-foliaged chestnut trees which gave a park-like appearance to this patch of ground hemmed in by the neighbouring houses.

Abbé Faujas glanced under the chestnut-trees, and at last remarked:

'These gardens are quite lively. There are some people, too, in the one on the left.'

Mouret raised his eyes.

'Oh, yes!' he said unconcernedly, 'it's like that every afternoon. They are the friends of Monsieur Péqueur des Saulaies, our sub-prefect. In the summer-time they meet in the evenings in the same way round the basin on the left, which you can't see from here. Ah! so Monsieur de Condamin has got back! That fine old man there, who is so well preserved and has such a bright colour; he is our conservator of rivers and forests; a jovial old fellow, who is constantly to be seen, gloved and tightly breeched, on horse-back. And the tales he can tell, too! He doesn't belong to this neighbourhood, and he has lately married a very young woman. However, that's fortunately no business of mine!'

He bent his head again as he heard Désirée, who was playing with Serge, break out into one of her childish laughs.

But the Abbé, whose face was now slightly flushed, recalled his attention by asking:

'Is that the sub-prefect, that fat gentleman with the white tie?'

This question seemed to amuse Mouret exceedingly.

'Oh, no!' he replied, with a laugh. 'It is very evident that you don't know Monsieur Péqueur des Saulaies. He isn't forty yet; he's a tall, handsome, very distinguished-looking young man. That fat gentleman is Doctor Porquier, the fashionable medical man of Plassans. He is a very well-to-do man, I can assure you, and he has only one trouble, his son Guillaume. Do you see those two people sitting on the bench with their backs towards us? They are Monsieur Paloque, the assistant judge, and his wife. They are the ugliest couple in the town. It is difficult to say which is the worse-looking, the husband or the wife. Fortunately they have no children.'

Mouret began to laugh more loudly; he was growing excited, and kept on striking the window-rail.

'I can never look at the assemblies in those grounds,' he continued, motioning with his head, first towards Monsieur Rastoil's garden and then towards the sub-prefect's, 'without being highly amused. You don't take any interest in politics, Monsieur l'Abbé, or I could tell you some things which would tickle you immensely. Rightly or wrongly, I myself pass for a republican. Business matters take me a good deal about the country; I am a friend of the peasantry, and people have even talked about proposing me for the Council-General—in short, I am a well-known man. Well, on my right here, at Monsieur Rastoil's, we have the cream of the Legitimists, and on the left, at the Sub-Prefecture, we have the big-wigs of the Empire. And so, you see, my poor old-fashioned garden, my little happy nook, lies between two hostile camps. I am continually afraid lest they should begin throwing stones at each other, for the stones, you see, might very well fall into my garden.'

Mouret appeared to be quite delighted with this witticism and drew closer to the Abbé, like some old gossip who is just going to launch out into a long story.

'Plassans is a very curious place from a political point of view. The Coup d'Etat succeeded here because the town is conservative. But first of all it is Legitimist and Orleanist; so much so, indeed, that at the outset of the Empire it wanted to dictate conditions. As its claims were disregarded, the town grew annoyed and went over to the opposition; yes, Monsieur l'Abbé, to the opposition. Last year we elected for our deputy the Marquis de Lagrifoul, an old nobleman of mediocre abilities, but one whose election was a very bitter pill for the Sub-Prefecture.—Ah, look! there is Monsieur Péqueur des Saulaies! He is with the mayor, Monsieur Delangre.'

The Abbé glanced keenly in the direction indicated by Mouret. The sub-prefect, a very dark man, was smiling beneath his waxed moustaches. He was irreproachably dressed, and preserved a demeanour which suggested both that of a fashionable officer and that of a good-natured diplomatist. The mayor was by his side, talking and gesticulating rapidly. He was a short man, with square shoulders, and a sunken face that was rather Punch-like in appearance. He seemed to be garrulously inclined.

'Monsieur Péqueur des Saulaies,' continued Mouret, 'had felt so confident of the return of the official candidate that the result of the election nearly made him ill. It was very amusing. On the evening of the election, the garden of the Sub-Prefecture remained as dark and gloomy as a cemetery, while in the Rastoils' grounds there were lamps and candles burning under the trees, and joyous laughter and a perfect uproar of triumph. Our people don't let things be seen from the street, but they throw off all restraint and give full vent to their feelings in their gardens. Oh, yes! I see singular things sometimes, though I don't say anything about them.'

He checked himself for a moment, as though he was unwilling to say more, but his gossiping propensities were too strong for him.

'I wonder what course they will now take at the Sub-Prefecture?' he continued. 'They will never get their candidate elected again. They don't understand the people about here, and besides they are very weak. I was told that Monsieur Péqueur des Saulaies was to have had a prefecture if the election had gone off all right. Ah! he will remain a sub-prefect for a long time yet, I imagine! What stratagem will they devise, I wonder, to overthrow the Marquis? They will certainly have recourse to one of some kind or other; they will do their best somehow to effect the conquest of Plassans.'

He turned his eyes upon the Abbé, at whom he had ceased to look for the last few moments, and he suddenly checked himself as he caught sight of the priest's eager face, his glistening eyes, and his ears that seemed to have grown bigger. All Mouret's *bourgeois* prudence then reasserted itself, and he felt that he had said too much. So he hastily added:

'But, after all, I really know nothing about it. People tell so many ridiculous stories. All I care about is to be allowed to live quietly in my own house.'

He would then have liked to leave the window, but he dared not go away so suddenly after gossiping in such an unrestrained and familiar fashion. He was beginning to think that if one of them had been having his laugh at the other, it certainly was not he.

The Abbé, for his part, was again glancing alternately at the two gardens in a calm, unconcerned manner, and did not make the slightest attempt to induce Mouret to continue talking. Mouret was already wishing, somewhat impatiently, that his wife or one of his children would call to him to come down, when he was greatly relieved by seeing Rose appear on the steps outside the house. She raised her head towards him.

'Well, sir!' she cried, 'aren't you coming at all to-day? The soup has been on the table for the last quarter of an hour!'

'All right, Rose! I'll be down directly,' he replied.

Then he made his apologies to the Abbé, and left the window. The chilly aspect of the room, which he had forgotten while his back had been turned to it, added to the confusion he felt. It seemed to him like a huge confessional-box, with its awful black crucifix, which must have heard everything he had said. When the Abbé took leave of him with a silent bow, this sudden finish of their conversation so disturbed him, that he again stepped back and, raising his eyes to the ceiling, said:

'It is in that corner, then?'

'What is?' asked the Abbé in surprise.

'The damp stain that you spoke to me about.'

The priest could not restrain a smile, but he again pointed out the stain to Mouret.

'Ah! I can see it quite plainly now,' said the latter. 'Well, I'll send the workmen up to-morrow.'

Then he at last left the room, and before he had reached the end of the landing, the door was noiselessly closed behind him. The silence of the staircase irritated him extremely, and as he went down, he muttered:

'The confounded fellow! He gets everything out of one without asking a single question!'

V

The next morning old Madame Rougon, Marthe's mother,[1] came to pay a visit to the Mourets. It was quite an event, for there was a coolness between Mouret and his wife's relations which had increased since the election of the Marquis de Lagrifoul, whose success the Rougons attributed to Mouret's influence in the rural districts. Marthe used to go alone when she went to see her parents. Her mother, 'that black Félicité,' as she was called, had retained at sixty-six years of age all the slimness and vivacity of a girl. She always wore silk dresses, covered with flounces, and was particularly partial to yellows and browns.

---

[1] One of the chief characters of 'The Fortune of the Rougons' and 'Dr. Pascal.'—Ed.

When she arrived, only Marthe and Mouret were in the dining-room.

'Hallo!' cried the latter in great surprise, as he saw her coming, 'here's your mother! I wonder what she wants! She was here less than a month ago. She's scheming after something or other, I know.'

The Rougons, whose assistant Mouret had been prior to his marriage, when their shabby little shop in the old quarter of the town had ever suggested bankruptcy, were the objects of his constant suspicions. They returned the feeling with bitter and deep-seated animosity, their rancour being especially aroused by the speedy success which had attended him in business. When their son-in-law said, 'I simply owe my fortune to my own exertions,' they bit their lips and understood quite well that he was accusing them of having gained theirs by less honourable means. Notwithstanding the fine house she now had on the Place of the Sub-Prefecture, Félicité silently envied the peaceful little home of the Mourets, with all the bitter jealousy of a retired shopkeeper who owed her fortune to something else than the profits of her business.

Félicité kissed Marthe on the forehead and then gave her hand to Mouret. She and her son-in-law generally affected a mocking tone in their conversations together.

'Well,' she said to him with a smile, 'the gendarmes haven't been for you yet then, you revolutionist?'

'No, not yet,' he replied with a responsive smile; 'they are waiting till your husband gives them the order.'

'It's very nice and polite of you to say that!' exclaimed Félicité, whose eyes were beginning to glisten.

Marthe turned a beseeching glance upon Mouret. He had gone too far; but his feelings were roused and he added:

'Good gracious! What are we thinking of to receive you in the dining-room? Let us go into the drawing-room, I beg you.'

This was one of his usual pleasantries. He affected all Félicité's fine airs whenever he received a visit from her. It was to no purpose that Marthe protested that they were very comfortable where they were; her husband insisted that she and her mother should follow him into the drawing-room. When they got there, he bustled about, opening the shutters and drawing out the chairs. The drawing-room, which was seldom entered, and the shutters of which were generally kept closed, was a great wilderness of a room, with furniture swathed in white dust-covers which were turning yellow from the proximity of the damp garden.

'It is really disgraceful!' muttered Mouret, wiping the dust from a small console; 'that wretched Rose neglects everything abominably.'

Then, turning towards his mother-in-law, he said with ill-concealed irony:

'You will excuse us for receiving you in this way in our poor dwelling. We cannot all be wealthy.'

Félicité was choking with rage. She scanned Mouret for a moment, and almost indulged in a burst of anger; but she made an effort to restrain herself and slowly dropped her eyes. When she again raised them she spoke in a pleasant tone.

'I have just been calling upon Madame de Condamin,' she said, 'and I thought I would look in here and see how you all were. The children are well, I hope, and you, too, my dear Mouret?'

'Yes, we are all wonderfully well,' he replied, quite astonished by this amiability.

But the old lady gave him no time to import any fresh unpleasantness into the conversation, for she began to question Marthe affectionately about all sorts of trifles, playing the part of a fond grandmother and scolding Mouret for not sending the dear children to see her oftener, for she was always so delighted to have them with her, said she.

'Well, here we are in October again,' she remarked carelessly, after awhile, 'and I shall be having my day again, Thursdays, as in former seasons. I shall count upon seeing you, my dear Marthe, of course; and you too, Mouret, you will look in occasionally, won't you, and not go on sulking with us for ever?'

Mouret, who was growing a little suspicious of all his mother-in-law's affectionate chatter, was at a loss how to reply. He had not expected such a thrust, but there was nothing in it to which he could take exception; so he merely said:

'You know very well that I can't go to your house; you receive a lot of people who would be delighted to have an opportunity of making themselves disagreeable to me. And, besides, I don't want to mix myself up with politics.'

'You are quite mistaken, Mouret, quite mistaken!' Félicité replied. 'My drawing-room is not a club; I would never allow it to become one. All the town knows that I do all I can to make my house as pleasant as possible; and if political matters ever are discussed there, it is only in corners, I assure you. Ah! believe me, I had quite enough of politics long ago. What makes you say such a thing?'

'Why, you receive all the Sub-Prefecture set,' Mouret said shortly.

'The Sub-Prefecture set!' she repeated, 'the Sub-Prefecture set! Certainly I receive those gentlemen. But I don't think that Monsieur Péqueur des Saulaies will be found very often in my house this winter. My husband has told him pretty plainly what he thought of his conduct in connection with the last elections. He allowed himself to be tricked like a mere nincompoop. But his friends are very pleasant men. Monsieur Delangre and Monsieur de Condamin are extremely amiable, and that worthy Paloque is kindness itself, while I'm sure you can have nothing to say against Doctor Porquier.'

Mouret shrugged his shoulders.

'Besides,' she continued, with ironic emphasis, 'I also receive Monsieur Rastoil's circle, worthy Monsieur Maffre and our clever friend Monsieur de Bourdeu, the former prefect. So you see we are not at all bigoted or exclusive, the representatives of all opinions find a welcome among us. Of course when I am inviting a party of people, I don't ask those to meet each other who would be likely to quarrel. But wit and cleverness are welcome in whomsoever they are found, and we pride ourselves upon having at our gatherings all the most distinguished persons in Plassans. My drawing-room is neutral ground, remember that, Mouret; yes, neutral ground that is the right expression.'

She had grown quite animated whilst talking. Her drawing-room was her great glory, and it was her desire to reign there, not as a chief of a party, but as a queen of society. It is true that her friends said that she was adopting conciliatory tactics merely in conformity with the advice of her son Eugène, the minister,[1] who had charged her to personify at Plassans the gentleness and amiability of the Empire.

'You may say what you like,' Mouret growled, 'but that Maffre of yours is a bigot, and your Bourdeu is a fool, and most of all the others are a pack of rascals. That's my opinion of them. I am much obliged to you for your invitation, but it would disturb my habits too much to accept it. I like to go to bed in good time, and I prefer stopping at home.'

Félicité rose from her seat, and turning her back upon Mouret, she said to her daughter:

'Well, at any rate I may expect you, mayn't I, my dear?'

'Of course you may,' replied Marthe, who wished to soften the bluntness of her husband's blunt refusal.

---

[1] The chief character in 'His Excellency.'

The old lady was just going to leave, when a thought seemed to strike her, and she asked if she might kiss Désirée, whom she had seen playing in the garden. She would not let them call the girl into the house, but insisted on going herself to the terrace, which was still damp from a slight shower which had fallen in the morning. When she found Désirée, she was profuse in her caresses of the girl, who seemed rather frightened of her. Then she raised her head as if by chance and looked at the curtains at the second-floor windows.

'Ah! you have let the rooms, then? Oh, yes! I remember now; to a priest, isn't it? I've heard it spoken of. What sort of a person is he, this priest of yours?'

Mouret looked at her keenly. A sudden suspicion flashed through his mind, and he began to guess that it was entirely on account of Abbé Faujas that his mother-in-law had favoured them with this visit.

'Upon my word,' he replied, without taking his eyes off her, 'I really know nothing about him. But perhaps you are able to give me some information concerning him yourself?'

'I!' she cried, with an appearance of great surprise. 'Why, I've never even seen him! Stay, though, I know he is one of the curates at Saint-Saturnin; Father Bourrette told me that. By the way, that reminds me that I ought to ask him to my Thursdays. The director of the seminary and the bishop's secretary are already amongst my circle of visitors.'

And, turning to Marthe, she added:

'When you see your lodger you might sound him, so as to be able to tell me whether an invitation from me would be acceptable.'

'We scarcely ever see him,' Mouret hastily interposed. 'He comes in and goes out without ever opening his mouth. And, besides, it is really no business of ours.'

He still kept his eyes fixed suspiciously upon her. He felt quite sure that she knew much more about Abbé Faujas than she was willing to admit. However, she did not once flinch beneath his searching gaze.

'Very well, it's all the same to me,' she said, with an appearance of unconcern. 'I shall be able to find out some other way of inviting him, if he's the right sort of person, I've no doubt. Good-bye, my children.'

As she was mounting the steps again, a tall old man appeared on the hall threshold. He was dressed very neatly in blue cloth, and had a fur cap pressed over his eyes. In his hand he carried a whip.

'Hallo! why there's Uncle Macquart!' cried Mouret, casting a curious glance at his mother-in-law.

An expression of extreme annoyance passed over Félicité's face. Macquart, Rougon's illegitimate brother, had, by the latter's aid, returned to France after he had compromised himself in the rising of 1851. Since arriving from Piedmont he had been leading the life of a sleek and well-to-do citizen. He had purchased, though where the money had come from no one knew, a small house at the village of Les Tulettes, about three leagues from Plassans. And by degrees he had fitted up an establishment there, and had now even become possessed of a horse and trap, and was constantly to be met on the high roads, smoking his pipe, enjoying the sunshine, and sniggering like a tamed wolf. Rougon's enemies whispered that the two brothers had perpetrated some black business together, and that Pierre Rougon was keeping Antoine Macquart.

'Good day, Uncle!' said Mouret affectedly; 'have you come to pay us a little visit?

'Yes, indeed,' Macquart replied, in a voice as guileless as a child's. 'You know that whenever I come to Plassans—Hallo, Félicité! I didn't expect to find you here! I came over to see Rougon. There was something I wanted to talk to him about.'

'He was at home, wasn't he?' she exclaimed with uneasy haste.

'Yes, he was at home,' Uncle Macquart replied tranquilly.

'I saw him, and we had a talk together. He is a good fellow, is Rougon.'

He laughed slightly, and while Félicité stamped her feet with restless anxiety, he went on talking in his drawling voice, which made it seem as if he was always laughing at those whom he addressed.

'Mouret, my boy, I have brought you a couple of rabbits,' he said. 'They are in a basket over there. I have given them to Rose. I brought another couple with me for Rougon.

You will find them at home, Félicité, and you must tell me how they turn out. They are beautifully plump; I fattened them up for you. Ah, my dears! it pleases me very much to be able to make you these little presents.'

Félicité turned quite pale, and pressed her lips tightly, while Mouret continued to look at her with a quiet smile.

She would have been glad to get away, if she had not been afraid of Macquart gossiping as soon as her back should be turned.

'Thank you, Uncle,' said Mouret. 'The plums that you brought us the last time you came were very good. Won't you have something to drink?'

'Well, that's an offer I really can't refuse.'

When Rose had brought him out a glass of wine, he sat down on the balustrade of the terrace and slowly sipped the beverage, smacking his tongue and holding up the glass to the light.

'This comes from the district of Saint-Eutrope,' he said. 'I'm not to be deceived in matters of this kind. I know the different districts thoroughly.'

He wagged his head and again sniggered.

Then Mouret, with an intonation that was full of meaning, suddenly asked him:

'And how are things getting on at Les Tulettes?'

Macquart raised his eyes and looked at them all. Then giving a final cluck of his tongue and putting down the glass on the stone-work by his side, he said, quite unconcernedly.

'Oh! very well. I heard of her the day before yesterday. She is still just the same.'

Félicité had turned her head away. For a moment no one spoke. Mouret had just put his finger upon one of the family's sore places, by alluding to old Adelaide, the mother of Rougon and Macquart, who for several years now had been shut up as a mad woman in the asylum at Les Tulettes. Macquart's little property was near the mad-house, and it seemed as though Rougon had posted the old scamp there to keep watch over their mother.

'It is getting late,' Macquart said at last, rising from his seat on the balustrade,' and I want to get back again before night I shall expect to see you over at my house one of these days, Mouret, my boy. You have promised me several times to come, you know.'

'Oh, yes! I'll come, Uncle, I'll come.'

'Ah! but that isn't enough. I want you all to come; all of you, do you hear? I am very dull out there all by myself. I will give you some dinner.'

Then, turning to Félicité, he added:

'Tell Rougon that I shall expect him and you, too. You needn't stop from coming just because the old mother happens to be near there. She is going on very well, I tell you, and is properly looked after. You may safely trust yourselves to me, and I will give you some wine from one of the slopes of La Seille, a light wine that will warm you up famously.'

He began to walk towards the gate as he spoke. Félicité followed him so closely that it almost seemed as if she were pushing him out of the garden. They all accompanied him to the street. While he was untethering his horse, which he had fastened by the reins to one of the house shutters, Abbé Faujas, who was just returning home, passed the group with a slight bow. He glided on as noiselessly as a black shadow, but Félicité quickly turned and watched him till he reached the staircase. Unfortunately she had not had time to catch sight of his face. Macquart on perceiving the priest had shaken his head in utter surprise.

'What! my boy,' said he, 'have you really got priests lodging with you now? That man has very strange eyes. Take care! take care! cassocks bring ill luck with them!'

Then he took his seat in his trap and clucked his horse on, going down the Rue Balande at a gentle trot. His round back and fur cap disappeared at the corner of the Rue Taravelle. As Mouret turned round again, he heard his mother-in-law speaking to Marthe.

'I would rather you do it,' she was saying; 'the invitation would seem less formal. I should be very glad if you could find some opportunity of speaking to him.'

She checked herself when she saw that she was overheard; and having kissed Désirée effusively, she went away, giving a last look round to make quite sure that Macquart was not likely to come back to gossip about her.

'I forbid you to mix yourself up in your mother's affairs, you know,' Mouret said to his wife as they returned into the house. 'She has always got some business or other on hand that no body can understand. What in the world can she want with the Abbé? She wouldn't invite him for his own sake, I'm sure. She must have some secret reason for doing so. That priest hasn't come from Besançon to Plassans for nothing. There is some mystery or other at the bottom of it all!'

Marthe had again set to work at the everlasting repairs of the family-linen which kept her busy for days together. But her husband went on chattering:

'Old Macquart and your mother amuse me very much. How they hate each other! Did you notice how angry she was when she saw him come? She always seems to be in a state of fear lest he should make some unpleasant revelation—I dare say that he'd willingly do so. But they'll never catch me in his house. I've sworn to keep clear of all that business. My father was quite right when he said that my mother's family, those Rougons and Macquarts, were not worth a rope to hang them with—They are my relations as well as yours, so you needn't feel hurt at what I am saying. I say it because it is true. They are wealthy people now, but their money hasn't made them any better—rather the contrary.'

Then he set off to take a turn along the Cours Sauvaire, where he met his friends and talked to them about the weather and the crops and the events of the previous day. An extensive transaction in almonds, which he undertook on the morrow, kept him busy for more than a week and made him almost forget all about Abbé Faujas. He was beginning, besides, to feel a little weary of the Abbé, who did not talk enough and was far too secretive. On two separate occasions he purposely avoided him, imagining that the priest only wanted to see him in order to make him relate the stories of the remainder of the Sub-Prefecture circle and Monsieur Rastoil's friends. Rose had informed him that Madame Faujas had tried to get her to talk, and this had made him vow that he would in future keep his mouth shut. This resolve furnished fresh amusement for his idle hours, and now, as he looked up at the closely drawn curtains of the second-floor windows, he would mutter:

'All right, my good fellow! Hide yourself as much as you like! I know very well that you're watching me from behind those curtains, but you won't be much the wiser for your trouble, and you'll find yourself much mistaken if you expect to get any more information out of me about our neighbours!'

He derived great pleasure from the thought that the Abbé Faujas was secretly watching, and he took every precaution to avoid falling into any trap that might be laid for him. One evening as he was coming home he saw Abbé Bourrette and Abbé Faujas standing before Monsieur Rastoil's gate. So he concealed himself behind the corner of a house and spied on them. The two priests kept him waiting there for more than a quarter of an hour. They talked with great animation, parted for a moment, and then joined each other again, and resumed their conversation. Mouret thought he could detect that Abbé Bourrette was trying to persuade Abbé Faujas to accompany him to the judge's; and that Faujas was making excuses for not going, and at last refusing to do so with some show of impatience. It was a Tuesday, the day of the weekly dinner. Finally Bourrette entered Monsieur Rastoil's house, and Faujas went off in his quiet fashion to his own rooms. Mouret stood for awhile thinking. What could be Abbé Faujas's reason for refusing to go to Monsieur Rastoil's? All the clergy of Saint-Saturnin's dined there, Abbé Fenil, Abbé Surin, and all the others. There was not a single priest in Plassans who had not enjoyed the fresh air by the fountain in the garden there. The new curate's refusal to go seemed a very extraordinary thing.

When Mouret got home again, he hurried to the bottom of his own garden to reconnoitre the second-floor windows. And after a moment or two he saw the curtain of the second window move to the right. He felt quite sure that Abbé Faujas was behind, it, spying upon what might be going on at Monsieur Rastoil's. Then Mouret thought that he could discover by certain movements of the curtain that the Abbé was in turn inspecting the gardens of the Sub-Prefecture.

The next day, a Wednesday, Rose told him just as he was going out that Abbé Bourrette had been with the second-floor people for at least an hour. Upon this he came back into the house and began to rummage about in the dining-room. When Marthe asked him what he was looking for, he replied sharply that he was trying to find a paper without which he could not go out. He even went upstairs, as if to see whether he had left it there. After waiting for a long time behind his bedroom door, he thought he could hear some chairs moving on the second floor, and thereupon he slowly went downstairs, stopping for a moment or two in the hall to give Abbé Bourrette time to catch him up.

'Ah! is that you, Monsieur l'Abbé? This is a fortunate meeting! You are going to Saint-Saturnin's, I suppose, and I am going that way too. We will keep each other company, if you have no objection.'

Abbé Bourrette replied that he would be delighted, and they both walked slowly up the Rue Balande towards the Place of the Sub-Prefecture. The Abbé was a stout man, with an honest, open face, and big, child-like blue eyes. His wide silk girdle which was drawn tightly round him threw his well-rounded stomach into relief. His arms were unduly short and his legs heavy and clumsy, and he walked with his head thrown slightly back.

'So you've just been to see our good Monsieur Faujas?' said Mouret, going to the point at once. 'I must really thank you for having procured me such a lodger as is rarely to be found.'

'Yes, yes,' said the priest, 'he is a very good and worthy man.'

'He never makes the slightest noise, and we can't really tell that there is anyone in the house. And he is so polite and courteous, too.

I've heard it said, do you know, that he is a man of unusual attainments, and that he has been sent here as a sort of compliment to the diocese.'

They had now reached the middle of the Place of the Sub-Prefecture. Mouret stopped short and looked at Abbé Bourrette keenly.

'Ah, indeed!' the priest merely replied, with an air of astonishment.

'So I've been told. The Bishop, it is said, intends to do something for him later on. In the meantime, the new curate has to keep himself in the background for fear of exciting jealousy.'

Abbé Bourrette went on walking again, and turned the corner of the Rue de la Banne.

'You surprise me very much,' he quietly remarked. 'Faujas is a very unassuming man; in fact, he is far too humble. For instance, at the church he has taken upon himself the petty duties which are generally left to the ordinary staff. He is a saint, but he is not very sharp. I scarcely ever see him at the Bishop's, and from the first he has always been very cold with Abbé Fenil, though I strongly impressed upon him that it was necessary he should be on good terms with the Grand-Vicar if he wished to be well received at the Bishop's. But he didn't seem to see it, and I'm afraid that he's deficient in judgment. He shows the same failing, too, by his continual visits to Abbé Compan, who has been confined to his bed for the last fortnight, and whom I'm afraid we are going to lose. Abbé Faujas's visits are most ill-advised, and will do him a deal of harm. Compan has always been on bad terms with Fenil, and it's only a stranger from Besançon who could be ignorant of a fact that is known to the whole diocese.'

Bourrette was growing animated, and in his turn he stopped short as they reached the Rue Canquoin and took his stand in front of Mouret.

'No, no, my dear sir,' he said, 'you have been misinformed: Faujas is as simple as a new-born babe. I'm not an ambitious man myself, and God knows how fond I am of Compan, who has a heart of gold, but, all the same, I keep my visits to him private. He said to me himself: "Bourrette, my old friend, I am not much longer for this world. If you want to succeed me, don't be seen too often knocking at my door. Come after dark and knock three times, and my sister will let you in." So now, you understand, I wait till night before I go to see him. One has plenty of troubles as it is, without incurring unnecessary ones!'

His voice quavered, and he clasped his hands across his stomach as he resumed his walk, moved by a naive egotism which made him commiserate himself, while he murmured:

'Poor Compan! poor Compan!'

Mouret was feeling quite perplexed. All his theories about Abbé Faujas were being upset.

'I had such very precise details furnished to me,' he ventured to say. 'I was told that he was to be promoted to some important office.'

'Oh dear, no!' cried the priest. 'I can assure you that there is no truth in anything of the kind. Faujas has no expectations of any sort. I'll tell you something that proves it. You know that I dine at the Presiding Judge's every Tuesday. Well, last week he particularly asked me to bring Faujas with me. He wanted to see him, and find out what sort of a person he was, I suppose. Now, you would scarcely guess what Faujas did. He refused the invitation, my dear sir, bluntly refused it. It was all to no purpose that I told him he would make his life at Plassans quite intolerable, and would certainly embroil himself with Fenil by acting so rudely to Monsieur Rastoil. He persisted in having his own way, and wouldn't be persuaded by anything that I said. I believe that he even exclaimed, in a moment of anger, that he wasn't reduced to accepting dinners of that kind.'

Abbé Bourrette began to smile. They had now reached Saint-Saturnin's, and he detained Mouret for a moment near the little side door of the church.

'He is a child, a big child,' he continued. 'I ask you, now, could a dinner at Monsieur Rastoil's possibly compromise him in any way? When your mother-in-law, that good Madame Rougon, entrusted me yesterday with an invitation for Faujas, I did not conceal from her my fear that it would be badly received.'

Mouret pricked up his ears.

'Ah! my mother-in-law gave you an invitation for him, did she?'

'Yes, she came to the sacristy yesterday. As I make a point of doing what I can to oblige her, I promised her that I would go and see the obstinate man this morning. I felt quite certain, however, that he would refuse.'

'And did he?'

'No, indeed; much to my surprise, he accepted.'

Mouret opened his lips and then closed them again without speaking. The priest winked with an appearance of extreme satisfaction.

'I had to manage the matter very skillfully, you know. For more than an hour I went on explaining your mother-in-law's position to him. He kept shaking his head, however; he could not make up his mind to go, and he was ever dwelling upon his desire for privacy. I had exhausted my stock of arguments when I recalled one point of the instructions which the dear lady gave me. She had told me to tell him that her drawing-room was entirely neutral ground, and that this was a fact well known to the whole town. When I pressed this upon his notice he seemed to waver, and at last he consented to accept the invitation, and even promised to go to-morrow. I shall send a few lines to that excellent Madame Rougon to inform her of my success.'

He lingered for a moment longer, rolling his big blue eyes, and saying—more to himself than to Mouret:

'Monsieur Rastoil will be very much vexed, but it's no fault of mine.'

Then he added: 'Good-morning, dear Monsieur Mouret; remember me very kindly to all your family.'

He entered the church, letting the padded doors close softly behind him. Mouret gazed at the doors and lightly shrugged his shoulders.

'There's a fine old chatterbox!' he muttered; 'one of those men who never give one a chance of getting in a word, but go on chattering away for hours without ever telling one anything worth listening to. So Faujas is going to Félicité's to-morrow! It's really very provoking that I am not on good terms with that fool Rougon!'

All the afternoon he was occupied with business matters, but at night, just as he and his wife were going to bed, he said to Marthe carelessly:

'Are you going to your mother's to-morrow evening?'

'No, not to-morrow,' Marthe replied, 'I have too many things to do. But I dare say I shall go next week.'

He made no immediate reply, but just before he blew out the candle, he resumed:

'It is wrong not to go out oftener than you do. Go to your mother's to-morrow evening; it will enliven you a little. I will stay at home and look after the children.'

Marthe looked at him in astonishment. He generally kept her at home with him, requiring all kinds of little services from her, and grumbling if she went out even for an hour.

'Very well,' she replied,' I will go if you wish me to.'

Then he blew out the candle, laid his head upon the pillow, and muttered:

'That's right; and you can tell us all about it when you come back. It will amuse the children.'

VI

About nine o'clock on the following evening, Abbé Bourrette called for Abbé Faujas. He had promised to go with him to the Rougons' and introduce him there. He found him ready, standing in the middle of his big bare room, and putting on a pair of black gloves that were sadly whitened at the finger-tips. Bourrette could not restrain a slight grimace as he looked at him.

'Haven't you got another cassock?' he asked.

'No,' quietly replied Abbé Faujas. 'This one is still very decent, I think.'

'Oh, certainly! certainly!' stammered the old priest; 'but it's very cold outside. Hadn't you better put something round your shoulders? Well! well! come along then!'

The nights had just commenced to be frosty. Abbé Bourrette, who was warmly wrapped in a padded silk over-coat, got quite out of breath as he panted along after Abbé Faujas, who wore nothing over his shoulders but his thin, threadbare cassock. They stopped at the corner of the Rue de la Banne and the Place of the Sub-Prefecture, in front of a house built entirely of white stone, one of the handsome mansions of the new part of the town. A servant in blue livery received them at the door and ushered them into the hall. He smiled at Abbé Bourrette as he helped him to take off his over-coat, and seemed greatly surprised at the appearance of the other priest, that tall, rough-hewn man, who had ventured out on such a bitter night without a cloak.

The drawing-room was on the first floor, and Abbé Faujas entered it with head erect, and grave, though perfectly easy, demeanour, while Abbé Bourrette, who was always very nervous when he went to the Rougons' house, although he never missed a single one of their receptions, made his escape into an adjoining apartment, thus cowardly leaving his companion in the lurch. Faujas, however, slowly traversed the whole drawing-room in order to pay his respects to the mistress of the house, whom he felt sure he could recognise among a group of five or six ladies. He was obliged to introduce himself, and he did so in two or three words. Félicité had immediately risen from her seat, and she closely if quickly scanned him from head to foot. Then her eyes sought his own, as she smilingly said:

'I am delighted, Monsieur l'Abbé; I am delighted indeed.'

The priest's passage through the drawing-room had created considerable sensation. One young lady who had suddenly raised her head, had quite trembled with alarm at the sight of that great black mass in front of her. The impression created by the Abbé was, indeed, an unfavourable one. He was too tall, too square-shouldered, his face was too hard and his hands were too big. His cassock, moreover, looked so frightfully shabby beneath the bright light of the chandelier that the ladies felt a kind of shame at seeing a priest so shockingly dressed. They spread out their fans, and began to giggle behind them, while pretending to be quite unconscious of the Abbé's presence. The men, meantime, exchanged very significant glances.

Félicité saw what a very churlish welcome the priest was receiving; she seemed annoyed at it, and remained standing, raising her voice in order to force her guests to hear the compliments which she addressed to Faujas.

'That dear Bourrette,' said she, in her most winning tone, 'has told me what difficulty he had in persuading you to come. I am really quite cross with you, sir. You have no right to deprive society of the pleasure of your company.'

The priest bowed without making any reply, and the old lady laughed as she began to speak again, laying a meaning emphasis on certain of her words.

'I know more about you than you imagine, in spite of all the care you have taken to hide your light under a bushel. I have been told about you; you are a very holy man, and I want to be your friend. We shall have an opportunity to talk about this, for I hope that you will now consider yourself as one of our circle.'

Abbé Faujas looked at her fixedly, as though he had recognised some masonic sign in the movements of her fan. He lowered his voice as he replied:

'Madame, I am entirely at your service.'

'I am delighted to hear you say so,' said Madame Rougon with another laugh. 'You will find that we do our best here to make everyone happy. But come with me and let me present you to my husband.'

She crossed the room, disturbing several of her guests in her progress to make way for Abbé Faujas, thus giving him an importance which put the finishing touch to the prejudice against him. In the adjoining room some card-tables were set out. She went straight up to her husband, who was gravely playing whist. He seemed rather impatient as she stooped down to whisper in his ear, but the few words she said to him made him spring briskly from his seat.

'Very good! very good!' he murmured.

Then, having first apologised to those with whom he was playing, he went and shook hands with Abbé Faujas.

At that time Rougon was a stout, pale man of seventy, and had acquired all a millionaire's gravity of expression. He was generally considered by the Plassans people to have a fine head, the white, uncommunicative head of a man of political importance. After he had exchanged a few courtesies with the priest he resumed his seat at the card-table. Félicité had just gone back into the drawing-room, her face still wreathed with smiles.

When Abbé Faujas at last found himself alone he did not manifest the slightest sign of embarrassment. He remained for a moment watching the whist-players, or appearing to do so, for he was, in reality, examining the curtains, and carpet, and furniture. It was a small wainscotted room, and bookcases of dark pear-tree wood, ornamented with brass headings, occupied three of its sides. It looked like a magistrate's private sanctum. At last the priest, who was apparently desirous of making a complete inspection, returned to the drawing-room and crossed it. It was hung with green, and was in keeping with the smaller *salon,* but there was more gilding about it, so that it suggested the soberness of a minister's private room combined with the brightness of a great restaurant. On the other side of it was a sort of boudoir where Félicité received her friends during the day. This was hung in straw colour, and was so full of easy-chairs and ottomans and couches, covered with brocade with a pattern of violet scroll-work, that there was scarcely room to move about in it.

Abbé Faujas took a seat near the fireplace and pretended to be warming his feet. He had placed himself in such a position that through the open doorway he could command a view of the greater part of the large drawing-room. He reflected upon Madame Rougon's gracious reception, and half closed his eyes, as though he were thinking out some problem which it was rather difficult to solve. A moment or two afterwards, while he was still absorbed in his reverie, he heard someone speaking behind him. His large-backed easy-chair concealed him from sight, and he kept his eyes still more tightly closed than before, as he remained there listening, looking for all the world as though the warmth of the fire had sent him to sleep.

'I went to their house just once at that time,' an unctuous voice was saying. 'They were then living opposite this place, on the other side of the Rue de la Banne. You were at Paris then; but all Plassans at that period knew of the Rougons' yellow drawing-room. A wretched room it was, hung with lemon-coloured paper at fifteen sous the piece, and containing some rickety furniture covered with cheap velvet. But look at black Félicité now, dressed in plum-coloured satin and seated on yonder couch! Do you see how she gives her hand to little Delangre? Upon my word, she is giving it to him to kiss!'

Then a younger voice said with something of a sneer:

'They must have managed to lay their hands on a pretty big share of plunder to be able to have such a beautiful drawing-room; it is the handsomest, you know, in the whole town.'

'The lady,' the other voice resumed, 'has always had a passion for receptions. When she was hard up she drank water herself so that she might be able to provide lemonade for her guests. Oh! I know all about the Rougons. I have watched their whole career. They are very clever people, and the Coup d'Etat has enabled them to satisfy the dreams of luxury and pleasure which had been tormenting them for forty years. Now you see what a magnificent style they keep up, how lavishly they live! This house which they now occupy formerly belonged to a Monsieur Peirotte, one of the receivers of taxes, who was killed in the affair at Sainte-Roure in the insurrection of '51. Upon my word, they've had the most extraordinary luck: a stray bullet removed the man who was standing in their way, and they stepped into his place and house. If it had been a choice between the receivership and the house, Félicité would certainly have chosen the house. She had been hankering after it for half a score years nearly, making herself quite ill by her covetous glances at the magnificent curtains that hung at the windows. It was her Tuileries, as the Plassans people used to say, after the 2nd of December.'

'But where did they get the money to buy this house?'

'Ah! no one knows that, my dear fellow. Their son Eugène, who has had such amazing political success in Paris, and has become a deputy, a minister and a confidential adviser at the Tuileries, had no difficulty in obtaining the receivership and the cross of the Legion of Honour for his father, who had played his cards very cleverly here. As for the house, they probably paid for it by borrowing the money from some banker. Anyhow, they are wealthy people to-day, and are fast making up for lost time. I fancy their son keeps up a constant correspondence with them, for they have not made a single false step as yet.'

The person who was speaking paused for a moment, then resumed with a low laugh:

'Ah! I really can't help laughing when I see that precious grasshopper of a Félicité putting on all her fine duchess's airs! I always think of the old yellow drawing-room with its threadbare carpet and shabby furniture and little fly-specked chandelier. And now, to-day, she receives the Rastoil young ladies. Just look how she is manoeuvring the train of her dress! Some day, my dear fellow, that old woman will burst of sheer triumph in the middle of her green drawing-room!'

Abbé Faujas had gently let his head turn so that he might peep at what was going on in the drawing-room. There he observed Madame Rougon standing in all her majesty in the centre of a group of guests. She seemed to have increased in stature, and every back around bent before her glance, which was like that of some victorious queen.

'Ah! here's your father!' said the person with the unctuous voice; 'the good doctor is just arriving. I'm quite surprised that he has never told you of all these matters. He knows far more about them than I do.'

'Oh! my father is always afraid lest I should compromise him,' replied the other gaily. 'You know how he rails at me and swears that I shall make him lose all his patients. Ah! excuse me, please; I see the young Maffres over there, I must go and shake hands with them.'

There was a sound of chairs being moved, and Abbé Faujas saw a tall young man, whose face already bore signs of physical weariness, cross the small room. The other person, the one who had given such a lively account of the Rougons, also rose from his seat. A lady who happened to pass near him allowed him to pay her some pretty compliments; and she smiled at him and called him 'dear Monsieur de Condamin.' Thereupon the priest recognised him as the fine man of sixty whom Mouret had pointed out to him in the garden of the Sub-Prefecture. Monsieur de Condamin came and sat down on the other side of the fireplace. He was startled to see Abbé Faujas, who had been quite concealed by the back of his chair, but he appeared in no way disconcerted. He smiled and, with amicable self-possession, exclaimed:

'I think, Monsieur l'Abbé, that we have just been unintentionally confessing ourselves. It's a great sin, isn't it, to backbite one's neighbour? Fortunately you were there to give us absolution.'

The Abbé, in spite of the control which he usually had over his features, could not restrain a slight blush. He perfectly understood that Monsieur de Condamin was reproaching him for having kept so quiet in order to listen to what was being said. Monsieur de Condamin, however, was not a man to preserve a grudge against anyone for their curiosity, but quite the contrary. He was delighted at the complicity which the matter seemed to have established between himself and the Abbé. It put him at liberty to talk freely and to while away the evening in relating scandalous stories about the persons present. There was nothing that he enjoyed so much, and this Abbé, who had only recently arrived at Plassans, seemed likely to prove a good listener, the more especially as he had an ugly face, the face of a man who would listen to anything, and wore such a shabby cassock -that it would be preposterous to think that any confidence to which he might be treated would lead to unpleasantness.

By the end of a quarter of an hour Monsieur de Condamin became quite at his ease, and gave Abbé Faujas a detailed account of Plassans with all the suave politeness of a man of the world.

'You are a stranger amongst us, Monsieur l'Abbé,' said he, 'and I shall be delighted if I can be of any assistance to you. Plassans is a little hole of a place, but one gets reconciled to it in time. I myself come from the neighbourhood of Dijon, and when I was appointed conservator of woods and rivers in this district, I found the place detestable, and thought I should be bored to death here. That was just before the Empire. After '51, the provinces were by no means cheerful places to live in, I assure you. In this department the folks were alarmed if they heard a dog bark, and they were ready to sink into the ground at the sight of a gendarme. But they calmed down by degrees, and resumed their old, monotonous, uneventful existences, and in the end I grew quite resigned to my life here. I live chiefly in the open air, I take long rides on horseback, and I have made a few pleasant friendships.'

He lowered his voice, and continued confidentially:

'If you will take my advice, Monsieur l'Abbé, you will be careful what you do. You can't imagine what a scrape I once nearly fell into. Plassans, you know, is divided into three absolutely distinct divisions: the old district, where your duties will be confined to administering consolation and alms; the district of Saint-Marc, where our aristocrats live, a district that is full of boredom and ill-feeling, and Where you can't be too much upon your guard; and, lastly, the new town, the district which is now springing up round the Sub-Prefecture, and which is the only one where it is possible to live with any degree of comfort. At first I was foolish enough to take up my quarters in the

Saint-Marc district, where I thought that my position required me to reside. There, alack! I found myself surrounded by a lot of withered old dowagers and mummified marquises. There wasn't an atom of sociability, not a scrap of gaiety, nothing but sulky mutiny against the prosperous peace that the country was enjoying. I only just missed compromising myself, upon my word I did. Péqueur used to chaff me, Monsieur Péqueur des Saulaies, our sub-prefect; you know him, don't you? Well, then I crossed the Cours Sauvaire, and took rooms on the Place. At Plassans, you must know, the people have no existence, and the aristocracy are a dreadful lot that it's quite impossible to get on with; the only tolerable folks are a few parvenus, some delightful persons who are ready to incur any expense in entertaining their official acquaintances. Our little circle of functionaries is a very delightful one. We live amongst ourselves after our own inclinations, without caring a rap about the townspeople, just as if we had pitched our camp in some conquered country.'

He laughed complacently, stretched himself further back in his chair, and turned up his feet to the fire; then he took a glass of punch from a tray which one of the servants banded to him, and sipped it slowly while still watching Abbé Faujas out of the corner of his eye. The latter felt that politeness required him to say something.

'This house seems a very pleasant one,' he remarked, turning slightly towards the green drawing-room, whence the sound of animated conversation was proceeding.

'Yes, yes,' resumed Monsieur de Condamin, who checked his remarks every now and then to take a little sip of punch. 'The Rougons almost make us forget Paris. You would scarcely fancy here that you were in Plassans. It is the only pleasant and amusing drawing-room in the whole place, because it is the only one where all shades of opinion elbow one another. Péqueur, too, has very pleasant assemblies. It must cost the Rougons a lot of money, and they haven't the public purse behind them like Péqueur has; though they have something better still, the pockets of the taxpayers.'

He seemed quite pleased with this witticism of his. He set his empty glass, which he had been holding in his hand, upon the mantelpiece, and then, drawing his chair near to Abbé Faujas and leaning towards him, he began to speak again:

'The most amusing comedies are continually being played here. But you ought to know the actors to appreciate them. You see Madame Rastoil over yonder between her two daughters—that lady of about forty-five with a head like a sheep's? Well, have you noticed how her eyelids trembled and blinked when Delangre came and sat down in front of her? Delangre is the man there on the left, with a likeness to Punch. They were acquainted intimately some ten years ago, and he is said to be the father of one of the girls, but it isn't known which. The funniest part of the business is that Delangre himself didn't get on very well with his wife about the same time; and people say that the father of his daughter is an artist very well known in Plassans.'

Abbé Faujas had considered it his duty to assume a very serious expression on being made the recipient of such confidences as these, and he even closed his eyes and seemed to hear nothing; while Monsieur de Condamin went on, as though in justification of himself:

'I allow myself to speak in this way of Delangre, as I know him so well. He is a wonderfully clever, pushing fellow. His father was a bricklayer, I believe. Fifteen years ago he used to take up the petty suits that other lawyers wouldn't be bothered with. Madame Rastoil extricated him from a condition of absolute penury; she supplied him even with wood in the winter-time to enable him to keep himself warm. It was through her influence that he won his first cases. It's worth mentioning that at that time Delangre had been shrewd enough to manifest no particular political proclivities; and so, in 1852, when people were looking out for a mayor, his name was at once thought of. He was the only man who could have been chosen without alarming one or other of the three divisions of the town. From that time everything has prospered with him, and he has a fine future before him. The only unfortunate part of the matter is that he doesn't get on very well with Péqueur; they are always wrangling about some silly trifles or other.'

He broke off as he saw the tall young man, with whom he had been chatting previously, come up to him again.

'Monsieur Guillaume Porquier,' he said, introducing him to the Abbé, 'the son of Doctor Porquier.'

Then, as Guillaume seated himself, he asked him with a touch of irony:

'Well! what did you see to admire over yonder?'

'Nothing at all, indeed!' replied the young man with a smile. 'I saw the Paloques. Madame Rougon always tries to hide them behind a curtain to prevent anything unpleasant happening. Paloque never takes his eyes off Monsieur Rastoil, hoping, no doubt, to kill him with suppressed terror. You know, of course, that the hideous fellow hopes to die presiding judge.'

They both laughed. The ugliness of the Paloques was a perpetual source of amusement amongst the little circle of officials. Porquier's son lowered his voice as he continued:

'I saw Monsieur Bourdeu, too. Doesn't it strike you that he's ever so much thinner since the Marquis de Lagrifoul's election? Bourdeu will never get over the loss of his prefecture; he had put all his Orleanist rancour at the service of the Legitimists in the hope that that course would lead him straight to the Chamber, where he would be able to win back that deeply-deplored prefecture. So he was horribly disgusted and hurt to find that instead of himself they chose the marquis, who is a perfect ass and hasn't the faintest notion of politics, whereas he, Bourdeu, is a very shrewd fellow.'

'That Bourdeu, with his tightly-buttoned frock-coat and broad-brimmed hat, is a most overbearing person,' said Monsieur de Condamin, shrugging his shoulders. 'If such people as he were allowed to have their own way they would turn France into a mere Sorbonne of lawyers and diplomatists, and would bore us all to death—Oh! by the way, Guillaume, I have been hearing about you. You seem to be leading a merry sort of life.'

'I?' exclaimed the young man with a smile.

'Yes, you, my fine fellow! and observe that I get my information from your father. He is much distressed about it: he accuses you of gambling and of staying out all night at the club and other places. Is it true that you have discovered a low café behind the gaol where you go with a company of scamps and play the devil's own game? I have even been told—'

Here Monsieur de Condamin, observing two ladies enter the room, began to whisper in Guillaume's ear, while the young man replied with affirmative signs and shook with suppressed laughter. Then he bent forward in turn and whispered to Monsieur de Condamin, and the pair of them, drawing close together with brightly glistening eyes, seemed to derive a prolonged enjoyment from this private story, which could not be told in the presence of ladies.

Abbé Faujas had remained where he was. He no longer listened to what was being said, but watched the many movements of Monsieur Delangre, who bustled about the green drawing-room trying to make himself extremely agreeable. The priest was so absorbed in his observations that he did not see Abbé Bourrette beckoning to him, so that the other had to come and touch his shoulder and ask him to follow. He then led him into the card-room with all the precaution of a man who has some very delicate communication to make.

'My dear friend,' he whispered, when they were alone in a quiet corner, 'it is excusable in you, as this is the first time you have been here, but I must warn you that you have compromised yourself very considerably by talking so long with the persons you have just left.'

Then, as Abbé Faujas looked at him with great surprise, he added:

'Those persons are not looked upon favourably. I myself am not passing any judgment upon them, and I don't want to repeat any scandal. I am simply warning you out of pure friendship, that's all.'

He was going away, but Abbé Faujas detained him, exclaiming hastily:

'You disquiet me, my dear Monsieur Bourrette; I beg of you to explain yourself. Without speaking any ill of anyone, you can surely be a little clearer.'

'Well then,' replied the old priest, after a momentary hesitation, 'Doctor Porquier's son causes his worthy father the greatest distress, and sets the worst example to all the studious youth of Plassans. He left nothing but debts behind him in Paris, and here he is turning the whole town upside down. As for Monsieur de Condamin—'

Here he hesitated again, feeling embarrassed by the enormity of what he had to relate; then, lowering his eyes, he resumed:

'Monsieur de Condamin is very free in his conversation, and I fear that he is deficient in a sense of morality. He spares no one, and he scandalises every honourable person. Then—I really hardly know how to tell you—but he has contracted, it is said, a scarcely creditable marriage. You see that young woman there, who is not thirty years old, and who has such a crowd around her? Well, he brought her to Plassans one day from no one knows where. From the time of her arrival she has been all-powerful here. It is she who has got her husband and Doctor Porquier decorated. She has influential friends in Paris. But I beg of you not to repeat any of this. Madame de Condamin is very amiable and charitable. I go to her house sometimes, and I should be extremely distressed if I thought that she considered me an enemy of hers. If she has committed faults, it is our duty —is it not?—to help her to return to a better way of life. As for her husband, he is, between ourselves, a perfect scamp. Have as little as possible to do with him.'

Abbé Faujas gazed into the worthy Bourrette's eyes. He had just noticed that Madame Rougon was following their conversation from the distance with a thoughtful air.

'Wasn't it Madame Rougon who told you to come and give me this good advice?' he suddenly asked the old priest.

'How did you know that?' the latter exclaimed in great astonishment. 'She asked me not to mention her name, but since you have guessed it—Ah! she is a good, kind-hearted lady who would be much distressed to see a priest compromising himself in her house. She is unfortunately compelled to receive all sorts of persons.'

Abbé Faujas expressed his thanks, and promised to be more prudent in the future. The card-players had not taken any notice of the two priests, who returned into the big drawing-room, where Faujas was again conscious of hostile surroundings. He even experienced greater coldness and more silent contempt than before. The ladies pulled their dresses out of his way as though his touch would have soiled them, and the men turned away from him with sneering titters. He himself maintained haughty calmness and indifference. Fancying that he heard the word Besançon meaningly pronounced in a corner of the room where Madame de Condamin was holding her court, he walked straight up to the folks by whom she was surrounded; but, at his approach, there was a dead silence amongst them, and they all stared him in the face with eyes that gleamed with uncharitable curiosity. He felt quite sure that they had been talking about him, and repeating some disgraceful story. While he was still standing there, behind the Rastoil young ladies, who had not observed him, he heard the younger one ask her sister:

'What was it that this priest, of whom everyone is talking, did at Besançon?'

'I don't quite know,' the elder sister replied. 'I believe he nearly murdered his vicar in a quarrel they had. Papa also said that he had been mixed up in some great business speculation which turned out badly.'

'He's in the small room over there, isn't he? Somebody saw him just now laughing with Monsieur de Condamin.'

'Oh! then people do quite right to distrust him if he laughs with Monsieur de Condamin.'

This gossip of the two girls made perspiration, start from Abbé Faujas's brows. He did not frown, but his lips tightened one upon the other, and his cheeks took an ashy tint. He seemed to hear the whole room talking of the priest whom he had tried to murder, and of the shady transactions in which he had been concerned.

Opposite him were Monsieur Delangre and Doctor Porquier, still looking very severe; Monsieur de Bourdeu's mouth pouted scornfully as he said something in a low voice to a lady; Monsieur Maffre, the justice of the peace, was casting furtive glances at him, as if he had piously resolved to examine him from a distance before condemning him; and at the other end of the room the two hideous Paloques craned out their malice-warped faces, in which shone a wicked joy at all the cruel stories that were being whispered about. Abbé Faujas slowly retired as he saw Madame Rastoil, who had been standing a few paces away, come up and seat herself between her two daughters, as though to keep them under the protection of her wing and shield them from his touch. He rested his elbow on the piano which he saw behind him, and there he stood with his head erect and his face as hard and silent as a face of stone. He felt that they were all in a plot to treat him as an outcast.

As he stood thus gazing at the company from under his partially lowered eyelids he suddenly gave a slight start, which he quickly suppressed. He had just caught sight of Abbé Fenil, leaning back in an easy-chair and smiling quietly behind a perfect wall of petticoats. The eyes of the two men met, and they gazed at each other for some moments with the fierce expression of duellists about to engage in mortal combat. Then there was a rustling of silk, and Abbé Fenil was hidden from sight by the ladies' gowns.

However, Félicité had contrived to reach the neighbourhood of the piano, and when she had succeeded in installing at it the elder of the Rastoil girls, who had a pleasant voice, and was able to speak to Abbé Faujas without being heard, she drew him towards one of the windows and asked:

'What have you done to Abbé Fenil?'

They talked together in very low tones. The priest at first feigned surprise, but when Madame Rougon had murmured a few words, accompanied by sundry shruggings of her shoulders, he seemed to become more open with her. They both smiled, and made a pretence of merely exchanging ordinary courtesies, but the glistening of their eyes spoke of something much more serious. The piano was silent for a moment, and then the elder Mademoiselle Rastoil began to sing 'La Colombo du Soldat,' which was a favourite song at that time.

'Your *début* has been most unfortunate,' Félicité continued. 'You have quite set people against you, and I should advise you not to come here again for a considerable time.

You must make yourself popular and a favourite, you understand. Any rash act would be fatal.'

Abbé Faujas seemed absorbed in thought.

'You say that it was Abbé Fenil who circulated these abominable stories?' he asked.

'Oh, he is much too wily to commit himself in such a way. He must just have faintly suggested them to his penitents. I don't know whether he has found you out, but he is certainly afraid of you. I am sure of that. And he will attack you in every possible way. The most unfortunate part of the matter is that he confesses the most important people in the town. It was he who secured the election of the Marquis de Lagrifoul.'

'I did wrong to come this evening,' the priest murmured.

Félicité bit her lips, then continued with animation:

'You did wrong to compromise yourself with such a man as that Condamin. I did what I thought was best. When the person whom you know of wrote to me from Paris I thought that I should be doing you a service by inviting you here. I imagined that you would he able to make it an opportunity for gaining friends. But, instead of doing what you could to make yourself popular, you have set everyone against you. Please excuse my freedom, but you really seem to be doing all you can to ensure your failure. You have committed nothing but mistakes: in going to lodge with my son-in-law, in persistently keeping yourself aloof from others, and in walking about in a cassock which makes the street-lads jeer at you.'

Abbé Faujas could not repress a movement of impatience. However, he merely replied:

'I will profit by your kind advice. Only, don't try to assist me; that would mar everything.'

'Yes, what you say is prudent,' replied the old lady. 'Only return here in triumph. One last word, my dear sir. The person in Paris is most anxious for your success, and it is for that reason that I am interesting myself in you. Well, then, don't make people frightened of you—shun you; be pleasant, and make yourself agreeable to the ladies. Remember that particularly. You must make yourself agreeable to the ladies if you want to get Plassans on your side.'

The elder Mademoiselle Rastoil had just finished her song with a final flourish, and the guests were softly applauding her. Madame Rougon left the Abbé to go and congratulate the singer. Then she took up a position in the middle of the room, and shook hands with the visitors who were beginning to retire. It was eleven o'clock. The Abbé was much vexed to find that the worthy Bourrette had taken advantage of the music to effect his escape. He had thought of leaving with him—a course which would have enabled him to make a respectable exit. Now, however, he would have to go away alone, which would be extremely prejudicial to him. It would be reported through the town in the morning that he had been turned out of the house. So he retired into a window-recess, whence he watched for an opportunity to effect an honourable retreat.

The room was emptying fast, however, and there were only a few ladies left. At last he noticed one who was very simply dressed; it was Madame Mouret, whose slightly waved hair made her look younger than usual. He looked with surprise at her tranquil face and her large, peaceful black eyes. He had not noticed her during the evening; she had quietly remained in the same corner without moving, vexed at wasting her time in this way, with her hands in her lap, doing nothing. While he was looking at her she rose to take leave of her mother.

It was one of Félicité's greatest delights to see the high society of Plassans leave her with profuse bows and thanks for her punch, her green drawing-room, and the pleasant evening they had spent there; and she thought how, formerly, these same fine folks had trampled her underfoot, whereas now the richest amongst them could not find sweet enough smiles for 'dear Madame Rougon.'

'Ah, madame!' murmured Maffre, the justice of the peace, 'one quite forgets the passage of time here.'

'You are the only pleasant hostess in all this uncivilised place,' whispered pretty Madame de Condamin.

'We shall expect you to dinner to-morrow,' said Monsieur Delangre; 'but you must take pot-luck, for we don't pretend to do as you do.'

Marthe was obliged to make her way through all this incense-offering crowd in order to reach her mother. She kissed her, and was about to retire, when Félicité detained her and looked around as if to trying to find someone. Then, on catching sight of Abbé Faujas, she inquired, with a smile:

'Is your reverence a gallant man?'

The Abbé bowed.

'Well, then, I should be much obliged to you if you would escort my daughter home. You both live in the same house, and so it will not put you to any inconvenience. On the road there is a little bit of dark lane which is not very pleasant for a lady by herself.'

Marthe assured her mother, in her quiet way, that she was not a little girl, and in no wise felt afraid; but as Félicité insisted, saying that she should feel easier if her daughter had someone with her, she at last accepted the Abbé's escort. As the latter retired with her, Félicité, who accompanied them to the landing, whispered in the priest's ear, with a smile:

'Don't forget what I told you. You must make yourself agreeable to the ladies if you want Plassans to belong to you.'

VII

That same night Mouret, who was still awake when his wife returned home, plied her with questions in his desire to find out what had taken place at Madame Rougon's. She told him that everything had gone off as usual, and that she had noticed nothing out of the common. She just added that Abbé Faujas had walked home with her, but had merely spoken of commonplace matters. Mouret was very much vexed, at what he called his wife's indolence.

'If anyone had committed suicide at your mother's,' he growled, as he angrily buried his head in his pillow, 'you would know nothing about it!'

When he came home to dinner the next day, he called to Marthe as soon as he caught sight of her:

'I was sure of it! I knew you had never troubled yourself to use your eyes! It's just like you! Sitting the whole evening in a room and never having the faintest notion of what was being said or done around you! Why, the whole town is talking about it! The whole town, do you hear? I couldn't go anywhere without somebody speaking to me about it'

'About what, my dear?' asked Marthe, in astonishment.

'About the fine success of Abbé Faujas, forsooth! He was turned out of the green drawing-room!'

'Indeed he wasn't! I saw nothing of the kind.'

'Haven't I told you that you never see anything? Do you know what the Abbé did at Besançon? He either murdered a priest or committed forgery! They are not quite certain which it was. However, they seem to have given him a nice reception! He turned quite green. Well, it's all up with him now!'

Marthe bent her head and allowed her husband to revel in the priest's discomfiture. Mouret was delighted.

'I still stick to my first idea,' he said; 'your mother and he have got some underhand plot together. I hear that she showed him the greatest civility. It was she, wasn't it, who asked him to accompany you home? Why didn't you tell me so?'

Marthe shrugged her shoulders without replying.

'You are the most provoking woman in the world!' her husband cried. 'All these little details are of the greatest importance. Madame Paloque, whom I have just met, told me that she and several other ladies had lingered behind to see how the Abbé would effect his departure, and that your mother availed herself of you to cover the parson's retreat. Just try to remember, now, what he said to you as he walked home with you.'

He sat down by his wife's side with his keen, questioning little eyes fixed upon her.

'Really,' said she quietly, 'he only talked to me about the trifling commonplace matters such as anyone might have talked of. He spoke about the cold, which was very sharp, and about the quietness of the town at night-time, and I think he mentioned the pleasant evening he had passed.'

'Ah, the hypocrite! Didn't he ask you any questions about your mother or her guests?'

'No. The Rue de la Banne is only a very short distance, you know, and it didn't take us three minutes. He walked by my side without offering me his arm, and he took such long strides that I was almost obliged to run. I don't know why folks should all be so bitter against him. He doesn't seem very well off, and he was shivering, poor man, in that threadbare old cassock of his.'

Mouret was not without pity and sympathy.

'Ah! he must have done,' he said; 'he can't feel very warm now that the frost has come.'

'I'm sure we have nothing to complain of in his conduct,' Marthe continued. 'He is very punctual in his payments, and he makes no noise and gives no trouble. Where could you find a more desirable tenant?'

'Nowhere, I grant you. What I was saying just now was to show you what little attention you pay, wherever you go, to what takes place around you. I know the set your mother receives too well to attach much weight to anything that happens in the green drawing-room: it's a perpetual source of lies and the most ridiculous stories. I don't suppose for a moment that the Abbé ever murdered anyone any more than that he was ever a bankrupt; and I told Madame Paloque that people ought to see that their own linen was clean before they found fault with that of others. I hope she took the hint to herself.'

This was a fib on Mouret's part, for he had said nothing of the kind to Madame Paloque; but Marthe's pity had made him feel rather ashamed of the delight which he had manifested at the Abbé's troubles. On the following days he went entirely over to the priest's side, and whenever he happened to meet any people whom he detested, Monsieur de Bourdeu, Monsieur Delangre, and Doctor Porquier, he launched out into warm praises of the Abbé just for the pleasure of astonishing and annoying them. The Abbé, said he, was a man of great courage and perfect guilelessness, but extremely poor, and some very base-minded person must have originated the calumnies about him. Then he went on to have a rap at the Rougons' guests, whom he called hypocrites, canting humbugs and stuck-up idiots, who were afraid of a man of real virtue. In a short time he had quite made the Abbé's quarrel his own, and availed himself of it to attack both the Rastoil gang and the gang of the Sub-Prefecture as well.

'Isn't it pitiable?' he sometimes said to his wife, forgetting that she had heard him tell a very different story, 'isn't it pitiable to see a lot of people who stole their money no one knows where, leaguing so bitterly against a poor man just because he hasn't got twenty francs to spare to buy a cart-load of firewood? Such conduct quite disgusts me! I'm quite willing to be surety for him. I ought to know what he does and what sort of a man he is, since he lives in my house; and so I'm not slack in telling them the truth, I give them all they deserve when I meet them. And I won't content myself with that, either. I want the Abbé to be my friend, and I mean to walk out with him arm-in-arm along the promenade to let people know that I'm not afraid of being seen with him, rich and well thought of as I am! I hope, too, that you will show all the kindness and consideration to these poor people that you can.'

Marthe smiled quietly, She was delighted at the friendly disposition her husband was now manifesting towards their lodgers. Rose was ordered to show them every civility; she was even told that she might volunteer to do Madame Faujas' shopping for her on wet mornings. The latter, however, always declined the cook's services, though she no longer manifested that silent stiffness of demeanour which she had shown during the earlier days of her residence in the house. One morning, as she met Marthe, who was coming down from an attic which was used as a storeroom for the fruit, she stopped and talked to her for a moment, and even unbent so far as to accept a couple of magnificent pears. Those pears were the beginning of a closer intimacy between them.

Abbé Faujas, too, did not now glide so hurriedly up and down the stairs as he had been wont to do. Almost every day, when Mouret heard the rustling of the priest's cassock as he came down, he hastened to the foot of the staircase and told the Abbé that it would give him great pleasure to walk part of the way with him. He had also thanked him for the little service he had done his wife, skillfully questioning him at the time to find out if he intended again calling on the Rougons. The Abbé had smiled and freely confessed that he was not fitted for society. This had delighted Mouret, who felt quite certain that he had had some influence in bringing about his lodger's decision. He even began to dream of preventing all future intercourse with the green drawing-room and of keeping him altogether to himself. So, when Marthe told him one evening that Madame Faujas had accepted a couple of pears, he looked upon this as a fortunate circumstance which would facilitate the execution of his designs.

'Haven't they really got a fire on the second floor this bitterly cold weather?' he asked, in Rose's presence.

'No, indeed, sir,' replied the cook, who understood that the question was meant for herself; 'they couldn't very well have one, for I've never seen the least bit of wood taken upstairs, unless indeed they're burning their four chairs or Madame Faujas manages to carry up the wood in her basket.'

'It is not right of you to talk in that way, Rose,' said Marthe. 'The poor things must be shivering with cold in those big rooms.'

'I should think so, indeed,' exclaimed Mouret; 'there were several degrees of frost last night and there was considerable fear felt about the olive-trees. The water in our jug upstairs was frozen. This room of ours here is a small one, however, and very warm.'

The doors and windows of the dining-room were provided with pads, so that no draught could find its way through any crevice, and a big earthenware stove made the place as warm as a bakehouse. During the winter evenings the young people read or played round the table, while Mouret made his wife play piquet till bed-time, which, by the way, was perfect torture to her. For a long time she had refused to touch the cards, saying that she did not know a single game, but at last he had taught her piquet, and she had then been forced to resign herself to her fate.

'Don't you think,' Mouret continued, 'that we really ought to ask the Faujases to come and spend the evenings here? They would at any rate be warm for two or three hours; and they would be company for us, too, and make us feel more lively. Ask them, and I don't think they'll refuse.'

The next day Marthe met Madame Faujas in the hall and gave the invitation, which the old lady at once accepted, both for herself and her son.

'I'm surprised she didn't make some little demur about coming,' said Mouret. 'I fancied that they would have required more pressing. But the Abbé is beginning to understand that he does wrong in living like a wild beast.'

In the evening Mouret took care that the table was cleared in good time, and he set out a bottle of sweet wine and a plateful of little cakes. Although he was not given to being lavish, he was anxious to show that the Rougons were not the only people who knew how things ought to be done. The tenants of the second floor came downstairs about eight o'clock. Abbé Faujas was wearing a new cassock, at the sight of which Mouret was so much surprised that he could only stammer a few words in answer to the priest's courtesies.

'Indeed, Monsieur l'Abbé, all the honour is for us. Come, children, put some chairs here.'

They all took their seats round the table. The room was uncomfortably warm, for Mouret had crammed the stove as full as possible in order to let his guests see that he made no account of a log more or less. Abbé Faujas made himself very pleasant, fondling Désirée and questioning the two lads about their studies. Marthe, who was knitting some stockings, raised her eyes every now and then in surprise at the flexible tones of that strange voice which she was not accustomed to hear sounding in the monotonous quietness of the dining-room. She looked at the priest's powerful face and square-cut features, and then bent her head again, without trying to hide the interest she took in this man who was so strong and kindly and whom she knew to be so poor. As for Mouret, he uncouthly stared at the new cassock, and could not restrain himself from saying, with a sly smile:

'You needn't have troubled to dress to come here, Monsieur l'Abbé. We don't go in for ceremony, as you know very well.'

Marthe blushed, while the priest gaily related that he had bought the cassock that very day. He had kept it on, he said, to please his mother, who thought that he looked finer than a king in it.

'Don't you, mother?' he asked the old lady.

Madame Faujas nodded without taking her eyes off her son. She was sitting opposite to him, gazing at him in the bright lamp light with an air of ecstacy.

They began to talk of various matters, and Abbé Faujas seemed to throw off his gloomy coldness. He still remained grave, but it was with a pleasant, good-natured gravity. He listened attentively to Mouret, replied to his most insignificant remarks, and seemed to take an interest in his gossip. His landlord explained to him the manner in which the family lived, and finished his account by saying:

'We spend our evenings in the way you see, always as quietly as this. We never invite anyone, as we are always more comfortable by ourselves. Every evening I have a game at piquet with my wife. It is a very old habit of ours, and I could scarcely go to sleep without it.'

'Pray don't let us interfere with it!' cried Abbé Faujas. 'I beg that you won't in any way depart from your usual habits on our account.'

'Oh dear no! I am not a monomaniac about it, and it won't kill me to go without it for once.'

The priest insisted for a time, but, when he saw that Marthe declined to play with even greater determination than her husband, he turned towards his mother, who had been sitting silent with her hands folded in front of her, and said:

'Mother, you have a game with Monsieur Mouret.'

She looked keenly into her son's eyes, while Mouret still continued to refuse, and declared that he did not want to break up the party. However, when the priest told him that his mother was a good player he gave way.

'Is she, indeed?' he said. 'Then, if madame really wishes it, and no one objects—'

'Come along, mother, and have a game!' said Abbé Faujas in a more decided tone.

'Certainly,' she replied, 'I shall be delighted; but I shall have to change my place.'

'Oh! there will be no difficulty about that,' said Mouret, who was quite charmed. 'You had better take your son's seat, and perhaps Monsieur l'Abbé will be good enough to sit next to my wife. Madame can sit next to me. There! that will do capitally.'

The priest, who had at first been opposite to Marthe on the other side of the table, was thus placed next to her. They sat quite apart by themselves, the two players having drawn their chairs close together to engage in their struggle. Octave and Serge had just gone up to their room. Désirée was sleeping with her head on the table after her usual custom. When ten o'clock struck, Mouret, who had lost the first game, did not feel inclined to go to bed but asked for his revenge. Madame Faujas consulted her son with a glance, and then in her tranquil fashion began to shuffle the cards. The Abbé had merely exchanged a few words with Marthe. On this the first evening that he spent in the dining-room he only spoke of commonplace topics; the household, the price of victuals at Plassans, and the anxieties which children caused. Marthe replied with a show of interest, looking up every now and then with her bright glance, and importing into the conversation some of her own sedate good sense.

It was nearly eleven o'clock when Mouret threw down the cards with some slight irritation.

'I have lost again!' he said. 'I haven't had a single good card all the evening. Perhaps I shall have better luck to-morrow. We shall see you again, I hope, madame?'

And when Abbé Faujas began to protest that they could not think of abusing the Mourets' kindness by disturbing them in this way every evening, he continued:

'But you are not disturbing us at all, you are giving us pleasure. Besides, I have been defeated, and I'm sure that madame can't refuse me another game.'

When the priest and his mother had accepted the invitation and had gone upstairs again, Mouret showed some ill-temper and began to excuse himself for having lost. He seemed quite annoyed about it.

'The old woman isn't as good a player as I am, I'm sure,' he said to his wife; 'but she has got such eyes! I could really almost fancy she was cheating, upon my word I could! Well! we shall see what happens to-morrow.'

From that time the Faujases came down regularly every day to spend the evening with the Mourets. There were tremendous battles between the old lady and her landlord.

She seemed to play with him, to let him win just frequently enough to prevent him from being altogether discouraged, and this made him fume with suppressed anger, for be prided himself on his skill at piquet. He used to indulge in dreams of beating her night after night for weeks in succession without ever letting her win a single game; while she ever preserved wonderful coolness, her square peasant-like face remaining quite expressionless as with her big hands she threw down the cards with all the regularity of a machine.

From eight o'clock till bed-time they would remain seated at their end of the table, quite absorbed in their game and never moving.

At the other end, near the stove, Abbé Faujas and Marthe were left entirely to themselves. The Abbé felt a masculine and priestly disdain for woman, and in spite of himself this disdain often made itself manifest in some slightly harsh expression. On these occasions Marthe was affected by a strange feeling of anxiety. She raised her eyes with one of those sudden thrills of alarm which cause people to cast a hurried glance behind them, half expecting to see some concealed enemy raising his hand to strike. At other times, on catching sight of the Abbé's cassock, she would check herself suddenly in the midst of a laugh, and would relapse into silence, quite confused, astonished at finding herself talking so freely to a man who was so different from other men. It was a long time before there was any real intimacy between them.

Abbé Faujas never directly questioned Marthe about her husband, or her children, or her house; but, nevertheless, he gradually made himself acquainted with every detail of their history and manner of life. Every evening, while Mouret and Madame Faujas were contending furiously one against the other, he contrived to learn some new fact. Upon one occasion he remarked that the husband and wife were surprisingly alike.

'Yes,' Marthe answered with a smile, 'when we were twenty years old we used to be taken for brother and sister; and, indeed, it was a little owing to that circumstance that we got married. People used to joke us about it, and were continually making us stand side by side, and saying what a fine couple we should make. The likeness was so striking that worthy Monsieur Compan, though he knew us quite well, hesitated to marry us.'

'But you are cousins, are you not?' the priest asked.

'Yes,' she replied, with a slight blush, 'my husband is a Macquart, and I am a Rougon.'

Then she kept silence for a moment or two, feeling ill at ease, for she was sure that the priest knew the history of her family which was so notorious at Plassans. The Macquarts were an illegitimate branch of the Rougons.

'The most singular part of it,' she resumed, to conceal her embarrassment, 'is, that we both resemble our grandmother. My husband's mother transmitted the likeness to him, while in me it has sprung up again after a break, passing my father by.'

Then the Abbé cited a similar instance in his own family. He had a sister, he said, who was the living image of her mother's grandfather. The likeness in this case had leapt over two generations. His sister, too, closely resembled the old man in her character and habits, even in her gestures and the tone of her voice.

'It was just the same with me when I was a little girl; I often heard people say of me,' remarked Marthe, '"She's Aunt Dide all over again!" The poor woman is now at Les Tulettes. She never had a strong head. For my part, in growing older, I have become less excitable and stronger, but I remember that when I was a child I hadn't good health at all. I used to have attacks of giddiness, and my head was filled with the strangest fancies. I often laugh now when I think of the extraordinary things I used to do.'

'And your husband?'

'Oh! he takes after his father, a journeyman hatter, a careful, prudent man. I should say that when we were young, though we were so much alike in face, it was quite a different matter as to our dispositions; however, as time has gone on, we have grown to resemble each other very much. We were so quiet and happy in our business at Marseilles! The fifteen years I spent there taught me to find happiness in my own home, in the midst of my children.'

Abbé Faujas noticed a touch of bitterness in her tone every time that he led her to speak on this subject. She was certainly happy, as she said; but he fancied that he could detect traces of old rebellion in her nervous nature, that was now calmed by the approach of her fortieth year. He imagined a little drama for himself, in which this husband and wife, who were so much alike, were considered by their relations to be made for each other, and were thus forced into marriage, whereas, in reality, they were of different and antagonistic temperaments. Then his mind dwelt upon the fatal outcome of a monotonous life, the wearing away of character by the daily cares of business, the soporific effect of fifteen years' fortune-making upon this couple, who were now living upon that fortune in a sleepy corner of a little town. To-day, though they were both still young, there seemed to be nothing but the ashes left of their former selves. The Abbé cleverly tried to discover whether Marthe was resigned to her existence, and he found her full of common sense.

'I am quite contented with my home,' she said; 'my children are all that I want. I was never much given to gaiety; I only felt a little dull at times. I dare say I should have been better if I had had some mental occupation, but I was never able to find one. And perhaps, after all, it's as well I didn't, for I should very likely have split my head. I could never even read a novel without giving myself a frightful headache, and for nights afterwards all the characters would dance about in my brain. Needlework is the only thing which never fatigues me, so I stay at home and keep out of the way of noise and chatter, and all the frivolous follies which weary me.'

She paused every now and then to glance at Désirée, who was still sleeping with her head upon the table, and smiling in her innocent way.

'Poor child!' she murmured. 'She can't even do any needlework. She gets dizzy directly. She is fond of animals, and that's all she's capable of. When she goes to stay with her nurse, as she does every now and then, she spends all her time in the poultry-yard, and she comes back to me with rosy cheeks and as strong and well as possible.'

Marthe often spoke of Les Tulettes, manifesting as she did so a lurking fear of insanity, and Abbé Faujas thus became aware of a strange dread haunting this peaceful home. Marthe loved her husband with a sober, unimpassioned love, but there was mingled with her affection for him considerable fear of his jokes and pleasantries, his perpetual teasing. She was hurt, too, by his selfishness, and the loneliness in which he left her; she felt a vague grudge against him for the quietude in which she lived—that very manner of life which she said made her happy. When she spoke of him, she said:

'He is very good to us. You've heard him, I dare say, get angry sometimes, but that arises from his passion for seeing everything in order, which he often carries to an almost ridiculous extent. He gets quite vexed if he sees a flower-pot a little out of place in the garden, or a plaything lying about on the floor; but in other matters he does quite right in pleasing himself. I know he is not very popular, because he has managed to accumulate some money, and still continues to do a good stroke of business every now and then; but he only laughs at what people say about him. They say nasty things, too, of him in connexion with me. They say that he is a miser, and won't let me go out anywhere, and even deprives me of boots. But all that is quite untrue. I am entirely free. He certainly prefers to see me here when he comes home, instead of finding that I am always off somewhere, paying calls and walking on the promenade. But he knows quite well what my tastes are. What, indeed, should I go out for?'

As she defended Mouret against the gossip of Plassans, Marthe's voice assumed a sudden animation, as though she felt the need of defending him quite as much from the secret accusations which arose within her own mind; and she kept reverting with nervous uneasiness to the subject of society life. She seemed to seek a refuge within the little dining-room and the old-fashioned garden with its box borders, as if everything else filled her with vague alarm, and made her doubtful of her strength, apprehensive of some possible catastrophe. Then she would smile at her fears, and shrug her shoulders as she resumed her knitting or the mending of some old skirt; and Abbé Faujas would see before him only a cold, reserved housewife, with listless face and inanimate eyes, who filled the house with a scent as of clean linen, and of blossoms gathered in the shade.

Two months passed away in this manner. Abbé Faujas and his mother had become quite a part of the Mourets' family life. They all had their recognised places every evening at the table, just as the lamp had its place; and the same intervals of silence were broken night after night by the same remarks from the card-players and the same subdued converse of the priest and Marthe. When Madame Faujas had not given him too tremendous a beating Mouret found his lodgers 'extremely nice people.'

All that curiosity of his, born of idleness, waned before the interest and occupation that the nightly parties afforded him, and he no longer played the spy upon the Abbé, whom he declared to be a very good fellow, now that he knew him better.

'Oh, don't bother me with your stories!' he used to exclaim to those who attacked Abbé Faujas. 'You get hold of a pack of nonsense and put absurd interpretations upon facts that admit of the simplest explanation. I know all about him. He very kindly comes and spends his evenings with us; but he's not a man to make himself cheap, and I can quite understand that people don't like him for it and accuse him of pride.'

Mouret greatly enjoyed being the only person in Plassans who could boast of knowing Abbé Faujas, and he even somewhat abused this advantage. Every time he met Madame Rougon he put on an air of triumph and made her understand that he had stolen her guest from her, while the old lady contented herself with smiling quietly. With his intimate acquaintances Mouret extended his confidences further, and remarked that those blessed priests could do nothing like other people. Then he gave them a string of little details, and told them in what manner the Abbé drank, how he talked to women, and how he always kept his knees apart without ever crossing his legs, and other trifling matters which the vague alarm that his free-thinking mind experienced in the presence of his guest's long, mystic-looking cassock made him notice.

The evenings passed away one after another, and at last the first days of February came round. In all the conversations between himself and Marthe Abbé Faujas had to all appearance carefully avoided the subject of religion. She had once remarked to him, almost lightly:

'No, Monsieur l'Abbé, I am not a very religious woman, and I seldom go to church. At Marseilles I was always too busy, and now I am too indolent to go out. And then I must confess to you that I wasn't brought up with religious ideas. My mother used to tell me that God would come to us quite as well at home.'

The priest bowed his head without making any reply, and seemed to signify that he would rather not discuss religious matters under such circumstances. One evening, however, he drew a picture of the unexpected comfort which suffering souls find in religion. They were talking of a poor woman whom troubles of every sort had driven to suicide.

'She did wrong to despair,' said the priest in his deep voice. 'She was ignorant of the comfort and consolation to be found in prayer. I have often seen heart-broken, weeping women come to us, and they have gone away again filled with a resignation that they had vainly sought elsewhere, and glad to live; and this had come from their falling upon their knees and tasting the blessedness of humiliating themselves before God in some quiet corner of the church. They came back there, they forgot their troubles, and became God's entirely.'

Marthe listened with a thoughtful expression to these remarks of the priest, whose last words fell in a gradually softening voice that seemed to breathe of superhuman felicity.

'Yes, it must be a blessed thing,' she murmured, as though she were speaking to herself. 'I have thought about it sometimes, but I have always felt afraid.'

If the Abbé seldom referred to such matters as this, he frequently spoke on the subject of charity. Marthe was very tender-hearted, and tears rose to her eyes at the slightest tale of trouble. It seemed to please the priest to see her so moved to pity; and every evening he told her some fresh story of sorrow, and kept her constantly excited with compassion. She would let her work fall, and clasp her hands as with a sad, pitying face, she gazed into his eyes and listened to him as he recounted heartrending details of how some poor persons had died of starvation, or how others had been goaded by misery into committing base crimes. At these times she fell completely under his influence, and he might have done what he willed with her.

About the middle of February a deplorable occurrence threw Plassans into dismay. It was discovered that a number of young girls, scarcely more than children, had fallen into evil courses while loafing about the streets, and it was even rumoured that some persons of high position in the town would be compromised. For a week Marthe was very painfully affected by this discovery, which caused the greatest sensation. She was acquainted with one of the unfortunate girls, who was the niece of her cook, Rose; and she could not think of the poor little creature without shuddering.

'It is a great pity,' said Abbé Faujas to her one evening, 'that there isn't a Home at Plassans on the model of the one at Besançon.'

Then, in reply to Marthe's pressing questions, the Abbé explained to her the constitution of this Home. It was a sort of refuge for girls from eight to fifteen years of age, the daughters of working men, whose parents were obliged to leave them alone during the day while they themselves went to their employment. During the day-time these girls were set to do needlework, and in the evening they were sent back to their parents, the latter having then returned home from their work. By this system the children were brought up out of the reach of vice and in the midst of good examples. Marthe thought the idea an admirable one, and she gradually became so prepossessed in its favour that she could talk of nothing else than the necessity of founding a similar institution at Plassans.

'We might put it under the patronage of the Virgin,' Abbé Faujas suggested. 'But there are such difficulties in the way! You have no idea of the trouble there is in effecting the least good work! What is quite essential to the success of such a scheme as this is some woman with a motherly heart, full of zeal and absolutely devoted to the work.'

Marthe lowered her head and looked at Désirée, who was asleep by her side, and she felt tears welling from beneath her eyelids. She made inquiries as to the steps that it would be necessary to take for founding such a Home, the cost of erecting it, and the annual expenses.

'Will you help me?' she suddenly asked the priest one evening.

Abbé Faujas gravely took her hand and held it within his own for a moment, telling her that she had one of the fairest souls he had ever known. He would willingly do what he could, he assured her, but he should rely altogether upon her, for the assistance that he himself would be able to give would be small. It would be for her to form a committee of the ladies of the town, to collect subscriptions, and to take upon herself, in a word, all the delicate and onerous duties which are connected with an appeal to the charity of the public. He appointed a meeting with her for the following day at Saint-Saturnin's to introduce her to the diocesan architect, who would be able to tell her much better than he himself could do about the expenses that would have to be incurred.

Mouret was very gay that evening when they went to bed. He had not allowed Madame Faujas to win a single game.

'You seem quite pleased about something to-night, my dear,' he said to his wife. 'Did you see what a beating I gave the old lady downstairs?'

Then as he observed Marthe taking a silk dress out of her wardrobe, he asked her with some surprise if she intended to go out in the morning. He had not heard anything of the conversation in the dining-room between his wife and the priest.

'Yes,' she replied, 'I have to go out. I have to meet Abbé Faujas at the church about a matter which I will tell you of.'

He stood motionless in front of her, and gazed at her with an expression of stupefaction, wondering if she were not really jesting with him. Then, without any appearance of displeasure, he said in his bantering fashion:

'Hallo! hallo! well I never expected that! So you've gone over to the priests now!'

VIII

The next morning Marthe began by calling on her mother, to whom she explained the pious undertaking which she was contemplating. She became almost angry when the old lady smilingly shook her head, and she gave her to understand that she considered her lacking in charity.

'It is one of Abbé Faujas's ideas, isn't it?' Félicité suddenly inquired.

'Yes,' Marthe replied in surprise: 'we have talked a good deal about it together. But how did you know?'

Madame Rougon shrugged her shoulders without vouchsafing any definite reply. Then she continued with a show of animation:

'Well, my dear, I think you are quite right. You ought to have some kind of occupation, and you have found a very good one. It has always distressed me very much to see you perpetually shut up in that lonely, death-like house of yours. But you mustn't count upon my assistance. I would rather not appear in the matter, for people would say that it was I who was really doing everything, and that we had come to an understanding together to try to force our ideas upon the town. I should prefer that you yourself should have all the credit of your charitable inspiration. I will help you with my advice, if you will let me, but with nothing more.'

'I was hoping that you would join the committee,' said Marthe, who felt a little alarmed at the thought of finding herself alone in such an onerous undertaking.

'No! no! my presence on it would only do harm, I can assure you. Make it well known, on the contrary, that I am not going to be on the committee, that I have been asked, and have refused, excusing myself on the ground that I am too much occupied. Let it be understood, even, that I have no faith in your scheme; and that, you will see, will influence the ladies at once. They will be delighted to take part in charitable work in which I have no share. Go and see Madame Rastoil, Madame de Condamin, Madame Delangre, and Madame Paloque. Be sure to see Madame Paloque; she will feel flattered, and will help you more than all the others. If you find any difficulty about anything, come here again and tell me.'

She accompanied her daughter to the head of the stairs; then she stopped and looked her in the face, saying with her sharp smile:

'I hope the dear Abbé keeps well.'

'Yes, he is quite well,' replied Marthe. 'I am going to Saint-Saturnin's, where I am to meet the diocesan architect.'

Marthe and the priest had considered that matters were still in too indefinite a stage for them to disturb the architect, and so they had planned just to meet him at Saint-Saturnin's, where he came every day to inspect a chapel that happened to be under repair at the time. It would seem like a chance meeting. When Marthe walked up the church, she caught sight of Abbé Faujas and Monsieur Lieutaud—the architect—talking together on some scaffolding, from which they descended as soon as they saw her. One of the Abbé's shoulders was quite white with plaster, and he seemed to be taking a great interest in the operations.

At this hour of the afternoon, there were no worshippers or penitents in the church, and the nave and aisles were quite deserted, encumbered only by a litter of chairs, which two vergers were noisily setting in order. Workmen were calling to each other from the tops of ladders, and trowels were scraping against the walls. There was so little appearance of devotion about Saint-Saturnin's that Marthe had not even crossed herself on entering. She took a seat opposite to the chapel that was being repaired, between Abbé Faujas and Monsieur Lieutaud, just as she would have done if she had gone to consult the latter in his office.

The conversation lasted for a good half-hour. The architect showed much kindly interest in the scheme. But he advised them not to erect a special building for the Home of the Virgin, as the Abbé called the projected refuge. It would cost too much money, he thought; and it would be better to buy some building already in existence, and adapt it to suit the requirements of their scheme. He suggested a house in the Faubourg which, after being used as a boarding-school, had passed into the hands of a forage dealer, and was now for sale. A few thousand francs would enable one to entirely transform the place and restore it from its present ruinous condition; and he promised them all kinds of wonderful things: a handsome entrance, spacious rooms, and a court planted with trees. By degrees, Marthe and the priest raised their voices, and they discussed details beneath the echoing vaults of the nave, while Monsieur Lieutaud scratched the flagstones with the tip of his stick to give them an idea of the façade he suggested.

'It is settled, then,' said Marthe, as she took leave of the architect. 'You will make a little estimate, won't you, so that we may know what we are about? And please keep our secret, will you?'

Abbé Faujas wished to escourt her as far as the door of the church. As they passed together before the high-altar, however, while she was still briskly talking to him, she was suddenly surprised to miss him from her side. She turned round and saw him bent almost double before the great cross, veiled with muslin. The sight of him, covered as he was with plaster, bent in this way before the cross, gave her a singular feeling. She recollected where she was, glanced round her with an uneasy expression and trod as silently as she could. When they reached the door, the Abbé, who had become very grave and serious, silently reached out his finger, which he had dipped in the holy water, and she crossed herself in great disquietude of mind. Then the muffled doors softly fell back behind her with a sound like a sigh.

From the church Marthe repaired to Madame de Condamin's. She felt quite happy as she walked through the streets in the fresh air; the few visits that she had now to make seemed to her almost like pleasure-parties. Madame de Condamin welcomed her with an air of friendly surprise. That dear Madame Mouret came so seldom! When she learned the business on hand, she declared herself charmed with it, and was quite ready to further it in every possible way. She was wearing a lovely mauve dress, with knots of pearl-grey ribbon, in that pretty boudoir of hers where she played the part of an exiled Parisienne.

'You did quite right to count upon me,' she exclaimed as she pressed Marthe's hands. 'Who ought to help those poor girls if it isn't we whom people accuse of setting them a bad example by our luxury? It is frightful to think of those children being exposed to all those horrible dangers. It has made me feel quite ill. I am entirely at your service.'

When Marthe told her that her mother could not join the committee she displayed still greater enthusiasm for the scheme.

'It is a pity Madame Rougon has so many things to do,' she said with a touch of irony; 'she would have been of great assistance to us. But it can't be helped. No one can do more than they are able. I have plenty of friends. I will go and see the Bishop; and move heaven and earth if it's necessary. I'll promise you that we shall succeed,'

She would not listen to any of the particulars about the expenses. She was quite sure, she said, that whatever money was wanted would be found, and she meant the Home to be a credit to the committee, as handsome and as comfortable as possible. She added with a laugh that she quite lost her head when she began to dabble in figures; but she undertook to charge herself with the preliminary steps and the general furtherance of the scheme. Dear Madame Mouret, said she, was not accustomed to begging, and she would accompany her on her visits and would even take several of them off her hands altogether. By the end of a quarter of an hour she had made the business entirely her own, and it was now she who gave instructions to Marthe. The latter was just about to take her leave when Monsieur de Condamin came into the room; so she lingered on, feeling very ill at ease, however, and not daring to say any more on the subject of her visit in the presence of a man who was rumoured to be compromised in that matter of the poor girls with whose shameful story the town was ringing.

But Madame de Condamin explained the great scheme to her husband, who listened with an appearance of perfect ease, and gave utterance to the most moral sentiments. He considered the scheme an extremely proper one.

'It is an idea which could only have occurred to a mother,' he said gravely, in a tone which made it impossible to tell whether he was serious or not. 'Plassans will be indebted to you, madame, for a purer morality.'

'But I must tell you that the idea is not my own! I have merely adopted it,' replied Marthe, made uneasy by these praises. 'It was suggested to me by a person whom I esteem very highly.'

'Who was that?' asked Madame de Condamin, with a show of curiosity.

'Abbé Faujas.'

Then Marthe, with great frankness, told them what a high opinion she had of the priest. She made no allusion to the unpleasant stories that had been circulated about him, but she represented him as a man worthy of the highest respect, whom she was very happy to receive in her home. Madame de Condamin nodded approvingly as she listened.

'I always said so!' she exclaimed. 'Abbé Faujas is a very distinguished priest. But there are such a lot of malicious people about! Now, however, that you receive him in your home, they don't venture to say anything more against him; all that calumnious talk has been cut short. The idea, you say, is his. We shall have to persuade him, then, to take a prominent part in putting it into execution. For the present we will keep the matter very quiet. I can assure you that I always liked and defended the Abbé.'

'I recollect talking with him, and I thought him a very good fellow,' remarked the conservator of rivers and forests.

His wife silenced him with a gesture. She occasionally treated him in a very cavalier style. Truth to tell, Monsieur de Condamin alone bore the shame attaching to the equivocal marriage which he was charged with having made; the young woman, whom he had brought from no one knew where, had got herself forgiven and liked by the whole town, thanks to her pleasant ways and taking looks, to which provincial folks are more susceptible than might be imagined.

Monsieur de Condamin understood that he was in the way in this virtuous consultation.

'I will leave you to your good designs,' he said with a slight touch of irony. 'I am going to smoke a cigar. Octavie, don't forget to be dressed in good time. We are going to the Sub-Prefecture this evening, you know.'

When he had left the room, the two women resumed their conversation for a few moments longer, returning to what they had previously been saying, expressing pity for the poor girls who yielded to temptation, and manifesting much anxiety to shelter them from danger. Madame de Condamin inveighed eloquently against vice.

'Well, then!' she said, as she pressed Marthe's hand for the last time, 'it is all settled, and I shall be entirely at your service as soon as you call for my help. If you go to see Madame Rastoil and Madame Delangre, tell them that I will undertake to do everything, and that all we want from them is their names. My idea is a good one, don't you think? We won't depart a hair's breadth from it. Give my compliments to Abbé Faujas.'

Marthe at once proceeded to call upon Madame Delangre, and then upon Madame Rastoil. She found them very polite, but less enthusiastic than Madame de Condamin. They discussed the pecuniary side of the scheme. A large sum of money would be required, they said; the charity of the public would certainly never provide it, and there was a great risk of the whole business coming to a ridiculous termination. Marthe tried to reassure them, and plied them with figures. Then they asked her what ladies had consented to join the committee. The mention of Madame de Condamin's name left them silent, but when they learned that Madame Rougon had excused herself from joining, they became more amiable.

Madame Delangre had received Marthe in her husband's private room. She was a pale little woman whose dissoluteness had remained a matter of legend in Plassans.

'Indeed,' she ended by saying, 'there is nothing I should like to see better. It would be a school of virtue for the youth of the working-classes, and it would be the means of saving many weak souls. I cannot refuse my assistance, for I feel that I could be of much use to you through my husband, who as mayor of the town is brought into continual contact with all the influential people. But I must ask you to allow me till to-morrow before I give a definite reply. Our position requires us to exercise circumspection, and I should like to consult Monsieur Delangre.'

In Madame Rastoil Marthe encountered a woman who was equally listless but more prudish, and who sought for irreproachable words when referring to the unfortunate girls who had fallen. She was a sleek, plump person, and Marthe found her embroidering a very gorgeous alb, between her two daughters, whom she sent away at her visitor's first words.

'I am much obliged to you for having thought of me, she said; 'but really I am very much occupied. I am already on several committees and I don't know whether I should have the time. I have had some such idea as your own myself, but my scheme was a larger one and, perhaps, more complete and comprehensive. For a whole month I have been intending to talk to the Bishop about it, but I have never been able to find the time. Well! we will unite our efforts, and I will tell you my own views, for I think you are making a mistake in some points. Since it seems necessary, I will surrender still more of my time. But it was only yesterday that my husband said to me: "Really, you never attend to your own affairs; you are always looking after other people's."'

Marthe glanced at her curiously, thinking of her old entanglement with Monsieur Delangre, which folks still chuckled over in the cafés of the Cour Sauvaire. The wives of the mayor and the presiding judge had received the mention of Abbé Faujas's name very suspiciously, the latter especially so. Marthe was a little vexed at this distrust of a person for whom she vouched; so she made a point of dwelling upon the Abbé's good qualities, and eventually forced the two women to acknowledge the merit of this priest, who lived a life of retirement and supported his mother.

On leaving Madame Rastoil's Marthe merely had to cross the road to reach Madame Paloque's, which was on the other side of the Rue Balande. It was seven o'clock, but she was anxious to make this last call, even if she were to keep Mouret waiting for dinner and get herself scolded in consequence.

The Paloques were just about to sit down to table in a chilly dining-room, whose prim coldness spoke of provincial penury. Madame Paloque hastened to cover up the soup-tureen, vexed at being thus found at table. She was very polite, humble almost, anxious as she really felt about this visit which she had not expected. Her husband, the judge, sat before his empty plate with his hands upon his knees.

'The hussies!' he exclaimed, when Marthe spoke of the girls of the old quarter of the town. 'I heard some nice accounts of them to-day at court. It was they who led some of our most respectable townspeople astray. You do wrong, madame, to interest yourself about such vermin.'

'I am very much afraid,' said Madame Paloque in her turn, 'that I cannot be of much assistance to you. I know no one, and my husband would cut his hand off rather than beg for the smallest trifle. We have held ourselves quite aloof from everyone, disgusted as we are with all the injustices we have witnessed. We live here very quietly and modestly, happy in being forgotten and let alone. Even if promotion were offered to my husband now, he would refuse it. Wouldn't you, my dear?'

The judge nodded his head in assent and they exchanged a slight smile, while Marthe sat ill at ease in the presence of that hideous wrinkled couple, livid with gall and bitterness, who played so well the little comedy of feigned resignation. Fortunately she recalled her mother's counsels.

'I had quite counted upon you,' she said, making herself very pleasant. 'We shall have Madame Delangre, Madame Rastoil, and Madame de Condamin; but, between ourselves, those ladies will only give us their names. I should have liked to find some lady of good status and kindly, charitable disposition, who would have taken a stronger interest and shown more energy in the matter, and I thought that you would be the very person. Think what gratitude Plassans would owe us if we could only bring such an undertaking to a successful issue!'

'Of course, of course!' Madame Paloque murmured, quite delighted at Marthe's insinuating words.

'I am sure you are wrong in fancying that you are without power to assist us. It is very well known that Monsieur Paloque is a favourite at the Sub-Prefecture; and between ourselves I may say that he is intended to succeed Monsieur Rastoil. Ah, now! don't try to depreciate yourselves; your merits are known, and it is no use your trying to hide them. This would be a very good opportunity for Madame Paloque to emerge a little from the obscurity and privacy in which she keeps herself, and to let the world see what a head and what a heart she has!'

The judge seemed very restless. He looked at his wife with blinking eyes.

'Madame Paloque has not refused,' said he.

'No, certainly not,' interposed the latter. 'If you really stand in need of me, that settles the matter. I dare say I am only committing another piece of folly, and shall give myself a lot of trouble without ever getting a word of thanks for it. Monsieur Paloque can tell you of all the good works we've done without ever saying a word about them; and you can see for yourself what they've brought us to. Well, well, we can't change our natures, and I suppose we shall continue being dupes to the end! You may count upon me, dear madame.'

The Paloques rose and Marthe took leave of them, thanking them for their kindly interest. As she stopped for a moment on the landing to liberate a flounce of her dress which had caught between the banisters and the steps, she heard them talking with animation on the other side of the door.

'They want to enlist you because they want to make use of you!' the judge was saying in a bitter voice. 'You will be their beast of burden.'

'Of course!' replied his wife, 'but you may be sure that I'll make them pay for it with the rest!'

When Marthe at last got back home, it was nearly eight o'clock. Mouret had been waiting a whole half-hour for his dinner, and she was afraid that there would be a terrible scene. But, when she had undressed and come downstairs, she found her husband seated astride an overturned chair, tranquilly beating a tattoo on the table-cloth with his fingers. He was in a very teasing, bantering mood.

'Well,' said he, 'I had quite made up my mind that you were going to spend the night in a confessional-box. Now that you have taken to going to church, you had better give me notice when the priests invite you, so that I can dine out.'

All through the dinner he indulged in witticisms of this kind, and Marthe was more distressed by them than if he had openly stormed at her. Two or three times she cast a glance at him as if beseeching him to leave her in peace. But her looks only appeared to stimulate his wit. Octave and Désirée laughed at it all, but Serge remained silent and mentally took his mother's side. During dessert Rose came into the room, looking quite scared, with the news that Monsieur Delangre had called and wished to see madame.

'Hallo! have you begun to associate with the authorities as well?' exclaimed Mouret in his sneering fashion.

Marthe went into the drawing-room to receive the mayor. With much politeness the latter told her that he had felt unwilling to wait until the morrow to congratulate her upon her charitable idea. Madame Delangre was a little timid; she had done wrong in not immediately promising her cooperation, and he had now come to say in her name that she would be delighted to serve on the committee of lady patronesses of the Home of the Virgin. As for himself, he would do all he could to further the success of a scheme that would be so useful, so conducive to morality.

Marthe accompanied him to the street-door; and there, as Rose held up the lamp to light the footpath, the mayor added:

'Will you tell Abbé Faujas that I shall be glad to have a little conversation with him, if he will kindly call on me? As he has had experience of an establishment of this kind at Besançon, he will be able to give me valuable information. I mean the town to pay for the building, at any rate. Goodbye, dear madame. Give my best compliments to Monsieur Mouret, whom I won't disturb.'

When Abbé Faujas came down with his mother at eight o'clock Mouret merely said to him, with a laugh:

'So you walked my wife off to-day, eh? Well, don't spoil her for me too much, and don't make a saint of her.'

Then he turned to his card-play. He was anxious to revenge himself on Madame Faujas, who had defeated him three evenings in succession; and so Marthe was left free to tell the Abbé of all she had done during the day. She seemed full of child-like pleasure, and was still quite excited with her afternoon. The priest made her repeat certain details, and then promised to call on Monsieur Delangre, although he would have preferred remaining altogether in the background.

'You did wrong to mention my name at all,' he said, when he saw her so moved and yielding. 'But you are like all other women; the best causes would be spoilt in your hands.'

She looked at him in surprise at this harsh exclamation, recoiling and feeling that thrill of fear which she still occasionally experienced in the presence of his cassock. It was as though iron hands were being laid upon her shoulders and were forcing her into compliance with their will. Every priest looks upon woman as an enemy; but when the Abbé saw that she was hurt by his stern reproof he softened his voice and said:

'I think only of the success of your noble design. I am afraid that I should compromise it if I myself were to appear in it. You know very well that I am not a favourite in the town.'

Marthe, seeing him so humble, assured him that he was mistaken, and that all the ladies had spoken of him in the highest terms. They knew that he was supporting his mother, and that he led a quiet, retired life worthy of the greatest praise. Then they talked over the great scheme, dwelling on the smallest details of it, till eleven o'clock struck. It was a delightful evening.

Mouret had caught a word or two of the talk every now and then between the deals.

'And so,' he said, as they were going to bed, 'so you two are going to stamp out vice? It's a fine invention.'

Three days later the committee of patronesses was formally constituted. The ladies having elected Marthe as president, she, upon her mother's advice which she had privately sought, immediately named Madame Paloque treasurer. They both gave themselves a great deal of trouble in directing circulars and looking after a host of other petty details. In the meantime Madame de Condamin went from the Sub-Prefecture to the Bishop's, and from the Bishop's to the houses of various other influential persons, exhibiting some lovely toilettes, explaining in her pretty fashion 'the happy idea that had occurred to her,' and carrying off subscriptions and promises of assistance. Madame Rastoil, on the other hand, told the priests who came to her house on the Tuesday how she had formed a plan for rescuing unfortunate girls from vice, and then contented herself with charging Abbé Bourrette to inquire of the Sisters of Saint-Joseph if they would come and serve in the projected refuge; while Madame Delangre confided to a little company of functionaries that the town was indebted for the Home to her husband, who had also kindly given the committee the use of a room at the town-hall, where they could meet and deliberate at their ease. Plassans was speedily excited by this pious turmoil, and soon nothing but the Home of the Virgin was spoken of. A chorus of praise went up, and the friends of each lady patroness made up little parties and worked strenuously for the success of the undertaking. Within a week subscriptions were opened in all three quarters of the town, and as the 'Plassans Gazette' published lists of the subscriptions, a feeling of pride was awakened, and the most notable families vied as to which should be the most generous.

Amidst all the talk on the subject Abbé Faujas's name frequently cropped up. Although each of the lady patronesses claimed the idea of the refuge as her own, there was a prevailing belief that it was the Abbé who had brought it with him from Besançon. Monsieur Delangre, indeed, made an express statement to that effect at the meeting of the municipal council when it was decided to purchase the building which the diocesan architect had suggested as being best suited to the requirements of the Home. On the previous evening the mayor had had a lengthy conversation with the priest. They had shaken hands most cordially on parting, and the mayor's secretary had even heard them call each other 'my dear sir.' This brought about quite a revolution in the Abbé's favour. From that time he had a group of partisans who defended him against the attacks of his enemies.

Besides, the Mourets vouched for Abbé Faujas's respectability.

Supported by Marthe's friendship, recognised as the originator of a good work, which he modestly refused to acknowledge as his own, he no longer manifested in the streets that appearance of humility which had led him to withdraw as much as possible from observation by keeping in the shadow of the houses. He bravely showed his new cassock in the sun and walked in the middle of the road. On his way from the Rue Balande to Saint-Saturnin's he now had to return a great number of bows. One Sunday Madame de Condamin stopped him after Vespers on the Place in front of the Bishop's house and kept him talking with her there for a good half-hour.

'Well, your reverence,' Mouret said to him with a laugh, 'you are quite in the odour of sanctity now. One would scarcely have anticipated that six months ago when I was the only one to say a good word for you! But if I were you I shouldn't trust too much to it all; you still have the Bishop's set against you.'

The priest lightly shrugged his shoulders. He knew quite well that what hostility he still met with came from the clergy. Abbé Fenil kept Monseigneur Rousselot trembling beneath his rough, hard will. However, when the grand-vicar, about the end of March, left Plassans on a short holiday, Abbé Faujas profited by his absence to make several calls upon the Bishop. Abbé Surin, the prelate's private secretary, reported that the 'wretched man' had been closeted for hours with his lordship, who had manifested an atrocious temper after each interview. When Abbé Fenil returned, Abbé Faujas discontinued his visits, and again drew into the background. But the Bishop still showed himself very much disturbed, and it was quite evident that something had occurred to upset his careless mind. At a dinner which he gave to his clergy he showed himself particularly friendly to Abbé Faujas, who was still only a humble curate at Saint-Saturnin's. Abbé Fenil then kept his thin lips more tightly closed than ever, but inwardly cursed his penitents when they politely asked him how he was in health.

And now at last Abbé Faujas manifested complete serenity. He still led a self-denying life, but he seemed permeated by a pleasant ease of mind. One Tuesday evening he triumphed definitively. He was looking out of the window of his room, enjoying the early warmth of springtide, when Monsieur Péqueur des Saulaies's guests came into the garden of the Sub-Prefecture and bowed to him from a distance. Madame de Condamin was there, and carried her familiarity so far as to wave her handkerchief to him. Just at the same time, on the other side, some guests came to sit on the rustic seats in front of the waterfall in Monsieur Rastoil's grounds. Monsieur Delangre, who was leaning over the terrace of the Sub-Prefecture, could see across Mouret's garden into the judge's place, owing to the sloping character of the ground.

'You will see,' he said, 'they won't deign even to notice him.'

But he was wrong. For Abbé Fenil, having turned his head as though by chance, took off his hat, whereupon all the other priests who happened to be present did the same, and Abbé Faujas returned their salute. Then, after slowly glancing over the two sets of guests on his right and his left, he quitted his window, carefully drawing his white and conventual-looking curtains.

IX

The month of April was very mild and warm, and in the evenings, after dinner, the young Mourets went to amuse themselves in the garden. Marthe and the priest, too, as they found the dining-room become very close, also went out on to the terrace. They sat a few steps from the open window, just outside the stream of light which the lamp cast upon the tall box hedges. Hid there in the deepening dusk, they discussed all the little details connected with the Home of the Virgin. This constant discussion of charitable matters seemed to give a tone of additional softness to their conversation. In front of them, between Monsieur Rastoil's huge pear-trees and the dusky chestnuts of the Sub-Prefecture, there was a large patch of open sky. The young people sported about under the arbours, while every now and then the voices of Mouret and Madame Faujas, who remained alone in the dining-room, deeply absorbed in their game, could be heard raised in passing altercations.

Sometimes Marthe, full of tender emotion, a gentle languor that made her words fall slowly from her lips, would check her speech as she caught sight of the golden train of some shooting star, and smile as she threw back her head a little and looked up at the heavens.

'There's another soul leaving purgatory and entering paradise!' she murmured, while, as the priest kept silent, she added: 'How pretty they are, those little beliefs! One ought to be able to remain a little girl, your reverence.'

She no longer now mended the family linen in the evening. She would have had to light a lamp on the terrace to see to do it, and she preferred the gloom of the warm night, which seemed to thrill her with peaceful happiness. Besides, she now went out every day, which fatigued her, and when dinner was over she had not energy enough to take up her needle. Rose had been obliged to undertake the mending, as Mouret was beginning to complain that his socks were all in holes.

To tell the truth Marthe was really very much occupied. Besides the committee meetings over which she presided, she had numerous other things to attend to, visits to make, and superintendence duties to exercise. She deputed much necessary writing and other little matters to Madame Paloque; but she was so eager to see the Home actually established, that she went off to the Faubourg, where the building stood, three times a week, to make sure that the workmen were not wasting their time. Whenever she thought that satisfactory progress was not being made, she hurried to Saint-Saturnin's to find the architect, and grumbled to him and begged him not to leave the men without his supervision, growing quite jealous, indeed, of the work which was being executed in the church, and saying that the chapel repairs were being much too quickly pushed forward. Monsieur Lieutaud smiled at all this, and assured her that everything would be completed within the stipulated time. But Abbé Faujas likewise protested that sufficient progress was not being made, and urged Marthe to give the architect no peace, so she ended by going to Saint-Saturnin's every day.

She went thither with her brain full of figures, or absorbed in thinking of walls that had to be pulled down and rebuilt. The chilliness of the church cooled her excitement a little. She dipped her fingers in the holy water and crossed herself, by way of doing as others did. The vergers grew to know her and bow to her, and she herself became quite familiar with the different chapels and the sacristy, whither she sometimes had to go in search of Abbé Faujas, and the wide corridor and low cloisters through which she had to pass. At the end of a month there was not a corner in Saint-Saturnin's which she did not know. Sometimes she had to wait for the architect, and then she would sit down in some retired chapel and rest after her hurried walk, recapitulating in her mind the host of things which she wanted to impress upon Monsieur Lieutaud. The deep, palpitating silence which surrounded her, and the dim religious light falling from the stained-glass windows, gradually plunged her into a vague, soft reverie. She began to love the lofty arches and the solemn bareness of the walls, the altars draped in protecting covers, and the chairs all arranged in order. As soon, indeed, as the padded doors swung to behind her, she began to experience a feeling of supreme restfulness, she forgot all the weary cares of the world, and perfect peace permeated her being.

'Saint-Saturnin's is such a pleasant place,' she said in an unguarded moment one evening before her husband, after a close, sultry day.

'Would you like us to go and sleep there?' Mouret asked, with a laugh.

Marthe felt hurt. The feeling of purely physical happiness which she experienced in the church began to distress her as being something wrong; and it was with a slight feeling of trouble that she thenceforward entered Saint-Saturnin's, trying to force herself to remain indifferent and uninfluenced by her surroundings, just as she would have been in the big rooms at the town hall. But in spite of herself she was deeply, distressfully affected. It was, however, a distress to which she willingly returned.

Abbé Faujas manifested no consciousness of the slow awakening which every day went on within her. He still retained with her the demeanour of a busy, obliging man, putting heaven on one side. He never showed anything of the priest. Sometimes, however, she would disturb him as he was going to read the burial office; and he would then speak to her for a moment between a couple of pillars in his surplice which exhaled a vague odour of incense and wax tapers. It was frequently a mere bricklayer's bill or some carpenter's claim that they spoke about, and the priest would just tell her the exact figures and then hurry away to attend to the funeral; she remaining there, lingering in the empty nave, while one of the vergers was extinguishing the candles. As Faujas, when he crossed the church with her, bowed before the high altar, she had acquired the habit of doing likewise, at first out of a feeling of mere propriety. But afterwards the action had become mechanical, and she now bowed when she was quite alone. Hitherto this act of reverence had been her only sign of devotion. Two or three times she had come to the church on days of high ceremonial of which she had not previously been aware: but when she saw the church was full of worshippers and heard the pealing of the organ, she hurried off, thrilled with sudden fear and not daring to cross the threshold.

'Well!' Mouret would frequently ask her with his sniggering laugh, 'when do you mean to take your first communion?'

He was perpetually teasing her, but she never replied, simply fixing upon him the gaze of her eyes, in which a passing brightness glistened when he went too far. By degrees he became more bitter, he was tired of mocking at her; and at the end of a month he quite lost his temper.

'What sense is there in going and mixing yourself up with a lot of priests?' he would growl at times when his dinner was not ready when he wanted it. 'You are always away from home now, there's no keeping you in the house for an hour at a time! I shouldn't mind it myself, if everything weren't going to pieces here. I never get any of my things mended, the table is not even laid by seven o'clock, there's no making anything out of Rose, and the whole place is left to rack and ruin.'

He picked up a house-cloth that was lying about, locked up a bottle of wine that had been left out, and began to wipe the dust off the furniture with his fingers, working himself up to a higher pitch of anger as he cried: 'There'll soon be nothing left for me to do but to take up a broom and put an apron on! You would see me do it without disturbing yourself, I know! I might do all the work of the house without your being any the wiser for it indeed! Do you know that I spent a couple of hours this morning in putting this cupboard in order? No, no, things can't go on any longer in this way!'

At other times there was a disturbance about the children. Once when Mouret came home he found Désirée 'wallowing like a young pig' in the garden, lying on her stomach before an ant-hole, and trying to find out what the ants might be doing in the ground.

'We may be very thankful, I'm sure, that you don't sleep away from the house as well!' he cried as soon as he caught sight of his wife. 'Come and look at your daughter! I wouldn't let her change her dress because I wished that you might see what a pretty sight she is.'

The girl cried bitterly while her father kept turning her round.

'Look at her now! Isn't she a nice spectacle? This is the way children go on when they are left to themselves! It isn't her fault, poor little innocent! At one time you couldn't leave her alone for five minutes: she would be getting into the fire, you said! Well, I expect she will be getting into the fire now, and everything will be burnt up, and then there'll be an end of it all!'

When Rose had taken Désirée away, he continued:

'You live now simply for other people's children. You don't give a moment to your own! What a goose you must be to go knocking yourself up for a parcel of hussies who only laugh at you! Go and walk about the ramparts any evening and you will see something of the conduct of those impudent creatures whom you talk of putting under the protection of the Virgin!'

He stopped to take breath and then went on again:

'At all events see that Désirée is properly taken care of before you go picking up girls from the gutter! There are holes as big as my fist in her dress. One of these days we shall be finding her in the garden with a leg or an arm broken. I don't say anything about Octave or Serge, though I should much prefer your being at home when they come back from college. They are up to all kinds of diabolical tricks. Only yesterday they split a couple of flag-stones on the terrace by letting off crackers. I tell you that if you don't keep yourself at home we shall find the whole house blown to bits one of these days!'

Marthe said a few words in self-defence. She had been obliged to go out, she urged. There was no doubt that Mouret, who possessed an ample fund of common sense, in spite of his proclivities for teasing and jeering, was right. The house was getting into a most unsatisfactory state. That once quiet spot indeed, where the sun had set so peacefully, was becoming uproarious, left to look after itself, suffering from the children's noisiness, the father's bursts of temper, and the mother's careless, indifferent lassitude. In the evening, at table, they dined badly and quarrelled amongst themselves. Rose did just what she liked, and she, by the way, was of opinion that her mistress was quite in the right.

Matters came to such a pass at last that Mouret, happening to meet his mother-in-law, complained to her bitterly of Marthe's conduct, although he was quite aware of the pleasure he afforded the old lady by revealing to her the troubles of his home.

'You astonish me extremely!' Félicité replied with a smile. 'Marthe always seemed to me to be afraid of you, and I considered her even too yielding and obedient. A woman ought not to tremble before her husband.'

'Ah, yes, indeed!' cried Mouret, with a hopeless look, 'once upon a time she would have sunk into the ground to avoid a quarrel; a mere glance was sufficient to make her do everything I desired. But that's all quite altered now. I may remonstrate and shout as much as I like, she still goes her own way. She doesn't reply, she hasn't as yet got to flying out at me, but that will come as well, I dare say, by-and-by.'

Félicité then answered with some hypocrisy:

'I will speak to Marthe if you like. But it might, perhaps, hurt her if I did. Matters of this kind are better kept between husband and wife. I don't feel very uneasy about them; I've no doubt that you'll soon get back again all the quiet peacefulness which you used to be so proud of.'

Mouret shook his head with downcast eyes.

'No! no!' he said; 'I know myself too well. I can make a noise, but it does no good. In reality I am as weak as a child. People are quite wrong in supposing that I gained my own way with my wife by force. She has generally done what I wanted her to do, because she was quite indifferent about everything, and would as soon do one thing as another. Mild as she looks, she is very obstinate, I can tell you. Well, I must try to make the best of it.'

Then, raising his eyes, he added:

'It would have been better if I had said nothing about all this to you; but you won't mention it to anyone, will you?'

When Marthe went to see her mother the next day, the latter received her with some show of coldness, and exclaimed:

'It is wrong of you, my dear, to show yourself so neglectful of your husband. I saw him yesterday and he is quite angry about it. I am well aware that he often behaves in a very ridiculous manner, but that does not justify you in neglecting your home.'

Marthe fixed her eyes upon her mother.

'Ah! he has been complaining about me!' she said curtly. 'The least he could do would be to keep silent, for I never complain about him.'

Then she began to talk of other matters, but Madame Rougon brought her back to the subject of her husband by inquiring after Abbé Faujas.

'Perhaps Mouret isn't very fond of the Abbé, and finds fault with you in consequence. Is that the case, do you think?'

Marthe showed great surprise.

'What an idea!' she exclaimed. 'What makes you think that my husband does not like Abbé Faujas? He has certainly never said anything to me which would lead me to imagine such a thing. He hasn't said anything to you, has he? Oh no! you are quite mistaken. He would go up to their rooms to fetch them if the mother didn't come down to have her game of cards with him.'

Mouret, indeed, never complained in any way about Abbé Faujas. He joked with him a little bluntly sometimes, and occasionally brought his name into the teasing banter with which he tormented his wife, but that was all.

One morning, as he was shaving, he said to Marthe:

'I'll tell you what, my dear; if ever you go to confession, take the Abbé for your director, and then your sins will, at any rate, be kept amongst ourselves.'

Abbé Faujas heard confessions on Tuesdays and Fridays, on which days Marthe used to avoid going to Saint-Saturnin's. She alleged that she did not want to disturb him; but she was really under the influence of that timid uneasiness which disquieted her whenever she saw him in his surplice redolent of the mysterious odours of the sacristy. One Friday, she went with Madame de Condamin to see how the works at the Home of the Virgin were getting on. The men were just finishing the frontage. Madame de Condamin found fault with the ornamentation, which, said she, was extremely mean and characterless. At the entrance there ought to have been two slender columns with a pointed arch, something at once light and suggestive of religion, something that would be a credit to the committee of lady patronesses. Marthe hesitated for a time, but she gradually admitted that the place looked very mean as it was. Then as the other pressed her, she promised to speak to Monsieur Lieutaud on the subject that very day. In order that she might keep her promise, she went to the cathedral before returning home. It was four o'clock when she got there, and the architect had just left. When she asked for Abbé Faujas, a verger told her that he was confessing in the chapel of Saint Aurelia. Then for the first time she recollected what day it was, and replied that she could not wait. But as she passed the chapel of Saint Aurelia on her way out, she thought that the Abbé might, perhaps, have already caught sight of her. The truth was that she felt singularly faint, and so she sat down outside the chapel, near the railing. And there she remained.

The sky was grey, and the church was steeped in twilight. Here and there in the aisles, already shrouded in darkness, gleamed a lamp, or some gilt candelabrum, or some Virgin's silver robe; and a pale ray filtered through the great nave and died away on the polished oak of the stalls and benches. Marthe had never before felt so completely overcome. Her legs seemed to have lost all their strength, and her hands were so heavy that she clasped them across her knees to save herself from having to support their weight. She allowed herself to drift into drowsiness, in which she still continued to hear and see, but in a very soft subdued fashion. The slight sounds wafted along beneath the vaulted roof, the falling of a chair, the slow step of some worshipper, all filled her with emotion, assumed a musical tone which thrilled her to the heart; while the last glimmers of daylight and the dusky shadows that crept up the pillars like covers of crape, assumed in her eyes all the delicate tints of shot silk. She gradually fell into a state of exquisite languor, in which she seemed to melt away and die. Everything around her then vanished, and she was thrilled with perfect happiness in her strange, trance-like condition.

The sound of a voice awoke her from this state of ecstasy.

'I am very sorry,' said Abbé Faujas; 'I saw you, but I could not get away.'

She then appeared to wake up with a start. She looked at him. He was standing before her in the dying light, in his surplice. His last penitent had just left, and the empty church seemed to be growing still more solemn.

'You want to speak to me?' he asked.

Marthe made an effort to recall her thoughts.

'Yes,' she murmured; 'but I can't remember now. Ah yes! it is about the frontage, which Madame de Condamin thinks too mean. There ought to be two columns instead of that characterless flat door. And up above one might put a pointed arch filled with stained glass. It would look very pretty. You understand what I mean, don't you?'

He gazed at her very gravely with his hands crossed over his surplice, and his head inclined towards her; and she, still seated, without strength to rise to her feet, went on stammering confusedly, as though she had been taken unawares in a sleep which she could not shake off.

'It would entail additional expense, of course; but we might have columns of soft stone with a very simple moulding. We might speak about it to the master mason, and he will tell us how much it would cost. But we had better pay him his last account first. It is two thousand one hundred and odd francs, I think. We have the money in hand; Madame Paloque told me so this morning. There will be no difficulty about that, Monsieur l'Abbé.'

She lowered her head, as though she felt oppressed by the gaze that was bent upon her. When she raised it again and met the priest's eyes, she clasped her hands together, after the manner of a child seeking forgiveness, and she burst into sobs. The priest allowed her to weep, still standing in silence in front of her. Then she fell on her knees before him, weeping behind her hands, with which she covered her face.

'Get up, I pray you,' said Abbé Faujas gently. 'It is before God that you should go and kneel.'

He helped her to rise and he sat down beside her. They talked together for a long time in low tones. The night had now fully fallen, and the lamps set golden specks gleaming through the black depths of the church. The murmur of their voices alone disturbed the silence in front of the chapel of Saint Aurelia. From the priest streamed a flood of words after each of Marthe's weak broken answers. When at last they rose, he seemed to be refusing her some favour which she was seeking with persistence. And leading her towards the door, he raised his voice as he said:

'No! I cannot, I assure you I cannot. It would be better for you to take Abbé Bourrette.'

'I am in great need of your advice,' Marthe murmured, beseechingly. 'I think that with your help everything would be easy to me.'

'You are mistaken,' he replied, in a sterner voice. 'On the contrary, I fear that my direction would be prejudicial to you to begin with. Abbé Bourrette is the priest you want, I assure you. Later on, I may perhaps give you a different reply.'

Marthe obeyed the priest's injunctions, and on the morrow the worshippers at Saint-Saturnin's were surprised to see Madame Mouret kneel before Abbé Bourrette's confessional. Two days later nothing but this conversion was spoken of in Plassans. Abbé Faujas's name was pronounced with subtle smiles by certain people, but on the whole the impression was a good one and in favour of the Abbé. Madame Rastoil complimented Madame Mouret in full committee, and Madame Delangre professed to see in the matter a first blessing vouchsafed by God who rewarded the lady patronesses for their good work by touching the heart of the only one amongst them who had not conformed with the requirements of religion. Madame de Condamin, taking Marthe aside, said to her:

'You have done right, my dear. What you have done is a necessity for a woman; and, besides, as soon as one begins to go about a little, it is necessary to go to church.'

The only matter of astonishment was her choice of Abbé Bourrette. That worthy man almost entirely confined himself to hearing the confessions of young girls. The ladies found him 'so very uninteresting.' On the Thursday at the Rougons' reception, before Marthe's arrival, the matter was talked over in a corner of the green drawing-room, and it was Madame Paloque with her waspish tongue who summed up the matter.

'Abbé Faujas has done quite right in not keeping her himself,' said she, with a twist of her mouth that made her still more hideous than usual; 'Abbé Bourrette is very successful in saving souls and appearances also.'

When Marthe came that evening her mother stepped forward to welcome her, and kissed her affectionately with some ostentation before the company. She herself had made her peace with God on the morrow of the Coup d'Etat. She was of opinion that Abbé Faujas might now venture to return to the green drawing-room; but he excused himself, making a pretext of his work and his love of privacy. Madame Rougon then fancied that he was planning a triumphal return for the following winter. The Abbé's success was certainly on the increase. For the first few months his only penitents had come from the vegetable-market held behind the cathedral, poor hawkers, to whose dialect he had quietly listened without always being able to understand it; but now, especially since all the talk there had been in connection with the Home of the Virgin, he had a crowd of well-to-do citizens' wives and daughters dressed in silk kneeling before his confessional-box. When Marthe quietly mentioned that he would not receive her amongst his penitents, Madame de Condamin was seized with a sudden whim, and deserted her director, the senior curate of Saint-Saturnin's, who was greatly distressed thereby, to transfer the guardianship of her soul to Abbé Faujas. Such a distinction as this gave the latter a firm position in Plassans society.

When Mouret learned that his wife now went to confession, he merely said to her:

'You have been doing something wrong lately, I suppose, since you find it necessary to go and tell all your affairs to a parson?'

In the midst of all this pious excitement he seemed to isolate himself and shut himself up in his own narrow and monotonous life still further. When his wife reproached him for complaining to her mother, he answered:

'Yes, you are right; it was wrong of me. It is foolish to give people any pleasure by telling them of one's troubles. However, I promise you that I won't give your mother this satisfaction a second time. I have been thinking matters over, and the house may topple down on our heads before I'll go whimpering to anyone again.'

From that time he never made any disparaging remarks about the management of the house or scolded his wife in the presence of strangers, but professed himself, as formerly, the happiest of men. This effort of sound sense cost him little, for he saw that it would tend to his comfort, which was the object of his constant thoughts. He even exaggerated his assumption of the part of a contented methodical citizen who took pleasure in living. Marthe only became aware of his impatience by his restless pacing up and down. For whole weeks he refrained from teasing or fault-finding as far as she was concerned, while upon Rose and his children he constantly poured forth his jeers, scolding them too from morning till night for the slightest shortcomings.

Previously he had only been economical, now he became miserly.

'There is no sense in spending money in the way we are doing,' he grumbled to Marthe. 'I'll be bound you are giving it all to those young hussies of yours. But it's quite sufficient for you to waste your time over them. Listen to me, my dear. I will give you a hundred francs a month for housekeeping, and if you will persist in giving money to girls who don't deserve it, you must save it out of your dress allowance.'

He kept firmly to his word, and the very next month he refused to let Marthe buy a pair of boots on the pretext that it would disarrange his accounts, and that he had given her full notice and warning. One evening his wife found him weeping bitterly in their bedroom. All her kindness of heart was aroused, and she clasped him in her arms and besought him to tell her what distressed him. But he roughly tore himself away from her and told her that he was not crying at all, but simply had a bad headache. It was that, said he, which made his eyes red.

'Do you think,' he exclaimed, 'that I am such a simpleton as you are to cry?'

She felt much hurt. The next day Mouret affected great gaiety; but some days afterwards, when Abbé Faujas and his mother came downstairs after dinner, he refused to play his usual game of piquet. He did not feel clear-headed enough for it, he said. On the next few nights he made other excuses, and so the games were broken off, and everyone went out on the terrace. Mouret seated himself in front of his wife and the Abbé, doing all he could to speak as much and as frequently as possible; while Madame Faujas sat a few yards away in the gloom, quite silent and still, with her hands upon her knees, like one of those legendary figures keeping guard over a treasure with the stern fidelity of a crouching dog.

'Fine evening!' Mouret used to say every night. 'It is much pleasanter here than in the dining-room. It is very wise of you to come out and enjoy the fresh air. Ah! there's a shooting-star! Did your reverence see it? I've heard say that it's Saint Peter lighting his pipe up yonder.'

He laughed, but Marthe kept quite grave, vexed by his attempts at pleasantry, which spoilt her enjoyment of the expanse of sky that spread between Monsieur Rastoil's pear-trees and the chestnuts of the Sub-Prefecture. Sometimes he would pretend to be unaware that she conformed with the requirements of religion, and he would take the Abbé aside and tell him that he relied on him to effect the salvation of the whole house. At other times he could never begin a sentence without saying in a bantering tone, 'Now that my wife goes to confession—' Then having grown tired of this subject, he began to listen to what was being said in the neighbouring gardens, trying to catch the faint sounds of voices which rose in the calm night air, as the distant noises of Plassans were hushed.

'Ah! those are the voices of Monsieur de Condamin and Doctor Porquier!' he said, straining his ear towards the Sub-Prefecture. 'They are making fun of the Paloques. Did you hear Monsieur Delangre saying in his falsetto, "Ladies, you had better come in, the air is growing cool"? Don't you think that little Delangre always talks as though he had swallowed a reed-pipe?'

Then he turned his head towards the Rastoils' garden.

'They haven't anyone there to-night,' he said; 'I can't hear anything. Ah, yes! those big geese the daughters are by the waterfall. The elder one talks just as though she were gobbling pebbles. Every evening they sit there jabbering for a good hour. They can't want all that time to tell each other about the matrimonial offers they have had. Ah! they are all there! There's Abbé Surin, with a voice like a flute; and Abbé Fenil, who would do for a rattle on Good Friday. There are sometimes a score of them huddled together, without stirring a finger, in that garden. I believe they all go there to listen to what we say.'

While he went chattering on in this manner Abbé Faujas and Marthe merely spoke a few words, chiefly in reply to his questions. Generally they sat apart from him with their faces raised to the sky and their eyes gazing into space. One evening Mouret fell asleep. Then, inclining their heads to-wards each other, they began to talk in subdued tones; while some few yards away, Madame Faujas, with her hands upon her knees, her eyes wide open and her ears on the strain, yet never seeing or hearing anything, seemed to be keeping watch for them.

X

The summer passed away, and Abbé Faujas seemed in no hurry to derive any advantage from his increasing popularity. He still kept himself in seclusion at the Mourets', delighting in the solitude of the garden, to which he now came down during the day-time. He read his breviary as he slowly walked with bent head up and down the green arbour at the far end. Sometimes he would close his book, still further slacken his steps, and seem to be buried in deep reverie. Mouret, who used to watch him, at last became impatient and irritated at seeing that black figure walking to and fro for hours together behind his fruit-trees.

'One has no privacy left,' he muttered. 'I can't lift my eyes now without catching sight of that cassock. He is like a crow, that fellow there, with his round eyes that always seem to be on the look-out for something. I don't believe in his fine disinterested airs.'

It was not till early in September that the Home of the Virgin was completed. In the provinces workmen are painfully slow; though it must be stated that the lady patronesses had twice upset Monsieur Lieutaud's designs in favour of ideas of their own. When the committee took possession of the building they rewarded the architect for the complaisance he had manifested by lavishing the highest praises upon him. Everything seemed to them perfectly satisfactory. The rooms were large, the communications were excellent, and there was a courtyard planted with trees and embellished with two small fountains. Madame de Condamin was particularly charmed with the façade, which was one of her own ideas. Over the door, the words 'Home of the Virgin' were carved in gold letters on a slab of black marble.

On the occasion of the opening of the Home there was a very affecting ceremony. The Bishop, attended by the Chapter, came in person to install the Sisters of Saint Joseph, who had been authorised to work the institution. A troop of some fifty girls of from eight to fifteen years of age had been collected together from the streets of the old quarter of the town, and all that had been required from the parents to obtain admission for their children had been a declaration that their avocations necessitated their absence from home during the entire day. Monsieur Delangre made a speech which was much applauded. He explained at considerable length, and in a magnificent style, the details and arrangements of this new refuge, which he called 'the school of virtue and labour, where young and interesting creatures would be kept safe from wicked temptations.' A delicate allusion, towards the end of the speech, to the real promoter of the Home, Abbé Faujas, attracted much notice. The Abbé was present amongst the other priests, and his fine, grave face remained perfectly calm and tranquil when all eyes were turned upon him. Marthe blushed on the platform, where she was sitting in the midst of the lady patronesses.

When the ceremony was over, the Bishop expressed a desire to inspect the building in every detail; and, notwithstanding the evident annoyance of Abbé Fenil, he sent for Abbé Faujas, whose big black eyes had never for a moment quitted him, and requested him to be good enough to act as his guide, adding aloud with a smile, that he was sure he could not find a better one. This little speech was circulated amongst the departing spectators, and in the evening all Plassans commented upon the Bishop's favourable demeanour towards Abbé Faujas.

The lady patronesses had reserved for themselves one of the rooms in the Home. Here they provided a collation for the Bishop, who ate a biscuit and drank two sips of Malaga, while saying a polite word or two to each of them. This brought the pious festival to a happy conclusion, for both before and during the ceremony there had been heart-burnings and rivalries among the ladies, whom the delicate praises of Monseigneur Rousselot quite restored to good humour. When they were left to themselves, they declared that everything had gone off exceedingly well, and they profusely praised the Bishop. Madame Paloque alone looked sour. The prelate had somehow forgotten her when he was distributing his compliments.

'You were quite right,' she said in a fury to her husband, when she got home again; 'I have just been made a convenience in that silly nonsense of theirs. It's a fine idea, indeed, to bring all those corrupt hussies together. I have given up all my time to them, and that big simpleton of a Bishop, who trembles before his own clergy, can't even say thank you. Just as if that Madame de Condamin had done anything, indeed. She is far too much occupied in showing off her dresses! Ah! we know quite enough about her, don't we? The world will hear something about her one of these days that will surprise it a little! Thank goodness, we've nothing to conceal. And that Madame Delangre and Madame Rastoil, too—well, it wouldn't be difficult to tell tales about them that would cover them with blushes! And they never stirred out of their drawing-rooms, they haven't taken half the trouble about the matter that I have! Then there's that Madame Mouret, with her pretence of managing the whole business, though she really did nothing but hang on to the cassock of her Abbé Faujas! She's another hypocrite of whom we shall hear some pretty things one of these days! And yet they could all get a polite speech, while there wasn't a word for me! I'm nothing but a mere convenience, they treat me like a dog! But things shan't go on like this, Paloque, I tell you. The dog will turn and bite them before long!'

From that time forward Madame Paloque showed herself much less accommodating. She became very irregular in her secretarial work, and declined to perform any duties that she did not fancy, till at last the lady patronesses began to talk of employing a paid secretary. Marthe mentioned these worries to Abbé Faujas and asked him if he could recommend a suitable man.

'Don't trouble yourself to look for anyone,' he said, 'I dare say I can find you a fit person. Give me two or three days.'

For some time past he had been frequently receiving letters bearing the Besançon postmark, They were all in the same handwriting, a large, ugly hand. Rose, who took them up to him, remarked that he seemed vexed at the mere sight of the envelopes.

'He looks quite put out,' she said. 'You may depend upon it that it's no great favourite of his who writes to him so often.'

Mouret's old curiosity was roused by this correspondence. One day he took up one of the letters himself with a pleasant smile, telling the Abbé, as an excuse for his own appearance, that Rose was not in the house. The Abbé probably saw through Mouret's cunning, for he assumed an expression of great pleasure, as though he had been impatiently expecting the letter. But Mouret did not allow himself to be deceived by this piece of acting, he stayed outside the door on the landing and glued his ear to the keyhole.

'From your sister again, isn't it?' asked Madame Faujas, in her hard voice. 'Why does she worry you in that way?'

There was a short silence, after which came a sound of paper being roughly crumpled, and the Abbé said, with evident displeasure:

'It's always the same old story. She wants to come to us and bring her husband with her, so that we may get him a situation somewhere. She seems to think that we are wallowing in gold. I'm afraid they will be doing something rash—perhaps taking us by surprise some fine morning.'

'No, no! we can't do with them here, Ovide!' his mother replied.

'They have never liked you; they have always been jealous of you. Trouche is a scamp and Olympe is quite heartless. They would want everything for themselves, and they would compromise you and interfere with your work.'

Mouret was too much excited by the meanness of the act he was committing to be able to hear well, and, besides, he thought that one of them was coming to the door, so he hurried away. He took care not to mention what he had done. A few days later Abbé Faujas, in his presence, while they were all out on the terrace, gave Marthe a definite reply respecting the Secretaryship at the Home.

'I think I can recommend you a suitable person,' he said, in his calm way. 'It is a connection of my own, my brother-in-law, who is coming here from Besançon in a few days.'

Mouret became very attentive, while Marthe appeared delighted.

'Oh, that is excellent!' she exclaimed. 'I was feeling very much bothered about finding a suitable person. You see, with all those young girls, we must have a person of unexceptionable morality, but of course a connection of yours—'

'Yes, yes,' interrupted the priest; 'my sister had a little hosiery business at Besançon, which she has been obliged to give up on account of her health; and now she is anxious to join us again, as the doctors have ordered her to live in the south. My mother is very much pleased.'

'I'm sure she must be,' said Marthe. 'I dare say it grieved you very much to have to separate, and you will be very glad to be together again. I'll tell you what you must do. There are a couple of rooms upstairs that you don't use; why shouldn't your sister and her husband have them? They have no children, have they?'

'No, there are only their two selves. I had, indeed, thought for a moment of giving them those two rooms; but I was afraid of displeasing you by bringing other people into your house.'

'Not at all, I assure you. You are very quiet people.'

She checked herself suddenly, for her husband was tugging at her dress. He did not want to have the Abbé's relations in the house, for he remembered in what terms Madame Faujas had spoken of her daughter and son-in-law.

'The rooms are very small,' he began; 'and Monsieur l'Abbé would be inconvenienced. It would be better for all parties that his sister should take lodgings somewhere else; there happen to be some rooms vacant just now at the Paloques' house, over the way.'

There was a dead pause in the conversation. The priest said nothing, but gazed up into the sky. Marthe thought he was offended, and she felt much distressed at her husband's bluntness. After a moment she could no longer endure the embarrassing silence. 'Well, it's settled then,' she said, without any attempt at skill in knitting the broken threads of the conversation together again, 'Rose shall help your mother to clean the rooms. My husband was only thinking about your own personal convenience; but, of course, if you wish it, it is not for us to prevent you from disposing of the rooms in any way you like.'

Mouret was quite angry when he again found himself alone with his wife.

'I can't understand you at all!' he cried. 'When first I let the rooms to the Abbé, you were quite displeased, and seemed to hate the thought of having even so much as a cat brought into the house; and now I believe you would be perfectly willing for the Abbé to bring the whole of his relations, down to his third and fourth cousins. Didn't you feel me tugging at your dress? You might have known that I didn't want those people. They are not very respectable folks.'

'How do you know that?' cried Marthe, annoyed by this accusation. 'Who told you so?'

'Who, indeed? It was Abbé Faujas himself. I overheard him one day while he was talking to his mother.'

She looked at him keenly; and he blushed slightly beneath her gaze as he stammered:

'Well, it is sufficient that I do know. The sister is a heartless creature and her husband is a scamp. It's of no use your putting on that air of insulted majesty; those were their own words, and I'm inventing nothing. I don't want to have those people here, do you understand? The old lady herself was the first to object to her daughter coming here. The Abbé now seems to have changed his mind. I don't know what has led him to alter his opinion. It's some fresh mystery of his. He's going to make use of them somehow.' Marthe shrugged her shoulders and allowed her husband to rail on. He told Rose not to clean the rooms, but Rose now only obeyed her mistress's orders. For five days his anger vented itself in bitter words and furious recriminations. In Abbé Faujas's presence he confined himself to sulking, for he did not dare to attack the priest openly. Then, as usual, he ended by submitting, and ceased to rail at the people who were coming. But he drew his purse-strings still tighter, isolated himself, shut himself up more and more in his own selfish existence. When the Trouches arrived one October evening, he merely exclaimed:

'The deuce! they don't look a nice couple. What faces they have!'

Abbé Faujas did not appear very desirous that his sister and brother-in-law should be seen on that occasion. His mother took up a position by the street-door, and as soon as she caught sight of them turning out of the Place of the Sub-Prefecture, she glanced uneasily behind her into the hall and the kitchen. Luck was, however, against her, for just as the Trouches arrived, Marthe, who was going out, came up from the garden, followed by her children.

'Ah! there you all are!' she said, with a pleasant smile.

Madame Faujas, who was generally so completely mistress of herself, could not suppress a slight show of confusion as she stammered a word or two of reply. For some moments they stood confronting and scrutinising each other in the hall. Mouret had hurriedly mounted the steps and Rose had taken up her position at the kitchen door.

'You must be very glad to be together again,' said Marthe, addressing Madame Faujas.

Then, noticing the feeling of embarrassment which was keeping them all silent, she turned towards Trouche and added:

'You arrived by the five o'clock train, I suppose? How long were you in getting here from Besançon?'

'Seventeen hours in the train,' Trouche replied, opening a toothless mouth. 'It is no joke that, in a third-class carriage, I can tell you. One gets pretty well shaken up inside.'

Then he laughed with a peculiar clattering of his jaws. Madame Faujas cast a very angry glance at him, and he began to fumble mechanically at his greasy overcoat, trying to fasten a button that was no longer there, and pressing to his thighs (doubtless in order to hide some stains) a couple of cardboard bonnet-boxes which he was carrying, one green and the other yellow. His red throat was perpetually gurgling beneath a twisted, ragged black neckcloth, over which appeared the edge of a dirty shirt. In his wrinkled face, which seemed to reek with vice, there glistened two little black eyes that rolled about incessantly, examining everybody and everything with an expression of astonishment and covetousness. They looked like the eyes of a thief studying a house to which he means to return in order to plunder it some night.

Mouret fancied that Trouche was examining the fastenings.

'That fellow,' he thought to himself, 'looks as though he were getting the patterns of the locks into his head!'

Olympe was conscious that her husband had made a vulgar remark. She was a tall, slight woman, fair and faded, with a flat plain face. She carried a little deal box and a big bundle tied up in a tablecloth.

'We have brought some pillows with us,' she said, glancing at the bundle. 'Pillows come in very usefully in a third-class carriage; they make one quite as comfortable as if one were travelling first-class. It is a great saving, going third, and it is of no use throwing money away, is it?'

'Certainly not,' Marthe replied, somewhat surprised by the appearance and language of the new-comers.

Olympe now came forward and went on talking in an ingratiating way.

'It's the same thing with clothes,' said she; 'when I set off on a journey I put on my shabbiest things. I told Honoré that his old overcoat was quite good enough. And he has got his old work-day trousers on too, trousers that he's quite tired of wearing. You see I selected my worse dress; it is actually in holes, I believe. This shawl was mother's; I used to iron on it at home; and this bonnet I'm wearing is an old one that I only put on when I go to the wash-house; but it's quite good enough to get spoilt with the dust, isn't it, madame?'

'Certainly, certainly,' replied Marthe, trying to force a smile.

Just at this moment a stern voice was heard from the top of the stairs, calling sharply: 'Well! now, mother!'

Mouret raised his head and saw Abbé Faujas leaning against the second-floor banisters, looking very angry, and bending over, at the risk of falling, to get a better view of what was going on in the passage. He had heard a sound of talking and had been waiting there for a moment or two in great impatience.

'Come, mother, come!' he cried again.

'Yes, yes, we are coming up,' answered Madame Faujas, trembling at the sound of her son's angry voice.

Then turning to the Trouches, she said:

'Come along, my children, we must go upstairs. Let us leave madame to attend to her business.'

But the Trouches did not seem to hear; they appeared quite satisfied to remain in the passage, and they looked about them with a well-pleased air, as though the house, had just been presented to them.

'It is very nice, very nice indeed, isn't it, Honoré?' Olympe said. 'After what Ovide wrote in his letters we scarcely expected to find it so nice as this, did we? But I told you that we ought to come here, and that we should do better here, and I am right, you see.'

'Yes, yes, we ought to be very comfortable here,' Trouche murmured. 'The garden, too, seems a pretty big one.'

Then addressing Mouret, he inquired:

'Do you allow your lodgers to walk in the garden, sir?'

Before Mouret had time to reply, Abbé Faujas, who had come downstairs, cried out in thundering tones:

'Come, Trouche! Come, Olympe!'

They turned round; and when they saw him standing on the steps looking terribly angry, they fairly quailed and meekly followed him. The Abbé went up the stairs in front of them without saying another word, without even seeming to observe the presence of Mouret, who stood gazing after the singular procession. Madame Faujas smiled at Marthe to take away the awkwardness of the situation as she brought up the rear.

Marthe then went out, and Mouret, left to himself, lingered a moment or two in the passage. Upstairs, on the second floor, doors were being noisily banged. Then loud voices were heard, and presently there came dead silence.

'Has he locked them up separately, I wonder?' said Mouret to himself, with a laugh. 'Well, anyhow, they are not a nice family.'

On the very next day, Trouche, respectably dressed, entirely in black, shaven, and with his scanty hair carefully brushed over his temples, was presented by Abbé Faujas to Marthe and the lady patronesses. He was forty-five years of age, wrote a first-rate hand, and was said to have kept the books of a mercantile house for a long time. The ladies at once installed him as secretary. His duties were to represent the committee, and employ himself in certain routine work from ten till four in an office on the first floor of the Home. His salary was to be fifteen hundred francs.

'Those good people are very quiet, you see,' Marthe remarked to her husband a few days afterwards.

Indeed the Trouches made no more noise than the Faujases. Two or three times Rose asserted that she had heard quarrels between the mother and daughter, but the Abbé's grave voice had immediately restored peace. Trouche went out every morning punctually at a quarter to ten, and came back again at a quarter past four. He never went out in the evening. Olympe occasionally went shopping with Madame Faujas, but she was never seen to come down the stairs by herself.

The window of the room in which the Trouches slept overlooked the garden. It was the last one on the right, in front of the trees of the Sub-Prefecture. Big curtains of red calico, with a yellow border, hung behind the glass panes, making a strong contrast, when seen from outside, with the priest's white ones. The window was invariably kept closed. One evening when Abbé Faujas and his mother were out on the terrace with the Mourets, a slight involuntary cough was heard, and as the priest raised his head with an expression of annoyance, he caught sight of Olympe and her husband leaning out of the window. For a moment or two he kept his eyes turned upwards, thus interrupting his conversation with Marthe. At this the Trouches disappeared; and those below heard the window-catch being fastened.

'You had better go upstairs, I think, mother,' said the priest. 'I am afraid you may be catching cold out here.'

Madame Faujas wished them all good-night; and, when she had retired, Marthe resumed the conversation by asking in her kindly way:

'Is your sister worse? I have not seen her for a week.'

'She has great need of rest,' the priest curtly answered. However, Marthe's sympathetic interest made her continue the subject.

'She shuts herself up too much,' said she; 'the fresh air would do her good. These October evenings are still quite warm. Why doesn't she ever come out into the garden? She has never set foot in it. You know that it is entirely at your disposal.'

The priest muttered a few vague words of excuse, and then Mouret, to increase his embarrassment, manifested still greater amiability than his wife's.

'That's just what I was saying this morning,' he began.

'Monsieur l'Abbé's sister might very well bring her sewing out here in the sun in the afternoons, instead of keeping herself shut in upstairs. Anyone would think that she daren't even show herself at the window. She isn't frightened of us, I hope! We are not such terrible people as all that! And Monsieur Trouche, too, he hurries up the stairs, four steps at a time. Tell them to come and spend an evening with us now and then. They must be frightfully dull up in that room of theirs, all alone.'

The Abbé did not seem to be in the humour that evening to submit to his landlord's pleasantry. He looked him straight in the face, and said very bluntly:

'I am much obliged to you, but there is little probability of their accepting your invitation. They are tired in the evening, and they go to bed. And, besides, that is the best thing they can do.'

'Just as they like, my dear sir,' replied Mouret, vexed by the Abbé's rough manner.

When he was alone again with Marthe, he said to her:

'Does the Abbé, I wonder, think he can persuade us that the moon is made of green cheese? It's quite clear that he is afraid that those scamps he has taken in will play him some bad trick or other. Didn't you see how sharply he kept his eye on them this evening when he caught sight of them at the window? They were spying out at us up there. There will be a bad end to all this!'

Marthe was now living in a state of blessed calm. She no longer felt troubled by Mouret's raillery; the gradual growth of faith within her filled her with exquisite joy, she glided softly and slowly into a life of pious devotion, which seemed to lull her with a sweet restfulness. Abbé Faujas still avoided speaking to her of God. He remained merely a friend, simply exercising influence over her by his grave demeanour and the vague odour of incense exhaled by his cassock. On two or three occasions when she was alone with him she had again broken out into fits of nervous sobbing, without knowing why, but finding a happiness in thus allowing herself to weep. On each of these occasions the Abbé had merely taken her hands in silence, calming her with his serene and authoritative gaze. When she wanted to tell him of her strange attacks of sadness, or her secret joys, or her need of guidance, he smiled and hushed her, telling her that these matters were not his concern, and that she must speak of them to Abbé Bourrette. Then she retired completely within herself and remained trembling; while the priest seemed to assume still colder reserve than before, and strode away from her like some unheeding god at whose feet she wished to pour put her soul in humiliation.

Marthe's chief occupation now was attending the various religious services and works in which she took part. In the vast nave of Saint-Saturnin's she felt perfectly happy; it was there that she experienced the full sweetness of that purely physical restfulness which she sought. She there forgot everything: it was like an immense window open upon another life, a life that was wide and infinite, and full of an emotion which thrilled and satisfied her. But she still felt some fear of the church, and she went there with a feeling of uneasy bashfulness, and a touch of nervous shame, that made her glance behind her as she passed through the doorway, to see if anyone was watching her. Then, once inside, she abandoned herself, everything around her seemed to assume a melting softness, even the unctuous voice of Abbé Bourrette, who, after he had confessed her, sometimes kept her on her knees for a few minutes longer, while he spoke to her about Madame Rastoil's dinners or the Rougons' last reception.

Marthe often returned home in a condition of complete prostration. Religion seemed to break her down. Rose had become all-powerful in the house. She scolded Mouret, found fault with him because he dirtied too much linen, and let him have his dinner at her own hours. She even tried to convert him.

'Madame does quite right to live a Christian life,' said she. 'You will be damned, sir, you will, and it will only be right, for you are not a good man at heart, no, you are not! You ought to go with your wife to mass next Sunday morning.'

Mouret shrugged his shoulders. He let things take their own course, and sometimes even did a bit of house-work himself, taking a turn or two with the broom when he thought that the dining-room looked particularly dusty. The children gave him most trouble. It was vacation-time, and, as their mother was scarcely ever at home, Désirée and Octave—who had again failed in his examination for his degree—turned the place upside down. Serge was poorly, kept his bed, and spent whole days in reading in his room. He had become Abbé Faujas's favourite, and the priest lent him books. Mouret thus spent two dreadful months, at his wits' end how to manage his young folks. Octave was a special trouble to him, and as he did not feel inclined to keep him at home till the end of the vacation, he determined that he should not again return to college, but should be sent to some business-house at Marseilles.

'Since you won't look after them at all,' he said to Marthe, 'I must find some place or other to put them in. I am quite worn out with them all, and I won't have them at home any longer. It's your own fault if it causes you any grief. Octave is quite unbearable. He will never pass his examination, and it will be much better to teach him at once how to gain his own living instead of letting him idle his time away with a lot of good-for-nothings. One meets him roaming all over the town.'

Marthe was very much distressed. She seemed to awake from a dream on hearing that one of her children was about to leave her. She succeeded in getting the departure postponed for a week, during which she remained more at home, and resumed her active life. But she quickly dropped back again into her previous state of listless languor; and on the day that Octave came to kiss her, telling her that he was to leave for Marseilles in the evening, she had lost all strength and energy, and contented herself with giving him some good advice.

Mouret came back from the railway station with a very heavy heart. He looked about him for his wife, and found her in the garden, crying under the arbour. Then he gave vent to his feelings.

'There! that's one the less!' he exclaimed. 'You ought to feel glad of it. You will be able to go prowling about the church now as much as you like. Make your mind easy, the other two won't be here long. I shall keep Serge with me as he is a very quiet lad and is rather young as yet to go and read for the bar; but if he's at all in your way, just let me know, and I will free you of him at once. As for Désirée, I shall send her to her nurse.'

Marthe went on weeping in silence.

'But what would you have?' he continued. 'You can't be both in and out. Since you have taken to keeping away from home, your children have become indifferent to you. That's logic, isn't it? Besides it is necessary to find room for all the people who are now living in our house. It isn't nearly big enough, and we shall be lucky if we don't get turned out of doors ourselves.'

He had raised his eyes as he spoke, and was looking at the windows of the second-floor. Then, lowering his voice, he added:

'Don't go on crying in that ridiculous way! They are watching you. Don't you see those eyes peeping between the red curtains? They are the eyes of the Abbé's sister; I know them well enough. You may depend on seeing them there all day long. The Abbé himself may be a decent fellow, but as for those Trouches, I know they are always crouching behind their curtains like wolves waiting to spring on one. I feel quite certain that if the Abbé didn't prevent them, they would come down in the night to steal my pears. Dry your tears, my dear; you may be quite sure that they are enjoying our disagreement. Even though they have been the cause of the boy's going away, that is no reason why we should let them see what a trouble his departure has been to us both.'

His voice broke, and he himself seemed on the point of sobbing. Marthe, quite heart-broken, deeply touched by his last words, was prompted to throw herself into his arms. But they were afraid of being observed; and besides they felt as if there were some obstacle between them that prevented them from coming together. So they separated, while Olympe's eyes still glistened between the red curtains upstairs.

XI

One morning Abbé Bourrette made his appearance, his face betokening the greatest distress. As soon as he caught sight of Marthe on the steps, he hurried up to her and, seizing her hands and pressing them, he stammered:

'Poor Compan! it is all over with him! he is dying! I am going upstairs, I must see Faujas at once.'

When Marthe showed him his fellow priest, who, according to his wont, was walking to and fro at the bottom of the garden, reading his breviary, he ran up to him, tottering on his short legs. He tried to speak and tell the other the sad news, but his grief choked him, and he could only throw his arms round Abbé Faujas's neck, while sobbing bitterly.

'Hallo! what's the matter with the two parsons?' cried Mouret, who had hastily rushed out of the dining-room.

'The Curé of Saint-Saturnin's is dying,' Marthe replied, showing much distress.

Mouret assumed an expression of surprise, and, as he went back into the house, he murmured:

'Pooh! that worthy Bourrette will manage to console himself tomorrow when he is appointed Curé in the other's place. He counts on getting the post; he told me so.'

Abbé Faujas disengaged himself from the old priest's embrace, quietly closed his breviary, and listened to the sad news with a grave face.

'Compan wants to see you,' said Abbé Bourrette in a broken voice; 'he will not last the morning out. Oh! he has been a dear friend to me! We studied together. He is anxious to say good-bye to you. He has been telling me all through the night that you were the only man of courage in the diocese. For more than a year now he has been getting weaker and weaker, and not a single Plassans priest has dared to go and grasp his hand; while you, a stranger, who scarcely knew him, you have spent an afternoon with him every week. The tears came into his eyes just now as he was speaking of you; you must lose no time, my friend.'

Abbé Faujas went up to his room for a moment, while Abbé Bourrette paced impatiently and hopelessly about the passage; and then at last they set off together. The old priest wiped his brow and swayed about on the road as he talked in disconnected fashion:

'He would have died like a dog without a single prayer being said for him if his sister had not come and told me about him at eleven o'clock last night. She did quite right, the dear lady, though he did not want to compromise any of us, and even would have foregone the last sacraments. Yes, my friend, he was dying all alone, abandoned and deserted, he who had so high a mind, and who has only lived to do good!'

Then Bourrette became silent; but after a few moments he resumed again in a different voice:

'Do you think that Fenil will ever forgive me for this? Never, I expect! When Compan saw me bringing the viaticum, he was unwilling to let me anoint him and told me to go away. Well, well! it's all over with me now, and I shall never be Curé! But I am glad that I did it, and that I haven't let Compan die like a dog. He has been at war with Fenil for thirty years, you know. When he took to his bed he said to me, "Ah! it's Fenil who is going to carry the day! Now that I am stricken down he will get the better of me!" So think of it! That poor Compan, whom I have seen so high-spirited and energetic at Saint-Saturnin's! Little Eusèbe, the choir-boy, whom I took to ring the viaticum bell, was quite embarrassed when he found where we were going. He kept looking behind him at each tinkle, as if he was afraid that Fenil would hear it.'

Abbé Faujas, who was stepping along quickly with bent head and a preoccupied air, kept perfectly silent, and did not even seem to hear what his companion was saying.

'Has the Bishop been informed?' he suddenly asked.

But Abbé Bourrette in his turn now appeared to be buried in thought and made no reply; however, just as they reached Abbé Compan's door he said to his companion:

'Tell him that we met Fenil and that he bowed to us. It will please him, for he will then think that I shall be appointed Curé.'

They went up the stairs in silence. The Curé's sister came to the landing, and on seeing them burst into tears. Then she stammered between her sobs:

'It is all over! He has just passed away in my arms. I was quite alone with him. As he was dying, he looked round him and murmured, "I must have the plague since they have all deserted me." Ah! gentlemen he died with his eyes full of tears.'

They went into the little room where Abbé Compan, with his head resting on his pillow, seemed to be asleep. His eyes had remained open, and tears yet trickled down his white sad face. Then Abbé Bourrette fell upon his knees, sobbing and praying, with his face pressed to the counterpane. Abbé Faujas at first remained standing, gazing at the dead man; and after having knelt for a moment, he quietly went away. Abbé Bourrette was so absorbed in his grief that he did not even hear his colleague close the door.

Abbé Faujas went straight to the Bishop's. In Monseigneur Rousselot's ante-chamber he met Abbé Surin, carrying a bundle of papers.

'Do you want to speak to his lordship?' asked the secretary, with his never-failing smile. 'You have come at an unfortunate time. His lordship is so busy that he has given orders that no one is to be admitted.'

'But I want to see him on a very urgent matter,' quietly said Abbé Faujas. 'You can at any rate let him know that I am here; and I will wait, if it is necessary.'

'I am afraid that it would be useless for you to wait. His lordship has several people with him. It would be better if you came again tomorrow.'

But the Abbé took a chair, and just as he was doing so the Bishop opened the door of his study. He appeared much vexed on seeing his visitor, whom at first he pretended not to recognise.

'My son,' he said to Surin, 'when you have arranged those papers, come to me immediately; there is a letter I want to dictate to you.'

Then turning to the priest, who remained respectfully standing, he said:

'Ah! is it you, Monsieur Faujas? I am very glad to see you. Perhaps you want to say something to me? Come into my study; you are never in the way.'

Monseigneur Rousselot's study was a very large and rather gloomy room, in which a great wood fire was kept burning in the summer as well as the winter. The heavy carpet and curtains kept out all the air, and the room was like a warm bath. The Bishop, like some dowager shutting herself up from the world, detesting all noise and excitement, lived a chilly life there in his armchair, committing to Abbé Fenil the care of his diocese. He delighted in the classics, and it was said that he was secretly making a translation of Horace. He was equally fond of the little verses of the Anthology, and broad quotations occasionally escaped from his lips, quotations which he enjoyed with the naïveté of a learned man who cares nothing for the modesty of the vulgar.

'There is no one here, you see,' said he, sitting down before the fire; 'but I don't feel very well to-day, and I gave orders that nobody was to be admitted. Now you can tell me what you have to say; I am quite at your service.'

His general expression of amiability was tinged with a kind of vague uneasiness, a sort of resigned submission. When Abbé Faujas had informed him of the death of Abbé Compan, he rose from his chair, apparently both distressed and alarmed.

'What!' he cried, 'my good Compan dead! and I was not able to bid him farewell! No one gave me any warning! Ah, my friend, you were right when you gave me to understand that I was no longer master here. They abuse my kindness.'

'Your lordship knows,' said Abbé Faujas, 'how devoted I am to you. I am only waiting for a sign from you.'

The Bishop shook his head as he murmured:

'Yes, yes; I remember the offer you made to me. You have an excellent heart; but what an uproar there would be, if I were to break with Abbé Fenil! I should have my ears deafened for a whole week! And yet if I could feel quite sure that you could really rid me of him, if I was not afraid that at a week's end he would come back and crush your neck under his heel—'

Abbé Faujas could not repress a smile. Tears were welling from the Bishop's eyes.

'Yes, I am afraid, I am afraid,' the prelate resumed, as he again sank down into his chair. 'I don't feel equal to it yet. It is that miserable man who has killed Compan and has kept his death agony a secret from me so that I might not go and close his eyes. He is capable of the most terrible things. But, you see, I like to live in peace. Fenil is very energetic and he renders me great services in the diocese. When I am no longer here, matters will perhaps be better ordered.'

He grew calmer again and his smile returned.

'Besides, everything is going on satisfactorily at present, and I don't see any immediate difficulty. We can wait.'

Abbé Faujas sat down, and calmly resumed:

'No doubt: but still you will have to appoint a Curé for Saint-Saturnin's in succession to the Abbé Compan.'

Monseigneur Rousselot lifted his hands to his temples with an expression of hopelessness.

'Indeed, you are right!' he ejaculated. 'I had forgotten that. Poor Compan doesn't know in what a hole he has put me, by dying so suddenly without my having had any warning. I promised you that place, didn't I?'

The Abbé bowed.

'Well, my friend, you will save me by letting me take back my word. You know how Fenil detests you. The success of the Home of the Virgin has made him quite furious, and he swears that he will prevent you from making the conquest of Plassans. I am talking to you quite openly, you see. Recently, when reference was made to the appointment of a Curé for Saint-Saturnin's, I let your name fall. But Fenil flew into a frightful rage and I was obliged to promise that I would give the place to a friend of his, Abbé Chardon, whom you know, and who is really a very worthy man. Now, my friend, do this much for me, and give up that idea. I will make you whatever recompense you like to name.'

The priest's face wore a grave expression. After a short interval of silence during which he seemed to be taking counsel of himself, he spoke:

'You know very well, my lord,' he said, 'that I am quite without personal ambition. I should much prefer to lead a life of privacy, and it would be a great relief to me to give up this appointment. But I am not my own master, I feel bound to satisfy those patrons of mine who take an interest in me. I trust that your lordship will reflect very seriously before taking a step which you would probably regret afterwards.'

Although Abbé Faujas spoke very humbly, the Bishop was not unconscious of the menace which his words veiled. He rose from his chair and took a few steps about the room, a prey to the painful perplexity.

'Well, well,' he said, lifting his hands, 'here's trouble and no mistake, for a long time. I should much have preferred to avoid all these explanations, but, since you insist, I must speak frankly. Well, my dear sir, Abbé Fenil brings many charges against you. As I think I told you before, he must have written to Besançon and learnt all the vexatious stories you know of. You have certainly explained those matters to me, and I am quite aware of your merits and of your life of penitence and solitude; but what can I do? Fenil has weapons against you and he uses them ruthlessly. I often don't know what to say in your defence. When the Minister requested me to receive you into my diocese, I did not conceal from him that your position would be a difficult one; but he continued to press me and said that that was your affair, and so in the end I consented. But you must not come to-day and ask me to do what is impossible.'

Abbé Faujas had not lowered his head during the Bishop's remarks. He now raised it still higher as he looked the prelate straight in the face and said in his sharp voice:

'You have given me your promise, my lord.'

'Certainly, certainly,' the Bishop replied. 'That poor Compan was getting weaker every day and you came and confided certain matters to me, and I then made the promise to you. I don't deny it. Listen to me, I will tell you everything, so that you may not accuse me of wheeling round like a weathercock. You asserted that the Minister was extremely desirous for you to be appointed Curé of Saint-Saturnin's. Well, I wrote for information on the subject, and a friend of mine went to the Ministry in Paris. They almost laughed in his face there, and they told him that they didn't even know you. The Minister absolutely denies that he is your supporter, do you hear? If you wish it, I will read you a letter in which he makes some very stern remarks about you.'

He stretched his arm towards a drawer, but Abbé Faujas rose to his feet without taking his eyes off him, and smiled with mingled irony and pity.

'Ah, my lord! my lord!' said he.

Then, after a moment's silence, as though he were unwilling to enter into further explanations, he said:

'I give your lordship back your promise; but believe that in all this I was working more for your own advantage than for mine. By-and-by, when it will be too late, you will call my warnings to mind.'

He stepped towards the door, but the Bishop laid his hand upon him and brought him back, saying with an expression of uneasiness:

'What do you mean? Explain yourself, my dear Monsieur Faujas. I know very well that I have not been in favour at Paris since the election of the Marquis de Lagrifoul. But people know me very little if they suppose that I had any hand in the matter. I don't go out of my study twice a month. Do you imagine that they accuse me of having brought about the marquis's return?'

'Yes, I am afraid so,' the priest curtly replied.

'But it is quite absurd! I have never interfered in politics; I live amongst my beloved books. It was Fenil who did it all. I told him a score of times that he would end by compromising me in Paris.'

He checked himself and blushed slightly at having allowed these last words to escape him. Abbé Faujas sat down again and said in a deep voice:

'My lord, by those words you have condemned your vicar-general. I have never said otherwise than you have just said. Do not continue to make common cause with him or he will lead you into serious trouble. I have friends in Paris, whatever you may believe. I know that the Marquis de Lagrifoul's election has strongly predisposed the Government against you. Rightly or wrongly, they believe that you are the sole cause of the opposition movement which has manifested itself in Plassans, where the Minister, for special reasons, is most anxious to have a majority. If the Legitimist candidate should again succeed at the next election, it would be very awkward, and I should be considerably alarmed for your comfort.'

'But this is abominable!' cried the unhappy Bishop, rocking himself in his chair; 'I can't prevent the Legitimist candidate from being returned! I haven't got the least influence, and I never mix myself up in these matters at all. Really, there are times when I feel that I should like to shut myself up in a monastery. I could take my books with me, and lead a quiet, peaceful life there. It is Fenil who ought to be Bishop instead of me. If I were to listen to Fenil, I should get on the very worst terms with the Government. I should hearken only to Rome, and tell Paris to mind its own business. But that is not my nature, and I want to die in peace. The Minister, then, you say, is enraged with me?'

The priest made no reply. Two creases which appeared at the corners of his mouth gave his face an expression of silent scorn.

'Really,' continued the Bishop, 'if I thought it would please him if I were to appoint you Curé of Saint-Saturnin's, I would try to manage it. But I can assure you that you are mistaken. You are but little in the odour of sanctity.'

Abbé Faujas made a hasty movement of his hands, as he broke out impatiently:

'Have you forgotten that calumnies are circulated about me, and that I came to Plassans in a threadbare cassock? When they send a compromised man to a post of danger, they deny all knowledge of him till the day of triumph. Help me to succeed, my lord, and then you will see that I have friends in Paris.'

Then, as the Bishop, surprised to find in a priest such a bold adventurer, continued to gaze at him in silence, Faujas lapsed into a less assertive manner and continued:

'These, however, are suppositions, and what I mean is, that I have much to be pardoned. My friends are waiting to thank you till my position is completely established.'

Monseigneur Rousselot kept silence for a moment longer. He was a man of sharp understanding, and he had gained a knowledge of human failings from books. He was conscious of his own yielding character, and he was even a little ashamed of it; but he consoled himself for it by judging men for what they were worth. In the life of a learned epicurean, which he led, there were times when he felt supreme disdain for the ambitious men about him, who fought amongst themselves for a few stray shreds of his power.

'Well,' he said, with a smile, 'you are a pertinacious man, my dear Monsieur Faujas, and since I have made you a promise I will keep it. Six months ago, I confess, I should have been afraid of stirring up all Plassans against me, but you have succeeded in making yourself liked, and the ladies of the town often speak to me about you in very eulogistic terms. In appointing you Curé of Saint-Saturnin's, I am only paying the debt which we owe you for the Home of the Virgin.'

The Bishop had recovered his usual pleasant amiability and charming manner. Just at this moment Abbé Surin put his handsome head through the doorway.

'No, my child,' said the Bishop to him, 'I shall not dictate that letter to you. I have no further need of you, and you can go.'

'Abbé Fenil is here,' muttered the young priest.

'Oh, very well, let him wait!'

Monseigneur Rousselot winced slightly; but he spoke to his secretary with an almost ludicrous expression of decision, and looked at Abbé Faujas with a glance of intelligence.

'See! go out this way,' he said to him, as he opened a door that was hidden behind a curtain.

He kept the priest standing on the threshold for a moment, and continued to look at him with a smile on his face.

'Fenil will be furious,' said he; 'but you will promise to defend me against him if he is too hard upon me! I am making him your enemy, I warn you of that. I am counting upon you, too, to prevent the re-election of the Marquis de Lagrifoul. Ah! it is upon you that I am leaning now, my dear Monsieur Faujas.'

He waved his white hand to the Abbé, and then returned with an appearance of perfect unconcern to the warmth of his study. The priest had remained bowing, feeling surprised at the quite feminine ease with which the Bishop changed his master and yielded to the stronger side. And only now did he begin to feel that Monseigneur Rousselot had been secretly laughing at him, even as he laughed at Abbé Fenil in that downy armchair of his where he read his Horace.

About ten o'clock on the following Thursday, just when the fashionable folks of Plassans were treading on each other's toes in the Rougons' green drawing-room, Abbé Faujas appeared at the door. He looked tall and majestic, there was a bright colour on his cheeks, and he wore a delicate cassock that glistened like satin. His face was still grave, though there was a slight smile upon it, just the pleasant turn of the lips that was necessary to light up his stern countenance with a ray of cheerfulness.

'Ah! here is the dear Curé!' Madame de Condamin gaily exclaimed.

The mistress of the house eagerly hastened up to him; she grasped one of his hands within both her own, and drew him into the middle of the room, with wheedling glances and a gentle swaying of her head.

'This is a surprise! a very pleasant surprise!' she cried. 'It's an age since we have seen you! Is it only when good fortune visits you that you can remember your friends?'

Abbé Faujas bowed with easy composure. All around him there was a flattering ovation, a buzzing of enthusiastic women. Madame Delangre and Madame Rastoil did not wait till he came up to them, but hastened to congratulate him upon his appointment, which had been officially announced that morning. The mayor, the justice of the peace, and even Monsieur de Bourdeu, all stepped up to him and shook his hand heartily.

'Ah, he's a fine fellow and will go a long way!' Monsieur de Condamin murmured into Doctor Porquier's ear. 'I scented him from the first day I saw him. That grimacing old Madame Rougon and he tell no end of lies. I have seen him slipping in here at dusk half a score of times. They must be mixed up in some queer things together.'

Doctor Porquier was terribly afraid of being compromised by Monsieur de Condamin, so he hurried away from him, and came like the others to grasp Abbé Faujas's hand, although he had never previously spoken to him.

The priest's triumphal entry was the great event of the evening. He had now seated himself and was hemmed in by a triple circle of petticoats. He talked with charming good nature on all sorts of subjects, but avoided replying to any hints or allusions. When Félicité directly questioned him, he merely said that he should not occupy the parsonage, as he preferred remaining in the lodgings where he had found himself so comfortable for nearly three years. Marthe was present among the other ladies, and was, as usual, extremely reserved. She had only just smiled at the Abbé, watching him from a distance, and looking the while a little pale and rather weary and uneasy. When he signified his intention of not quitting the Rue Balande, she blushed and rose to go into the small drawing-room as if she felt incommoded by the heat. Madame Paloque, beside whom Monsieur de Condamin had seated himself, said to him quite loud enough to be heard:

'It's very decorous, isn't it? She certainly might refrain from making assignations with him here, since they have the whole day to themselves!'

Only Monsieur de Condamin laughed; everyone else received the sally very coldly. Then Madame Paloque, recognising that she had made a mistake, tried to turn the matter off as a joke. Meantime in the corners of the room the guests were discussing Abbé Fenil. Great curiosity was manifested as to whether he would put in an appearance. Monsieur de Bourdeu, who was one of his friends, said with an air of authority that he was indisposed—a statement which was received by the company with discreet smiles. Everyone was quite aware of the revolution that had taken place at the Bishop's. Abbé Surin gave the ladies some very interesting details of the terrible scene that had taken place between his lordship and the grand-vicar. The latter, on getting the worst of the struggle, had caused it to be reported that he was confined to his room by an attack of gout. But the fight was not over, and Abbé Surin hinted that a good deal more would happen yet, a remark which was whispered about the room with many little exclamations, shakings of heads and expressions of surprise and doubt. For the moment, at any rate, Abbé Faujas was carrying everything before him: and so the fair devotees sunned themselves pleasantly in the rays of the rising luminary.

About the middle of the evening Abbé Bourrette arrived. Conversation ceased and people looked at him with curiosity. They all knew that he had expected to be appointed Curé of Saint-Saturnin's himself. He had taken over the Abbé Compan's duties during the latter's long illness, and he had a lien upon the appointment. He lingered for a moment by the door, a little out of breath and with blinking eyes, without being aware of the interest which his appearance excited. Then, catching sight of Abbé Faujas, he eagerly hastened up to him, and seizing both his hands with a show of much pleasure exclaimed:

'Ah I my dear friend, let me congratulate you! I have just come from your rooms, where your mother told me that you were here. I am delighted to see you.'

Abbé Faujas had risen from his seat, and notwithstanding his great self-control, he seemed annoyed, taken by surprise, as it were, by this unexpected display of affection.

'Yes,' he murmured, 'I felt bound to accept his lordship's offer in spite of my lack of merit. I refused it, indeed, at first, mentioning the names of several more deserving priests than myself. I mentioned your own name.'

Abbé Bourrette blinked, and taking Abbé Faujas aside he said to him in low tones:

'His lordship has told me all about it. Fenil, it seems, would not hear of me. He would have set the whole diocese in a blaze if I had been appointed. Those were his very words. My crime is having closed poor Compan's eyes. He demanded, as you know, the appointment of Abbé Chardon, a pious man, no doubt, but not of sufficient reputation. Fenil counted on reigning at Saint-Saturnin's in his name. It was then that his lordship determined to give you the place and checkmate him. I am quite avenged, and I am delighted, my dear friend. Did you know the full story?'

'No, not in all its details.'

'Well, it is all just as I have told you, I can assure you. I have the facts from his lordship's own lips. Between ourselves, he has hinted to me of a very sufficient recompense. The deputy vicar-general, Abbé Vial, has for a long time been desirous of settling in Borne, and his place will be vacant, you understand. But don't say anything about this. I wouldn't take a big sum of money for my day's work.'

He continued pressing both Abbé Faujas's hands, while his broad face beamed with satisfaction. The ladies around them were smiling and looking at them in surprise. But the worthy man's joy was so frank and unreserved that it communicated itself to all in the green drawing-room, where the ovation in the new Curé's honour took a more familiar and affectionate turn. The ladies grouped themselves together and spoke of the cathedral organ which wanted repairing, and Madame de Condamin promised a magnificent altar for the procession on the approaching festival of Corpus Christi. Abbé Bourrette was sharing in the general triumph when Madame Paloque, craning out her hideous face, touched him on the shoulder and murmured in his ear:

'Your reverence won't, I suppose, hear confessions tomorrow in Saint-Michael's chapel?'

The priest, while taking Abbé Compan's duty, had occupied the confessional in Saint-Michael's chapel, which was the largest and most convenient in the church and was specially reserved for the Curé. He did not at first understand the force of Madame Paloque's remark, and he looked at her, again blinking his eyes.

'I ask you,' she continued, 'if you will resume your old confessional in the chapel of the Holy Angels, to-morrow.'

He turned rather pale and remained silent for a moment longer. Then he bent his gaze to the floor, and a slight shiver coursed down his neck, as though he had received a blow from behind. And, seeing that Madame Paloque was still there staring at him, he stammered out:

'Certainly; I shall go back to my old confessional. Come to the chapel of the Holy Angels, the last one on the left, on the same side as the cloisters. It is very damp, so wrap yourself up well, dear madame, wrap yourself up well.'

Tears rose to his eyes. He was filled with regretful longing for that handsome confessional in the chapel of Saint-Michael, into which the warm sun streamed in the afternoon just at the time when he heard confessions. Until now he had felt no sorrow at relinquishing the cathedral to Abbé Faujas; but this little matter, this removal from one chapel to another, affected him very painfully; and it seemed to him that he had missed the goal of his life. Madame Paloque told him in her loud voice that he appeared to have grown melancholy all at once, but he protested against this assertion and tried to smile and look cheerful again. However he left the drawing-room early in the evening.

Abbé Faujas was one of the last to go. Rougon came up to him to offer his congratulations and they remained talking earnestly together on a couch. They spoke of the necessity of religious feeling in a wisely ordered state. Each lady, on retiring from the room, made a low bow as she passed in front of them.

'You know, Monsieur le Curé,' said Félicité graciously, 'that you are my daughter's cavalier.'

The priest rose from his seat. Marthe was waiting for him at the door. When they got out into the street, they seemed as if blinded by the darkness, and crossed the Place of the Sub-Prefecture without exchanging a word; but in the Rue Balande, as they stood in front of the house, Marthe touched the priest's arm at the moment when he was about to insert the key in the lock.

'I am so very pleased at your success,' she said to him, in a tone of great emotion. 'Be kind to me to-day, and grant me the favour which you have hitherto refused. I assure you that Abbé Bourrette does not understand me. It is only you who can direct and save me.'

He motioned her away from him, and, when he had opened the door and lighted the little lamp which Rose had left at the foot of the staircase, he went upstairs, saying to her gently as he did so:

'You promised me to be reasonable—well, I will think over what you have asked. We will talk about it.'

Marthe did not retire to her own room until she had heard the priest close his door on the upper floor. While she was undressing and getting into bed she paid no attention whatever to Mouret, who, half asleep, was retailing to her at great length some gossip that was being circulated in the town. He had been to his club, the Commercial Club, a place where he rarely set foot.

'Abbé Faujas has got the better of Abbé Bourrette,' he repeated for the tenth time as he slowly rolled his head upon the pillow. 'Poor Abbé Bourrette! Well, never mind! it's good fun to see those parsons devouring one another. The other day when they were hugging each other in the garden —you remember it, don't you?—anyone would have thought that they were brothers. Ah! they rob each other even of their very penitents. But why don't you say anything, my dear? You don't agree with me, eh? Or is it because you are going to sleep? Well, well, good-night then, my dear.'

He fell asleep, still muttering disjointed words, while Marthe, with widely opened eyes, stared up into the air and followed over the ceiling, faintly illumined by the night-light, the pattering of the Abbé's slippers while he was retiring to rest.

XII

At the return of summer Abbé Faujas and his mother again came downstairs to enjoy the fresh air on the terrace. Mouret had become very cross-grained. He declined the old lady's invitations to play piquet and sat swaying himself about on a chair. Seeing him yawn, without making any attempt to conceal how bored he was feeling, Marthe said to him:

'Why don't you go to your club, my dear?'

He now went there more frequently than he had been used to do. When he returned he found his wife and the Abbé still in the same place on the terrace, while Madame Faujas, a few yards away from them, preserved the demeanour of a blind and dumb guardian.

When anyone in the town spoke to Mouret of the new Curé he still continued to sound his praises. Faujas, said he, was decidedly a superior sort of man, and he himself had never felt any doubt of his great abilities. Madame Paloque could never succeed in drawing a hostile word from him on the subject of the priest, in spite of the malicious way in which she would ask him after his wife in the midst of his remarks about Abbé Faujas. Old Madame Rougon had no better success in her attempts to unveil the secret troubles which she thought she could detect beneath Mouret's outward show of cheerfulness. She laid all sorts of traps for him as she watched his face with her sharp shrewd smile; but that inveterate chatterer, whose tongue was a regular town-crier's bell, now showed the greatest reserve when any reference was made to his household.

'So your husband has become reasonable at last?' Félicité remarked to her daughter one day. 'He leaves you free.'

Marthe looked at her mother with an air of surprise.

'I have always been free,' she said.

'Ah! my dear child, I see that you don't want to say anything against him. You told me once that he looked very unfavourably upon Abbé Faujas.'

'Nothing of the kind, I assure you! You must have imagined it. My husband is upon the best terms with Abbé Faujas. There is nothing whatever to make them otherwise.'

Marthe was much astonished at the persistence with which everybody seemed to imagine that her husband and the Abbé were not good friends. Frequently at the committee-meetings at the Home of the Virgin the ladies put questions to her which made her quite impatient. She was really very happy and contented, and the house in the Rue Balande had never seemed pleasanter to her than it did now. Abbé Faujas had given her to understand that he would undertake her spiritual direction as soon as he should be of opinion that Abbé Bourrette was no longer sufficient, and she lived in this hope, her mind full of simple joy, like a girl who is promised some pretty religious pictures if she keeps good. Every now and then indeed she felt as though she were becoming a child again; she experienced a freshness of feeling and child-like impulses that filled her with gentle emotion. One day, in the spring-time, as Mouret was pruning his tall box plants, he found her sitting at the bottom of the garden beneath the young shoots of the arbour with her eyes streaming with tears.

'What is the matter, my dear?' he asked anxiously. 'Nothing,' she said, with a smile, 'nothing at all, really; I am very happy, very.'

He shrugged his shoulders, and went on delicately cutting the box plants into an even line. He took considerable pride in having the neatest trimmed hedges in the neighbourhood. Marthe had wiped her eyes, but she soon began to weep again, feeling a choking heart-rending sensation at the scent of the severed verdure. She was forty years old now, and it was for her past-away youth that she was weeping.

Since his appointment as Curé of Saint-Saturnin's, Abbé Faujas had shown a dignity which seemed to increase his stature. He carried his breviary and his hat with an air of authority, which he had exhibited at the cathedral in such wise as to ensure himself the respect of the clergy. Abbé Fenil, having sustained another defeat on two or three matters of detail, now seemed to have left his adversary free to do as he pleased. Abbé Faujas, however, was not foolish enough to make any indiscreet use of his triumph, but showed himself extremely supple. He was quite conscious that Plassans was still far from being his; and so, though he stopped every now and then in the street to shake hands with Monsieur Delangre, he merely exchanged passing salutations with Monsieur de Bourdeu, Monsieur Maffre, and the other guests of Monsieur Rastoil. A large section of society in the town still looked upon him with suspicion. They found fault with him for the want of frankness in his political opinions. In their estimation he ought to explain himself, declare himself in favour of one party or another. But the Abbé only smiled and said that he belonged to 'the honest men's party,' a reply which spared him a more explicit declaration. Moreover he showed no haste or anxiety, but continued to keep aloof till the drawing-rooms should open their doors to him of their own accord.

'No, my friend, not now; later on we will see about it,' he said to Abbé Bourrette, who had been pressing him to pay a visit to Monsieur Rastoil.

He was known to have refused two invitations to the Sub-Prefecture, and the Mourets were still the only people with whom he continued intimate. There he was, as it were, occupying a post of observation between two hostile camps. On Tuesdays, when the two sets of guests assembled in the gardens on his right and left, he took up his position at his window and watched the sunset in the distance behind the forests of the Seille, and then, before withdrawing, he lowered his eyes and replied with as much amiability to the bows of Monsieur Rastoil's guests as to those of the Sub-Prefect's. His intercourse with his neighbours as yet went no further than this.

On Tuesday, however, he went down into the garden. He was quite at home now in Mouret's grounds and no longer confined himself to pacing up and down beneath the arbour as he read his breviary. All the walks and beds seemed to belong to him; his cassock glided blackly past all the greenery. On that particular Tuesday, as he made a tour of the garden, he caught sight of Monsieur Maffre and Madame Rastoil below him and bowed to them; and then as he passed below the terrace of the Sub-Prefecture, he saw Monsieur de Condamin leaning there in company with Doctor Porquier. After an exchange of salutations, the priest was turning along the path, when the doctor called to him.

'Just a word, your reverence, I beg.'

Then he asked him at what time he could see him the following day. This was the first occasion on which any one of the two sets of guests had spoken to the priest from one garden to the other. The doctor was in great trouble however. His scamp of a son had been caught in a gambling den behind the gaol in company with other worthless characters. The most distressing part of the matter was that Guillaume was accused of being the leader of the band, and of having led Monsieur Maffre's sons, much younger than himself, astray.

'Pooh!' said Monsieur de Condamin with his sceptical laugh; 'young men must sow their wild oats. What a fuss about nothing! Here's the whole town in a state of perturbation because some young fellows have been caught playing baccarat and there happened to be a lady with them!'

The doctor seemed very much shocked at this.

'I want to ask your advice,' he said, addressing himself to the priest. 'Monsieur Maffre came to my house boiling over with anger, and assailed me with the bitterest reproaches, crying out that it was all my fault, as I had brought my son up badly. I am extremely distressed and troubled about it. Monsieur Maffre ought to know me better. I have sixty years of stainless life behind me.'

He went on wailing, dwelling upon the sacrifices that he had made for his son and expressing his fears that he would lose his practice in consequence of the young man's misconduct. Abbé Faujas, standing in the middle of the path, raised his head and gravely listened.

'I shall be only too glad if I can be of any service to you,' he said kindly. 'I will see Monsieur Maffre and will let him understand that his natural indignation has carried him too far. I will go at once and ask him to appoint a meeting with me for to-morrow. He is over there, on the other side.'

The Abbé crossed the garden and went towards Monsieur Maffre, who was still there with Madame Rastoil. When the justice of the peace found that the priest desired an interview with him, he would not hear of his taking any trouble about it, but put himself at his disposition, saying that he would do himself the honour of calling upon him the next day.

'Ah! Monsieur le Curé,' Madame Rastoil then remarked, 'let me compliment you upon your sermon last Sunday. All the ladies were much affected by it, I assure you.'

The Abbé bowed and crossed the garden again in order to reassure Doctor Porquier. Then he continued slowly pacing about the walks till nightfall, without taking part in any further conversations, but ever hearing the merriment of the groups of guests on his right hand and his left.

When Monsieur Maffre appeared the next day, Abbé Faujas was watching a couple of men who were at work repairing the fountain in the garden. He had expressed a desire to see the fountain play again, for the empty basin, said he, had such a melancholy appearance. At first Mouret had not seemed very willing to have anything done, alleging the probability of accidents with Désirée, but Marthe had prevailed upon him to let the repairs be executed upon the understanding that the basin should be protected by a railing.

'Monsieur le Curé,' said Rose, 'the justice of the peace wishes to see you.'

Abbé Faujas hastened indoors. He wanted to take Monsieur Maffre up to his own room on the second floor, but Rose had already opened the drawing-room door.

'Go in,' she said; 'aren't you at home here? It is useless to make the justice go up two flights of stairs. If you had only told me this morning, I would have given the room a dusting.'

As she closed the door upon the Abbé and the magistrate, after opening the shutters, Mouret called her into the dining-room.

'That's right, Rose,' he cried, 'you had better give my dinner to your priest this evening, and if he hasn't got sufficient blankets of his own upstairs you can take mine off my bed.'

The cook exchanged a meaning glance with Marthe, who was working by the window, waiting till the sunshine should leave the terrace. Then, shrugging her shoulders, she said:

'Ah! sir, you have never had a charitable heart!'

She took herself off, while Marthe continued sewing without raising her head. For the last few days she had, with feverish energy, again applied herself to her needlework. She was embroidering an altar-frontal as a gift for the cathedral. The ladies were desirous of giving a complete set of altar furniture. Madame Rastoil and Madame Delangre had undertaken to present the candlesticks, and Madame de Condamin had ordered a magnificent silver crucifix from Paris.

Meantime, in the drawing-room, Abbé Faujas was gently remonstrating with Monsieur Maffre, telling him that Doctor Porquier was a religious man and a person of the highest integrity, and that no one could be more pained than he by his son's deplorable conduct. The magistrate listened with a sanctimonious air, and his heavy features and big prominent eyes assumed quite an ecstatic expression at certain pious remarks which the priest uttered in a very moving manner. He allowed that he had been rather too hasty, and declared that he was willing to make every apology as his reverence thought he had been in the wrong.

'You must send your own sons to me,' said the priest, 'and I will talk to them.'

Monsieur Maffre shook his head with a slight sneering laugh.

'Oh! you needn't be afraid about them, Monsieur le Curé. The young scamps won't play any more tricks. They have been locked up in their rooms for the last three days with nothing but bread and water. If I had had a stick in my hand when I found out what they had been doing, I should have broken it across their backs.'

The Abbé looked at him and recollected how Mouret had accused him of having killed his wife by harshness and avarice; then, with a gesture of protest, he added:

'No, no; that is not the way to treat young men. Your elder son, Ambroise, is twenty years old and the younger is nearly eighteen, isn't he? They are no longer children, remember. You must allow them some amusements.'

The magistrate remained silent with surprise. 'Then you would let them go on smoking and allow them to frequent cafés?' he said, presently.

'Well,' replied the priest, with a smile. 'I think that young men should be allowed to meet together to talk and smoke their cigarettes and even to play a game of billiards or chess. They will give themselves every license if you show no tolerance. Only remember that it is not to every café that I should be willing for them to go. I should like to see a special one provided for them, a sort of club, as I have seen done in several towns.'

Then he unfolded a complete scheme for such a club. Monsieur Maffre gradually seemed to appreciate it. He nodded his head as he said:

'Capital, capital! It would be a worthy pendant to the Home of the Virgin. Really, Monsieur le Curé, we must put such a splendid idea as this into execution.'

'Well, then,' the priest concluded, as he accompanied Monsieur Maffre to the door, 'since you approve of the plan, just advocate it among your friends. I will see Monsieur Delangre, and speak to him about it. We might meet in the cathedral on Sunday after vespers and come to some decision.'

On the Sunday, Monsieur Maffre brought Monsieur Rastoil with him. They found Abbé Faujas and Monsieur Delangre in a little room adjoining the sacristy. The gentlemen displayed great enthusiasm in favour of the priest's idea, and the institution of a young men's club was agreed upon in principle. There was considerable discussion, however, as to what it should be called. Monsieur Maffre was strongly desirous that it should be known as the Guild of Jesus.

'Oh, no! no!' the priest impatiently cried at last. 'You would get scarcely anyone to join, and the few members would only be jeered at. There must be no attempt to tack religion on to the business; indeed, I intend that we should leave religion outside its doors altogether. All we want to do is to win the young people over to our side by providing them with some innocent recreation; that is all.'

The justice of the peace gazed at the priest with such an expression of astonishment and anxiety that Monsieur Delangre was obliged to bend his head to conceal a smile, while he slyly pulled the Abbé's cassock. Then the priest went on in a calmer voice:

'I am sure, gentlemen, that you do not feel any distrust of me, and I ask you to leave the management of the matter in my hands. I propose to adopt some very simple name, such a one, for instance, as the Young Men's Club, which fully expresses all that is required.'

Monsieur Rastoil and Monsieur Maffre bowed, although this title seemed to them a little weak. They next spoke of nominating the Curé as president of a provisional committee.

'I fancy,' said Monsieur Delangre, glancing at the priest, 'that this suggestion will scarcely meet with his reverence's approbation.'

'Oh dear, no!' the Abbé exclaimed, slightly shrugging his shoulders. 'My cassock would frighten the timid and lukewarm away. We should only get the pious young people, and it is not for them that we are going to found our club. What we want is to gather in the wanderers; to win converts, in a word; isn't that so?'

'Clearly,' replied the presiding judge.

'Very well, then, it will be better for us to keep ourselves in the background, myself especially. What I propose is this: your son, Monsieur Rastoil, and yours, Monsieur Delangre, will alone come forward. It must appear as if they themselves had formed the idea of this club. Send them to me in the morning, and I will talk the matter over at length with them. I already have a suitable building in my mind and a code of rules quite prepared. Your two sons, Monsieur Maffre, will naturally be enrolled at the head of the list of members.'

The presiding judge seemed flattered at the part assigned to his son; and so matters were arranged in this way, notwithstanding the resistance of the justice of the peace, who had hoped to win some personal distinction from the founding of the club. The next day Séverin Rastoil and Lucien Delangre put themselves in communication with Abbé Faujas. Séverin was a tall young man of five-and-twenty, with a badly shaped skull and a dull brain, who had just been called to the bar, thanks to the position which his father held. The latter was anxiously dreaming of making him a public prosecutor's assessor, despairing of his ever succeeding in winning any practice for himself. Lucien, on the other hand, was short and sharp-eyed, had a crafty mind, and pleaded with all the coolness of an old practitioner, although he was a year younger than Séverin. The 'Plassans Gazette' spoke of him as a future light of the bar. It was more particularly to him that the Abbé gave the minutest instructions as to his scheme. As for young Rastoil he simply went fussing about, bursting with importance. In three weeks the Young Men's Club was founded and opened.

There was at that time beneath the church of the Minimes, situated at the end of the Cours Sauvaire, a number of very large rooms and an old monastery refectory, which were no longer put to any use. This was the place that Abbé Faujas had thought of for the club, and the clergy of the parish very willingly allowed him to use the rooms. One morning, when the provisional committee of the Young Men's Club had set workmen going in this cellar-like place, the citizens of Plassans were quite astounded to see what appeared to be a café being fitted up under the church. Five days afterwards there was no longer any room for doubt on the point. The place was certainly going to be a café. Divans were being brought thither, with marble-topped tables, chairs, two billiard-tables, and even three crates of crockery and glass. An entrance was contrived at the end of the building, as far as possible from the doorway of the church, and great crimson curtains, genuine restaurant-curtains, were hung behind the glass panes. You descended five stone steps, and on opening the door found yourself in a large hall; to the right of which there was a smaller one and a reading-room, while in a square room at the far end were placed the two billiard-tables. They were exactly beneath the high altar.

'Well, my poor boys,' said Guillaume Porquier one day to Monsieur Maffre's two sons, whom he had met on the Cours, 'so they are going to make you serve at mass between your games at bézique,'

However, Ambroise and Alphonse besought him not to speak to them in public, as their father had threatened to send them to sea if they continued to associate with him.

When the first astonishment was over, the Young Men's Club proved a great success. Monseigneur Rousselot accepted the honorary presidency, and even visited it in person one evening, attended by his secretary, Abbé Surin. Each of them drank a glass of currant-syrup in the smaller room, and the glass which his lordship used was preserved with great respect upon a sideboard. The Bishop's visit is still talked of with much emotion at Plassans, and it brought about the adherence of all the fashionable young men of the town. It was soon considered very bad style not to belong to the Young Men's Club.

Guillaume Porquier, however, used to prowl about the entrance, sniggering like a young wolf who dreams of making his way into a sheep-fold. Notwithstanding all the fear they had of their father, Monsieur Maffre's sons quite worshipped this shameless young man who regaled them with stories of Paris, and entertained them at secret little parties in the suburbs. They had got into the habit of meeting him regularly every Saturday evening at nine o'clock near a certain seat on the Mall. They slipped away from the club and sat gossiping till eleven, concealed beneath the dark shade of the plane-trees. On these occasions Guillaume always twitted them about the evenings they spent underneath the church of the Minimes.

'It is very kind of you,' he would say, 'to let yourselves be led by the nose. The verger gives you glasses of sugar and water as though he were administering the communion to you, doesn't he?'

'Nothing of the sort! you are quite mistaken, I assure you,' Ambroise exclaimed. 'You might fancy you were in the Café du Cours, or the Café de France, or the Café des Voyageurs. We drink beer, or punch, or madeira, whatever we like, whatever is drunk in other places.'

Guillaume continued jeering however.

'Well, I shouldn't like to go drinking their dirty stuff,' he said. 'I should be afraid that they had mixed some drug with it to make me go to confession. I suppose you amuse yourselves by playing at hot-cockles and puss-in-the-corner!'

The young Maffres gaily laughed at his pleasantries, but they took care to undeceive him. They told him that even cards were allowed, and that there was no flavour of a church about the place at all. The club was extremely pleasant, there were very comfortable couches, and mirrors all over.

'Well,' said Guillaume, 'you'll never make me believe that you can't hear the organ when there is an evening service at the church. It would make me swallow my coffee the wrong way only to know that there was a baptism, or a marriage, or a funeral going on over my cup.'

'Well, there's something in that,' Alphonse allowed.

'Only the other day, while I was playing at billiards with Séverin in the day-time, we could distinctly hear a funeral going on. It was the funeral of the butcher's little girl, the butcher at the corner of the Rue de la Banne. That fellow Séverin is a big jackass, he tried to frighten me by telling me that the whole funeral would fall through on our heads.'

'Ah well! it must be a very pleasant place, that club of yours!' cried Guillaume. 'I wouldn't set foot in it for all the money in the world! I'd as soon go and drink my coffee in a sacristy.'

The truth of the matter was that Guillaume felt very much vexed that he did not belong to the Young Men's Club. His father had forbidden him to offer himself for election, fearing that he would be rejected. At last, however, the young man grew so annoyed about the matter that he sent in an application to be allowed to join the club, without mentioning what he had done to his people. The question was a very serious one. The committee which elected the members then comprised the young Maffres amongst its number, and Lucien Delangre was its president and Séverin Rastoil its secretary. These young men felt terribly embarrassed. While they did not dare to grant Guillaume's application, they were unwilling to do anything to hurt the feelings of Doctor Porquier, so worthy and irreproachable a person, one, too, who was so completely trusted by all the fashionable ladies. At last Ambroise and Alphonse begged Guillaume not to press his application, giving him to understand that he had no chance of being admitted.

'You are a couple of pitiful poltroons!' he replied to them.

'Do you suppose that I care a fig about joining your brotherhood? I was only amusing myself. I wanted to see if you would have the courage to vote against me. I shall have a good laugh when those hypocrites bang the door in my face.

As for you, my good little boys, you can go and amuse yourselves where you like; I shall never speak to you again.'

The young Maffres, in great consternation, then besought Lucien Delangre to try to arrange matters in such a way as would prevent any unpleasantness. Lucien submitted the difficulty to his usual adviser, Abbé Faujas, for whom he had conceived a genuine disciple's admiration. The Abbé came to the Young Men's Club every afternoon from five o'clock till six. He walked through the big room with a pleasant smile, nodding and sometimes stopping for a few minutes at one of the tables to chat with some of the young men. However, he never accepted anything to drink, not even a glass of water. Afterwards he passed into the reading-room, and, taking a seat at the long table covered with a green cloth, he attentively pored over the newspapers which the club received, the Legitimist organs of Paris and the neighbouring departments. Occasionally he made a rapid note in a little pocket-book. Then he went quietly away, again smiling at the members who were present, and shaking hands with them. On some occasions, however, he remained for a longer time to watch a game at chess, or chat merrily about all kinds of matters. The young men, who were extremely fond of him, used to say that when he talked no one would take him for a priest.

When the mayor's son told him of the embarrassment which Guillaume's application had caused the committee, Abbé Faujas promised to arrange the affair; and next morning he went to see Doctor Porquier, to whom he related everything. The doctor was aghast. His son, he cried, was determined to kill him with distress by dishonouring his grey hairs. What could be done now? Even if the application were withdrawn, the shame and disgrace would be none the less. The priest then advised him to send Guillaume away for two or three months to an estate which he possessed a few leagues from Plassans, and undertook to charge himself with the further conduct of the affair. As soon as Guillaume had left the town, the committee postponed the consideration of his application, saying that there was no occasion for haste in the matter, as the applicant was absent and that a decision could be taken later on.

Doctor Porquier heard of this solution from Lucien Delangre one afternoon when he was in the garden of the Sub-Prefecture. He immediately hastened to the terrace. It was the hour when Abbé Faujas read his breviary, Doctor Porquier caught sight of him under the Mourets' arbour.

'Ah, Monsieur le Curé!' he cried, 'how can I thank you? I should like very much to shake hands with you.'

'The wall is rather high,' said the priest, looking at it with a smile.

But Doctor Porquier was an effusive individual who did not allow himself to be discouraged by obstacles.

'Wait a moment!' he cried. 'If you will allow me, Monsieur le Curé, I will come round.'

Then he disappeared. The Abbé, still smiling, slowly bent his steps towards the little door which opened into the Impasse des Chevillottes. The doctor was already gently knocking at it.

'Ah! this door is nailed up,' said the priest. 'One of the nails is broken though. If I had any sort of a tool, there would be no difficulty in getting the other one out.'

He glanced round him and caught sight of a spade. Then, after he had drawn back the bolts with a slight effort, he opened the door, and stepped out into the alley, where Doctor Porquier overwhelmed him with thanks and compliments. As they walked along, talking, Monsieur Maffre, who happened at the time to be in Monsieur Rastoil's garden, opened a little door that was hidden away behind the presiding judge's waterfall. The gentlemen were much amused to find themselves all three in this deserted little lane.

They remained there for a few moments, and, as they took leave of the Abbé, the magistrate and the doctor poked their heads inside the Mourets' garden, looking about them with curiosity.

Mouret, however, who was putting stakes to his tomatoes, raised his head and caught sight of them. He was fairly lost in astonishment.

'Hallo! so they've made their way in here!' he muttered. 'The Curé now only has to bring in both gangs!'

XIII

Serge was now nineteen years of age. He occupied a small room on the second floor, opposite the priest's, and there led an almost cloistered life, spending much time in reading.

'I shall have to throw those old books of yours into the fire,' Mouret said to him angrily. 'You'll end by making yourself ill and having to take to your bed.'

The young man was, indeed, of such a nervous temperament, that the slightest imprudence made him poorly, as though he were a young girl, and thus he was frequently confined to his room for two or three days together. At these times Rose inundated him with herb tea, and whenever Mouret went upstairs to shake him up a little, as he called it, the cook, if she happened to be there, would turn her master out of the room, crying out at him:

'Leave the poor dear alone! Can't you see that you are killing him with your rough ways? It isn't after you that he takes: he is the very image of his mother; and you'll never be able to understand either the one or the other of them.'

Serge smiled. After he had left college his father, seeing him so delicate, had hesitated to send him to Paris to read for the bar there. He would not hear, however, of a provincial faculty; Paris, he felt sure, was necessary for a young man who wanted to climb to a high position. He tried, indeed, to instill ambitious ideas into the lad, telling him that many with much weaker wits than his own, his cousins, the Rougons, for instance, had attained to great distinction. Every time that the young man seemed to grow more robust, his father settled that he should leave home early the following month; but his trunk was never packed, for Serge was always catching a fresh cold, and then his departure would be again postponed.

On each of these occasions Marthe contented herself with saying in her gentle, indifferent way:

'He isn't twenty yet. It's really not prudent to send so young a lad to Paris; and, besides, he isn't wasting his time here; you even think that he studies too much.'

Serge used to accompany his mother to mass. He was very piously minded, very gentle and grave. Doctor Porquier had recommended him to take a good deal of exercise, and he had become enthusiastically fond of botany, going off on long rambles to collect specimens which he spent his afternoons in drying, mounting, classifying and naming. It was about this time that he struck up a great friendship with Abbé Faujas. The Abbé himself had botanised in earlier days, and he gave Serge much practical advice for which the young man was very grateful. They also lent each other books, and one day they went off together to try to discover a certain plant which the priest said he thought would be found in the neighbourhood. When Serge was ill, his neighbour came to see him every morning, and sat and talked for a long while at his bedside. At other times, when the young man was well, it was he who went and knocked at Abbé Faujas's door, as soon as he heard him stirring in his room. They were only separated by a narrow landing, and they ended by almost living together.

In spite of Marthe's unruffled tranquillity and Rose's angry glances, Mouret still often indulged in bursts of anger.

'What can the young scamp be after up there?' he would growl. 'Whole days pass without my catching more than a glimpse of him. He never seems to stir from the Abbé; they are always talking together in some corner or other. He shall be off to Paris at once. He's as strong as a Turk. All those ailments of his are mere shams, excuses to get himself petted and coddled. You needn't both of you look at me in that way; I don't mean to let the priest make a hypocrite of the boy.'

Then he began to keep a watch over his son, and when he thought that he was in Faujas's room he called for him angrily.

'I would rather he went to the bad!' he cried one day in a fit of rage.

'Oh, sir!' said Rose, 'it is abominable to say such things.'

'Well, indeed I would! And I'll put him in the way myself one of these days, if you irritate me much more with these parsons of yours!'

Serge naturally joined the Young Men's Club, though he went there but little, preferring the solitude of his own room. If it had not been for Abbé Faujas, whom he sometimes met there, he would probably never have set foot in the place. The Abbé taught him to play chess in the reading-room. Mouret, on learning that the lad met the priest at the café, swore that he would pack him off by the train on the following Monday. His luggage was indeed got ready, and quite seriously this time, but Serge, who had gone out to spend a last day in the open country, returned home drenched to the skin by a sudden downpour of rain. He was obliged to go to bed, shivering with fever. For three weeks he hung between life and death; and then his convalescence lasted for two long months. At the beginning of it he was so weak that he lay with his head on the pillow and his arms stretched over the sheets, as motionless as if he were simply a wax figure.

'It is your fault, sir!' cried the cook to Mouret. 'You will have it on your conscience if the boy dies.'

While his son continued in danger, Mouret wandered silently about the house, plunged in gloomy melancholy, his eyes red with crying. He seldom went upstairs, but paced up and down the passage to intercept the doctor as he went away. When he was told that Serge was at length out of danger, he glided quietly into the lad's room and offered his help. But Rose turned him away. They had no occasion for him, she said, and the boy was not yet strong enough to bear his roughness. He had much better go and attend to his business instead of getting in the way there. Mouret then remained in complete loneliness downstairs, more melancholy and unoccupied than ever. He felt no inclination for anything, said he. As he went along the passage, he often heard on the second floor the voice of Abbé Faujas, who spent whole afternoons by Serge's bedside, now that he was growing better.

'How is he to-day, Monsieur l'Abbé?' Mouret asked the priest timidly, as he met the latter going down into the garden.

'Oh, fairly well; but it will be a long convalescence, and very great care will be required.'

The priest tranquilly read his breviary, while the father, with a pair of shears in his hand, followed him up and down the garden walks, trying to renew the conversation and to get more detailed information about his boy. As his son's convalescence progressed, he remarked that the priest scarcely ever left Serge's room. He had gone upstairs several times in the women's absence, and he had always found the Abbé at the young man's bedside, talking softly to him, and rendering him all kinds of little services, sweetening his drink, straightening his bed-clothes, or getting him anything he happened to want. There was a hushed murmur throughout the house, a solemn calm which gave quite a conventual character to the second floor. Mouret seemed to smell incense, and could almost fancy sometimes, as he heard a muttering of voices, that they were saying mass upstairs.

'What can they be doing?' he wondered. 'The youngster is out of danger now; they can't be giving him extreme unction.'

Serge himself caused him much disquiet. He looked like a girl as he lay in bed in his white night-dress. His eyes seemed to have grown larger; there was a soft ecstatic smile upon his lips, which still played there even amidst his keenest pangs of suffering. Mouret no longer ventured to say anything about Paris; his dear sick boy seemed too girlish and tender for such a journey.

One afternoon he went upstairs, carefully hushing the sound of his steps. The door was ajar, and he saw Serge sitting in an easy chair in the sunshine. The young fellow was weeping with his eyes turned upward, and his mother stood sobbing in front of him. They both turned as they heard the door open, but they did not wipe away their tears. As soon as Mouret entered the room, the invalid said to him in his feeble voice:

'I have a favour to ask you, father. Mother says that you will be angry and will refuse me permission, though it would fill me with joy—I want to enter the Seminary.'

He clasped his hands together with a sort of feverish devotion.

'You! you!' exclaimed Mouret.

He looked at Marthe, who turned away her head. Then saying nothing further, he walked to the window, returned, and sat down mechanically by the bedside, as though overwhelmed by the blow.

'Father,' resumed Serge, after a long silence, 'in my nearness to death I have seen God, and I have sworn to be His. I assure you that all my happiness is centred in that. Believe me that it is so, and do not cause me grief.'

Mouret, looking very mournful, with his eyes lowered, still kept silence. At last, with an expression of utter hopelessness, he murmured:

'If I had the least particle of courage, I should wrap a couple of shirts in a handkerchief and go away.'

Then he rose from his seat, went to the window and drummed on the panes with his fingers; and when Serge again began to implore him, he said very quietly:

'Very well, my boy; be a priest.'

Immediately afterwards he left the room.

The next day, without the least warning to anyone, he set off for Marseilles, where he spent a week with his son Octave. But he came back looking careworn and aged. Octave had afforded him very little consolation. He had found the young man leading a fast life, overwhelmed with debts and in all sorts of scrapes. However, Mouret did not say a word about these matters. He began to lead a perfectly sedentary existence, and no longer made any of those good strokes of business, those fortunate purchases of standing crops, in which he had formerly taken such pride. Rose noticed that he maintained almost unbroken silence, and that he even avoided saluting Abbé Faujas.

'Do you know that you are not very polite?' she boldly said to him one day. 'His reverence the Curé has just gone past, and you turned your back upon him. If you behave in this way because of the boy, you are under a great mistake. The Curé was quite against his going to the Seminary, and I often heard him talking to him against it. This house is getting a very cheerful place, indeed, now! You never speak a word, even to madame, and when you have your meals, anyone would think that it was a funeral that was going on. For my part, sir, I'm beginning to feel that I've had quite enough of it.'

Mouret went out of the room, but the cook followed him into the garden.

'Haven't you every reason to be happy, now that your son is on his feet again? He ate a cutlet yesterday, the darling, and with such a good appetite too. But you care nothing about that, do you? What you want is to make a pagan of him like yourself. Ah! you stand in great need of some one to pray for you. But God Almighty wishes to save us all. If I were you I should weep with joy, to think that that poor little dear was going to pray for me. But you are made of stone, sir! And how sweet he will look too, the darling, in his cassock!'

Mouret thereupon went up to the first floor, and shut himself up in a room which he called his study, a big bare room, furnished only with a table and a couple of chairs. This room became his refuge whenever the cook worried him. When he grew weary of staying there, he went down again into the garden, upon which he expended greater care than ever. Marthe no longer seemed to be conscious of her husband's displeasure. Sometimes he kept silent for a week, but she was in no way disquieted or distressed by it. Every day she withdrew more and more from her surroundings, and she even began to fancy, now that the house seemed so quiet and peaceable and she had ceased to hear Mouret scolding, that he had grown more reasonable and had discovered for himself, as she had done, some little nook of happiness. This thought tranquillised her and induced her to plunge more deeply into her dreamy life. When her husband looked at her with his blurred eyes, scarcely recognising in her the wife of other days, she only smiled at him and did not notice the tears which were welling beneath his eyelids.

On the day when Serge, now completely restored to health, entered the Seminary, Mouret remained at home alone with Désirée. He now frequently looked after her; for this big 'innocent' girl, who was nearly sixteen, might have fallen into the basin of the fountain or have set the house on fire with matches just like a child of six. When Marthe returned home, she found the doors open and the rooms empty. The house seemed quite deserted. She went on to the terrace, and there, at the end of one of the walks, she saw her husband playing with his daughter. He was sitting on the gravel, and with a little wooden scoop was gravely filling a cart which Désirée was pulling along with a piece of string.

'Gee up! gee up!' cried the girl.

'Wait a little,' said her father patiently, 'it is not full yet. As you are the horse, you must wait till the cart is full.'

Then she stamped her feet like an impatient horse, and, at last, not being able to stand still any longer, she set off with a loud burst of laughter. The cart fell over and lost its load. When she had dragged it round the garden, she came back to her father crying:

'Fill it again! Fill it again!'

Mouret loaded it again with the little scoop. For a moment Marthe remained upon the terrace watching them, full of uneasy emotion. The open doors, the sight of the man playing with the child, the empty deserted house all touched her with sadness, though she was not clearly conscious of the feelings at work in her. She went upstairs to take off her things, on hearing Rose, who also had just returned, exclaim from the terrace steps:

'Good gracious! how silly the master is!'

His friends, the retired traders with whom he took a turn or two every day on the promenade in the Cours Sauvaire, declared that he was a little 'touched.' During the last few months his hair had grizzled, he had begun to get shaky on his legs, and was no longer the biting jeerer, feared by the whole town. For a little time it was thought that he had been venturing upon some risky speculations and had been overcome by a heavy loss of money.

Madame Paloque, as she leaned over the window-rail of her dining-room which overlooked the Rue Balande, said every time she saw him, that he was certainly going to the bad. And if, a few moments later, she happened to catch sight of Abbé Faujas passing along the street, she took a delight in exclaiming—the more especially if she had visitors with her:

'Just look at his reverence the Curé! Isn't he growing sleek? If he eats out of the same dish as Mouret, he can leave him nothing but the bones.'

Then she laughed, as did those who heard her. Abbé Faujas was, indeed, becoming quite an imposing object; he now always wore black gloves and a shimmering cassock. A peculiar smile played about his face, a sort of ironical twist of his lips, when Madame de Condamin complimented him upon his appearance. The ladies liked to see him nicely and comfortably dressed; though the priest himself would probably have preferred fighting his way with bare arms and clenched fists, and never a thought about what he wore. Whenever he appeared to grow neglectful of his appearance, the slightest hint of reproach from old Madame Rougon sufficed to cure him, and he hurried off to buy silk stockings and a new hat and girdle. He was frequently requiring new clothes, for his big frame seemed to wear out his garments very quickly.

Since the foundation of the Home of the Virgin, all the women had been on his side; and defended him against the malicious stories which were still occasionally repeated, though no one was able to get at their origin. Now and then they found him a little blunt, but this roughness of his by no means offended them, least of all in the confessional, where they rather liked to feel his iron hand pressing down their necks.

'He gave me such a scolding yesterday, my dear,' said Madame de Condamin to Marthe one day. 'I believe he would have struck me if there had not been the partition between us. He is not always very easy to get on with!'

She laughed gently and seemed to enjoy the recollection of this scene with her spiritual director. Madame de Condamin had observed Marthe turn pale whenever she made her certain confidences as to Abbé Faujas's manner of hearing confessions; and divining her jealousy, she took a mischievous delight in tormenting her, with which object she gave her many further private details.

When Abbé Faujas had founded the Young Men's Club, he there became quite sociable and gay; in fact he seemed to have undergone a transformation. Thanks to his will power he moulded his stern nature like wax. He allowed the part which he had taken in the founding of the club to be made public, and he became the friend of all the young men in the town, keeping a strict watch over his manners, for he well knew that young men just fresh from college had not the same taste for roughness of speech and demeanour as the women had. He one day narrowly escaped losing his temper with young Rastoil, whose ears he threatened to pull, over a disagreement about the club management; but with surprising command over himself, he put out his hand to him almost immediately afterwards, humbling himself and winning over to his side all who were present by his gracious apologies to 'that big fool Séverin,' as the other was called.

However, although the Abbé had conquered the women and the young men, he still remained on a footing of mere formal politeness with the fathers and husbands. The grave gentlemen continued to distrust him as they saw that he still refrained from identifying himself with any political party. At the Sub-Prefecture Monsieur Péqueur des Saulaies discussed him with much animation, while Monsieur Delangre, without definitely defending him, said with a sharp smile that they ought to wait before judging him. At the Rastoils' he had become a source of much tribulation to the Presiding Judge, whom Séverin and his mother never ceased wearying with their constant eulogies of the priest.

'Well! well! let him have every good quality under the sun!' cried the unhappy man. 'I won't dispute one of them, only leave me at peace. I asked him to dinner, but he wouldn't come. I can't go and drag him here by force!'

'No, but, my dear,' said Madame Rastoil, 'when you meet him you scarcely bow to him. It's that, I dare say, that has made him rather cold.'

'Of course it is,' interposed Séverin; 'he sees very well that you are not as polite to him as you ought to be.'

Monsieur Rastoil shrugged his shoulders. When Monsieur de Bourdeu was there, the pair of them accused Abbé Faujas of leanings towards the Sub-Prefecture, though Madame Rastoil directed their attention to the fact that he never dined there, and had never even set foot in the house.

'Oh, don't imagine that I accuse him of being a Bonapartist,' said the president. 'I only remarked that he had leanings that way; that was all. He has had communications with Monsieur Delangre.'

'Well! and so have you!' cried Séverin; 'you have had communications with the mayor! They are absolutely necessary under certain circumstances. Tell the truth and say you detest Abbé Faujas; it would be much more straightforward.'

For whole days at a time the Rastoils sulked with one another. Abbé Fenil came to see them very rarely now, excusing himself upon the ground that he was kept at home by his gout; but twice, when he had been forced to express an opinion on the Curé of Saint-Saturnin's, he had said a few words in his praise. Abbé Surin and Abbé Bourrette, as well as Monsieur Maffre, held the same views as the mistress of the house concerning the Curé, and the opposition to him came only from Monsieur Rastoil, backed up by Monsieur de Bourdeu, both of whom gravely declared that they could not compromise their political positions by receiving a man who concealed his views.

Séverin, however, now began to knock at the door in the Impasse des Chevillottes whenever he wanted to say anything to the priest, and gradually the little lane became a sort of neutral ground. Doctor Porquier, who had been the first to avail himself of it, young Delangre, and the magistrate, all came thither to talk to Abbé Faujas. Sometimes the little doors of both the gardens, as well as the cart-entrance to the Sub-Prefecture, were kept open for a whole afternoon, while the Abbé leant against the wall, smiling and shaking hands with those members of the two groups who wished to have a word with him. Monsieur Péqueur des Saulaies, however, carefully refrained from leaving the garden of the Sub-Prefecture; and Monsieur Rastoil and Monsieur de Bourdeu, equally persistent, remained seated beneath the trees in front of the former's waterfall. It was very seldom that the priest's little court invaded the Mourets' arbour. Now and then a head just peeped inside, took a hasty glance around, and then quickly disappeared.

Abbé Faujas now seemed to trouble about nothing. At the most he glanced with an expression of disquietude at the Trouches' windows, through which Olympe's eyes were constantly glistening. The Trouches kept themselves in ambush there behind the red curtains, full of an envious desire to come down like the Abbé and eat the fruit, and talk to the fashionable folks. They tapped on the shutters, leant out of the window for a moment, and then withdrew, infuriated by the authoritative glances of the priest. Soon afterwards, however, they would return with stealthy steps, press their pale faces to one of the panes, and keep watch over his every movement, quite tortured to see him enjoying that paradise which was forbidden to them.

'It is really abominable!' Olympe exclaimed one day to her husband. 'He would lock us up in a cupboard, if he could, so as to deprive us of every atom of enjoyment. Well go down if you like, and we'll see what he says.'

Trouche had just returned from his office. He put on a clean collar and dusted his boots, anxious to make himself as neat as possible. Olympe put on a light dress, and then they both boldly came downstairs into the garden, walking slowly alongside the tall box plants, and stopping in front of the flower-beds.

At that moment Abbé Faujas happened to have his back turned towards them. He was standing at the little door that opened into the lane talking to Monsieur Maffre. When he heard the Trouches' steps grating upon the gravel, they were close behind him under the arbour.

He turned round, and stopped short in the middle of a sentence, quite astounded at seeing them there. Monsieur Maffre, who did not know them, was looking at them with curiosity.

'A beautiful day, isn't it, gentlemen?' said Olympe, who had turned pale beneath her brother's gaze.

The Abbé abruptly dragged the justice of the peace into the lane; where he quickly got rid of him.

'He is furious!' murmured Olympe. 'Well, so much the worse; we had better stay where we are now. If we go back upstairs, he will think we are afraid of him. I've had quite enough of this kind of thing, and you will see what I will say to him.'

She made Trouche seat himself on one of the chairs which Rose had brought out a short time previously, and when the Abbé returned he found them tranquilly settled there. He fastened the bolts of the little door, glanced quickly around to assure himself that the trees screened them from observation, and then came up close to the Trouches, saying in a muffled voice:

'You forget our agreement. You undertook to remain in your own rooms.'

'It was too hot up there,' Olympe replied. 'We are not committing any crime by coming down here to get a little fresh air.'

The priest was on the point of exploding, but his sister, still quite pale from the effort she had made in resisting him, added in a peculiar tone:

'Don't make a noise, now! There are some people over there, and you might do yourself harm.'

Then both the Trouches laughed slightly. The Abbé fixed his eyes upon them with a terrible expression, but without speaking.

'Sit down,' said Olympe. 'You want an explanation, don't you? Well, you shall have one. We are tired of imprisoning ourselves. You are living here in clover; the house seems to belong to you, and so does the garden. So much the better, indeed; we are delighted to see how well things appear to be going with you, but you mustn't treat us as dirt beneath your feet. You have never thought of bringing me up a single bunch of grapes; you have given us the most wretched of the rooms; you hide us away and are ashamed of us; you shut us up as though we had the plague. You must understand that it can't go on any longer!'

'I am not the master here,' replied Abbé Faujas. 'You must address yourselves to Monsieur Mouret if you want to strip his garden.'

The Trouches exchanged a fresh smile.

'We don't want to pry into your affairs,' Olympe continued. 'We know what we know, and that is sufficient for us. But all this proves what a bad heart you have. Do you think that if we were in your position we shouldn't invite you to come and take your share in the good things that were going?'

'What is it that you want me to do?' demanded the Abbé. 'Do you suppose that I am rolling in wealth? You know what sort of a room I occupy myself; it is more scantily furnished than your own. The house isn't mine, and I can't give it you.'

Olympe shrugged her shoulders. She silenced her husband who was beginning to speak, and then calmly continued:

'Everyone has his own ideas of life. If you had millions you wouldn't buy a strip of carpet for your bedside; you would spend them all in some foolish scheme or other. We, on the other hand, like to be comfortable. Dare you say that if you had a fancy for the handsomest furniture in the house and for the linen and food and anything else it contains, you couldn't have them this very evening? Well, in such circumstances a good brother would think of his relations, and wouldn't leave them in wretchedness and squalor as you leave us!'

Abbé Faujas looked keenly at the Trouches. They were both swaying backwards and forwards on their chairs.

'You are a pair of ungrateful people,' he said after a moment's silence. 'I have already done a great deal for you. You have me to thank for the food that you eat now. I still have letters of yours, Olympe, letters in which you beseech me to rescue you from your misery by bringing you over to Plassans. Now that you are here and your livelihood is assured, you break out into fresh demands.'

'Stuff!' Trouche impudently interrupted. 'You sent for us here because you wanted us. I have learned to my cost not to believe in anyone's fine talk. I have allowed my wife to speak, but women can never come to the point. In two words, my good friend, you are making a mistake in keeping us cooped up like dogs, who are only brought out in the hour of danger. We are getting weary of it, and we shall perhaps end by doing something foolish. Confound it all! give us a little liberty. Since the house isn't yours and you despise all luxury, what harm can it do you if we make ourselves comfortable? We shan't eat the walls!'

'Of course!' exclaimed Olympe, 'it's only natural that we should rebel against being constantly locked up. We will take care to do nothing to prejudice you. You know that my husband only requires the least sign from you. Go your own way, and you may depend upon us; but let us go ours. Is that understood, eh?'

Abbé Faujas had bent his head; he remained silent for a moment, and then, raising his eyes, and avoiding a direct reply, he said:

'Listen to what I say. If ever you do anything to hamper me, I swear to you that I will send you away to starve in a garret on the straw.'

Then he went back into the house, leaving them under the arbour. From that time the Trouches went down into the garden almost every day, but they conducted themselves with considerable discretion, and refrained from going there at the times when the priest was talking with the guests from the neighbouring gardens.

The following week Olympe complained so much of the room she was occupying that Marthe kindly offered her Serge's, which was now at liberty. The Trouches then kept both rooms. They slept in the young man's old bedchamber, from which not a single article of furniture had been removed, and turned the other apartment into a sort of drawing-room, for which Rose found them some old velvet-covered furniture in the lumber-room. Olympe, in great delight, ordered a rose-coloured dressing-gown from the best maker in Plassans.

Mouret, who had forgotten that Marthe had asked his permission to let the Trouches have Serge's room, was quite surprised to find them there one evening. He had gone up to look for a knife which he thought his son must have left in one of the drawers, and, as he entered the room, he saw Trouche trimming with this very knife a switch which he had just cut from one of the pear-trees in the garden. Thereupon he apologised and went downstairs.

XIV

During the public procession on the Feast of Corpus Christi, when Monseigneur Rousselot came down the steps of the magnificent altar, set up through the generosity of Madame de Condamin on the Place of the Sub-Prefecture, close to the very door of the small house she occupied, it was noticed with much surprise by the spectators that the Bishop abruptly turned his back upon Abbé Faujas.

'Ah! has there been some disagreement between them!' exclaimed Madame Rougon, who was looking out of her drawing-room window.

'Didn't you know about it?' asked Madame Paloque, who was leaning over by the old lady's side. 'It has been the talk of the town since yesterday. Abbé Fenil has been restored to favour.'

Monsieur de Condamin, who was standing behind the ladies, began to laugh. He had made his escape from his own house, saying that it smelt like a church.

'Do you attach any importance to such trifles?' said he. 'The Bishop is merely an old weathercock, turning one way or the other according as Faujas or Fenil blows against him; to-day it is one of them, to-morrow it will be the other. They have quarrelled and made it up again half a score times already. Before three days are over, you will see that Faujas will be the pet again.'

'I don't believe it,' exclaimed Madame Paloque; 'it is serious this time. It seems that Abbé Faujas has caused his lordship a great deal of worry. It appears that he formerly preached some sermons which excited great displeasure at Rome. I can't explain the matter quite clearly, but I know that the Bishop has received reproachful letters from Borne, in which he is recommended to be on his guard. It is said that Abbé Faujas is simply a political agent.'

'Who says so?' asked Madame Rougon, blinking her eyes as though to see the procession, which was then passing through the Rue de la Banne, more distinctly.

'I heard it said, but I really don't remember by whom,' the judge's wife replied carelessly.

Then she retired, saying that one would be able to get a better view from the side-window. Monsieur de Condamin, however, took the vacant place by Madame Rougon, and whispered in the old lady's ear:

'I have already twice seen her going to Abbé Fenil's. They have some plot or other in hand, I'm sure. Abbé Faujas must have trodden somehow or other on that viper of a woman, and she's trying to bite him. If she were not so ugly I would do her the service of telling her that her husband will never be presiding judge.'

'Why? I don't understand,' murmured the old lady, with a guileless expression.

Monsieur de Condamin looked at her curiously, and then began to smile.

The last two gendarmes in the procession had just disappeared round the corner of the Cours Sauvaire, and the few guests whom Madame Rougon had invited to witness the blessing of the altar returned into the drawing-room, where they chatted for a moment about the

Bishop's graciousness and the new banners of the different congregations, and especially the one belonging to the girls of the Home of the Virgin, which had attracted much attention. The ladies were loud in their praises, and Abbé Faujas's name was mentioned every moment in the most eulogistic terms.

'He is clearly a saint!' sniggered Madame Paloque to Monsieur de Condamin, who had taken a seat near her. Then, bending forward towards him, she added: 'I could not speak openly before Madame Rougon, you know, but there is a great deal of talk about Abbé Faujas and Madame Mouret. I dare say those unpleasant reports have reached the Bishop's ears.'

'Madame Mouret is a charming woman, and extremely winning notwithstanding her forty years,' was all that Monsieur de Condamin said in reply.

'Oh, yes! she is very charming, very charming, indeed,' murmured Madame Paloque, whose face turned quite green with spleen.

'Extremely charming,' persisted the conservator of rivers and forests. 'She is at the age of genuine passion and great happiness. You ladies are given to judging each other unfavourably.'

Thereupon he left the drawing-room, chuckling over Madame Paloque's suppressed rage.

The town was now indeed taking an absorbing interest in the continual struggle that went on between Abbé Faujas and Abbé Fenil for influence over the Bishop. It was a ceaseless combat, like the struggles of a couple of buxom housekeepers for the affection of an old dotard. The Bishop smiled knowingly; he had discovered how to maintain a kind of equilibrium between these opposing forces which he pitted one against the other, amused at seeing them overthrown in turn, and securing peace for himself by accepting the services of the one who temporarily gained the upper hand. To the dreadful stories which were told him to the detriment of his favourites, he paid but little attention, for he knew that the rival Abbés were capable of accusing each other of murder.

'They are getting worse, my child,' the Bishop said, in one of his expansive moments to Abbé Surin. 'I fancy that in the end Paris will carry the day, and Rome will get the worst of it; but I am not quite sure, and I shall leave them to wear each other out. When one has made an end of the other, things will be settled—By the way, just read me the third Ode of Horace; I'm afraid I've translated one of the lines rather badly.'

On the Tuesday after the public procession the weather was lovely. Laughter was heard both in the garden of the Rastoils and in that of the Sub-Prefect, and numerous guests were sitting under the trees. Abbé Faujas read his breviary in the Mourets' garden after his usual custom, while slowly walking up and down beside the tall hedges of box. For some days past he had kept the little door that led to the lane bolted; he was indeed coquetting with his neighbours and keeping aloof, in order that he might make them more anxious to see him. Possibly too he had noticed a slight coldness in their manner after his last misunderstanding with the Bishop, and the abominable reports that his enemies had circulated against him.

About five o'clock, just as the sun was sinking, Abbé Surin proposed a game of shuttlecock to Monsieur Rastoil's daughters. He was very clever at it himself; and, notwithstanding the approach of their thirtieth year, both Angéline and Aurélie were immensely fond of games. When the servant brought the battledores, Abbé Surin, looking about him for a shady spot, for the garden was still bright with the last rays of the sun, was struck with an idea of which the young ladies cordially approved.

'Shall we go and play in the Impasse des Chevillottes?' he asked. 'We shall be shaded by the chestnut-trees there, and have more room.'

They left the garden and started a most delightful game in the lane. The two girls began, and Angéline was the first who failed to keep the shuttlecock going. Abbé Surin, who took her place, handed his battledore with professional skill and ease. Having tucked his cassock between his legs, he sprang backwards and forwards and sideways without cessation. His battledore caught the shuttlecock as it reached the ground and sent it flying, now to a surprising height, and now straight ahead like a bullet; and at times made it describe the most graceful curves. As a rule he preferred to be pitted against poor players, who, as they struck the shuttlecock at random, or, to use his own phrase, without any rhythm, brought all the skilful agility of his own play into exercise. Mademoiselle Aurélie, however, played a fair game. She vented a little cry like a swallow's every time she struck a blow with the battledore, and she laughed distractedly when the shuttlecock alighted on the young Abbé's nose. Gathering up her skirts, she waited for its return, or leaped backward with a great rustling of petticoats when he vengefully gave it a smarter blow than usual. At last the shuttlecock fell into her hair, and she almost toppled over upon her back. This greatly amused them all. Angéline now took her sister's place; and every time that Abbé Faujas raised his eyes from his breviary as he paced the Mourets' garden, he saw the white feathers of the shuttlecock skimming above the wall like a big butterfly.

'Are you there, your reverence?' all at once cried Angéline, at the little door. 'Our shuttlecock has fallen into your garden.'

The Abbé picked up the shuttlecock, which had dropped at his feet, and made up his mind to open the door.

'Oh, thank you! your reverence,' said Aurélie, who had already taken the battledore. 'Only Angéline would ever make such a stroke. The other day when papa was watching us she sent the shuttlecock right against his ear with such a bang that he was quite deaf till the next day.'

There was more laughter at this; and Abbé Surin, as rosy as a girl, delicately dabbed his brow with a handkerchief of fine texture. He pushed his fair hair behind his ears, and stood there with glistening eyes and flexible figure, using his battledore as a fan. In the excitement of the game his bands had got slightly displaced.

'Monsieur le Curé,' said he, as he took up his position again, 'you shall be umpire.'

Abbé Faujas, holding his breviary under his arm and smiling paternally, stood on the threshold of the little doorway. Through the cart-entrance of the Sub-Prefecture, which was half open, he could see Monsieur Péqueur des Saulaies seated in front of the cascade amidst his friends. The priest looked straight in front of him, however, and counted the points of the game, while complimenting Abbé Surin and consoling the young ladies.

'I tell you what, Péqueur,' said Monsieur de Condamin, in a whisper, in the sub-prefect's ear, 'you make a mistake in not inviting that little Abbé to your parties. He is a great favourite with the ladies, and he looks as though he could waltz to perfection.'

Monsieur Péqueur des Saulaies, who was talking to Monsieur Delangre with much animation, did not however appear to bear the other, but went on with his conversation with the mayor.

'Really, my dear sir,' he said, 'I don't know where you see all the merits that you profess to find in him. On the contrary, indeed, Abbé Faujas appears to me to be of very doubtful character. There is considerable suspicion attached to his past career, and strange things are said about him here. I really don't see why I should go down on my knees to this priest, especially as the clergy of Plassans are hostile to us. I should gain no advantage by doing so.'

Monsieur Delangre and Monsieur de Condamin exchanged glances of intelligence, and then, by way of reply, nodded their heads.

'None, whatever,' continued the sub-prefect. 'It is no use pretending to look mysterious; I may tell you that I have myself written to Paris. I was a good deal bothered, and I wanted to be quite certain about this Faujas, whom you seem to look upon as a sort of prince in disguise. Well! do you know what reply I got? They told me that they did not know him and could tell me nothing about him, and that I must carefully avoid mixing myself up with clerical matters. They are grumpy enough in Paris as it is, since the election of that jackass Lagrifoul, and I have to be prudent, you understand.'

The mayor exchanged another glance with the conservator of rivers and forests. He even slightly shrugged his shoulders before the correctly twirled moustaches of Monsieur Péqueur des Saulaies.

'Just listen to me,' he said to him after a moment's silence; 'you would like to be a prefect, wouldn't you?'

The sub-prefect smiled as he rocked himself in his chair.

'Well, then, go at once, and shake hands with Abbé Faujas, who is waiting for you down there, while he is watching them play at shuttlecock.'

Monsieur Péqueur des Saulaies was silent with astonishment. He seemed quite puzzled, turned towards Monsieur de Condamin, and asked, with some show of uneasiness:

'Is that your advice also?'

'Certainly; go and offer him your hand,' replied the conservator of rivers and forests.

Then, with a slight touch of irony, he added:

'Consult my wife, if you like; I know you have perfect confidence in her.'

Madame de Condamin was just approaching them. She was wearing a lovely pink and pearl-grey dress. When they spoke to her of the Abbé she said graciously to the sub-prefect:

'It is very wrong of you to neglect your religious duties; one never sees you at church except perhaps when there is some official ceremony. It really distresses me very much, and I must try to convert you. What sort of opinion do you expect people will have of the government you represent, if they see you are not on the side of religion?—Leave us, gentlemen; I am going to confess Monsieur Péqueur.'

She took a seat, smiling playfully.

'Octavie,' said the sub-prefect, in an undertone, when they were alone together, 'don't make fun of me. You weren't a very pious person in the Rue du Helder in Paris. It's all I can do to keep from laughing when I see you worshipping in Saint-Saturnin's.'

'You are too flippant, my friend,' she replied,' and your flippancy will play you a bad turn one of these days. Seriously, you quite distress me. I gave you credit for having more intelligence. Are you so blind that you cannot see that you are tottering in your position? Let me tell you that it is only from fear of alarming the Legitimists at Plassans that you haven't already been recalled. If the Legitimists saw a new sub-prefect arriving here, they would take alarm, whereas so long as you remain here they will continue quietly sleeping, feeling certain of victory at the next election. All this is not very flattering for you; I am aware of that, and the more so as I know positively that the authorities are acting without taking you into their confidence. Listen to me, my friend; I tell you that you are ruined if you don't divine certain things.'

He looked at her with unfeigned alarm.

'Has "the great man" been writing to you?' he asked, referring to a personage whom they thus designated between themselves.

'No; he has broken entirely with me. I am not a fool, and I saw, before he did, the necessity of the separation. And I have nothing at all to complain of. He has shown me the greatest kindness. He found me a husband and gave me some excellent advice, which has proved extremely useful to me. But I have retained friends in Paris; and I swear to you that you have only just got time left to cling on to the branches if you don't want to fall. Don't be a pagan any longer, but go and offer your hand to Abbé Faujas. You will understand why later on, even if you can't guess it to-day.'

Monsieur Péqueur des Saulaies lowered his eyes and seemed a little humiliated by the lesson he was receiving. He was very conceited, and, showing his white teeth, he tried to re-assert himself by murmuring tenderly:

'Ah! if you had only been willing, Octavie, we might have governed Plassans between us. I asked you to resume that delightful life—'

'Really now, you are a great idiot!' she interrupted in a tone of vexation. 'You annoy me with your "Octavie." I am Madame de Condamin to everyone, my friend. Can't you understand anything? I have an income of thirty thousand francs; I am queen of a whole

Sub-Prefecture; I go everywhere; I am respected everywhere, bowed to and liked. What in the world should I do with you? You would only inconvenience me. I am a respectable woman, my friend.'

She rose from her seat and walked towards Doctor Porquier, who, according to his custom, had come to spend an hour in the garden chatting to his fair patients, after a round of visits.

'Oh, doctor!' she exclaimed, with one of her pretty grimaces, 'I have got such a headache. It pains me just here, under the left eyebrow.'

'That is the side of the heart, madame,' said the doctor, gallantly.

Madame de Condamin smiled and did not carry the consultation any further. Madame Paloque, who was present, bent, however, towards her husband, whom she brought with her every time she came, in order that she might recommend him to the sub-prefect's influence, and whispered in his ear:

'That's the only way Porquier has of curing them.'

When Monsieur Péqueur des Saulaies had joined Monsieur de Condamin and Monsieur Delangre he manoeuvred cleverly in such wise as to draw them towards the gateway. When he was within a few yards of it, he stopped and appeared to be interested in the game of shuttlecock which was still going on in the lane. Abbé Surin, with his hair blown about by the wind, the sleeves of his cassock rolled up, and his slender, white, womanly wrists displayed, had just stepped backwards, putting some twenty yards between himself and Mademoiselle Aurélie. He felt that he was being watched, and he quite surpassed himself. Mademoiselle Aurélie was also playing extremely well, spurred on, as it were, by the skill of her partner. Thus the shuttlecock described long gentle curves with such regularity that it seemed to light of its own accord upon the battledores, going from one to the other player without either of them having to stir from their places. Abbé Surin, inclined slightly backwards, displayed his well-shaped bust to advantage.

'Excellent! excellent!' cried the sub-prefect. 'Ah! Monsieur l'Abbé, I must compliment you upon your skill.'

Then, turning towards Madame de Condamin, Doctor Porquier and the Paloques, he exclaimed:

'I've really never seen anything like it before. You will allow us to admire your play, I hope, Monsieur l'Abbé?'

The whole set of the Sub-Prefecture now formed into a group at the far end of the lane. Abbé Faujas had not moved from the position he had taken up. Having acknowledged with a nod the salutations of

Monsieur Delangre and Monsieur de Condamin, he went on counting the points of the game. When Aurélie at last missed the shuttlecock, he said good-naturedly:

'That makes you three hundred and ten points, for the distance was altered; your sister has only forty-seven.'

However, while he appeared to follow the flight of the shuttlecock with all-absorbing interest, he every now and then glanced at the door of the Rastoils' garden, which still remained open. Monsieur Maffre was as yet the only person who had shown himself there; but at last a voice called from inside the garden:

'What is amusing them so much out there?' It was Monsieur Rastoil, who was chatting with Monsieur de Bourdeu beside the rustic table, that asked the question.

'His lordship's secretary is playing at shuttlecock,' Monsieur Maffre replied. 'He is making some wonderful strokes and everybody is watching him. His reverence the Curé is there, and seems quite amazed.'

Monsieur de Bourdeu took a big pinch of snuff as he exclaimed:

'Ah! Monsieur l'Abbé Faujas is there, is he?'

He glanced at Monsieur Rastoil, and they both seemed ill at ease.

'I have heard,' remarked the presiding judge, 'that the Curé has been restored to the Bishop's favour.'

'Yes, indeed; this very morning,' said Monsieur Maffre.

'There has been a complete reconciliation, and I have heard some touching particulars about it. His lordship shed tears. Ah, there can be no doubt that Abbé Fenil has cause for self-reproach.'

'I thought that you were the grand vicar's friend,' observed Monsieur de Bourdeu.

'So I am, but I am also the Curé's friend,' replied the justice of the peace. 'Thank goodness! he is a man of sufficient piety to be able to despise all the calumnies of his enemies. They haven't even hesitated to question his morality! It is disgraceful!'

The ex-prefect again glanced at the presiding judge with a singular expression.

'And they've tried to compromise him in political matters,' continued Monsieur Maffre. 'They said that he had come here to overturn everything, to bestow places right and left and bring about the triumph of the Paris clique. Why, if he had been the chief of a band of brigands folks couldn't have said worse things about him than they have done. A pack of lies, all of them!'

Monsieur de Bourdeu was drawing a face on the gravel of the walk with the tip of his walking-stick.!

'Yes,' he said, carelessly,' I have heard these things mentioned. But it is very unlikely that a minister of religion would allow himself to play such a part; and besides, to the honour of Plassans, I think it may be said that he would have failed completely. There is no one here who could be bought.'

'Oh! it's all stuff and nonsense, that!' cried the presiding judge, shrugging his shoulders. 'A town can't be turned inside out like an old coat. Paris may send us as many spies and agents as she likes, but Plassans will always keep Legitimist. Look at that little Péqueur now! We've only made a single mouthful of him! Folks must be very stupid to believe in mysterious personages running about the provinces offering places and appointments. I should be very curious to see one of those gentlemen.'

He seemed to be getting a little angry, and Monsieur Maffre, with some show of uneasiness, appeared to think it necessary to defend himself.

'Pardon me,' he exclaimed. 'I have never asserted that Abbé Faujas was a Bonapartist agent; on the contrary, I have always considered the accusation a most absurd one.'

'Oh! it's not a question of Abbé Faujas. My remarks are quite general. People don't sell themselves in that way! Abbé Faujas is above all suspicion.'

There was an interval of silence. Monsieur de Bourdeu finished the face he was drawing on the gravel by adding a long pointed beard to it.

'Abbé Faujas has no political views,' he at last said in his dry voice.

'Evidently,' replied Monsieur Rastoil; 'we found fault with him for his indifference, but now I approve of it. With all this gossip in the air, it would have had a prejudicial effect upon religion. You know as well as I do, Bourdeu, that he can't be accused of the slightest suspicious step. He has never been seen at the Sub-Prefecture, has he? He kept with great propriety in his fitting place. If he were a Bonapartist, he wouldn't be likely to conceal it, would he?'

'Certainly not.'

'Then, too, he leads a most exemplary life. My wife and my son have told me things about him which have affected me very much.'

The merriment in the little lane was now louder than ever. Abbé

Faujas could be heard complimenting Mademoiselle Aurélie on some wonderful stroke of her battledore. Monsieur Rastoil, who had checked himself for a moment, continued, with a smile:

'Just listen to them! What can they find in it to amuse them so much? It makes one quite long to be young again!'

Then, in a more serious tone, he added:

'Yes, my wife and my son have made me feel a strong liking for Abbé Faujas; and we are very sorry that his discreet reserve keeps him from joining our circle.'

As Monsieur Bourdeu nodded his head approvingly, shouts of applause were heard in the alley. There was a perfect uproar of hand-clapping, laughter and shouts, as though some troop of schoolboys had just rushed out to play. Monsieur Rastoil rose from his rustic chair.

'Good gracious!' he said, with a smile; 'let us go and see what they are up to. My legs are beginning to feel a little cramped.'

The others followed him, and they all three went and stood by the little door. It was the first time that the presiding judge and the ex-prefect had ventured so far. When they saw the group formed by the sub-prefect's guests at the end of the lane, their faces assumed a serious expression.

Monsieur Péqueur des Saulaies, for his part, drew himself up and put on an official attitude. Madame de Condamin went flitting to and fro along the lane laughing and smiling and filling the place with the rustle of her pink and grey dress. The two sets of guests kept glancing at one another, neither being willing to retire, while Abbé Faujas still maintained his position between them at Mouret's door, quietly enjoying himself without seeming in the least degree conscious of the delicacy of the situation.

All the spectators held their breath; for Abbé Surin, seeing that their number had increased, was desirous of winning their applause by a last exhibition of skill. He brought all his science into play, created difficulties for himself on purpose to overcome them, turned round and struck at the shuttlecock without looking at it, but seemingly divining its position, and thus sending it back over his head to Mademoiselle Aurélie with mathematical precision. He was very much flushed and was perspiring freely. He had thrown his hat off, and his bands were now hanging over his right shoulder. But he was the victor, and he looked as he always did, amiable and charming. The two groups of guests lingered there admiring him, and Madame de Condamin had to repress the applause, which burst out prematurely and inopportunely, by shaking her lace handkerchief. Then the young Abbé, introducing still further refinements into his play, began to skip about first to right and then to left, each time receiving the shuttlecock in a fresh position. This was the grand final flourish. He accelerated the rapidity of his play, and at last, just as he was jumping aside, his foot slipped and he nearly fell upon the bosom of Madame de Condamin, who had stretched out her arms with a little cry. The spectators, thinking he was hurt, rushed up, but the Abbé, who was pressing the ground with his hands and knees, sprang up again by a strong effort, and sent the shuttlecock, which had not yet fallen, spinning back to Mademoiselle Aurélie. Then, flourishing his battledore, he triumphed.

'Bravo! bravo!' cried Monsieur Péqueur des Saulaies, stepping up to him.

'Bravo! it was a magnificent stroke!' exclaimed Monsieur Rastoil, who also came up.

The game was interrupted, for the two sets of guests had now invaded the lane, and were mingled with each other, crowding around Abbé Surin, who leant, quite out of breath, against the wall by Abbé Faujas's side. Everybody began talking at once.

'I was afraid that he had split his skull,' said Doctor Porquier to Monsieur Maffre, in a voice full of emotion.

'Yes, these games generally have a bad ending,' remarked Monsieur de Bourdeu, addressing himself to Monsieur Delangre and the Paloques, while he received a shake of the hand from Monsieur de Condamin, whom he always tried to avoid in the streets, so that he might not have to bow to him.

Madame de Condamin went from the sub-prefect to the presiding judge, bringing them face to face, and exclaiming:

'But really, I am more upset than he is! I thought that we were going to fall together. There is a big stone there; did you notice it?'

'Yes, I see it there,' said Monsieur Rastoil; 'it must have caught against his heel.'

'Was it this round stone, do you think?' asked Monsieur Péqueur des Saulaies, picking up a pebble.

They had never spoken to each other before, except at official ceremonies. Now, however, they began to examine the stone, and passed it from one to the other, remarking that it was very sharp, and must have cut the Abbé's shoe. Madame de Condamin stood smiling between them, and assured them that she was beginning to feel better.

'Oh! the Abbé is feeling ill!' suddenly cried Monsieur Rastoil's daughters.

Abbé Surin had, indeed, turned very pale at hearing of the danger he had run. He was reeling with faintness, when Abbé Faujas, who had kept aloof, took him in his powerful arms, and carried him into Mouret's garden, where he seated him upon a chair. The two sets of guests soon swarmed into the arbour, where the young Abbé completely fainted away.

'Get some water and some vinegar, Rose!' cried Abbé Faujas, running towards the steps.

Mouret, who was in the dining-room, came to the window, but, on seeing all those people in his garden, he recoiled as though he were struck with fear, and kept himself out of sight. Rose soon came up with a collection of drugs, muttering, as she hastened along:

'If only madame were here! But she has gone to the Seminary to see the lad. I am all alone, and I can't do impossibilities, can I? The master won't stir an inch; anybody might die for all he cared. There he is in the dining-room, hiding himself! He would let you die, before he would get you even a glass of water.'

By the time she had got through this grumble, she had reached Abbé Surin, who was lying in a swoon. 'Oh! the cherub!' she exclaimed, overcome with womanly pity.

The young Abbé, with his closed eyes and his pale brow wreathed with long, fair hair, looked like one of the sweet-faced martyrs that one sees expiring in sacred pictures. The elder of the Rastoil girls was supporting his head, which lay back, allowing his delicate, white neck to be seen. They were all in great excitement over him. Madame de Condamin gently dabbed his brow with a rag soaked in vinegar and water, and the others stood anxiously looking at her. At last the young Abbé opened his eyes, but closed them again immediately. He had two more swoons before he recovered.

'You have given me a terrible fright!' at last said Doctor Porquier, who had kept his hand fast in his own.

Abbé Surin, still sitting on the chair, stammered out confused thanks, and assured them all that it was a mere nothing. Then he saw that his cassock had been unbuttoned, and he smiled as he buttoned it and readjusted his bands. To prove that he was all right again, when the company advised him to keep quiet, he went back to the lane with the Rastoil girls in order to finish the game.

'You have a very nice place here,' said Monsieur Rastoil to Abbé Faujas, whose side he had not quitted.

'The air on this slope is delightful,' added Monsieur Péqueur des Saulaies, in his charming manner.

Then both sets of guests began looking with curiosity at Mouret's house.

'Perhaps the ladies and gentlemen would like to stay in the garden a little while,' exclaimed Rose; 'I will go and get some chairs.'

She made three journeys in quest of them, in spite of the protestations of the company. Then, after glancing at each other for a moment, the two sets of guests felt constrained by courtesy to seat themselves. The sub-prefect installed himself on Abbé Faujas's right band, while the presiding judge took a chair on his left, and a friendly conversation at once began.

'You are a very quiet neighbour, Monsieur le Curé,' said Monsieur Péqueur des Saulaies very graciously; 'you can't imagine what pleasure it gives me to see you every day at the same hour in this little paradise. It seems to bring me a feeling of restfulness, after all the noise and worry I have.'

'A pleasant neighbour is a very rare thing,' observed Monsieur Rastoil.

'Quite true,' said Monsieur de Bourdeu. 'But his reverence seems to have filled this spot with the peaceful tranquillity of a cloister.'

While the Abbé was smiling and acknowledging these complimentary remarks, Monsieur de Condamin, who had not yet seated himself, stooped and whispered in Monsieur Delangre's ear:

'There's Rastoil, hoping to get that lout of a son of his made assessor to the public prosecutor.'

Monsieur Delangre, however, gave him an angry glance, trembling at the thought that this incorrigible chatterer might spoil everything. But this did not prevent the conservator of rivers and forests from adding:

'And Bourdeu, too, is flattering himself that he has already won back his prefecture.'

Meantime, Madame de Condamin had caused a great sensation by saying, in a meaning way:

'What I like about this garden is the tender charm it seems to possess, which makes it a nook apart from all the cares and wretchedness of the world. It is a spot where even Cain and Abel might have become reconciled.'

She emphasized her last words and gave two glances, one to the right and the other to the left, towards the neighbouring gardens. Monsieur Maffre and Doctor Porquier nodded approvingly; while the

Paloques looked at each other inquisitively, feeling uneasy and fearing to compromise themselves should they open their mouths.

At the end of a quarter of an hour Monsieur Rastoil rose from his seat.

'My wife will be wondering where we have got to,' said he.

And thereupon the whole company rose, feeling somewhat embarrassed as to the manner of their leave-taking. But Abbé Faujas spread out his hands and said, with the pleasantest possible smile:

'My paradise is always open to you.'

The presiding judge then promised to come and see the Curé every now and then, and the sub-prefect, with more effusiveness, declared that he would do the same. For another five minutes they all lingered there, exchanging compliments, while, out in the lane, the laughter of the Rastoil girls and Abbé Surin was again heard. A fresh game was going on with all the animation of the previous one, and the shuttlecock could be seen passing backwards and forwards in its regular flight above the garden wall.

XV

One Friday, as Madame Paloque was entering Saint-Saturnin's, she was greatly surprised to see Marthe kneeling in front of Saint Michael's chapel. The Abbé Faujas was hearing confessions.

'Ah!' she muttered, 'has she succeeded in touching the Abbé's heart? I must wait a little while and watch. It would be very fine if Madame de Condamin were to come.'

She took a chair a little in the rear, and, half kneeling, covered her face with her hands as though she was absorbed in earnest prayer; but she held her fingers apart so that she might glance between them. The church was very gloomy. Marthe, with her head bent over her prayer-book, looked as though she were asleep. Her figure showed blackly against a white pillar. Only her shoulders, heaving with deep-drawn sighs, seemed to be alive. She was, indeed, so profoundly overcome with emotion that she was constantly allowing her turn to be taken by some other of Abbé Faujas's penitents. The Abbé waited for a few moments, and then, seemingly a little impatient, he began tapping the woodwork of the confessional. Thereupon one of the women who were waiting, seeing that Marthe showed no sign of moving, decided to take her place. The chapel gradually grew empty, and Marthe still remained motionless as if in ecstasy.

'She seems in a terrible state,' thought Madame Paloque. 'It is really quite indecent to make such an exhibition of one's self in church. Ah! here comes Madame de Condamin!'

Madame de Condamin was indeed just entering the church. She stopped for a moment before the holy-water basin, removed her glove, and crossed herself with a pretty gesture. Her silk dress made a murmuring sound as she passed along the narrow space between the chairs. As she knelt down, she filled the lofty vault with a rustling of skirts. She had her usual affable expression, and smiled through the gloom. Soon she and Marthe were the only two penitents left. The priest grew more and more impatient, and tapped yet more loudly upon the woodwork of the confessional.

'It is your turn, madame; I am the last,' Madame de Condamin whispered politely, bending towards Marthe, whom she had not recognised.

Marthe raised her face, pinched and pale from her extreme emotion, and did not appear to understand. It was as though she were awakening from some ecstatic trance, and her eyelids trembled.

'Come, ladies, come!' exclaimed Abbé Faujas, who had now half-opened the door of the confessional.

Madame de Condamin smilingly rose to obey the priest's summons; but Marthe, recognising her, hastened into the chapel, to fall again upon her knees, however, a few paces away from the confessional-box.

Madame Paloque felt much amused. She hoped that the two ladies would seize each other by the hair. Marthe could hear all that was said, for Madame de Condamin had a clear flute-like voice. She dallied over the recital of her sins, and quite animated the confessional with her pretty gossiping ways. Once she even vented a little muffled laugh, at the sound of which Marthe raised her pain-racked face. Soon afterwards Madame de Condamin finished her confession, and rose as if to retire, but she quickly stepped back and commenced talking afresh, this time merely bending her head without kneeling down.

'That she-devil is making sport of Madame Mouret and the Abbé,' thought the judge's wife to herself. 'It's all put on, is this.'

At last Madame de Condamin really withdrew. Marthe watched her as if waiting till she disappeared. Then she went forward, leant against the confessional-box, and fell heavily on her knees. Madame Paloque had slipped a little nearer and was craning out her head, but she could only see the penitent's dark dress spread out around her.

For nearly half an hour there was not the slightest movement. Now and then she thought she could detect some smothered sobs in the throbbing silence, which was also broken at times by a creak from the confessional-box. She began to feel a little weary of her watching, for all she would be able to do now would be to stare at Marthe as she left the chapel.

Abbé Faujas was the first to leave, closing the door of the confessional-box with an appearance of annoyance. Madame Mouret lingered there for a long time, bent and motionless. When she at last went away, her face covered with her veil, she seemed quite broken down, and even forgot to cross herself.

'There has been a row; the Abbé hasn't made himself pleasant,' thought Madame Paloque. Then she followed Marthe as far as the Place de l'Archevêché, where she stopped and seemed to hesitate for a moment. At last, having glanced cautiously around to make sure that nobody was watching her, she stealthily slipped into the house where Abbé Fenil resided, at one of the corners of the Place.

Marthe now almost lived at Saint-Saturnin's. She carried out her religious duties with the greatest fervour. Even Abbé Faujas often had to remonstrate with her about her excessive zeal. He only allowed her to communicate once a month, fixed the hours which she should devote to pious exercises, and insisted that she should not entirely shut herself up in religious practices. She for a long time requested him to let her attend a low mass every morning before he would accede to her desire. One day, when she told him that she had lain for a whole hour on the cold floor of her room to punish herself for some fault she had committed, he was very angry with her, and declared that her confessor alone had the right to inflict penance. He treated her throughout very sternly, and threatened to send her back to Abbé Bourrette if she did not absolutely follow his directions.

'I was wrong to take you at all,' he often said; 'I do not like disobedient souls.'

She felt a pleasure in his harshness. That iron hand which bent her, and which held her back upon the edge of the adoration in the depths of which she would have liked to annihilate herself, thrilled her with ever-renewed desire. She remained like a neophyte, making but little advance in her journey of love, being constantly pulled up, and vaguely divining some yet greater bliss beyond. The sense of deep restfulness which she had first experienced in the church, that forgetfulness of herself and the outside world, now changed, however, into positive actual happiness. It was the happiness for which she had been vaguely longing since her girlhood, and which she was now, at forty years of age, at last finding; a happiness which sufficed her, which compensated her for all the past-away years, and made her egotistical, absorbed in the new sensations that she felt within her like sweet caresses.

'Be kind to me,' she murmured to Abbé Faujas,' be kind to me, for I stand in need of great kindness.'

And when he did show her kindness, she could have gone down upon her knees and thanked him. At these times he unbent, spoke to her in a fatherly way, and pointed out to her that her imagination was too excited and feverish. God, said he, did not like to be worshipped in that way, in wild impulses. She smiled, looking quite pretty and young again with her blushing face, and promised to restrain herself in the future. But sometimes she experienced paroxysms of devotion, which cast her upon the flagstones in some dark corner, where, almost grovelling, she stammered out burning words. Even her power of speech then died away, and she continued her prayers in feeling only, with a yearning of her whole being, an appeal for that divine kiss which seemed ever hovering about her brow without pressing it.

At home Marthe became querulous, she who till now had been indifferent and listless, quite happy so long as her husband left her at peace. Now, however, that he had begun to spend all his time in the house, had lost his old spirit of raillery, and had grown mopish and melancholy, she grew impatient with him.

'He is always hanging about us,' she said to the cook one day.

'Oh, he does it out of pure maliciousness,' replied Rose. 'He isn't a good man at heart. I haven't found that out today for the first time. He has only put on that woebegone look, he who is so fond of hearing his tongue wag, in order to try to make us pity him. He's really bursting with anger, but he won't show it, because he thinks that if he looks wretched we shall be sorry for him and do just what he wants. You are quite right, madame, not to let yourself be influenced by all those grimaces and pretences.'

Mouret kept a hold upon the women with his purse. He did not care to wrangle and argue with them, for fear of making his life still less comfortable than it already was; but, though he no longer grumbled and meddled and interfered, he showed his displeasure by refusing a single extra crown piece to either Marthe or Rose. He gave the latter a hundred francs a month for the purchase of provisions;

wine, oil, and preserves were in the house. The cook was obliged to make the sum stated last her till the end of the month, even if she had to pay for something out of her own pocket. As for Marthe, she had absolutely nothing; her husband never even gave her a sou, and she was compelled to appeal to Rose, and ask her to try to save ten francs out of the monthly allowance. She often found herself without a pair of boots to put on, and was obliged to borrow from her mother the money she needed to buy either a dress or a hat.

'But Mouret must surely be going mad!' Madame Rougon cried. 'You can't go naked! I will speak to him about it.'

'I beg you to do nothing of the kind, mother,' Marthe said. 'He detests you, and he would treat me even worse than he does already if he knew that I talked of these matters to you.'

She began to cry as she added:

'I have shielded him for a long time, but I really can't keep silent any longer. You remember that he was once most unwilling for me even to set foot in the street; he kept me shut up, and treated me like a mere chattel. Now he behaves so unkindly because he sees that I have escaped from him, and that I won't submit any longer to be a mere servant. He is a man utterly without religion, selfish and bad-hearted.'

'He doesn't strike you, does he?'

'No; but it will come to that. At present he contents himself with refusing me everything. I have not bought any chemises for the last five years, and yesterday I showed him those I have. They are quite worn out, so patched and mended that I am ashamed of wearing them. He looked at them and examined them and said that they would do perfectly well till next year. I haven't a single centime of my own. The other day I had to borrow two sous from Rose to buy some thread to sew up my gloves, which were splitting all over.'

She gave her mother many other details of the straits to which she was reduced—how she had to make laces for her boots out of blackened string, how she had to wash her ribbons in tea to make her hat look a little fresher, and how she had to smear the threadbare folds of her only silk dress with ink to conceal the signs of wear. Madame Rougon expressed great pity for her, and advised her to rebel. Mouret was a monster, said she. Rose asserted that he carried his avarice so far as to count the pears in the store-room and the lumps of sugar in the cupboard, while he also kept a close eye on the preserves, and ate himself all the remnants of the loaves.

It was a source of especial distress to Marthe that she was not able to contribute to the offertories at Saint-Saturnin's. She used to conceal ten-sou pieces in scraps of paper and carefully preserve them for high mass on Sundays. When the lady patronesses of the Home of the Virgin made some offering to the cathedral, such as a pyx, or a silver cross, or a banner, she felt quite ashamed, and kept out of the way, affecting ignorance of their intentions. The ladies felt much pity for her. She would have robbed her husband if she could have found the key of his desk, so keenly was she tortured at being able to do nothing for the honour of the church to which she was so passionately attached. She felt all the jealousy of a deceived woman when Abbé Faujas used a chalice which had been presented by Madame de Condamin; whereas on the days when he said mass in front of the altar cloth which she herself had embroidered she was filled with fervent joy, and said her prayers with ecstatic thrills, as though some part of herself lay beneath the priest's extended hands. She would have liked to have had a whole chapel of her own; and even dreamt of expending a fortune upon one, and of shutting herself up in it and receiving the Deity alone by herself at her own altar.

Rose, of whom she made a confidant, had recourse to all sorts of plans to obtain money for her. That year she secretly gathered the finest fruit in the garden and sold it, and she also disposed of a lot of old furniture that was stowed away in an attic, managing her sales so well that she succeeded in getting together a sum of three hundred francs, which she handed to Marthe with great triumph. The latter kissed the old cook.

'Oh! how good you are!' she said to her, affectionately. 'Are you quite sure that he knows nothing about what you have done? I saw the other day, in the Rue des Orfèvres, two little cruets of chased silver, such dear little things; they are marked two hundred francs. Now, you'll do me a little favour, won't you? I don't want to go and buy them myself, because someone would certainly see me going into the shop. Tell your sister to go and get them. She can bring them here after dark, and can give them to you through the kitchen window.'

This purchase of the cruets seemed like a clandestine intrigue to Marthe, and thrilled her with the sweetest pleasure. For three days she kept the cruets at the bottom of a chest, hidden away beneath layers of linen; and when she gave them to Abbé Faujas in the sacristy of Saint-Saturnin's she trembled so much that she could scarcely speak. The Abbé scolded her in a kindly fashion. He was not fond of presents, and spoke of money with the disdain of a strong-minded man who only cares for power and authority. During his earlier years of poverty, even at times when he and his mother had no food beyond bread and water, he had never thought of borrowing even a ten-franc piece from the Mourets.

Marthe found a safe hiding-place for the hundred francs which were still left her. She also was becoming a little miserly; and she schemed how she should best expend this money, making some fresh plan every morning. While she was still in a state of hesitation, Rose told her that Madame Trouche wished to see her privately. Olympe, who used to spend hours in the kitchen, had become Rose's intimate friend, and often borrowed a couple of francs of her to save herself from going upstairs at times when she said that she had forgotten to bring down her purse.

'Go upstairs and see her there,' said the cook; 'you will be better able to talk there. They are good sort of people, and they are very fond of his reverence. They have had a lot of trouble. Madame Olympe has quite made my heart ache with all the things she has told me.'

When Marthe went upstairs she found Olympe in tears. They, the Trouches, were too soft-hearted, said she, and their kindness was always being abused. Then she entered upon an explanation of their affairs at Besançon, where the rascality of a partner had saddled them with a heavy burden of debt. To make matters worse, their creditors were getting angry, and she had just received an insulting letter, the writer of which threatened to communicate with the Mayor and the Bishop of Plassans.

'I don't mind what happens to me,' she sobbed, 'but I would give my head to save my brother from being compromised. He has already done too much for us, and I don't want to speak to him on the matter, for he is not rich, and he would only distress himself to no purpose. Good heavens! what can I do to keep that man from writing? My brother would die of shame if such a letter were sent to the Mayor and the Bishop. Yes, I know him well; he would die of shame!'

Tears rushed to Marthe's eyes. She was quite pale, and fervently pressed Olympe's hands. Then, without the latter having preferred any request, she offered her the hundred francs she had.

'It is very little, I know; but perhaps it might be sufficient to avert the danger,' she said with an expression of great anxiety.

'A hundred francs, a hundred francs!' exclaimed Olympe. 'Oh, no! he would never be satisfied with a hundred francs.'

Marthe lost all hope. She swore that she had not a centime more. She so far forgot herself as to speak of the cruets. If she had not bought them she would have been able to give three hundred francs. Madame Trouche's eyes sparkled.

'Three hundred francs, that is just what he demands,' she said. 'Ah! you would have rendered my brother a much greater service by not giving him that present, which, by the way, will have to remain in the church. What a number of beautiful things the ladies of Besançon presented to him! But he isn't a bit the better off for them to-day! Don't give him anything more; it is really nothing but robbery! Consult me about what you do; there is so much hidden misery—No! a hundred francs will certainly not be sufficient!'

At the end of half an hour spent in lamentation, however, she accepted the hundred francs when she saw that Marthe really had no more.

'I will send them so as to pacify the man a little,' she said, 'but he won't leave us at peace long. Whatever you do, I beg of you not to mention anything about it to my brother. It would nearly kill him. And I think it would be better, too, if my husband knew nothing of what has passed between us; he is so proud that he would be sure to be doing something rash to be able to acquit himself of our obligation to you. We women can understand each other, you know.'

This loan was a source of much pleasure to Marthe, who henceforth had a fresh care, that of warding off from Abbé Faujas the danger that threatened him without his being aware of it. She frequently went upstairs to the Trouches' rooms and stayed there for hours, discussing with Olympe the best means of discharging the debts. The latter had told her that a good many promissory notes had been endorsed by the priest, and that there would be a terrible scandal if they should ever be sent to any bailiff in Plassans to be protested. The sum total of their liabilities was so great, she said, that for a long time she refused to disclose it, only weeping the more bitterly when Marthe pressed her. One day, however, she mentioned the sum of twenty thousand francs. Marthe was quite frozen upon hearing this. She would never be able to procure anything like twenty thousand francs, and thought that she would certainly have to wait for Mouret's death before she could hope to have any such sum at her disposal.

'I say twenty thousand francs in all,' Olympe hastily added, disquieted by Marthe's grave appearance: 'but we should be quite satisfied if we were able to pay by small installments spread over half a score of years. The creditors would wait for any length of time, if they were only sure of getting their installments regularly. It is a great pity that we can't find anyone who has sufficient confidence in us to make the small necessary advances.'

This matter became an habitual topic of conversation. Olympe also frequently spoke of Abbé Faujas, whom she seemed almost to worship. She gave Marthe all kinds of private details about the priest: such as, for instance, that he could not bear anything that tickled him, that he could sleep on his left side, and that he had a strawberry-mark on his right shoulder, which turned red in May like the natural fruit. Marthe smiled and never tired of hearing of these little matters; and she questioned the young woman about her childhood and that of her brother. When the subject of the money cropped up she seemed painfully overcome by her inability to do anything, and she even complained bitterly of Mouret, to whom Olympe, emboldened by Marthe's language, now always referred in her presence as the 'old miser.' Sometimes when Trouche returned from his office he found the two women still talking together, but at his appearance they checked themselves and changed the subject. Trouche conducted himself in the most satisfactory way, and the lady patronesses of the Home of the Virgin were highly pleased with him. He was never seen in any of the cafés in the town.

In order to be able to render some assistance to Olympe, who sometimes talked about throwing herself out of the window, Marthe made Rose take all the useless old odds and ends that were lying about the house to a second-hand dealer at the market. At first the two women were a little timid about the matter, and only disposed of broken-down chairs and tables when Mouret was out of the way, but afterwards they began to lay hands upon more important articles, and sold ornaments, pieces of china, and anything else they could remove without its absence appearing too conspicuous. They were slipping down a fatal incline, and would have ended by carting off all the furniture in the house and leaving nothing but the bare walls, if Mouret had not one day charged Rose with thieving and threatened to send for the police.

'What, sir! A thief! I!' she cried. 'Just because you happened to see me selling one of madame's rings. Be careful of what you are saying! The ring was mine; madame gave it to me. Madame isn't such a mean wretch as you are. You ought to be ashamed of yourself for leaving your wife without a sou! She hasn't even a pair of shoes to put on! The other day I had to pay the milkman myself! Yes, I did sell the ring, and what of that? Isn't madame's ring her own? She is obliged to turn it into money, since you won't give her any. If I were she, I would sell the whole house! The whole house, do you hear? It distresses me beyond everything to see her going about as naked as Saint John the Baptist!'

Mouret now began to keep a close watch at all times. He locked up the cupboards and drawers, and kept the keys in his own possession. Whenever Rose went out he would look at her hands distrustfully, and even feel at her pockets if he saw any suspicious swelling beneath her skirt. He brought certain articles back from the second-hand dealer's and restored them to their places, dusting and wiping them ostentatiously in Marthe's presence in order to remind her of what he called Rose's thefts. He never directly accused his wife. There was a cut-glass water-bottle which he turned into a special instrument of torture. Rose, having sold it for twenty sous, had pretended to Mouret that it was broken. But now he made her bring it and put it on the table at every meal. One day, at lunch, she quite lost her temper over it, and purposely let it fall.

'There, sir, it's really broken this time, isn't it?' she cried, laughing in his face.

As he threatened to dismiss her, she exclaimed:

'You had better! I've been in your service for five-and-twenty years. If I went madame would go with me!'

Marthe, reduced to extremities and egged on by Rose and Olympe, at last rebelled. She was desperately in want of five hundred francs. For the last week Olympe had been crying and sobbing, asserting that if she could not get five hundred francs by the end of the month one of the bills which had been endorsed by Abbé Faujas would be published in one of the Plassans newspapers. The threatened publication of this bill, this terrible threat which she did not quite understand, threw Marthe into a state of dreadful alarm, and she resolved to dare everything. In the evening, as they were going to bed, she asked Mouret for the five hundred francs, and when he looked at her in amazement she began to speak of the fifteen years which she had spent behind a counter at Marseilles, with a pen behind her ear like a clerk.

'We made the money together,' she said; 'and it belongs to us both. I want five hundred francs.'

Mouret thereupon broke his long maintained silence in the most violent fashion, and all his old raillery burst forth again.

'Five hundred francs!' he cried. 'Do you want them for your priest? I play the simpleton now and keep my peace for fear I might say too much; but you must not imagine that you can go on for ever making a fool of me! Five hundred francs! Why not say the whole house? The whole house certainly does seem to belong to him! He wants some money, does he? And he has told you to ask me for it? I might be among a lot of robbers in a wood instead of being in my own home! I shall have my very handkerchief stolen out of my pocket before long! I'll be bound that if I were to go and search his room I should find his drawers full of my property. There are seven pairs of my socks missing, four or five shirts, and three pairs of pants. I was going over the things yesterday. Everything I have is disappearing, and I shan't have anything left very soon! No, not a single sou will I give you, not a single sou!'

'I want five hundred francs; half of the money belongs to me,' Marthe tranquilly replied.

For a whole hour Mouret stormed and fumed and repeated the same reproaches. His wife was no longer the same, he said. He did not know her now. Before the priest's arrival, she had loved him and obeyed him and looked after the house. Those who set her to act in opposition to him must be very wicked persons. Then his voice grew thick, and he let himself fall into a chair, broken down and as weak as a child.

'Give me the key of your desk!' said Marthe.

He got up from his chair and gathered his strength together for a last cry of protest.

'You want to strip me of everything, eh? to leave your children with nothing but straw for a bed? You won't even leave us a loaf of bread? Well! well! clear out everything, and send for Rose to fill her apron! There's the key!'

He threw the key at Marthe and she placed it under her pillow. She was quite pale after this quarrel, the first violent quarrel that she had ever had with her husband. She got into bed, but Mouret passed the night in an easy-chair. Towards morning Marthe heard him sobbing. She would then have given him back the key, if he had not wildly rushed into the garden, though it was still pitch dark.

Peace again seemed to be re-established between them. The key of the desk remained hanging upon a nail near the mirror. Marthe, who was quite unaccustomed to the sight of large sums, felt a sort of fear of the money. She was very bashful and shamefaced at first whenever she went to open the drawer in which Mouret always kept some ten thousand francs in cash to pay for his purchases of wine. She strictly confined herself to taking only what was necessary. Olympe, too, gave her the most excellent advice, and told her that now she had the key she ought to be careful and economical; and, indeed, seeing the trembling nervousness which she exhibited at the sight of the hoard of money, she ceased for some time to speak to her of the Besançon debts.

Mouret meantime relapsed into his former moody silence. Serge's admission to the Seminary had been another severe blow to him. His friends of the Cours Sauvaire, the retired traders who promenaded there regularly between four o'clock and six, began to feel very uneasy about him, when they saw him arrive with his arms swaying about and his face wearing a stupefied expression. He hardly made any reply to their remarks and seemed a prey to some incurable disease.

'He's breaking up; he's breaking up,' they murmured to each other; 'and he's only forty-four; it's scarcely credible. He will end by having softening of the brain.'

Mouret no longer seemed to hear the malicious allusions which were made before him. If he was questioned directly about Abbé Faujas, he coloured slightly as he replied that the priest was an excellent tenant and paid his rent with great punctuality. When his back was turned, the retired shopkeepers grinned as they sat and basked in the sun on one of the seats on the Cours.

'Well, after all, he is only getting what he deserves,' said a retired almond-dealer. 'You remember how hotly he stood up for the priest, how he sang his praises in the four corners of Plassans; but when one talks to him on that subject now rather an odd expression comes over his face.'

These worthy gentlemen then regaled themselves with certain scandalous stories which they whispered into each other's ears, passing them on in this way from one end of the bench to the other.

'Well,' said a master-tanner in a half whisper, 'there isn't much pluck about Mouret; if I were in his place I would soon show the priest the door.'

Thereupon they all repeated that Mouret was certainly a very timid fellow, he who had formerly jeered so much at those husbands who allowed their wives to lead them by the nose.

These stories, however, in spite of the persistence with which certain persons kept them afloat, never got beyond a particular set of idle gossiping people, and the reason which the Curé himself gave for not taking up his residence at the parsonage, namely, his liking for the Mourets' beautiful garden, where he could read his breviary in such perfect peace, was generally accepted as the true one. His great piety, his ascetic life and his contempt for all the frivolities and coquetries which other priests allowed themselves placed him beyond suspicion. The members of the Young Men's Club accused Abbé Fenil of trying to ruin him. All the new part of the town was on his side, and it was only the Saint-Marc quarter that was against him, its aristocratic inhabitants treating him with great reserve whenever they met him in Monseigneur Rousselot's saloons. However, in spite of his popularity, he shook his head when old Madame Rougon told him that he might now dare everything.

'Nothing is quite safe and solid yet,' he said. 'I am not sure of anyone. The least touch might bring the whole edifice toppling down.'

Marthe had been causing him anxiety for some time past. He felt that he was incapable of calming the fever of devotion which was raging within her. She escaped his control and disobeyed him, and advanced further than he wished her to do. He was afraid lest this woman, this much-respected patroness, who was so useful, might yet bring about his ruin. There was a fire burning within her which seemed to discolour her flesh, and redden her eyes and make them heavy. It was like an ever-growing disease, an infatuation of her whole being, that was gradually weakening her heart and brain. She often seemed to lapse into some ecstatic trance, her hands were shaken by a nervous trembling, and a dry cough occasionally shook her from head to foot without consciousness apparently on her part of how it was rending her. The Curé then showed himself sterner to her than before, tried to crush the passion which was dawning within her, and even forbade her to come to Saint-Saturnin's.

'The church is very cold,' he said, 'and you cough so much there. I don't want you to do anything to make yourself worse.'

She protested that there was nothing the matter with her beyond a slight irritation of the throat, but at last she yielded and accepted his prohibition as a well-deserved punishment which closed the doors of heaven upon her. She wept, believed that she was damned, and dragged herself listlessly through the blank weary days; and then, in spite of herself, like a woman returning to some forbidden love, when Friday came she humbly glided into Saint-Michael's chapel and laid her burning brow against the woodwork of the confessional-box. She did not speak a word, but simply knelt there, completely crushed, quite overwhelmed. At this Abbé Faujas, who was greatly irritated, treated her as harshly as though she was some unworthy woman, and hastily ordered her away. Then she left the church, feeling happy and consoled.

The priest was afraid of the effect of the gloomy darkness of Saint-Michael's chapel. He spoke upon the subject to Doctor Porquier, who persuaded Marthe to go to confession at the little oratory of the Home of the Virgin in the suburb. Abbé Faujas promised to be there to hear her every other Saturday. This oratory, which had been established in a large whitewashed room with four big windows, was bright and cheerful, and would, he thought, have a calming effect upon the excited imagination of his penitent. There, he thought, he would be able to bring her under control, reduce her to obedience, without possible fear of any scandal. As a guard against all calumnious gossip, he asked his mother to accompany Marthe, and while he confessed the latter Madame Faujas remained outside the door. As the old lady did not like to waste her time, she used to take her knitting with her and work away at a stocking.

'My dear child,' she often said to Marthe, as they were returning together to the Rue Balande, 'I could hear very well what Ovide was saying to you to-day. You don't seem to be able to please him. You can't care for him. Ah! I wish I were in your place to be able to kiss his feet! I shall grow to hate you, if you go on causing him nothing but annoyance.'

Marthe bent her head. She felt deep shame in Madame Faujas's presence. She did not like her, she felt jealous of her at finding her always coming between herself and the priest. The old lady's dark eyes, too, troubled her when they constantly bent upon her, full as they seemed of strange and disquieting thoughts.

Marthe's weak state of health sufficed to account for her meetings with Abbé Faujas at the oratory of the Home of the Virgin. Doctor Porquier stated that she went there simply in obedience to his orders, and the promenaders on the Cours were vastly amused by this saying of the doctor's.

'Well, all the same,' remarked Madame Paloque to her husband one day, as she watched Marthe going down to the Rue Balande, accompanied by Madame Faujas, 'I should like to be in some corner and watch the vicar and his sweetheart. It is very amusing to hear her talk of her bad cold! As though a bad cold was any reason why one shouldn't make one's confession in church! I have had colds, but I never made them an excuse for shutting myself up in a little chapel with a priest.'

'It is very wrong of you to interfere in Abbé Faujas's affairs,' the judge replied to his wife. 'I have been spoken to about him. He is a man with whom we must keep on good terms, and you will prevent us from doing so; you are too spiteful.'

'Stuff!' she retorted angrily; 'they have trampled me under foot and I will let them know who I am! Your Abbé Faujas is a big imbecile! Don't you suppose that Abbé Fenil would be very grateful to me if I could catch the vicar and his sweetheart? Ah! he would give a great deal to have a scandal like that! Just you leave me alone; you don't understand anything about such matters.'

A fortnight later, Madame Paloque watched Marthe go out on the Saturday. She was standing ready dressed, hiding her hideous face behind her curtains, but keeping watch over the street through a hole in the muslin. When the two women disappeared round the corner of the Rue Taravelle, she sniggered, and leisurely drawing on her gloves went quietly on to the Place of the Sub-Prefecture, and walked slowly round it. As she passed in front of Madame de Condamin's little house, she thought for a moment of going in and taking her with her, but she reflected that the other might, perhaps, have some scruples. And, all considered, it was better she should be without witnesses, and manage the business by herself.

'I have given them time,' she thought, after a quarter of an hour's promenade. 'I think I may present myself now.'

Thereupon she quickened her pace. She frequently went to the Home of the Virgin to discuss the accounts with Trouche, but that day, instead of repairing to the secretary's office, she went straight along the corridor towards the oratory. Madame Faujas was quietly knitting on a chair in front of the door.

The judge's wife had foreseen that obstacle, and went straight on to the door with the hasty manner of a person who has important business on hand. But before she could reach out her hand to turn the handle the old lady had risen from her chair and pushed her aside with extraordinary energy.

'Where are you going?' she asked in her blunt peasant-woman's tones.

'I am going where I have business,' Madame Paloque replied, her arm smarting and her face convulsed with anger. 'You are an insolent, brutish woman! Let me pass! I am the treasurer of the Home of the Virgin, and I have a right to go anywhere here I want.'

Madame Faujas, who stood leaning against the door, straightened her spectacles upon her nose, and with unruffled tranquillity resumed her knitting.

'Well,' she said bluntly, 'you can't go in there.'

'Can't, indeed! And may I ask why?'

'Because I don't wish that you should.'

The judge's wife felt that her plan was frustrated, and she almost choked with spleen and anger. She was positively frightful to look at as she gasped and stammered:

'I don't know who you are, and I don't know what you are doing here. If I were to call out, I could have you arrested, for you have struck me. There must be some great wickedness going on at the other side of that door for you to have been put there to keep people from entering. I belong to the house, I tell you! Let me pass, or I shall call for help.'

'Call for anyone you like,' replied the old lady, shrugging her shoulders. 'I have told you that you shall not go in, that I won't let you. How am I to know that you belong to the house? But it makes no difference whether you do or you don't. No one can go in. I won't let them.'

Thereupon Madame Paloque lost all control of herself, raised her voice, and shrieked out:

'I have no occasion to go in now! I have learnt quite sufficient! You are Abbé Faujas's mother, are you not? This is a very decent and pretty part for you to be playing! I wouldn't enter the room now; I wouldn't mix myself up with all this wickedness!'

Madame Faujas laid her knitting upon the chair, and, bending slightly forward, gazed with glistening eyes through her spectacles at Madame Paloque, holding her hands the while a little in front of her, as though she were about to spring upon the angry woman and silence her. She was, indeed, going to throw herself forward, when the door suddenly opened and Abbé Faujas appeared on the threshold. He was in his surplice and looked very stern.

'Well, mother,' he asked, 'what is going on here?'

The old lady bent her head, and stepped back like a dog that is taking its place at its master's heels.

'Ah! is it you, dear Madame Paloque?' the Curé continued; 'do you want to speak to me?'

By a supreme effort of will, the judge's wife forced her face into a smile. She answered the priest in a tone that was terrible in its amiability and mingled irony.

'Ah! you were inside were you, your reverence? If I had known that, I would not have insisted upon entering. But I want to see the altar-cloth, which must, I think, be getting into a bad condition. I am a careful superintendent here, you know, and I keep an eye upon all these little details. But, of course, if you are engaged in the oratory, I wouldn't think of disturbing you. Pray go on with what you are doing; the house is yours. If madame had only just dropped me a word, I would have left her quietly to continue guarding you from being disturbed.'

Madame Faujas allowed a growl to escape her, but a glance from her son reduced her to silence.

'Come in, I beg you,' he said; 'you won't disturb me in the least. I was confessing Madame Mouret, who is not very well. Come in, by all means. The altar-cloth might very well be changed, I think.'

'Oh, no! I will come some other time,' Madame Paloque replied. 'I am quite distressed to have interrupted you. Pray go on, your reverence, pray go on!'

Notwithstanding her protestations, however, she entered the room. While she was examining the altar-cloth with Marthe, the priest began to chide his mother in a low voice:

'Why did you prevent her coming in, mother? I never told you to allow no one to enter.'

She gazed straight in front of her with her obstinate determined glance. 'She would have had to walk over my body before she got inside,' she muttered.

'But why?'

'Because—. Listen to me, Ovide; don't be angry; you know that it pains me to see you angry. You told me to accompany our landlady here, didn't you? Well, I thought you wanted me to stop inquisitive people's curiosity. So I took my seat out here, and no one should have entered, be sure of that.'

But the priest caught hold of his mother's hands and shook her, exclaiming:

'Why, mother, you couldn't have supposed—'

'I suppose nothing,' she replied, with sublime indifference. 'You are free to do whatever pleases you. You are my child; I would steal for you, I would."

The priest was no longer listening to her. He had let her hands drop, and, as he gazed at her, he seemed to be lost in reflections, which made his face look sterner and more austere than ever.

'No, never!' he exclaimed with lofty pride. 'You are greatly mistaken, mother. It is only the chaste who are powerful.'

XVI

At seventeen years of age, Désirée still retained the childlike laugh of an 'innocent.' She was now a fine, tall girl, plump and well-developed, with the arms and shoulders of a full-grown woman. She grew like a healthy plant, happy in her growth, and quite untouched by the unhappiness which was wrecking and saddening the house.

'Why do you never laugh?' she cried to her father one day. 'Come and have a game at skipping! It's such fun!'

She had taken possession of one of the garden-beds, which she dug, planted with vegetables, and carefully watered. The hard work delighted her. Then she desired to have some fowls, which devoured her vegetables and which she scolded with motherly tenderness. With these occupations of hers, gardening and fowl-keeping, she made herself dreadfully dirty.

'She's perfectly filthy!' cried Rose. 'I won't have her coming into my kitchen any more; she dirties everything! It is no use your trying to keep her neatly dressed, madame. If I were you I should just let her mess about as she likes.'

Marthe, now ever preoccupied, no longer took care even that Désirée should change her under-linen regularly. The girl sometimes wore the same chemise for three weeks together; her stockings fell over her shoes, which were sadly worn down at the heels, and her tattered skirts hung about her like a beggar's rags. Mouret was one day obliged to take up a needle himself, for the girl's dress was torn behind from top to bottom. She, however, laughed gleefully at her nakedness, at her hair that fell over her shoulders, and at her black hands and dirty face.

Marthe came to feel a sort of disgust of her. When she returned home from mass, still retaining in her hair the vague perfume of the church, she quite shuddered at the strong scent of earth which exhaled from her daughter. She sent her into the garden again immediately lunch was over. She could not bear to have her near her, distressed, disquieted as she was by the girl's robust vigour and clear laugh, which seemed to find amusement in everything.

'Oh, dear! how wearisome the child is!' she murmured sometimes, with an air of nerveless lassitude.

As Mouret heard her complain, he exclaimed in an impulse of anger:

'If she's in your way, we will turn her out of the house, as we have done the other two.'

'Indeed, I should be very glad if she were to go away,' Marthe answered unhesitatingly.

One afternoon, about the end of the summer, Mouret was alarmed at no longer being able to hear Désirée, who, a few minutes previously, had been making a tremendous noise at the bottom of the garden. He ran to see what had happened to her, and found her lying on the ground. She had fallen from a ladder on to which she had climbed to gather some figs: fortunately the box-plants had broken the force of her fall. Mouret, in a great fright, lifted her up in his arms and called for assistance. He thought she was dead; but she quickly came to herself, declared that she was none the worse for the accident, and wanted to climb the ladder again.

Marthe, however, had meantime come into the garden. When she heard Désirée laugh she seemed quite annoyed.

'That child will kill me one of these days,' she exclaimed. 'She doesn't know what to invent to alarm me. I'm sure that she threw herself down on purpose. I can't endure it any longer. I shall shut myself up in my own room, or go out in the morning and not return till evening. Yes, you may laugh, you great goose! To think that I am the mother of such a ninny! You are making me pay for it very dearly!'

'Yes, that she is!' cried Rose, who had run down from the kitchen; 'she's a great burden, and, unfortunately, there's no chance of our ever being able to get her married.'

Mouret looked at them and listened with a pang at the heart. He said nothing, but stayed with the girl at the bottom of the garden, and there they remained chatting affectionately till nightfall. The next day, Marthe and Rose were away from the house the whole morning. They went to hear mass at a chapel, a league from Plassans, dedicated to Saint-Januarius, whither all the pious folks of the town made a pilgrimage on that particular day. When they returned, the cook hastily served up a cold lunch. Marthe went on eating for a few minutes before she noticed that her daughter was not at table.

'Isn't Désirée hungry?' she asked. 'Why hasn't she come to lunch?'

'Désirée is no longer here,' answered Mouret, who left his food almost untouched upon his plate; 'I took her this morning to her nurse at Saint-Eutrope.'

Marthe laid down her fork, and turned a little pale, seeming both surprised and hurt.

'You might have consulted me,' she said.

Her husband, without making any direct reply, continued:

'She is all right with her nurse. The good woman is very fond of her, and will look well after her, and the child will no longer be in your way, and everyone will be happy.'

Then, as his wife said nothing, he added:

'If the house is not yet sufficiently quiet for you, just tell me, and I will go away myself.'

She half rose from her seat, and a light glistened in her eyes. Mouret had wounded her so cruelly that she stretched out her hand as though she were going to throw the water-bottle at his head. In her long submissive nature angry promptings were now being fanned into life, and she was growing to hate this man who was ever prowling round her. She made a show of eating again, but she said nothing further about her daughter. Mouret had folded his napkin, and remained sitting in front of her, listening to the sound of her fork, and casting lingering glances round the dining-room, which had once been so merry with the chatter of the children, but was now so empty and mournful. The room seemed to him to be quite chilly, and tears were mounting to his eyes when Marthe called to Rose to bring in the dessert.

'You must be very hungry, I should think, madame,' said the cook, as she put a plateful of fruit upon the table. 'We had quite a long walk; and if the master, instead of playing the pagan, had come with us, he would not have left you to eat the mutton all by yourself.'

Then she changed the plates, without pausing in her chatter.

'It is very pretty is that chapel of Saint-Januarius, but it is too small. Did you see that the ladies who came late were obliged to kneel down outside on the grass, in the open air? I can't understand why Madame de Condamin came in a carriage. There's no merit in making the pilgrimage if you come like that. We spent a delightful morning, didn't we, madame?'

'Yes, a very delightful morning,' Marthe replied. 'Abbé Mousseau, who preached, was very affecting.'

When Rose in her turn noticed Désirée's absence and learnt of the girl's departure, she exclaimed:

'Well, really, it was a very good idea of the master's! She was always walking off with my saucepans to water her plants. We shall be able to have a little peace now.'

'Yes, indeed,' said Marthe, who was cutting a pear.

Mouret was almost choking. He rose and left the dining-room without paying any attention to Rose, who cried out to him that the coffee would be ready directly. Marthe, now left alone in the room, quietly finished her pear.

Just as the cook was bringing the coffee, Madame Faujas came downstairs.

'Go in,' Rose said to her; 'you will be company for madame, and you can have the master's coffee, for he has just rushed off like a madman.'

The old lady sat down in Mouret's place.

'I thought you did not take coffee,' she remarked as she put some sugar into her cup.

'No, indeed, she didn't do so when the master kept the purse,' interposed Rose. 'But madame would be very silly now to deny herself what she likes.'

They talked for a good hour together, and Marthe ended by relating all her troubles to Madame Faujas, telling her how her husband had just inflicted a most painful scene upon her on account of her daughter, whom he had removed to her nurse's in a sudden pet. She defended herself, and told Madame Faujas that she was really very fond of the girl, and should go to fetch her back before long.

'Well, she was rather noisy,' Madame Faujas remarked. 'I have often pitied you. My son was thinking about giving up going into the garden to read his breviary. She almost distracted him with the noise she made.'

From that day forward Marthe and Mouret took their meals in silence. The autumn was very damp, and the dining-room looked intensely melancholy with only two covers laid, one at each end of the big table. The corners were dark, and a chill seemed to fall from the ceiling. As Rose would say, it looked as though a funeral were going on.

'Well, indeed,' she often exclaimed, as she brought the plates into the room, 'you couldn't make much less noise, sir, however you tried! There isn't much danger of your wearing the skin of your tongue off! Do try to be a little livelier, sir! You look as though you were following a corpse to the grave! You will end by making madame quite ill. It is bad for the health to eat without speaking.'

When the first frosts came, Rose, who sought in every way to oblige Madame Faujas, offered her the use of her cooking-stove. The old lady had begun by bringing down kettles to get her water boiled, as she had no fire, she said, and the Abbé was in a hurry to shave. Then she borrowed some flat-irons, begged the use of some saucepans, asked for the loan of the dutch-oven to cook some mutton, and finally, in the end, as she had no conveniently arranged fireplace upstairs, she accepted Rose's repeated offers, and the cook lighted her a fire of vine branches, big enough to roast a whole sheep, in the kitchen.

'Don't show any diffidence about it,' she said, as she herself turned the leg of mutton round; 'the kitchener is a large one, isn't it? and big enough for us both. I don't know how you've been able to do your cooking upstairs as long as you have, with only that wretched iron stove there. I should have been afraid of falling down in an apoplectic fit myself. Monsieur Mouret ought to know better than to let a set of rooms without any kitchen. You must be very enduring kind of people, and very easily satisfied.'

Thus Madame Faujas gradually began to cook her lunch and dinner in the Mourets' kitchen. On the first few occasions she provided her own coal and oil and spices. But afterwards, when she forgot to bring any article with her, Rose would not allow her to go upstairs for it, but insisted upon supplying the deficiency from the house stores.

'Oh, there's some butter there! The little bit which you will take with the tip of your knife won't ruin us. You know very well that everything here is at your service. Madame would be quite angry with me if I didn't make you at home here.'

A close intimacy now sprang up between Rose and Madame Faujas. The cook was delighted to have some one always at hand who was willing to listen to her while she stirred her sauces. She got on extremely well with the priest's mother, whose print dresses and rough face and unpolished demeanour put her almost on a footing of equality. They sat chatting together for hours before the fireplace, and Madame Faujas soon gained complete sway in the kitchen, though she still maintained her impenetrable attitude, and only said what she chose to say, while contriving to worm out all that she wanted to know. She settled the Mourets' dinner, tasted the dishes which she had arranged they should have, and Rose herself often made savoury little luxuries for the Abbé's delectation, such as sugared apples or rice-cakes or fritters. The provisions of the two establishments often got mixed together, mistakes were made with the different pans, the two dinners being so intermingled that Rose would cry out with a laugh:

'Tell me, madame, are these poached eggs yours? Really, I don't know. Upon my word, it would be much better if you were all to dine together!'

It was on All Saints Day that Abbé Faujas lunched for the first time in the Mourets' dining-room. He was in a great hurry, as he had to return to Saint-Saturnin's at once, and so, to give him as much time as possible, Marthe asked him to sit down at their table, saying that it would save his mother from climbing a couple of flights of stairs. A week later it had become a regular thing; the Faujases came downstairs at every meal and took their seats at table, just as if they were entering a restaurant. For the first few days their provisions were cooked and served separately, but Rose declared this was a very silly arrangement, that she could easily cook for four persons, and that she would arrange it all with Madame Faujas.

'Pray don't thank me,' she said to the Abbé and his mother; 'it is a kindness on your part to come down and keep madame company. You will cheer her up a little. I scarcely dare go into the dining-room now; it is just like going into the chamber of death. It quite frightens me, it feels so desolate. If the master chooses to go on sulking, he will have to do so all by himself.'

They kept up a roaring fire, the room was very warm, and the winter proved a delightful one. Rose had never before taken such pains to lay the tablecloth nicely. She placed his reverence's chair near the stove, so that he might have his back to the fire. She paid particular attention to his glass and his knife and fork, she took care that whenever the slightest stain made its appearance upon the cloth it should not be put on his side, and she paid him numberless other delicate little attentions.

When she had prepared any dish of which he was particularly fond, she gave him notice so that he might reserve himself for it; though sometimes, on the other hand, she made a surprise of it for him, and brought it into the room under a cover, smiling at the inquisitive glances directed towards it, and exclaiming with an air of triumph:

'This is for his reverence! It is a wild-duck stuffed with olives, just what he is so fond of. Give his reverence the breast, madame. I cooked it specially for him.'

Marthe carved the duck, and with beseeching looks pressed the choicest morsels upon the Abbé. She always helped him the first, and searched the dish for him, while Rose bent over her and pointed out what she thought the best parts. They occasionally even had little disputes as to the superiority of this or that part of a fowl or rabbit. Then, too, Rose used to push an embroidered hassock under the priest's feet, while Marthe insisted that he should always have his bottle of Bordeaux and his roll, specially ordering one of the latter for him from the baker every day.

'We can never do too much for you,' said Rose, when the Abbé expressed his thanks. 'Who should be well looked after, if it isn't good kind hearts like yours? Don't you trouble about it, the Lord will pay your debt for you.'

Madame Faujas smiled at all these flattering civilities as she sat at table opposite her son. She was beginning to feel quite fond of Marthe and Rose. She considered their adoration only natural, and thought it a great happiness for them to be allowed to cast themselves in this way at the feet of her idol. It was really she with her square head and peasant manner who presided over the table, eating slowly but plentifully, noticing everything that happened without once setting down her fork, and taking care that Marthe should play the part of servant to her son, at whom she was constantly gazing with an expression of content. She never opened her lips except to make known in as few words as possible the Abbé's various tastes or to over-rule the polite refusals in which he still occasionally indulged. Sometimes she shrugged her shoulders and pushed him with her foot. Wasn't everything on the table at his service? He might eat the whole contents of the dish, if he liked, and the others would be quite happy to nibble their dry bread and look at him.

Abbé Faujas himself, however, seemed quite indifferent to all the tender care which was lavished upon him. Of a very frugal disposition and a quick eater, his mind always occupied with other matters, he was frequently quite unconscious of the dainties which were specially reserved for him. He had yielded to his mother's entreaties in consenting to join the Mourets, but the only satisfaction he experienced in the dining-room on the ground-floor was the pleasure of being set entirely free from the everyday cares of life. He manifested unruffled serenity, gradually grew accustomed to seeing his least wish anticipated and fulfilled, and ceased to manifest any surprise or express any thanks, lording it haughtily between the mistress of the house and the cook, who kept anxious watch over the slightest motions of his stern face.

Mouret sat opposite his wife, quite forgotten and unnoticed. He let his hands rest upon the edge of the table, and waited, like a child, till Marthe should be willing to attend to him. She helped him the last, scantily, and to whatever might happen to be left. Rose stood behind her and warned her whenever by mistake she was going to give her husband some of the more delicate morsels in the dish.

'No, no; not that. The master likes the head, you know. He enjoys sucking the little bones.'

Mouret, snubbed and slighted, ate his food with a sort of shame, as though he was subsisting unworthily on other people's bounty. He could see Madame Faujas watching him keenly as he cut his bread. He kept his eyes fixed on the bottle for a whole minute, full of doubtful hesitation, before he dare venture to help himself to wine. Once he made a mistake and took a little of the priest's choice Bordeaux. There was a tremendous fuss made about it, and for a whole month afterwards Rose reproached him for those few drops of wine. Whenever she made any sweet dish, she would say:

'I don't want the master to have any of that. He never thinks anything I make nice. He once told me that an omelet I had made was burnt, and then I said, "They shall be burnt altogether for you." Don't give any of it to the master, I beg you, madame.'

She also did all she could to worry and upset him. She gave him cracked plates, contrived that one of the table legs should come between his own, left shreds of the glass-cloth clinging to his glass, and placed the bread and wine and salt as far from him as possible. Mouret was the only one in the family who liked mustard, and he used to go himself to the grocers and buy canisters of it, which the cook promptly caused to disappear, saying that they 'stank so.' The deprivation of mustard spoilt his enjoyment of his meals. But what made him still more miserable, and robbed him of all appetite, was his expulsion from his own seat, which he had always previously occupied, in front of the window, which was now given to the priest, as being the pleasantest in the room. Mouret had to sit with his face towards the door, and he felt as though he were eating amongst strangers, now that he could not at each mouthful cast a glance at his fruit-trees.

Marthe was not so bitter against him as Rose was. She treated him at first like a poor relation, whose presence is just tolerated, and then gradually grew to ignore him, scarcely ever addressing a remark to him, and acting as though Abbé Faujas alone had the right to give orders in the house. Mouret, however, showed no inclination to rebel. He occasionally exchanged a few polite phrases with the priest, though he generally ate in perfect silence, and only replied to the cook's attacks by looking at her. He always finished before any of the others, folded up his napkin tidily, and then left the room, frequently before the dessert was placed upon the table.

Rose alleged that he was bursting with anger, and when she gossiped in the kitchen with Madame Faujas she discussed his conduct freely.

'I know him very well; I've never been afraid of him. Before you came madame used to tremble before him, for he was always scolding and blustering and trying to appear very terrible. He used to worry our lives out of us, always poking about, never finding anything right, and trying to show us that he was master. Now he is as docile as a lamb, isn't he? It's just because madame has asserted herself. Ah! if he weren't a coward, and weren't afraid of what might happen, you would hear a pretty row. But he is afraid of your son; yes, he is afraid of his reverence the Curé. Anyone would say, to look at him, that he lost his senses every now and then. But after all, as long as he doesn't bother us any longer, he is welcome to act as he pleases; isn't he, madame?'

Madame Faujas replied that Monsieur Mouret seemed to her to be a very worthy man, and that his only fault was his lack of religion. But he would certainly adopt a better mode of life in time, she said. The old lady was gradually making herself mistress of the whole of the ground floor, going from kitchen to dining-room as she pleased, and ever bustling about in the hall and passages. When Mouret met her he used to recall the day when the Faujases first arrived; when, wearing that shabby black dress of hers, she had tenaciously clung to her basket with both hands and poked her head inquisitively into each room, with all the unruffled serenity of a person inspecting some property for sale.

Since the Faujases had begun to take their meals downstairs the Trouches were left in possession of the second floor. They made a great deal of noise, and the constant moving of furniture, the stamping of feet and the violent banging of doors, were heard by those downstairs. Madame Faujas would then uneasily raise her head in the midst of her gossiping in the kitchen. Rose, for the sake of putting her at her ease, used to say that poor Madame Trouche suffered a great deal of pain. One night the Abbé, who had not yet gone to bed, heard a strange commotion on the stairs. He left his room with his candle in his hand, and saw Trouche, disgracefully drunk, climbing up the stairs on his knees. He seized the sot in his strong arms and threw him into his room. Olympe was in bed there, quietly reading a novel and sipping a glass of spirits and water that stood on a little table at the bedside.

'Listen to me,' said Abbé Faujas, livid with rage; 'you will pack up your things in the morning and take yourselves off!'

'Why? What for?' asked Olympe, quite calmly; 'we are very comfortable here.'

The priest sternly interrupted her.

'Hold your tongue! You are a wretched woman! You have never tried to do anything but injure me. Our mother was right; I ought never to have rescued you from your state of wretchedness. I've just had to pick your husband up on the stairs. It is disgraceful. Think of the scandal there would be if he were to be seen in this state. You will go away in the morning.'

Olympe sat up to sip her grog.

'No, no, indeed!' she said.

Trouche laughed. He was drunkenly merry, and fell back into an arm-chair in a state of happy self-satisfaction.

'Don't let us quarrel,' he stammered. 'It is a mere nothing; only a little giddiness. The air, which is very cold, made me dizzy, that's all. And your streets in this confounded town are so very confusing. I say, Faujas, there are some very nice young fellows about here. There's Doctor Porquier's son. You know Doctor Porquier, don't you? Well, I meet the son at a café behind the gaol. It is kept by a woman from Aries, a fine handsome woman with a dark complexion.'

The priest crossed his arms and looked at him with a terrible expression.

'No, really, Faujas, I assure you that it is quite wrong of you to be angry with me. You know that I have been well brought up, and that I know how to behave myself. Why, in the daytime I wouldn't touch a drop of syrup for fear of compromising you. Since I have been here I have gone to my office just like a boy going to school, with slices of bread and jam in a little basket. It's a very stupid sort of life, I can assure you, and I only do it to be of service to you. But at night, I'm not likely to be seen, and I can go about a little. It does me good, and, in fact, I should die if I always kept myself locked up here. There is no one in the streets, you know. What funny streets they are, eh?'

'Sot!' growled the priest between his clenched teeth.

'You won't be friends, then? Well, that's very wrong of you, old chap. I'm a jolly fellow myself, and I don't like sour looks, and if what I do doesn't please you, I'll leave you to get on with your pious ladies by yourself. That little Condamin is the only decent one amongst them, and even she doesn't come up to the café-keeper from Aries. Oh, yes! you may roll your eyes about as much as you like. I can get on quite well without you. See! would you like me to lend you a hundred francs?'

He drew out a bundle of bank-notes and spread them on his knees, laughing loudly as he did so. Then he swept them under the Abbé's nose and threw them up in the air. Olympe sprang out of bed, half naked, picked up the notes and placed them under the bolster with an expression of vexation. Abbé Faujas glanced around him with great surprise. He saw bottles of liqueurs ranged all along the top of the chest of drawers, a scarcely touched patty was on the mantelpiece, and there were some sweetmeats in an old box. The room was, indeed, full of recent purchases; dresses thrown over the chairs, an open parcel of lace, a magnificent new overcoat hanging from the window-catch, and a bearskin rug spread out in front of the bed. By the side of Olympe's glass of grog on the little table there also lay a small gold lady's watch glittering in a porcelain tray.

'Whom have they been plundering, I wonder?' thought the priest.

Then he recollected having seen Olympe kissing Marthe's hands.

'You wretched people!' he cried; 'you have been thieving!'

Trouche sprang up, but his wife pushed him down upon the sofa. 'Keep quiet!' she said to him, 'go to sleep, you need it.'

Then, turning to her brother, she continued:

'It is one o'clock, and you might let us go to sleep if you have only disagreeable things to say. It is certainly wrong of my husband to intoxicate himself, but that's no reason why you should abuse him. We have already had several explanations; this one must be the last, do you understand, Ovide? We are brother and sister, are we not? Well, then, as I have told you before, we must go halves. You gorge yourself downstairs, you have all kinds of dainty dishes provided for you, and you live a fat life between the landlady and the cook. Well, you please yourself about that. We don't go and look into your plate or try to pull the dainty morsels out of your mouth. We let you manage your affairs as you like. Very well then, just you leave us alone and allow us the same liberty. I don't think I am asking anything unreasonable.'

The priest made a gesture of impatience.

'Oh yes, I understand,' she continued; 'you are afraid lest we should compromise you in your schemes. The best way to ensure our not doing so is to leave us in peace and cease from worrying us. Ah! in spite of all your grand airs, you are not so very clever. We have the same interests as you have, we are all of the same family, and we might very well hunt together. It would be much the best plan, if you would only see it. But there, go to bed, now! I'll scold Trouche in the morning, and I'll send him to you and you can give him your instructions.'

For a moment the priest, who was a little pale, remained thinking; then, without another word, he left the room, and Olympe resumed the perusal of her novel, while Trouche lay snoring on the sofa.

The next morning, Trouche, who had recovered his wits, had a long interview with Abbé Faujas. When he returned to his wife, he informed her of the conditions upon which peace had again been patched up.

'Listen to me, my dear,' Olympe replied. 'Give way to him and do what he asks. Above all try to be useful to him, since he gives you the chance of being so. I put a bold face on the matter when he is here, but in my own heart I know very well that he would turn us out into the street like dogs if we pushed him too far, and I don't want to have to go away. Are you sure that he will let us stay?'

'Oh yes; don't be afraid,' replied the secretary. 'He has need of me, and he will leave us to feather our nest.'

From this time forward Trouche used to go out every evening about nine o'clock, when the streets were quiet. He told his wife that he went into the old quarter of the town to further the Abbé's cause. Olympe was not at all jealous of his nightly absences, and laughed heartily whenever he brought her back some broad story. She preferred being left quietly to herself, to sip her glass and nibble her cakes in privacy, or to spend her long evenings snugly in bed, devouring the old novels of a circulating-library which she had discovered in the Rue Canquoin. Trouche used to come back slightly under the influence of liquor, but he took off his boots in the hall so as to make no noise as he went upstairs. When he had drunk too much, and reeked of tobacco and brandy, his wife would not let him get into bed, but made him sleep on the sofa. If he became annoying, she caught hold of him, looked him sternly in the face, and said:

'Ovide will hear you. Ovide is coming.'

At this he was as frightened as a child that is threatened with a wolf, and went off to sleep, muttering excuses. In the morning he dressed himself in serious, sedate fashion, wiped from his face all the marks of the previous night's dissipation, and put on a certain cravat, which gave him, he said, quite the air of a parson. As he passed the cafés he bent his head to the ground. At the Home of the Virgin he was held in great respect. Now and then, when the girls were playing in the courtyard, he raised a corner of his curtain and glanced at them with an affectation of fatherliness, though his eyes glistened beneath their lowered lids.

The Trouches were still kept in check by Madame Faujas. The mother and the daughter were perpetually quarrelling, Olympe complaining that she was sacrificed to her brother, and Madame Faujas treating her like a viper whom she ought to have crushed to death in her cradle. Both grasping after the same prey, they kept a close watch on one another, anxious to know which would secure the larger share. Madame Faujas wanted to obtain everything in the house, and she tried to keep the very sweepings from Olympe's clutching fingers. On seeing what large sums her daughter drew from Marthe, she quite burst with anger. When her son shrugged his shoulders at it like a man who despises such matters, and is forced to close his eyes to them, she, on her side, had a stormy explanation with her daughter, whom she branded as a thief, as though the money had been taken from her own pocket.

'There, mother, that will do!' cried Olympe impatiently. 'It isn't your purse, you know, that I have been lightening. Besides, I have only been borrowing a little money; I don't make other people keep me.'

'What do you mean, you wicked hussy?' gasped Madame Faujas with indignation. 'Do you suppose that we don't pay for our food? Ask the cook, and she will show you our account book.'

Olympe broke out into a loud laugh.

'Oh, yes, that's very nice!' she cried; 'I know that account book of yours! You pay for the radishes and butter, don't you? Stay downstairs by all means, mother; stay downstairs on the ground floor. I don't want to interfere with your arrangements. But don't come up here and worry me any more, or I shall make a row, and you know that Ovide has forbidden any noise up here.'

At this Madame Faujas went downstairs muttering and growling. The threat of making a disturbance always compelled her to beat a retreat. Olympe began to sing jeeringly as soon as her mother's back was turned. But whenever she went down into the garden the other took her revenge, keeping everlastingly at her heels, watching her hands, never ceasing to play the spy upon her. She would not allow her in the kitchen or dining-room for a moment. She embroiled her with Rose about a saucepan that had been borrowed and never returned; but she did not dare to attempt to undermine Marthe's friendship for her for fear of causing some scandal which might prove prejudicial to the priest.

'Since you are so regardless of your own interests,' she said to her son one day, 'I must look after them for you. Make yourself easy. I shan't do anything foolish; but if I were not here, your sister would snatch the very bread out of your hands.'

Marthe had no notion of the drama that was being played around her. To her the house simply seemed more lively and cheerful, now that all these people thronged the hall and the stairs and the passages. The place was as noisy as an hotel, what with all the echoes of quarrelling, the banging of doors, the free and independent life of each of the tenants, and the flaming fire in the kitchen, where Rose seemed to have a whole table d'hote to provide for. There was a continual procession of tradesmen to the house. Olympe, who became very particular about her hands and refused to risk spoiling them by washing plates and dishes, had everything sent from a confectioner's in the Rue de la Banne, who catered for the townspeople. Marthe smiled and said she enjoyed the present bustle of the house. She now greatly disliked being left alone, and felt the necessity of occupation of some sort to allay the fever that was consuming her.

Mouret, however, to escape from all the racket, used to shut himself up in a room on the first floor, which he called his office. He had overcome his distaste for solitude; he now scarcely ever went down into the garden, but kept himself locked up from morning till night.

'I should very much like to know what he finds to do in there,' said Rose to Madame Faujas. 'One can't hear him move, and you might almost fancy he was dead. If he wants to hide himself in that way, it must be because he is doing something that's neither right nor proper; don't you think so, eh?'

When the summer came round once more, the house grew still livelier. Abbé Faujas received the guests of both the sub-prefect and the presiding judge beneath the arbour at the bottom of the garden. Rose, by Marthe's orders, purchased a dozen rustic chairs, so that the visitors might enjoy the fresh air without it being necessary to carry the dining-room chairs hither and thither. It was now the regular thing for the doors communicating with the little lane to remain open every

Tuesday afternoon, and the ladies and gentlemen came to salute Abbé Faujas like friendly neighbours, the men often in their slippers and with their coats carelessly unbuttoned, and the ladies in straw hats and with skirts looped up with pins. The visitors arrived one by one, and gradually the two sets of guests found themselves mixing together, gossiping and amusing themselves with perfect familiarity.

'Aren't you afraid,' said Monsieur Bourdeu to Monsieur Rastoil one day, 'that these meetings with the sub-prefect's friends may be ill advised? The general elections are getting near.'

'Why should they be ill advised?' asked Monsieur Rastoil. 'We don't go to the Sub-Prefecture; we keep on neutral ground. Besides, my good friend, there is no ceremony about the matter. I keep my linen jacket on, and it's a mere private friendly visit. No one has any right to pass judgment upon what I do at the back of my house. In the front it's another matter. In the front we belong to the public. When Monsieur Péqueur and I meet each other in the streets we merely bow.'

'Monsieur Péqueur de Saulaies improves much on acquaintance,' the ex-prefect ventured to remark after a short pause.

'Certainly, certainly,' replied the presiding judge; 'I am delighted to have made his acquaintance. And what a worthy man Abbé Faujas is! No, no; I have no fear of any slander arising from our going to pay our respects to our excellent neighbour.'

Since the general election had begun to be the subject of conversation, Monsieur de Bourdeu had felt very uneasy. He declared that it was the increasing warmth of the weather that affected him; but he was frequently assailed with doubts and scruples, which he confided to Monsieur Rastoil in order that the latter might reassure him. However, politics were never mentioned in the Mourets' garden. One afternoon, Monsieur de Bourdeu, after vainly trying to devise some means of bringing political matters forward, exclaimed abruptly, addressing himself to Doctor Porquier:

'I say, doctor, have you seen the "Moniteur" this morning? I see that the marquis has at last spoken! He uttered just thirteen words; I counted them. Poor Lagrifoul! He has made himself very ridiculous!'

Abbé Faujas raised his finger with an arch look. 'No politics, gentlemen, no politics,' said he.

Monsieur Péqueur des Saulaies was chatting with Monsieur Rastoil, and they both pretended that they had not heard what was said. Madame de Condamin smiled as she continued her conversation with Abbé Surin.

'Aren't your surplices stiffened with a weak solution of gum?' she inquired.

'Yes, madame, with a weak solution of gum,' replied the young priest. 'Some laundresses use boiled starch, but it spoils the material and is worthless.'

'Well,' rejoined the young woman, 'I never can get my laundress to use gum for my petticoats.'

Thereupon Abbé Surin politely gave her the name and address of his own laundress upon the back of one of his visiting cards. Then the company chatted about dress and the weather and the crops and the events of the week, spending a delightful hour together; and there were also games of shuttlecock in the alley. Abbé Bourrette frequently made his appearance, and told in his enthusiastic manner divers pious little stories to which Monsieur Maffre listened with the greatest attention. Upon one occasion only had Madame Delangre met Madame Rastoil there; they had treated each other with the most scrupulous politeness, but in their faded eyes still flashed the sparks of their old-time rivalry. Monsieur Delangre for his part did not make himself too cheap, and though the Paloques were constantly at the Sub-Prefecture, they contrived to be absent when Monsieur Péqueur des Saulaies went to make one of his neighbourly calls upon Abbé Faujas. The judge's wife had been much perplexed in mind ever since her unfortunate expedition to the oratory at the Home of the Virgin. On the other hand, the person who was oftenest to be seen in the garden was certainly Monsieur de Condamin, who always wore the most perfect fitting gloves, and came thither to make fun of the company, telling fibs and indelicate stories with extraordinary coolness and unconcern, and deriving a perfect fund of amusement for the whole week from the little intrigues which he scented out. This tall old buck, whose coat fitted so closely to his slim figure, was devoted to youth; he scoffed at the 'old ones,' went off with the young ladies, and laughed gaily in the snug little corners of the garden.

'This way, youngsters!' he would say, with a smile, 'let us leave the old ones together.'

One day he almost defeated Abbé Surin in a tremendous battle at shuttlecock. He was very fond of plaguing young people, and made a special victim of Monsieur Rastoil's son, a simple young fellow, to whom he told the most prodigious stories. He ended, indeed, by accusing him of making love to his wife, and rolled his eyes about in such a terrible way, that the wretched Séverin broke out into a perspiration from very fear. The youth did, as it happened, actually fancy that he was in love with Madame de Condamin, in whose presence he behaved in a tender, simpering manner that extremely amused her husband.

The Rastoil girls, for whom the conservator of rivers and forests manifested all the gallantry of a young widower, also supplied subjects of his raillery. Although they were approaching their thirtieth birthdays, he spurred them on to indulge in childish games, and spoke to them as though they were yet schoolgirls. His great amusement was to gaze at them when Lucien Delangre, the mayor's son, was present. He would then take Doctor Porquier aside, and whisper in his ear, alluding to the former entanglement between Monsieur Delangre and Madame Rastoil:

'There's a young man there, Porquier, who is very much embarrassed in his mind—Is it Angéline or is it Aurélie whom he ought to choose? Guess, if you can, and name, if you dare.'

Meantime Abbé Faujas was very polite and amiable to all his visitors, even to the terrible Condamin who caused so much disquietude. He effaced himself as much as possible, spoke but little, and allowed the rival sets of guests to coalesce, seemingly experiencing the quiet satisfaction of a host who is happy to be the means of bringing together a number of distinguished people intended by nature to be on good terms with one another. Marthe had upon two occasions made her appearance, thinking that she would put the visitors more at their ease by doing so; but it distressed her to find the Abbé in the midst of so many people; she much preferred to see him walking slowly and seriously in the quiet of the arbour. The Trouches on their side had resumed their Tuesday watchings behind their curtains, while Madame Faujas and Rose craned their heads from the door-way and admired the graceful manner in which his reverence received the chief people of Plassans.

'Ah, madame!' said the cook, 'it is very easy to see that he is a distinguished man. Look at him bowing to the sub-prefect. I admire his reverence the most; though, indeed, the sub-prefect is a fine man. Why do you never go into the garden to them? If I were you, I would put on a silk dress and join them. You are his mother, you know, after all.'

But the old peasant woman shrugged her shoulders.

'Oh! he isn't ashamed of me,' she said; 'but I should be afraid of putting him out. I prefer to watch him from here; and I enjoy it more.'

'Yes, I can understand that. Ah! you must be very proud of him. He isn't a bit like Monsieur Mouret, who nailed the door up, so that no one might open it. We never had a visitor, there was never a dinner to be prepared for anyone, and the garden was so desolate that it made one feel quite frightened in the evenings. Monsieur Mouret would certainly never have known how to receive visitors. He always pulled a sour face if one ever happened to come by chance. Don't you think, now, that he ought to take an example from his reverence? If I were he, I should come down and amuse myself in the garden with the others, instead of shutting myself up all alone. I would take my proper place. But there he is, shut up in his room, as though he were afraid they would give him some nasty illness! By the way, shall we go up sometime and try to find out what he does?'

One Tuesday they did go upstairs together. The visitors were very merry that afternoon, and the sound of their laughter floated into the house through the open windows, while a tradesman, who had brought a hamper of wine for the Trouches, made a clatter on the second floor as he collected the empty bottles together. Mouret was securely locked up in his office.

'The key prevents me from seeing,' said Rose, who had applied her eye to the key-hole.

'Wait a moment,' murmured Madame Faujas, and she carefully turned the end of the key, which protruded slightly through the lock. Mouret was sitting in the middle of the room in front of a big empty table, covered with a thick layer of dust. There was not a single paper nor book upon it. He was lying back in his chair, his arms hanging listlessly beside him while he gazed blankly into space. He sat perfectly still, without the slightest movement.

The two women looked at him in silence, one after the other.

'He has made me feel cold to the very marrow,' exclaimed Rose, as they went downstairs again. 'Did you notice his eyes? And what a filthy state the room is in! He hasn't laid a pen on that desk for a couple of months past, and to think that I fancied he spent all his time there writing. Fancy him amusing himself like that—shutting himself up all alone like a corpse, when the house is so bright and cheerful!'

XVII

Marthe's health was causing Doctor Porquier much anxiety. He still smiled in his pleasant way, and talked to her after the manner of a fashionable medical man for whom disease never has any existence, and who grants a consultation just as a dressmaker fits on a new dress; but there was a certain twist on his lips which indicated that 'dear madame' had something more seriously wrong with her than a slight cough and spitting of blood, as he tried to persuade her. He advised her, now that the warm weather had come, to get a little change of surroundings and occupation by taking an occasional drive, without, however, over-fatiguing herself. In obedience to the doctor's directions, Marthe, who was more and more possessed by a vague feeling of anguish, and a need of finding some occupation to assuage her nervous impatience, started on a series of excursions to the neighbouring villages. Twice a week she drove off, after luncheon, in an old refurbished carriage, hired from a Plassans coachbuilder. She generally drove some six or seven miles out, so as to get back home by six o'clock. Her great desire was to induce Abbé Faujas to go with her, and it was only in the hope of accomplishing this that she had conformed with the doctor's directions; but the Abbé, without distinctly refusing, always excused himself on the ground that he was too busy to spare the time, and Marthe was obliged to content herself with the companionship of Olympe or Madame Faujas.

One afternoon as she was driving with Olympe towards the village of Les Tulettes, past the little estate of her uncle Macquart, the latter caught sight of her as he stood upon his terrace, which was ornamented with a couple of mulberry trees.

'Where is Mouret?' he cried. 'Why hasn't Mouret come as well?'

Marthe was obliged to stop for a moment or two to speak to her uncle, and to explain to him that she was not well, and could not stay to dine with him. He had expressed his determination to kill a fowl for the meal.

'Well,' he said at last, 'I'll kill it all the same, and you shall take it away with you.'

Then he hurried off to kill the fowl at once. When he came back with it, he laid it on a stone table in front of the house, and exclaimed with an expression of satisfaction:

'Isn't it a plump, splendid fellow?'

At the moment of Marthe's arrival Macquart had been on the point of drinking a bottle of wine under the shade of his mulberry trees, in company with a tall thin young fellow, dressed entirely in grey. He persuaded the two women to leave the carriage and sit down beside him for a time, bringing them chairs, and doing the honours of his house with a snigger of satisfaction.

'I have a very nice little place here, haven't I? My mulberries are very fine ones. In the summer I smoke my pipe out here in the fresh air. In the winter I sit down yonder with my back to the wall in the sun. Do you see my vegetables? The fowl-house is at the bottom of the garden. I have another strip of ground as well, behind the house, where I grow potatoes and lucern. I am getting old now, worse luck, and it's quite time that I should enjoy myself a little.'

He rubbed his hands together and gently wagged his head, as he cast an affectionate glance over his little estate. Then some thought seemed to sadden him.

'Have you seen your father lately?' he abruptly asked. 'Rougon isn't very amiable, you know. That corn-field over yonder to the left is for sale. If he had been willing we might have bought it. What would it have been for a man of his means? A paltry three thousand francs is all that is asked, but he refuses to have anything to do with it. The last time I went to see him he even made your mother tell me that he wasn't at home. But, you'll see, it will be all the worse for them in the end.'

He wagged his head and indulged in his unpleasant laugh, as he repeated:

'Yes, yes; it will be all the worse for them.'

Then he went to fetch some glasses, for he insisted upon making the two women taste his wine. It was some light wine which he had discovered at Saint-Eutrope, and in which he took great pride. Marthe scarcely wetted her lips, but Olympe finished the bottle. And afterwards she even accepted a glass of syrup, saying that the wine was very strong.

'And what have you done with your priest?' Uncle Macquart suddenly asked his niece.

Marthe looked at him in surprise and displeasure without replying.

'I heard that he was sponging on you tremendously,' Macquart loudly continued. 'Those priests are fond of good living. When I heard about him, I said that it served Mouret quite right. I warned him. Well, I shall be glad to help you to turn him out of the house. Mouret has only got to come and ask me, and I'll give him a helping hand. I've never been able to endure those fellows. I know one of them, Abbé Fenil, who has a house on the other side of the road. He is no better than the rest of them, but he is as malicious as an ape, and he amuses me. I fancy that he doesn't get on very well with that priest of yours; isn't that so, eh?'

Marthe had turned very pale.

'Madame here is the sister of his reverence Abbé Faujas,' she said, turning to Olympe, who was listening with much curiosity.

'What I said has no reference to madame,' replied Macquart quite unconcernedly. 'Madame is not offended, I'm sure. She will take another glass of syrup?'

Olympe accepted another glass of the syrup, but Marthe rose from her seat and wished to leave. Her uncle, however, insisted upon taking her over his grounds. At the end of the garden she stopped to look at a large white building that was on the slope of the hill, at a few hundred yards from Les Tulettes. Its inner courts looked like prison-yards, and the narrow symmetrical windows which streaked its front with black lines gave it the cheerless aspect of a hospital.

'That is the Lunatic Asylum,' exclaimed Macquart, who had followed the direction of Marthe's eyes. 'The young man here is one of the warders. We get on very well together, and he comes every now and then to have a bottle of wine with me.'

Then, turning towards the man in grey, who was finishing his glass beneath the mulberry tree, he called out:

'Here, Alexandre, come and show my niece our poor old woman's window.'

Alexandre came up to them politely. 'Do you see those three trees?' he said, stretching out his forefinger, as though he were drawing a plan in the air. 'Well, a little below the one to the left, you can see a fountain in the corner of a courtyard. Follow the windows on the ground floor to the right; it is the fifth one.'

Marthe stood there in silence, her lips white and her gaze fixed, in spite of herself, on the window pointed out to her. Uncle Macquart was looking at it as well, but with complaisance manifest in his blinking eyes.

'I see her sometimes of a morning,' he said, 'when the sun is on the other side. She keeps very well, doesn't she, Alexandre? I always tell them so when I go to Plassans. I am very well placed here to keep a watch on her. I couldn't be anywhere better.'

He again gave a snigger of satisfaction. 'The Rougons, you know, my dear, haven't got any stronger heads than the Macquarts have, and I often think, as I sit out here in front of that big house, that the whole lot will, perhaps, join the mother there some day. Thank Heaven, I've no fear about myself. My noddle is firmly fixed on. But I know some of them who are a little shaky. Well, I shall be here to receive them, and I shall see them from my den, and recommend them to Alexandre's kind attention, though they haven't all of them always been particularly kind to me.'

Then with that hideous smile of his that was like a captive wolf's, he added:

'It's very lucky for you all that I am here on the spot at Les Tulettes.'

Marthe could not help trembling. Though she was well aware of her uncle's taste for savage pleasantries, and the pleasure he took in torturing the people to whom he presented his rabbits, she could not help fancying that he was perhaps speaking the truth, and that the rest of the family would indeed be quartered eventually in those gloomy cells. She insisted upon taking her immediate departure in spite of the pressing entreaties of Macquart, who wanted to open another bottle of wine.

'Ah! where is the fowl?' he cried, just as she was getting into the carriage.

He went back for it, and placed it upon her knees.

'It is for Mouret, you understand,' he said, with a malicious expression; 'for Mouret, and for no one else. When I come to see you, I shall ask him how he liked it.'

He winked as he glanced at Olympe. Then, just as the coachman was going to whip his horse forward, he laid hold of the carriage again, and said:

'Go and see your father and talk to him about the cornfield. See, it's that field just in front of us. Rougon is making a mistake. We are too old friends to quarrel about the matter; besides, as he very well knows, it would be worse for him if we did. Let him understand that he is making a mistake.'

The carriage set off, and as Olympe turned round she saw Macquart grinning under his mulberry trees with Alexandre, and uncorking that second bottle of which he had spoken. Marthe gave the coachman strict orders that he was never to take her to Les Tulettes again. She was beginning to feel a little tired of these drives into the country, and she took them less frequently, and at last gave them up altogether, when she found that she could never prevail upon Abbé Faujas to accompany her.

Marthe was now undergoing a complete change; she was becoming quite another woman. She had grown much more refined, through the life of nervous excitement which she had been leading. The stolid heaviness and dull lifelessness which she had acquired from having spent fifteen years behind a counter at Marseilles seemed to melt away in the bright flame of her new-born piety. She dressed better than she had been used to do, and joined in the conversation when she now went to the Rougons' on Thursdays.

'Madame Mouret is becoming quite a young girl again,' exclaimed Madame de Condamin in amazement.

'Yes, indeed,' replied Doctor Porquier, nodding his head; 'she is going through life backwards.'

Marthe, who had now grown much slimmer, with rosy cheeks and magnificent black flashing eyes, burst for some months into singular beauty. Her face beamed with animation, extraordinary vitality seemed to flood her being and thrill her with warmth. Her forgotten and joyless youth appeared to blaze in her now, at forty years of age. At the same time she was overwhelmed by a perpetual craving for prayer and devotion, and no longer obeyed Abbé Faujas's injunctions. She wore out her knees upon the flag-stones at Saint-Saturnin's, lived in the midst of canticles and offerings of praise and worship, and took comfort in the presence of the gleaming monstrances and the brightly lit chapels, and priests and altars that glittered with starry sheen through the dark gloom of the cathedral nave. She had a sort of physical craving for those glories, a craving which tortured and racked her. She was compelled by her very suffering—she would have died if she had not yielded—to seek sustenance for her passion, to come and prostrate herself in confession, to bow in lowly awe amidst the thrilling peals of the organ, and to faint with melting joy in the ecstasy of communion. Then all consciousness of trouble left her, she was no longer tortured, she bowed herself to the ground in a painless trance, etherealised, as it were, becoming a pure, unsullied flame of self-consuming love.

But Faujas's severity increased, he tried to check her by roughness. He was amazed at this passionate awakening of Marthe's soul, this ardour for love and death. He frequently questioned her on the subject of her childhood; he even went to see Madame Rougon, and remained for a long time in great perplexity and dissatisfaction.

'Our landlady has been complaining of you,' his mother said to him. 'Why won't you allow her to go to church whenever she likes? It is very unkind of you to vex her; she is very kindly to us.'

'She is killing herself,' replied the priest.

Madame Faujas shrugged her shoulders after her usual fashion.

'That is her own business. We all have our ways of finding pleasure. It is better to die of praying than to give one's self indigestion like that hussy Olympe. Don't be so severe with Madame Mouret. You will end by making it impossible for us to live here.'

One day when she was advising him in this way, he exclaimed in a gloomy voice:

'Mother, this woman will be the obstacle!'

'She!' cried the old peasant woman, 'why, she worships you, Ovide! You may do anything you like with her, if you will only treat her a little more kindly. She would carry you to the cathedral if it rained, to prevent you wetting your feet, if you would only let her!'

Abbé Faujas himself at last came to understand the necessity of no longer treating Marthe so harshly. He began to fear an outburst. So he gradually allowed her greater liberty, permitted her to seclude herself, to tell her beads at length, to offer prayers at each of the Stations of the Cross, and even to come twice a week to his confessional at Saint-Saturnin's. Marthe, no longer hearing the terrible voice which had seemed to impute her piety to her as a vice, believed that God was pouring His grace upon her. Now at last, she thought, she was entering into all the joys of Paradise. She was overcome by trances of sweet emotion, inexhaustible floods of tears, which she shed without being conscious of their flow, and nervous ecstasies from which she emerged weak and faint as though all her life-blood had left her veins. At these times, Rose would take her and lay her upon her bed, where she would lie for hours with pinched lips and half-closed eyes like a dead woman.

One afternoon the cook, alarmed by her stillness, was really afraid that she might be dead. She did not think of knocking at the door of the room in which Mouret had shut himself, but she went straight to the second floor and besought Abbé Faujas to come down to her mistress. When he reached Marthe's room, Rose hastened to fetch some ether, leaving the priest alone with the swooning woman. He merely took her hands within his own. At last Marthe began to move about and talk incoherently. When she at last recognised him at her bedside her blood surged to her face.

'Are you better, my dear child?' he asked her. 'You make me feel very uneasy.'

She felt too much oppressed at first to be able to reply to him, and burst into tears, as she let her head slip between his arms.

'I am not ill,' she murmured at last, in so feeble a voice that it was scarcely more than a breath; 'I am too happy. Let me cry; I feel delight in my tears. How kind of you to have come! I had been expecting you and calling you for a long time.'

Then her voice grew weaker and weaker till it was nothing more than a mere murmur of ardent prayer.

'Oh! who will give me wings to fly towards thee? My soul languishes without thee, it longs for thee passionately and sighs for thee, O my God, my only good thing, my consolation, my sweet joy, my treasure, my happiness, my life, my God, my all—'

Her face broke into a smile as she breathed these passionate words, and she clasped her hands fancying that she saw Abbé Faujas's grave face circled by an aureole. The priest, who had hitherto always succeeded in checking anything of this sort, felt alarmed for a moment and hastily withdrew his arms. Then he exclaimed authoritatively:

'Be calm and reasonable; I desire you to be so. God will refuse your homage if you do not offer it to Him in calm reason. What is most urgent now is to restore your strength.'

Rose returned to the room, quite distracted at not having been able to find any ether. The priest told her to remain by the bedside, while he said to Marthe in a more gentle tone:

'Don't distress yourself. God will be touched by your love. When the proper time comes, He will come down to you and fill you with everlasting felicity.'

Then he quitted the room, leaving the ailing woman quite radiant, like one raised from the dead. From that day forward he was able to mould her like soft wax beneath his touch. She became extremely useful to him in certain delicate missions to Madame de Condamin, and she also frequently visited Madame Rastoil when he expressed a desire that she should do so. She rendered him absolute obedience, never seeking the reason of anything he told her to do, but saying just what he instructed her to say and no more. He no longer observed any precautions with her, but bluntly taught her her lessons and made use of her as though she were a machine. She would have begged in the streets if he had ordered her to do so. When she became restless and stretched out her hands to him, with bursting heart and passion-swollen lips, he crushed her with a single word beneath the will of Heaven. She never dared to make any reply. Between her and the priest there was a wall of anger and scorn. When Abbé Faujas left her after one of the short struggles which he occasionally had with her, he shrugged his shoulders with the disdain of a strong wrestler who has been opposed by a child.

Though Marthe was so pliant in the hands of the priest, she grew more querulous and sour every day amidst all the little cares of household life. Rose said that she had never before known her to be so fractious. It was towards her husband that she specially manifested increasing bitterness and dislike. The old leaven of the Rougons' rancour was reviving in presence of this son of a Macquart, this man whom she accused of being the torture of her life. When Madame Faujas or Olympe came downstairs to sit with her in the dining-room she no longer observed any reticence, but gave full vent to her feelings against Mouret.

'For twenty years he kept me shut up like a mere clerk, with a pen behind my ear, between his jars of oil and bags of almonds! He never allowed me a pleasure or gave me a present. He has robbed me of my children; and he is quite capable of taking himself off any day to make people believe that I have made his life unendurable. It is very fortunate that you are here and can tell the truth.'

She fell foul of Mouret in this way without any provocation from him. Everything that he did, his looks, his gestures, the few words he spoke, all seemed to infuriate her. She could not even see him without being carried away by an unreasoning anger. It was at the close of their meals, when Mouret, without waiting for dessert, folded his napkin and silently rose from table, that quarrels more especially occurred.

'You might leave the table at the same time as other people,' Marthe would bitterly remark; 'it is not very polite of you to behave in that way.'

'I have finished, and I am going away,' Mouret replied in his drawling voice.

Marthe began to imagine that her husband's daily retreat from table was an intentional slight to Abbé Faujas, and thereupon she lost all control over herself.

'You are a perfect boor, you make me feel quite ashamed!' she cried. 'I should have a nice time of it with you if I had not been fortunate enough to make some friends who console me for your boorish ways! You don't even know how to behave yourself at table, you prevent me from enjoying a single meal. Stay where you are, do you hear? If you don't want to eat any more, you can look at us.'

He finished folding his napkin as calmly as though he had not heard a word of what his wife had said, and then, with slow and deliberate steps, he left the room. They could hear him go upstairs and lock himself in his office. Thereupon Marthe, choking with anger, burst out:

'Oh, the monster! He is killing me; he is killing me!'

Madame Faujas was obliged to console and soothe her. Rose ran to the foot of the stairs and called out at the top of her voice, so that Mouret might hear her through the closed door:

'You are a monster, sir! Madame is quite right to call you a monster!'

Some of their quarrels were particularly violent. Marthe, whose reason was on the verge of giving way, had got it into her head that her husband wished to beat her. It was a fixed idea of hers. She asserted that he was only waiting and watching for an opportunity. He had not dared to do it yet, she said, because he had never found her alone, and in the night-time he was afraid lest she should cry out for assistance. Rose on her side swore that she had seen her master hiding a thick stick in his office. Madame Faujas and Olympe showed no hesitation in believing these stories, expressed the greatest pity for their landlady, and constituted themselves her protectors. 'That brute,' as they now called Mouret, would not venture, they said, to ill-treat her in their presence; and they told her to come for them at night if he should show the least sign of violence. The house was now in a constant state of alarm.

'He is capable of any wickedness,' exclaimed the cook.

That year Marthe observed all the religious ceremonies of Passion Week with the greatest fervour. On Good Friday she knelt in agony in the black-draped church, while the candles were extinguished, one by one, midst the mournful swell of voices rising through the gloomy nave. It seemed to her as though her own breath were dying away with the light of the candles. When the last one went out, and the darkness in front of her seemed implacable and repelling, she fainted away, remaining for an hour bent in an attitude of prayer without the women around her being aware of her condition. When she came to herself, the church was deserted. She imagined that she was being scourged with rods and that blood was streaming from her limbs; she experienced too such excruciating pains in her head that she raised her hands to it, as if to pull out thorns whose points she seemed to feel piercing her skull. She was in a strange condition at dinner that evening. She was still suffering from nervous shock; when she closed her eyes, she saw the souls of the expiring candles flitting away through the darkness, and she mechanically examined her hands for the wounds whence her blood had streamed. All the Passion bled within her.

Madame Faujas, seeing her so unwell, persuaded her to go to rest early, accompanied her to her room and put her to bed. Mouret, who had a key of the bedroom, had already retired to his office, where he spent his evenings. When Marthe, covered up to her chin with the blankets, said that she was quite warm and felt better, Madame Faujas went to blow out the candle that she might be better able to sleep; but at this Marthe sprang up in fear and cried out beseechingly:

'No! no! don't put out the light! Put it on the drawers so that I can see it. I should die if I were left in the dark.'

Then, with staring eyes, trembling as though at the recollection of some dreadful tragedy, she murmured in tones of terrified pity: 'Oh, it is horrible! it is horrible!'

She fell back upon the pillow and seemed to drop asleep, and Madame Faujas then silently left the room. That evening the whole house was in bed by ten o'clock. As Rose went upstairs, she noticed that Mouret was still in his office. She peeped through the key-hole and saw him asleep there with his head on the table, and a kitchen-candle smoking dismally by his side.

'Well, I won't wake him,' she said to herself as she continued her journey upstairs. 'Let him get a stiff neck, if he likes.'

About midnight, when the whole house was wrapped in slumber, cries were heard proceeding from the first floor. At first they were but wails, but they soon grew into loud howls, like the hoarse, choking calls of one who is being murdered, Abbé Faujas, awaking with a start, called his mother, who scarcely gave herself time to slip on a petticoat before she went to knock at Rose's door.

'Come down immediately!' she said, 'I'm afraid Madame Mouret is being murdered.'

The screams became louder than ever. The whole house was soon astir. Olympe with her shoulders simply hidden by a kerchief, made her appearance with Trouche, who had only just returned home, slightly intoxicated. Rose hastened downstairs, followed by the lodgers.

'Open the door, madame, open the door!' she cried excitedly, hammering with her fist on Madame Mouret's door.

Deep sighs alone answered her; then there was the sound of a body falling, and a terrible struggle seemed to be taking place on the floor in the midst of overturned furniture. The walls shook with repeated heavy blows, and a sound like a death-rattle passed under the door, so terrible that the Faujases and the Trouches turned pale as they looked at each other.

'Her husband is murdering her,' murmured Olympe.

'Yes, you are right; the brute is killing her,' said the cook. 'I saw him pretending to be asleep when I came up to bed. But he was planning it all then.'

She once more thundered on the door with both her fists, repeating:

'Open the door, sir! We shall go for the police if you don't. Oh, the scoundrel! he will end his days on the scaffold!'

Then the groans and cries began again. Trouche declared that the blackguard must be bleeding the poor lady like a fowl.

'We must do something more than knock at the door,' said Abbé Faujas, coming forward. 'Wait a moment.'

He put one of his broad shoulders to the door and with a slow persistent effort forced it open. The women then rushed into the room, where the most extraordinary spectacle met their eyes.

Marthe, her night-dress torn, lay panting on the floor, bruised, scratched, and bleeding. Her dishevelled hair was twined round the leg of a chair, and her hands had so firmly gripped hold of the chest of drawers, that it was pulled from its place and now stood in front of the door. Mouret was standing in a corner, holding the candle and gazing at his wife with an expression of stupefaction.

Abbé Faujas had to push the chest of drawers on one side.

'You are a monster!' cried Rose, rushing up to Mouret and shaking her fist at him. 'To treat a woman like that! He would have killed her, if we hadn't come in time to prevent him.'

Madame Faujas and Olympe bent down over Marthe.

'Poor dear!' said the former. 'She had a presentiment of something this evening. She was quite frightened.'

'Where are you hurt?' asked Olympe. 'There is nothing broken, is there? Look at her shoulder, it's quite black; and her knee is dreadfully grazed. Make yourself easy; we are with you, and we will protect you.'

But Marthe was now simply wailing like a child. While the two women were examining her, forgetting that there were men in the room, the Abbé quietly put the furniture in order. Then Rose helped Madame Faujas and Olympe to carry Marthe back to bed, and when they had done so and had knotted up her hair, they lingered for a moment, looking curiously round the room and waiting for explanations. Mouret still stood in the same corner holding the candle, as though petrified by what he had seen.

'I assure you,' he said, 'that I didn't hurt her; I didn't touch her with the tip of my finger even.'

'You've been waiting for your opportunity this month past,' cried Rose in a fury; 'we all know that well enough; we have watched you. The dear lady was quite expecting your brutality. Don't tell lies about it; they put me quite beside myself!'

The other women cast threatening glances at him, though they did not feel at liberty to speak to him in the same way as Rose had done.

'I assure you,' repeated Mouret in a gentle voice, 'that I did not strike her. I was just about to get into bed, but the moment I touched the candle, which was standing on the drawers, she awoke with a start, stretched out her arms with a cry, and then began to beat her forehead with her fists and tear her flesh with her nails.'

The cook shook her head furiously.

'Why didn't you open the door?' she cried; 'we knocked loud enough.'

'I assure you that I have done nothing,' he reiterated still more gently than before. 'I could not tell what was the matter with her. She threw herself upon the floor, bit herself and leapt about so violently as almost to break the furniture. I did not dare to go near her; I was quite overcome. I twice called to you to come in, but she was screaming so loudly that she must have prevented you from hearing me. I was in a terrible fright, but I have done nothing, I assure you.'

'Oh yes! She's been beating herself, hasn't she?' jeered Rose.

Then, addressing herself to Madame Faujas, she added:

'He threw his stick out of the window, no doubt, when he heard us coming.'

Mouret at last put the candle back upon the chest of drawers and seated himself on a chair, with his hands upon his knees. He made no further attempt to defend himself, but gazed with stupefaction at the women who were shaking their skinny arms in front of the bed. Trouche had exchanged a glance with Abbé Faujas. That poor fellow, Mouret, certainly had no very ferocious appearance as he sat there in his nightgown, with a yellow handkerchief tied round his bald head. However, the others all closed round the bed and looked at Marthe, who, with distorted face, seemed to be waking from a dream.

'What is the matter, Rose?' she asked. 'What are all these people doing here? I am quite exhausted. Ask them to leave me in peace.'

Rose hesitated for a moment.

'Your husband is in the room, madame,' she said at last. 'Aren't you afraid to remain alone with him?'

Marthe looked at her in astonishment.

'No, no; not at all,' she replied. 'Go away; I am very sleepy.'

Thereupon the five people quitted the room, leaving Mouret seated on the chair, staring blankly towards the bed.

'He won't be able to fasten the door again,' the cook exclaimed as she went back upstairs. 'At the very first sound I shall fly down and be at him. I shall go to bed with my things on. Did you hear what stories the dear lady told to prevent him from appearing such a brute? She would let herself be murdered rather than accuse him. What a hypocritical face he has, hasn't he?'

The three women remained for a few moments on the landing of the second floor, holding their candlesticks the while. No punishment, said they, would be severe enough for such a man. Then they separated. The house fell into its wonted quietness, and the remainder of the night passed off peacefully. The next morning, when the three women eagerly referred to the terrible scene, they found Marthe nervous, shamefaced and confused. She gave them no answer but cut the conversation short. When she was alone she sent for a workman to come and mend the door. Madame Faujas and Olympe came to the conclusion that Madame Mouret's reticence was caused by a desire to avoid scandal.

The next day, Easter Day, Marthe tasted at Saint-Saturnin's all the sweetness of an awakening of the soul amidst the triumphant joys of the Resurrection. The gloom of Good Friday was swept away by the brightness of Easter; the church was decked in white, and was full of perfume and light, as though for the celebration of some divine nuptials; the voices of the choir-boys sounded flute-like, and Marthe, amidst their songs of joyful praise, felt transported by even more thrilling, overwhelming sensations than during the celebration of the crucifixion. She returned home with glistening eyes and hot dry tongue, and sat up late, talking with a gaiety that was unusual in her. Mouret was already in bed when she at last went upstairs. About midnight, terrible cries again echoed through the house.

The scene that had taken place two days previously was repeated: only on this occasion, at the first knock, Mouret came in his nightgown and with distracted face to open the door. Marthe, still dressed, was lying on her stomach, sobbing violently and beating her head against the foot of the bed. The bodice of her dress looked as though it had been torn open, and there were two big scratches on her throat.

'He has tried to strangle her this time!' exclaimed Rose.

The women undressed her. Mouret, after opening the door, had got back into bed, trembling all over and as pale as a sheet. He made no attempt to defend himself; he did not even appear to hear the indignant remarks that were made about him, but simply covered himself up and lay close to the wall. Similar scenes now took place at irregular intervals. The house lived in a state of fear lest a crime should be committed; and, at the slightest noise, the occupants of the second floor were astir. Marthe, however, still avoided all allusions to the matter, and absolutely forbade Rose to prepare a folding bed for Mouret in his office. When the morning came, it seemed to take away from her the very recollection of the scene of the night.

However, it was gradually reported about the neighbourhood that strange things happened at the Mourets'. It was said that the husband belaboured his wife every night with a bludgeon. Rose had made Madame Faujas and Olympe swear that they would say nothing on the subject, as her mistress seemingly wished to keep silence upon it; but she herself, by her expressions of pity and her allusions and her reservations, materially contributed to set afloat amongst the tradesmen the stories that became current. The butcher, who was a great jester, asserted that Mouret had thrashed his wife on account of the priest, but the greengrocer's wife defended 'the poor lady,' who was, she declared, an innocent lamb quite incapable of doing any wrong. The baker's spouse, on the other hand, considered that Mouret was one of those men who ill-treat their wives for mere pleasure and amusement. In the market-place people raised their eyes to heaven when they spoke of the matter, and referred to Marthe in the same terms of caressing endearment that they would have used in speaking of a sick child. Whenever Olympe went to buy a pound of cherries or a basket of strawberries, the conversation inevitably turned upon the Mourets, and for a quarter of an hour there was a stream of sympathetic remarks.

'Well, and how are things getting on in your house?'

'Oh, don't speak of it! She is weeping her life away. It is most pitiable. One could almost wish to see her die.'

'She came to buy some anchovies the other day, and I noticed that one of her cheeks was scratched.'

'Oh, yes! he nearly kills her! If you could only see her body as I have seen it! It is nothing but one big sore. When she is down on the ground he kicks her with his heels. I am in constant fear of finding in the morning that he has split her head open during the night.'

'It must be very unpleasant for you, living in such a house. I should go somewhere else, if I were in your place. It would make me quite ill to be mixed up with such horrors every night.'

'But what would become of the poor woman? She is so refined and gentle! We stay on for her sake—five sous, isn't it, this pound of cherries?'

'Yes; five sous. Well, it's very good of you; you show a kind heart.'

This story of a husband who waited till midnight to fall upon his wife with a bludgeon excited the greatest interest amongst the gossips of the market-place. There were further terrible details every day. One pious woman asserted that Mouret was possessed by an evil spirit, and that he seized his wife by the neck with his teeth with such violence that Abbé Faujas was obliged to make the sign of the cross three times in the air with his left thumb before the monster could be made to let go his hold. Then, she added, Mouret fell to the ground like a great lump, and a huge black rat leapt out of his mouth and vanished, though not the slightest hole could be discovered in the flooring. The tripe-seller at the corner of the Rue Taravelle terrified the neighbourhood by promulgating the theory that 'the scoundrel had perhaps been bitten by a mad dog.'

The story, however, was not credited among the higher classes of the inhabitants of Plassans. When it was mooted about the Cours Sauvaire it afforded the retired traders much amusement, as they sat on the benches there, basking in the warm May sun.

'Mouret is quite incapable of beating his wife,' said the retired almond-dealers; 'he looks as though he had had a whipping himself, and he no longer even comes out for a turn on the promenade. His wife must be keeping him on dry bread.'

'One can never tell,' said a retired captain. 'I knew an officer in my regiment whose wife used to box his ears for a mere yes or no. That went on for ten years. Then one day she took it into her head to kick him; but that made him quite furious and he nearly strangled her. Perhaps Mouret has the same dislike to being kicked as my friend had.'

'He probably has a yet greater dislike to priests,' said another of the company with a sneer.

For some time Madame Rougon appeared quite unconscious of the scandal which was occupying the attention of the town. She preserved a smiling face and ignored the allusions which were made before her. One day, however, after a long visit from Monsieur Delangre, she arrived at her daughter's house looking greatly distressed, her eyes filled with tears.

'Ah, my dear!' she cried, clasping Marthe in her arms, 'what is this that I have just heard? Can your husband really have so far forgotten himself so as to have raised his hand against you? It is all a pack of falsehoods, isn't it? I have given it the strongest denial. I know Mouret. He has been badly brought up, but he is not a wicked man.'

Marthe blushed. She was overcome by that embarrassment and shame which she experienced every time this subject was alluded to in her presence.

'Ah! madame will never complain!' cried Rose with her customary boldness. 'I should have come and informed you a long time ago if I had not been afraid of madame being angry with me.'

The old lady let her hands fall with an expression of extreme grief and surprise.

'It is really true, then,' she exclaimed, 'that he beats you! Oh, the wretch! the wretch!'

Thereupon she began to weep.

'For me to have lived to *my* age to see such things! A man whom we have overwhelmed with kindnesses ever since his father's death, when he was only a little clerk with us! It was Rougon who desired your marriage. I told him more than once that Mouret looked like a scoundrel. He has never treated us well; and he only came to live at Plassans for the sake of setting us at defiance with the few sous he has got together. Thank heaven, we stand in no need of him; we are richer than he is, and it is that which annoys him. He is very mean-spirited, and so jealous that he has always refused to set foot in my drawing-room. He knows he would burst with envy there. But I won't leave you in the power of such a monster, my dear. There are laws, happily.'

'Oh don't be uneasy! There has been much exaggeration, I assure you,' said Marthe, who was growing more and more ill at ease.

'You see that she is trying to defend him!' cried the cook.

At this moment, Abbé Faujas and Trouche, who had been conferring together at the bottom of the garden, came up, attracted by the sound of the conversation.

'I am a most unhappy mother, your reverence,' said Madame Rougon piteously. 'I have only one daughter near me now, and I hear she is weeping her eyes out from ill-treatment. But you live in the same house, and I beg you to protect and console her.'

The Abbé fixed his eyes upon the old woman, as though he were trying to guess the real meaning of this sudden manifestation of distress.

'I have just seen some one whom I would rather not name,' she continued, returning the Abbé's glance. 'This person has quite alarmed me. God knows that I don't want to do anything to injure my son-in-law! But it is my duty— is it not?—to defend my daughter's interests. Well, my son-in-law is a wretch; he ill-treats his wife, he scandalises the whole town, and mixes himself up in all sorts of dirty affairs. You will see that he will also compromise himself in political matters when the elections come on. The last time it was he who put himself at the head of the riff-raff of the suburbs. It will kill me, your reverence!'

'Monsieur Mouret would not allow anybody to make remarks to him about his conduct,' the Abbé at last ventured to say.

'But I can't abandon my daughter to such a man!' cried Madame Rougon. 'I will not allow it that we should be dishonoured. Justice is not made for dogs.'

Trouche, who was swaying himself about, took advantage of a momentary pause to exclaim:

'Monsieur Mouret is mad!'

The words seemed to fall with all the force of a blow from a club, and everybody looked at the speaker.

'I mean that he has a weak head,' continued Trouche. 'You've only got to look at his eyes. I may tell you that I don't feel particularly easy myself. There was a man at Besançon who adored his daughter, but he murdered her one night without knowing what he was doing.'

'The master has been cracked for a long time past,' said Rose.

'But this is frightful!' cried Madame Rougon. 'Really, I fear you may be right. The last time I saw him he had a most extraordinary expression on his face. He never had very sharp wits. Ah! my poor dear, promise to confide everything to me. I shall not be able to sleep quietly after this. Listen to me now; at the first sign of any extravagant conduct on your husband's part, don't hesitate, don't run any further risk—madmen must be placed in confinement.'

After this speech, she went off. When Trouche was again alone with Abbé Faujas, he gave one of those unpleasant grins that exposed his black teeth to view.

'Our landlady will owe me a big taper,' he said. 'She will be able to kick about at nights as much as she likes.'

The priest, with his face quite ashy and his eyes turned to the ground, made no reply. Then he shrugged his shoulders and went off to read his breviary under the arbour at the bottom of the garden.

XVIII

On Sundays Mouret, like many of the other retired traders of Plassans, used to take a stroll about the town. It was on Sundays only that he now emerged from that lonely seclusion in which he buried himself, overcome by a sort of shame. And his Sunday outing was gone through quite mechanically. In the morning he shaved himself, put on a clean shirt, and brushed his coat and hat; then, after breakfast, without quite knowing how, he found himself in the street, walking along slowly, with his hands behind his back and looking very sedate and neat.

As he was leaving his house one Sunday, he saw Rose talking with much animation to Monsieur Rastoil's cook on the pathway of the Rue Balande. The two servants became silent when they caught sight of him. They looked at him with such a peculiar expression that he felt behind him to ascertain whether his handkerchief was hanging out of his pocket. When he reached the Place of the Sub-Prefecture he turned his head, looked back, and saw them still standing in the same place. Rose was imitating the reeling of a drunken man, while the president's cook was laughing loudly.

'I am walking too quickly and they are making fun of me,' thought Mouret.

He thereupon slackened his pace. As he passed through the Rue de la Banne towards the market, the shopkeepers ran to their doors and watched him curiously. He gave a little nod to the butcher, who looked confused and did not return the salutation. The baker's wife, to whom he raised his hat, seemed quite alarmed and hastily stepped backwards. The greengrocer, the pastrycook and the grocer pointed him out to each other from opposite sides of the street. As he went along there was ever excitement behind him, people clustered together in groups, and a great deal of talking, mingled with laughs and grins, ensued.

'Did you notice how quickly he was walking?'

'Yes, indeed, when he wanted to stride across the gutter he almost jumped.'

'It is said that they are all like that.'

'I felt quite frightened. Why is he allowed to come out? It oughtn't to be permitted.'

Mouret was beginning to feel timid, and dared not venture to look round again. He experienced a vague uneasiness, though he could not feel quite sure that it was about himself that the people were all talking. He quickened his steps and began to swing his arms about. He regretted that he had put on his old overcoat, a hazel-coloured one and no longer of a fashionable cut. When he reached the market-place, he hesitated for a moment, and then boldly strode into the midst of the greengrocers' stalls. The mere sight of him caused quite a commotion there.

All the housewives of Plassans formed in a line about his path, the market-women stood up by their stalls, with their hands on their hips, and stared hard at him. People even pushed one another to get a sight of him, and some of the women mounted on to the benches in the corn-market. Mouret still further quickened his steps and tried to disengage himself from the crowd, not as yet able to believe that it was he who was causing all this excitement.

'Well, anyone would think that his arms were windmill sails,' said a peasant-woman who was selling fruit.

'He flies on like a shot; he nearly upset my stall,' exclaimed another woman, a greengrocer.

'Stop him! stop him!' the millers cried facetiously. Then Mouret, overcome by curiosity, halted and rose on tiptoes to see what was the matter. He imagined that someone had just been detected thieving. But a loud burst of laughter broke out from the crowd, and there were shouts and hisses, all sorts of calls and cries.

'There's no harm in him; don't hurt him.'

'Ah! I'm not so sure of that. I shouldn't like to trust myself too near him. He gets up in the night and strangles people.'

'He certainly looks a bad one.'

'Has it come upon him suddenly?'

'Yes, indeed, all at once. And he used to be so kind and gentle! I'm going away; all this distresses me. Here are the three sous for the turnips.'

Mouret had just recognised Olympe in the midst of a group of women, and he went towards her. She had been buying some magnificent peaches, which she carried in a very fashionable-looking handbag. And she was evidently relating some very moving story, for all the gossips around her were breaking out into exclamations and clasping their hands with expressions of pity.

'Then,' said she, 'he caught her by the hair, and he would have cut her throat with a razor which was lying on the chest of drawers if we hadn't arrived just in time to prevent the murder. But don't say anything to her about it: it would only bring her more trouble.'

'What trouble?' asked Mouret in amazement. The listeners hurried away, and Olympe assumed an expression of careful watchfulness as, in her turn, she warily slipped off, saying:

'Don't excite yourself, Monsieur Mouret. You had better go back home.'

Mouret took refuge in a little lane that led to the Cours Sauvaire. Thereupon the shouts increased in violence, and for a few moments he was pursued by the angry uproar of the market-folk.

'What is the matter with them to-day?' he wondered. 'Could it be me that they were jeering at? But I never heard my name mentioned. Something out of the common must have happened.'

He then took off his hat and examined it, imagining that perhaps some street lad had thrown a handful of mud at it. It was all right, however, and there was nothing fastened on to his coat-tails. This examination soothed him a little, and he resumed his sedate walk through the silent lane, and quietly turned on to the Cours Sauvaire.

The usual groups of friends were sitting on the benches there.

'Hallo! here's Mouret!' cried the retired captain, with an expression of great astonishment.

The liveliest curiosity became manifest on the sleepy faces of the others. They stretched out their necks without rising from their seats, while Mouret stood in front of them. They examined him minutely from head to foot.

'Ah! you are taking a little stroll?' said the captain, who seemed the boldest.

'Yes, just a short stroll,' replied Mouret, in a listless fashion. 'It's a very fine day.'

The company exchanged meaning smiles. They were feeling chilly and the sky had just become overcast.

'Very fine,' said a retired tanner; 'you are easily pleased. It is true, however, that you are already wearing winter clothes. What a funny overcoat that is of yours!'

The smiles now grew into grins and titters. A sudden idea seemed to strike Mouret.

'Just look and tell me,' said he, suddenly turning round, 'have I got a sun on my back?'

The retired almond-dealers could no longer keep serious, but burst into loud laughter. The captain, who was the jester of the company, winked.

'A sun?' he asked, 'where? I can only see a moon.' The others shook with laughter. They thought the captain excessively witty.

'A moon?' said Mouret; 'be kind enough to remove it. It has caused me much inconvenience.'

The captain gave him three or four taps on the back, and then exclaimed:

'There, you are rid of it now. But it must, indeed, be extremely inconvenient to have a moon on one's back. You are not looking very well.'

'I am not very well,' Mouret replied in his listless indifferent way.

Then, imagining that he heard a titter, he added: 'But I am very well taken care of at home. My wife is very kind and attentive, and quite spoils me. But I need rest, and that is the reason why I don't come out now as I used to do. Directly I am better, I shall look after business again.'

'But they say it is your wife who is not very well,' interrupted the retired tanner bluntly.

'My wife! There is nothing the matter with her! It is a pack of falsehoods! There is nothing the matter with her—nothing at all. People say things against us because—because we keep quietly at home. Ill, indeed! my wife! She is very strong, and never even has so much the matter with her as—as a headache.'

He went on speaking in short sentences, stammering and hesitating in the uneasy way of a man who is telling falsehoods; full too of the embarrassment of a whilom gossip who has become tongue-tied. The retired traders shook their heads with pitying looks, and the captain tapped his forehead with his finger. A former hatter of the suburbs who had scrutinised Mouret from his cravat to the bottom button of his overcoat, was now absorbed in the examination of his boots. The lace of the one on the left foot had come undone, and this seemed to the hatter a most extraordinary circumstance. He nudged his neighbours' elbows, and winked as he called their attention to the loosened lace. Soon the whole bench had eyes for nothing else but the lace. It was the last proof. The men shrugged their shoulders in a way that seemed to imply that they had lost their last spark of hope.

'Mouret,' said the captain, in a paternal fashion, 'fasten up your boot-lace.'

Mouret glanced at his feet, but did not seem to understand; and he went on talking. Then, as no one replied, he became silent, and after standing there for a moment or two longer he quietly continued his walk.

'He will fall, I'm sure,' exclaimed the master-tanner, who had risen from his seat that he might keep Mouret longer in view.

When Mouret got to the end of the Cours Sauvaire, and passed in front of the Young Men's Club, he was again greeted with the low laughs which had followed him since he had set foot out of doors. He could distinctly see Séverin Rastoil, who was standing at the door of the club, pointing him out to a group of young men. Clearly, he thought, it was himself who was thus providing sport for the town. He bent his head and was seized with a kind of fear, which he could not explain to himself, as he hastily stepped past the houses. Just as he was about to turn into the Rue Canquoin, he heard a noise behind him, and, turning his head, he saw three lads following him; two of them were big, impudent-looking boys, while the third was a very little one, with a serious face. The latter was holding in his hand a dirty orange which he had picked out of the gutter. Mouret made his way along the Rue Canquoin, and then, crossing the Place des Récollets, he reached the Rue de la Banne. The lads were still following him.

'Do you want your ears pulled?' he called out, suddenly stepping up to them.

They dashed on one side, shouting and laughing, and made their escape on their hands and knees. Mouret turned very red, realising that he was an object of ridicule. He felt a perfect fear of crossing the Place of the Sub-Prefecture, and passing in front of the Rougons' windows with a following of street-arabs, whom he could hear, increasing in numbers and boldness, behind him. As he went on, he was obliged to step out of his way to avoid his mother-in-law, who was returning from vespers with Madame de Condamin.

'Wolf! Wolf!' cried the lads.

Mouret, with perspiration breaking out on his brow, and his feet stumbling against the flagstones, overheard old Madame Rougon say to the wife of the conservator of rivers and forests:

'See! there he is, the scoundrel! It is disgraceful; we can't tolerate it much longer.'

Thereupon Mouret could no longer restrain himself from setting off at a run. With swinging arms and a look of distraction upon his face, he rushed into the Rue Balande while some ten or a dozen street-arabs dashed after him. It seemed to him as though all the shopkeepers of the Rue de la Banne, the market-women, the promenaders of the Cours, the young men from the club, the Rougons, the Condamins —all the people of Plassans, in fact—were surging onwards behind his back, breaking out into laughs and jeers, as he sped up the hilly street. The lads stamped and slid over the pavement, making indeed as much noise in that usually quiet neighbourhood as a pack of hounds might have made.

'Catch him!' they screamed.

'Hie! What a scarecrow he looks in that overcoat of his!'

'Some of you go round by the Rue Taravelle, and then you'll nab him!'

'Cut along! cut along as hard as you can go!'

Mouret, now quite frantic, made a desperate rush towards his door, but his foot slipped and he tumbled upon the footpavement, where he lay for a few moments, utterly overcome. The lads, afraid lest he should kick out at them, formed a circle around and vented screams of triumph, while the smallest of them, gravely stepping forward, threw the rotten orange at Mouret. It flattened itself against his left eye. He rose up with difficulty, and went in to his house without attempting to wipe himself. Rose was forced to come out with a broom and drive the young ragamuffins away.

From that Sunday forward all Plassans was convinced that Mouret was a lunatic who ought to be placed under restraint. The most surprising statements were made in support of this belief. It was said, for instance, that he shut himself up for days together in a perfectly empty room which had not been touched with a broom for a whole year; and those who circulated this story vouched for its truth, as they had it, they said, from Mouret's own cook. The accounts differed as to what he did in that empty room. The cook said that he pretended to be dead, a statement which thrilled the whole neighbourhood with horror. The market-people firmly believed that he kept a coffin concealed in the room, laid himself at full length in it, with his eyes open and his hands upon his breast, and remained like that from morning till night.

'The attack had been threatening him for a long time past,' Olympe remarked in every shop she entered. 'It was brooding in him; he had for a long time been very melancholy and low-spirited, hiding in out-of-the-way corners, just like an animal, you know, that feels ill. The very first day I set foot in the house I said to my husband, "The landlord seems to be in a bad way." His eyes were quite yellow and he had such a queer look about him. Afterwards he went on in the strangest way; he had all sorts of extraordinary whims and crotchets. He used to count every lump of sugar, and lock everything up, even the bread. He was so dreadfully miserly that his poor wife hadn't even a pair of boots to put on. Ah! poor thing, she has a dreadful time of it, and I pity her from the bottom of my heart. Imagine the life she leads with a madman who can't even behave decently at table! He throws his napkin away in the middle of dinner, and stalks off, looking stupefied, after having made a horrible mess in his plate. And such a temper he has, too! He used to make the most terrible scenes just because the mustard pot wasn't in its right place. But now he doesn't speak at all, though he glares like a wild beast, and springs at people's throats without uttering a word. Ah! I could tell you some strange stories, if I liked.'

When she had thus excited her listeners' curiosity, and they began to press her with questions, she added:

'No, no; it is no business of mine. Madame Mouret is a perfect saint, and bears her suffering like a true Christian. She has her own ideas on the matter, and one must respect them. But, would you believe it, he tried to cut her throat with a razor!'

The story she told was always the same, but it never failed to produce a great effect. Fists were clenched, and women talked of strangling Mouret. If any incredulous person shook his head, he was put to confusion by a summons to explain the dreadful scenes which took place every night. Only a madman, people said, was capable of flying in that way at his wife's throat the moment she went to bed. There was a spice of mystery in the affair which helped materially to spread the story about the town. For nearly a month the rumours went on gaining strength. Yet, in spite of Olympe's tragical gossipings, peace had been restored at the Mourets' and the nights now passed in quietness. Marthe exhibited much nervous impatience when her friends, without openly speaking on the subject, advised her to be very careful.

'You will only go your own way, I suppose,' said Rose. 'Well, you'll see, he will begin again, and we shall find you murdered one of these fine mornings.'

Madame Rougon now ostentatiously called at the house every other day. She entered it with an air of extreme uneasiness, and, as soon as the door was opened, she asked Rose:

'Well! has anything happened to-day?' Then, as soon as she caught sight of her daughter, she kissed her, and threw her arms round her with a great show of affection, as though she had been afraid that she might not find her alive. She passed the most dreadful nights, she said; she trembled at every ring of the bell, imagining that it was the signal of the tidings of some dreadful calamity; and she no longer had any pleasure in living. When Marthe told her that she was in no danger whatever she looked at her with an expression of admiration, and exclaimed:

'You are a perfect angel! If I were not here to look after you, you would allow yourself to be murdered without raising even a sigh. But make yourself easy; I am watching over you, and am taking all precautions. The first time your husband raises his little finger against you, he will hear from me.'

She did not explain herself any further. The truth of the matter was that she had visited every official in Plassans, and had in this way confidentially related her daughter's troubles to the mayor, the sub-prefect, and the presiding judge of the tribunal, making them promise to observe absolute secrecy about the matter.

'It is a mother in despair who tells you this,' she said with tears in her eyes. 'I am giving the honour and reputation of my poor child into your keeping. My husband would take to his bed if there were to be a public scandal, but I can't wait till there is some fatal catastrophe. Advise me, and tell me what I ought to do.'

The officials showed her the greatest sympathy and kindness. They did their best to reassure her, they promised to keep a careful watch over Madame Mouret without in any way letting it be known, and to take some active step at the slightest sign of danger. In her interviews with Monsieur Péqueur des Saulaies and Monsieur Rastoil, she drew their especial attention to the fact that, as they were her son-in-law's immediate neighbours, they would be able to interfere at once in the event of anything going wrong.

This story of a lunatic in his senses, who awaited the stroke of midnight to become mad, imparted much interest to the meetings of the guests in Mouret's garden. They showed great alacrity in going to greet Abbé Faujas. The priest came downstairs at four o'clock, and did the honours of the arbour with much urbanity, but in talking he persisted in keeping in the background, merely nodding in answer to what was said to him. For the first few days, only indirect allusions were made to the drama which was being acted in the house, but one Tuesday Monsieur Maffre, who was gazing at it with an uneasy expression, fixing his eyes upon one of the windows of the first floor, ventured to ask:

'That is the room, isn't it?'

Then, in low tones, the two parties began to discuss the strange story which was exciting the neighbourhood. The priest made some vague remarks: it was very sad, and much to be regretted, said he, and then he pitied everybody, without venturing to say anything more explicit.

'But you, Doctor,' asked Madame de Condamin of Doctor Porquier, 'you who are the family doctor, what do you think about it all?'

Doctor Porquier shook his head for some time before making any reply. He at first affected a discreet reserve.

'It is a very delicate matter,' he muttered. 'Madame Mouret is not robust, and as for Monsieur Mouret—'

'I have seen Madame Rougon,' said the sub-prefect. 'She is very uneasy.'

'Her son-in-law has always been obnoxious to her,' Monsieur de Condamin exclaimed bluntly. 'I met Mouret myself at the club the other day, and he gave me a beating at piquet. He seemed to me to be as sensible as ever. The good man was never a Solomon, you know.'

'I have not said that he is mad, in the common interpretation of the word,' said the doctor, thinking that he was being attacked: 'but neither will I say that I think it prudent to allow him to remain at large.'

This statement caused considerable emotion, and Monsieur Rastoil instinctively glanced at the wall which separated the two gardens. Every face was turned towards the doctor,

'I once knew,' he continued, 'a charming lady, who kept up a large establishment, giving dinner-parties, receiving the most distinguished members of society, and showing much sense and wit in her conversation. Well, when that lady retired to her bedroom, she locked herself in, and spent a part of the night in crawling round the room on her hands and knees, barking like a dog. The people in the house long imagined that she really had a dog in the room with her. This lady was an example of what we doctors call lucid madness.'

Abbé Surin's face was wreathed with twinkling smiles as he glanced at Monsieur Rastoil's daughters, who appeared much amused by this story of a fashionable lady turning herself into a dog. Doctor Porquier blew his nose very gravely.

'I could give you a score of other similar instances,' he continued, 'of people who appeared to be in full possession of their senses, and who yet committed the most extravagant actions as soon as they found themselves alone.'

'For my part,' said Abbé Bourrette, 'I once had a very strange penitent. She had a mania for killing flies, and could never see one without feeling an irresistible desire to capture it. She used to keep them at home strung upon knitting needles. When she came to confess, she would weep bitterly and accuse herself of the death of the poor creatures, and believe that she was damned. But I could never correct her of the habit.'

This story was very well received, and even Monsieur Péqueur des Saulaies and Monsieur Rastoil themselves condescended to smile.

'There is no great harm done,' said the doctor, 'so long as one confines one's self to killing flies. But the conduct of all lucid madmen is not so innocent as that. Some of them torture their families by some concealed vice, which has reached the degree of a mania; there are other wretched ones who drink and give themselves up to secret debauchery, or who steal because they can't help stealing, or who are mad with pride or jealousy or ambition. They are able to control themselves in public, to carry out the most complicated schemes and projects, to converse rationally and without giving any one any reason to suspect their mental weakness, but as soon as they get back to their own private life, and are alone with their victims, they surrender themselves to their delirious ideas and become brutal savages. If they don't murder straight out, they do it gradually.'

'Well, now, what about Monsieur Mouret?' asked Madame de Condamin.

'Monsieur Mouret has always been a teasing, restless, despotic sort of man. His cerebral derangement has increased with his years. I should not hesitate now to class him amongst dangerous madmen. I had a patient who used to shut herself up, just as he does, in an unoccupied room, and spend the whole day in contriving the most abominable actions.'

'But, doctor, if that is your opinion, you ought to proffer your advice,' exclaimed Monsieur Rastoil; 'you ought to warn those who are concerned.'

Doctor Porquier seemed slightly embarrassed.

'Well, we will see about it,' he said, smiling again with his fashionable doctor's smile. 'If it should be necessary and matters should become serious, I will do my duty.'

'Pooh!' cried Monsieur de Condamin satirically; 'the greatest lunatics are not those who have the reputation of being so. No brain is sound for a mad-doctor. The doctor here has just been reciting to us a page out of a book on lucid madness, which I have read, and which is as interesting as a novel.'

Abbé Faujas had been listening with curiosity, though he had taken no part in the conversation. Then, as soon as there was a pause, he remarked that their talk about mad people had a depressing effect upon the ladies, and suggested that the subject should be changed. Everybody's curiosity was fully awakened, however, and the two sets of guests began to keep a sharp watch upon Mouret's behaviour. The latter now came out into the garden for an hour a day, while the Faujases remained at table with his wife. Directly he appeared there, he came under the active surveillance of the Rastoils and the frequenters of the Sub-Prefecture. He could not stand for a moment in front of a bed of vegetables or examine a plant, or even make a gesture of any sort, without exciting in the gardens on his right and left the most unfavourable comments. Everyone was turning against him. Monsieur de Condamin was the only person who still defended him. One day the fair Octavie said to him as they were at luncheon:

'What difference can it make to you whether Mouret is mad or not?'

'To me, my dear? Absolutely none,' he said in astonishment.

'Very well, then, allow that he is mad, since everyone says he is. I don't know why you always persist in holding a contrary opinion to your wife's. It won't prove to your advantage, my dear. Have the intelligence, at Plassans, not to be too intelligent.'

Monsieur de Condamin smiled.

'You are right, my dear, as you always are,' he said gallantly; 'you know that I have put my fortune in your hands—don't wait dinner for me. I am going to ride to Saint-Eutrope to have a look at some timber they are felling.'

Then he left the room, biting the end off a cigar.

Madame de Condamin was well aware that he had a flame for a young girl in the neighbourhood of Saint-Eutrope; but she was very tolerant and had even saved him twice from the consequences of scandalous intrigues. On his side, he felt very easy about his wife; he knew that she was much too prudent to give cause for scandal at Plassans.

'You would never guess how Mouret spends his time in that room where he shuts himself up!' the conservator of rivers and forests said the next morning when he called at the Sub-Prefecture. 'He is counting all the s's in the Bible. He is afraid of making any mistake about the matter, and he has already recommenced counting them for the third time. Ah! you were quite right; he is cracked from top to bottom!'

From this time forward Monsieur de Condamin was very hard upon Mouret. He even exaggerated matters and used all his skill to invent absurd stories to scare the Rastoils; but it was Monsieur Maffre whom he made his special victim. He told him one day that he had seen Mouret standing at one of the windows overlooking the street in a state of complete nudity, having only a woman's cap on his head and bowing to the empty air. Another day he asserted with amazing assurance that he had seen Mouret dancing like a savage in a little wood three leagues away; and when the magistrate seemed to doubt this story, he appeared to be vexed and declared that Mouret might very easily have got down out of his house by the water-spout without being noticed. The frequenters of the Sub-Prefecture smiled, but the next morning the Rastoils' cook spread these extraordinary stories about the town, where the legend of the man who beat his wife was assuming extraordinary proportions.

One afternoon Aurélie, the elder of Monsieur Rastoil's two daughters, related with a blushing face how on the previous night, having gone to look out of her window about midnight, she had seen their neighbour promenading about his garden, carrying a big altar candle. Monsieur de Condamin thought the girl was making fun of him, but she gave the most minute details.

'He held the candle in his left hand; and he knelt down on the ground and dragged himself along on his knees, sobbing as he did so.'

'Can it be possible that he has committed a murder and has buried the body of his victim in his garden?' exclaimed Monsieur Maffre, who had turned quite pale.

Then the two sets of guests agreed to watch some evening till midnight if necessary, to clear the matter up. The following night, indeed, they kept on the alert, in both gardens, but Mouret did not appear. Three nights were wasted in the same way. The Sub-Prefecture party was going to abandon the watch, and Madame de Condamin declared that she could not stay any longer under the chestnut trees, where it was so dreadfully dark, when all at once a light was seen flickering through the inky blackness of the ground floor of Mouret's house. When Monsieur Péqueur des Saulaies' attention was drawn to this, he slipped into the Impasse des Chevillottes to invite the Rastoils to come on to his terrace, which overlooked the neighbouring garden. The presiding judge, who was on the watch with his daughters behind the cascade, hesitated for a moment, reflecting whether he might not compromise himself politically by going to the sub-prefect's in this way, but as the night was very black, and his daughter Aurélie was most anxious to have the truth of her report manifested, he followed Monsieur Péqueur des Saulaies with stealthy steps through the darkness. It was in this manner that a representative of Legitimacy at Plassans for the first time entered the grounds of a Bonapartist official.

'Don't make a noise,' whispered the sub-prefect. 'Lean over the terrace.'

There Monsieur Rastoil and his daughters found Doctor Porquier and Madame de Condamin and her husband. The darkness was so dense that they exchanged salutations without being able to see one another. Then they all held their breath. Mouret had just appeared upon the steps, with a candle, which was stuck in a great kitchen candlestick.

'You see he has got a candle,' whispered Aurélie.

No one dissented. The fact was quite incontrovertible; Mouret certainly was carrying a candle. He came slowly down the steps, turned to the left and then stood motionless before a bed of lettuces. Then he raised his candle to throw a light upon the plants. His face looked quite yellow amidst the black night.

'What a dreadful face!' exclaimed Madame de Condamin. 'I shall dream of it, I'm certain. Is he asleep, doctor?'

'No, no,' replied Doctor Porquier, 'he is not a somnambulist; he is wide awake. Do you notice how fixed his gaze is? Observe, too, the abruptness of his movements—'

'Hush! hush!' interrupted Monsieur Péqueur des Saulaies; 'we don't require a lecture just now.'

The most complete silence then fell. Mouret had stridden over the box-edging and was kneeling in the midst of the lettuces. He held his candle down, and began searching along the trenches underneath the spreading leaves of the plants. Every now and then he made a slight examination and seemed to be crushing something and stamping it into the ground. This went on for nearly half an hour.

'He is crying; it is just as I told you,' Aurélie complacently remarked.

'It is really very terrifying,' Madame de Condamin exclaimed nervously. 'Pray let us go back into the house.'

Mouret dropped his candle and it went out. They could hear him uttering exclamations of annoyance as he went back up the steps, stumbling against them in the dark. The Rastoil girls broke out into little cries of terror, and did not quite recover from their fright till they were again in the brightly lighted drawing-room, where Monsieur Péqueur des Saulaies insisted upon the company refreshing themselves with some tea and biscuits. Madame de Condamin, who was still trembling with alarm, huddled up on a couch, said, with a touching smile, that she had never felt so overcome before, not even on the morning when she had had the reprehensible curiosity to go and see a criminal executed.

'It is strange,' remarked Monsieur Rastoil, who had been buried in thought for a moment or two; 'but Mouret looked as if he were searching for slugs amongst his lettuces. The gardens are quite ravaged by them, and I have been told that they can only be satisfactorily exterminated in the nighttime.'

'Slugs, indeed!' cried Monsieur de Condamin. 'Do you suppose he troubles himself about slugs? Do people go hunting for slugs with a candle? No; I agree with Monsieur Maffre in thinking that there is some crime at the bottom of the matter. Did this man Mouret ever have a servant who disappeared mysteriously? There ought to be an inquiry made.'

Monsieur Péqueur des Saulaies thought that his friend the conservator of rivers and forests was theorising a little further than the facts warranted. He took a sip at his tea and said:

'No, no; my dear sir. He is mad and has extraordinary fancies, but that is all. It is quite bad enough as it is.'

He then took a plate of biscuits, handed it to Monsieur Rastoil's daughter with a gallant bow, and after putting it down again continued:

'And to think this wretched man has mixed himself up in politics! I don't want to insinuate anything against your alliance with the Republicans, my dear judge, but you must allow that in Mouret the Marquis de Lagrifoul had a very peculiar supporter.'

Monsieur Rastoil, who had become very grave, made a vague gesture, without saying anything.

'And he still busies himself with these matters. It is politics, perhaps, which have turned his brain,' said the fair Octavie, as she delicately wiped her lips. 'They say he takes the greatest interest in the approaching elections, don't they, my dear?'

She addressed this question to her husband, casting a glance at him as she spoke.

'He is quite bursting over the matter!' cried Monsieur de Condamin. 'He declares that he can entirely control the election, and can have a shoemaker returned if he chooses.'

'You are exaggerating,' said Doctor Porquier. 'He no longer has the influence he used to have; the whole town jeers at him.'

'Ah! you are mistaken! If he chooses, he can lead the old quarter of the town and a great number of villages to the poll. He is mad, it is true, but that is a recommendation. I myself consider him still a very sensible person, for a Republican.'

This attempt at wit met with distinct success. Monsieur Rastoil's daughters broke out into school-girl laughs and the presiding judge himself nodded his head in approval. He threw off his serious expression, and, without looking at the sub-prefect, he said:

'Lagrifoul has not rendered us, perhaps, the services we had a right to expect, but a shoemaker would be really too disgraceful for Plassans!'

Then, as though he wanted to prevent any further remarks on the subject, he added quickly: 'Why, it is half-past one o'clock! This is quite an orgie we are having, my dear sub-prefect; we are all very much obliged to you.'

Madame de Condamin wrapped her shawl round her shoulders and contrived to have the last word.

'Well,' she said, 'we really must not let the election be controlled by a man who goes and kneels down in the middle of a bed of lettuces after twelve o'clock at night.'

That night became quite historical, and Monsieur de Condamin derived much amusement from relating the details of what had occurred to Monsieur de Bourdeu, Monsieur Maffre, and the priests, who had not seen Mouret with his candle. Three days later all the neighbourhood was asserting that the madman who beat his wife had been seen walking about with his head enveloped in a sheet. Meantime, the afternoon assemblies under the arbour were much exercised by the possible candidature of Mouret's radical shoemaker. They laughed as they studied each other's demeanour. It was a sort of political pulse-feeling. Certain confidential statements of his friend the presiding judge induced Monsieur de Bourdeu to believe that a tacit understanding might be arrived at between the Sub-Prefecture and the moderate opposition to promote the candidature of himself, and thus inflict a crushing defeat upon the Republicans. Possessed by this idea, he waxed more and more sarcastic against the Marquis de Lagrifoul, and made the most of the latter's blunders in the Chamber. Monsieur Delangre, who only called at long intervals, alleging the pressure of his municipal duties as an excuse for his infrequent appearance, smiled softly at each fresh sally of the ex-prefect.

'You've only got to bury the marquis, now, your reverence,' he said one day in Abbé Faujas's ear.

Madame de Condamin, who heard him, turned her head and laid her finger upon her lips with a pretty look of mischief.

Abbé Faujas now allowed politics to be mentioned in his presence. He even occasionally expressed an opinion in favour of the union of all honest and religious men. Thereupon all present, Monsieur Péqueur des Saulaies, Monsieur Rastoil, Monsieur de Bourdeu, and even Monsieur Maffre, grew quite warm in their expressions of desire for such an agreement. It would be so very easy, they said, for men with a stake in the country to come to an understanding together to work for the firm establishment of the great principles without which no society could hold together. Then the conversation turned upon property, and family and religion. Sometimes Mouret's name was mentioned, and Monsieur de Condamin once said:

'I never let my wife come here without feeling uneasy. I am really getting alarmed. You will see some strange things happen at the next elections if that man is still at liberty.'

Trouche did his best to frighten Abbé Faujas during the interviews which he had with him every morning. He told him the most alarming stories. The working men of the old quarter of the town, said he, were showing too much interest in Mouret; they talked of coming to see him, of judging his condition for themselves, and taking his advice.

As a rule, the priest merely shrugged his shoulders; but one day Trouche came away from him looking quite delighted. He went off to Olympe and kissed her, exclaiming:

'This time, my dear, I've managed it!'

'Has he given you leave?' she asked.

'Yes, full leave. We shall be delightfully comfortable when we have got rid of the old man.'

Olympe was still in bed. She dived under the bedclothes, and wriggled about and laughed gleefully.

'We shall have everything to do as we like with, then, shan't we? I shall take another bedroom, and go out into the garden whenever I like, and do all my cooking in the kitchen. My brother will have to let us do all that. You must have managed to frighten him very much.'

It was not till about ten o'clock that evening that Trouche made his appearance at the low café where he was accustomed to meet Guillaume Porquier and other wild young fellows. They joked him about the lateness of the hour, and playfully accused him of having been out on the ramparts courting one of the girls of the Home of the Virgin. Jests of this kind generally pleased him, but that night he remained very grave. He declared that he had been engaged with business—very serious business. It was only about midnight, when he had emptied the decanters on the counter, that he became more expansive. Then he began to talk familiarly to Guillaume, leaning the while against the wall, stammering, and lighting his pipe afresh between every two sentences.

'I saw your father this evening. He is a very good fellow. I wanted a paper from him. He was very kind, very kind indeed. He gave it to me. I have it here in my pocket. He didn't want to give it me at first, though. He said it was only the family's business. But I told him, "I am the family; I have got the wife's orders." You know her, don't you? a dear little woman. She seemed quite pleased when I went to talk the matter over with her beforehand. Then he gave me the paper. You can feel it here in my pocket.'

Guillaume looked at him, concealing his extreme curiosity with an incredulous laugh.

'I'm telling you the truth,' continued the drunkard. 'The paper's here in my pocket. Can't you feel it?'

'Oh, it's only a newspaper!' said Guillaume.

At this, Trouche sniggered, and drew a large envelope from the pocket of his overcoat, and laid it on the table amidst the cups and glasses. For a moment, though Guillaume had reached out his hand, he prevented him from taking it, but then he allowed him to have it, laughing loudly the while. The paper proved to be a most detailed statement by Doctor Porquier with respect to the mental condition of François Mouret, householder, of Plassans.

'Are they going to shut him up, then?' asked Guillaume, handing back the paper.

'That's no business of yours, my boy,' replied Trouche, who had now become distrustful again. 'This paper here is for his wife. I am merely a friend who is glad to do a service. She will act as she pleases. However, she can't go on letting herself be half murdered, poor lady!'

By the time they were turned out of the café he was so drunk that Guillaume had to accompany him to the Rue Balande. He wanted to lie down and go to sleep on every seat on the Cours Sauvaire. When they reached the Place of the Sub-Prefecture, he began to shed tears and stutter:

'I've no friends now; everyone despises me just because I'm poor. But you are a good-hearted young fellow, and you shall come and have coffee with us when we get into possession. If the Abbé interferes with us, well send him to keep the other one company. He isn't very sharp, the Abbé, in spite of all his grand airs. I can persuade him into believing anything. But you are a real friend, aren't you? Mouret is done for, old chap; we'll drink his wine together.'

When Guillaume had seen Trouche to his door, he walked back through the sleeping town and went and whistled softly before Monsieur Maffre's house. It was a signal he was making. The young Maffres, whom their father locked up in their bedroom, opened a window on the first floor and descended to the ground by the help of the bars with which the ground-floor windows were protected. Every night they thus went off to the haunts of vice in the company of Guillaume Porquier.

'Well,' he said to them, when they had reached the dark paths near the ramparts, 'we needn't trouble ourselves now. If my father talks any more about sending me off anywhere, I shall have something serious to say to him. I'll bet you that I can get elected into the Young Men's Club whenever I like now.'

The following night Marthe had a dreadful attack. She had been present in the morning at a long religious ceremony, the whole of which Olympe had insisted upon seeing. When Rose and the lodgers ran into the room upon hearing her piercing screams, they found her lying at the foot of the bed with her forehead gashed open. Mouret was kneeling in the midst of the bed-clothes, trembling all over.

'He has killed her this time!' cried the cook.

She seized Mouret in her arms, although he was in his night-dress, pushed him out of the room and into his office— the door of which was on the other side of the landing—then she went back to get a mattress and some blankets, which she threw to him. Trouche had set off at a run for Doctor Porquier. When the doctor arrived he dressed Marthe's wound. If the cut had been a trifle lower down, he said, it would have been fatal. Downstairs in the hall, he declared in the presence of them all that it was necessary to take some active steps, and that Madame Mouret's life could no longer be left at the mercy of a violent madman.

The next morning Marthe was obliged to keep her bed. She was still slightly delirious, and fancied that she saw an iron hand driving a flaming sword into her skull. Rose absolutely declined to allow Mouret to enter the room. She served him his lunch on a dusty table in his own office. He was still gazing at his plate with a look of stupefaction when Rose ushered into the room three men dressed in black.

'Are you the doctors?' he asked. 'How is she getting on?'

'She is better than she was,' replied one of the men.

Mouret began to cut his bread mechanically as though he were going to eat it.

'I wish the children were here,' he said. 'They would look after her, and we should be more lively. It is since the children went away that she has been ill. I am no longer good for anything.'

He raised a piece of bread to his mouth, and heavy tears trickled down his face. The man who had already spoken to him now said, casting at the same time a glance at his companions:

'Shall we go and fetch your children?'

'I should like it very much?' replied Mouret, rising from his seat. 'Let us start at once.'

As he went downstairs he saw no one except Trouche and his wife, who were leaning over the balustrade on the second floor, following each step he took with gleaming eyes. Olympe hurried down behind him and rushed into the kitchen, where Rose, in a state of great emotion, was watching out of the window. When a carriage, which was waiting at the door, had driven off with Mouret, she sprang up the staircase again, four steps at a time, and seizing Trouche by his shoulders, made him dance round the landing in a paroxysm of delight.

'He's packed off!' she cried.

Marthe kept her bed for a week. Her mother came to see her every afternoon and manifested the greatest affection. The Faujases and the Trouches succeeded each other in attendance at her bedside; and even Madame de Condamin called to see her several times. Nothing was said about Mouret, and Rose told her mistress that she thought he had gone to Marseilles. When Marthe, however, was able to come downstairs again, and took her place at table in the dining-room, she began to manifest some astonishment, and inquired uneasily where her husband was.

'Now, my dear lady, don't distress yourself,' said Madame Faujas, 'or you will make yourself ill again. It was absolutely necessary that something should be done, and your friends felt bound to consult together and take steps for your protection.'

'You've no reason to regret him, I'm sure,' cried Rose harshly. 'The whole neighbourhood breathes more freely now that he's no longer here. One was always afraid of him setting the place on fire or rushing out into the street with a knife. I used to hide all the knives in my kitchen and Monsieur Rastoil's cook did the same. And your poor mother nearly died of fright. Everybody who has been here while you have been ill, those ladies and gentlemen, they all said to me as I let them out, "It is a good riddance for Plassans." A place is always on the alert when a man like that is free to go about as he likes.'

Marthe listened to this stream of words with dilated eyes and pale face. She had let her spoon fall from her hand, and she gazed out of the window in front of her as though some dreadful vision rising from behind the fruit-trees in the garden was filling her with terror.

'Les Tulettes! Les Tulettes!' she gasped, as she buried her face in her trembling hands.

She fell backwards and was fainting away, when Abbé Faujas, who had finished his soup, grasped her hands, pressing them tightly, and saying in his softest tone:

'Show yourself strong before this trial which God is sending you. He will afford you consolation if you do not prove rebellious—He will grant you the happiness you deserve.'

At the pressure of the priest's hands and the tender tone of his voice, Marthe revived and sat up again with flushing cheeks.

'Oh, yes!' she cried, as she burst into sobs, 'I have great need of happiness; promise me great happiness, I beg you.'

XIX

The general elections were to take place in October. About the middle of September, Monseigneur Rousselot suddenly set off to Paris, after having a long interview with Abbé Faujas. It was said that one of his sisters, who lived at Versailles, was seriously ill. Five days later he was back in Plassans again, and he called Abbé Surin into his study to read to him. Lying back in his easy chair, closely enveloped in a padded robe of violet silk, although the weather was still quite warm, he smilingly listened to the young Abbé's womanish voice as he softly lisped the strophes of Anacreon.

'Good, very good,' he said; 'you express the music of that beautiful tongue excellently.'

Then, glancing at the timepiece with an expression of uneasiness, he added:

'Has Abbé Faujas been here yet this morning? Ah, my child, what a dreadful time I've had! My ears are still buzzing with the abominable uproar of the railway. It was raining the whole time I was in Paris. I had to rush all over the place, and saw nothing but mud everywhere.'

Abbé Surin laid his book on the corner of a small table.

'Is your lordship satisfied with the results of your journey?' he asked, with the familiarity of a petted favourite.

'I have learnt what I wanted to know,' the Bishop replied with his subtle smile. 'I ought to have taken you with me. You would have learnt a good many things that it would be useful for you to know at your age, destined as you are by your birth and connections for the episcopate.'

'I am listening, my lord,' said the young priest with a beseeching expression.

But the prelate shook his head.

'No, no; these matters are not to be spoken of. Make a friend of Abbé Faujas. He may be able to do much for you some day. I have received full information about him.'

Abbé Surin, however, clasped his hands with such a wheedling look of curiosity that Monseigneur Rousselot went on to say:

'He had some bother or other at Besançon. Afterwards he was living in great poverty in furnished apartments in Paris. He went and offered himself. Just at that time the minister was on the look-out for some priests devoted to the government. I was told that Faujas at first quite frightened him with his fierce looks and his old cassock. It was quite by chance that he was sent here. The minister was most pleasant and courteous to me.'

The Bishop finished his sentences with a slight wave of his hand, as he sought for fitting words, fearing, as it were, to say too much. But at last the affection which he felt for his secretary got the better of his caution, and he continued with more animation:

'Take my advice and try to be useful to the vicar of Saint-Saturnin's. He will want all the assistance he can get, and he seems to me to be a man who never forgets either an injury or a kindness. But don't ally yourself with him. He will end badly. That is my impression.'

'End badly?' exclaimed the young priest in surprise.

'Oh! just now he is in the full swing of triumph. But his face disquiets me, my child. He has a terrible face. That man will never die in his bed. Don't you do anything to compromise me. All I ask is to be allowed to live tranquilly—quietness is all I want.'

Abbé Surin was just taking up his book again, when Abbé Faujas was announced. Monseigneur Rousselot advanced to meet him with outstretched hands and a smiling face, addressing him as his 'dear Curé.'

'Leave us, my child,' he said to his secretary, who thereupon retired.

He spoke of his journey. His sister was better than she had been, he said, and he had been able to shake hands with some old friends.

'And did you see the minister?' asked Abbé Faujas, fixing his eves upon him.

'Yes; I thought it my duty to call upon him,' replied the Bishop, who felt that he was blushing. 'He spoke to me very favourably indeed of you.'

'Then you no longer have any doubts—you trust me absolutely?'

'Absolutely, my dear Curé. Besides, I know nothing about politics myself, and I leave everything in your hands.'

They remained talking together the whole morning. Abbé Faujas persuaded the Bishop to undertake a visitation of his diocese, and said he would go with him and prompt him as to what he should say. It would be necessary to summon all the rural deans so that the priests of the smallest villages might receive their instructions. There would be no difficulty in all this, for the clergy would act as they were told. The most delicate task would be in Plassans itself, in the district of Saint-Marc. The aristocrats there, shutting themselves up in the privacy of their houses, were entirely beyond the reach of Abbé Faujas's influence, and he had so far only been able to work upon certain ambitious royalists, such men as Rastoil and Maffre and Bourdeu. The Bishop, however, undertook to sound the feelings of various drawing-rooms in the district of Saint-Marc where he visited. But even allowing that the aristocracy should vote adversely, they would be in a ridiculous minority if they were deserted by those electors of the middle classes who were amenable to clerical influence.

'Now,' said Monseigneur Rousselot as he rose from his seat, 'it would perhaps be as well if you told me the name of your candidate, so that I may recommend him in my letters.'

Abbé Faujas smiled.

'It is dangerous to mention names,' he said. 'There wouldn't be a scrap of our candidate left in a week's time if we made his name known now. The Marquis de Lagrifoul has become quite out of the question. Monsieur de Bourdeu, who reckons upon being a candidate, is still more so. We shall leave them to destroy each other, and then, at the last moment, we shall come forward. Just say that an election on purely political grounds would be very regrettable, and that what is needed for the interests of Plassans is somebody who is not a party man, but has an intimate knowledge of the requirements of the town and the department. And you may let it be understood that such a man has been found; but don't go any further.'

The Bishop now in his turn smiled. He detained the priest for a moment as he was about to take leave.

'And Abbé Fenil?' he said, lowering his voice. 'Are you not afraid that he will do all he can to thwart your plans?'

Abbé Faujas shrugged his shoulders. 'He has made no sign at all,' he said.

'It is precisely that quietness of his that makes me uneasy,' rejoined the prelate. 'I know Fenil well. He is the most vindictive priest in my diocese. He may possibly have abandoned the ambition of beating you in the political arena, but you may be sure he will wreak personal vengeance upon you. I have no doubt that he is keeping a watch on you in his retirement.'

'Pooh!' said Abbé Faujas, showing his white teeth. 'I'll take care that he doesn't eat me up.'

Abbé Surin had just returned into the room, and when the vicar of Saint-Saturnin's had gone he made the Bishop laugh by exclaiming:

'Ah! if they could only devour each other like a couple of foxes, and leave nothing but their tails!'

The electoral campaign was on the point of commencing. Plassans, which generally remained quite calm, unexcited by political questions, was growing a little feverish and perturbed. From some invisible mouth a breath of war seemed to sweep through its quiet streets. The Marquis de Lagrifoul, who lived at La Palud, a large straggling village in the neighbourhood, had been in Plassans for the last fortnight, staying at the house of a relative of his, the Count de Valqueyras, whose mansion was one of the largest in the Saint-Marc district. The Marquis showed himself about the town, promenaded on the Cours Sauvaire, attended Saint-Saturnin's, and bowed to sundry influential townspeople, but without succeeding in throwing aside his haughty ways. His attempts to acquire popularity seemed to fail. Fresh charges against him, originating from some unknown source, were bandied about every day. It was asserted that he was a miserably incompetent man. With any other representative Plassans would long ago have had a branch line of railway connecting it with Nice. It was said, too, that if anyone from the district went to see him in Paris he had to call three or four times before he could obtain the slightest service. However, although the candidature of the Marquis was much damaged by gossip of this kind, no other candidate had openly entered the lists. There was some talk of Monsieur de Bourdeu coming forward, though it was considered that it would be extremely difficult to obtain a majority for an ex-prefect of Louis-Philippe, who had no strong connection with the place. There seemed also to be some unknown influence at work in Plassans upsetting all the previous prospects of the election by breaking the alliance between the Legitimists and the Republicans. The prevailing feeling was one of general perplexity and confusion, mingled with weariness and a desire to get the affair over as quickly as possible.

'The majority is shifting,' said the politicians of the Cours Sauvaire. 'The question is which way will it finally incline?'

Amid the excitement and restlessness which this doubtful state of things was causing in the town, the Republicans became anxious to run a candidate of their own. Their choice fell upon a master-hatter, one Maurin, a plain simple man, who was very much liked by the working-classes. In the cafés, in the evenings, Trouche expressed an opinion that Maurin was by no means sufficiently advanced in his views, and proposed in his stead a wheelwright of Les Tulettes, whose name had appeared in the list of the December proscripts.[1] This man, however, had the good sense to decline the nomination. It should be said that Trouche now gave himself out as an extreme Republican. He would have come forward himself, he said, if his wife's brother had not been a parson, but as he was—to his great regret, he declared—forced to eat the bread of the hypocrites, he felt bound to remain in the background. He was one of the first to circulate reports to the detriment of the Marquis de Lagrifoul, and he also favoured the rupture of the Republicans and the Legitimists. Trouche's greatest success was obtained by accusing the Sub-Prefecture party and the

[1]Those proscribed by Louis Napoleon at the Coup d'Etat of 1851.

adherents of Monsieur Rastoil of having brought about the confinement of poor Mouret, with the view of depriving the democratic party of one of its worthiest chiefs. On the evening when he first launched this accusation at a spirit-dealer's in the Rue Canquoin, the company assembled there looked at one other with a peculiar expression. The gossips of the old quarter of the town spoke quite feelingly about 'the madman who beat his wife,' now that he was shut up at Les Tulettes, and told one another that Abbé Faujas had simply wanted to get an inconvenient husband out of his way. Trouche repeated his charge every evening, banging his fists upon the tables of the cafés with such an air of conviction that he succeeded in persuading his listeners of the truth of his story, in which, by the way, Monsieur Péqueur des Saulaies was made to play the most extraordinary part imaginable. There was a complete reaction in Mouret's favour. He was considered to be a political victim, a man whose influence had been feared so much that he had been put out of the way in a cell at a madhouse.

'Just leave it all to me,' Trouche said with a confidential air. 'I'll expose all these precious pious folks, and I'll tell some fine stories about their Home of the Virgin. It's a nice place is that Home—a place where the ladies make assignations!'

Meanwhile Abbé Faujas almost seemed to have the power of multiplying himself. For some time past he was to be seen everywhere. He bestowed much attention upon his appearance, and was careful always to have a pleasant smile upon his face; though now and then his eyelids dropped for an instant to hide the stern fire kindling in his glance. Often with his patience quite worn out, weary of his wretched struggles, he returned to his bare room with clenched fists. Old Madame Rougon, whom he continued to see in secret, proved his good genius. She lectured him soundly whenever he felt despondent, and kept him bent before her while she told him that he must strive to please, and that he would ruin everything if he let the iron hand appear from under the velvet glove. Afterwards, when he had made himself master, he might seize Plassans by the throat and strangle it, if he liked. She herself certainly had no great affection for Plassans, against which she owed a grudge for forty years' wretchedness, and which had been bursting with jealousy of her ever since the Coup d'Etat.

'It is I who wear the cassock,' she said sometimes, with a smile; 'you carry yourself like a gendarme, my dear Curé.'

The priest showed himself particularly assiduous in his attendance at the Young Men's Club. He listened with an indulgent air to the young men talking politics, and told them, with a shake of his head, that honesty was all that was necessary. His popularity at the Club was still increasing. One evening he consented to play at billiards, and showed himself extremely skilful at the game, and sometimes, when they formed a quiet little party, he would even accept a cigarette. The club took his advice on every question that arose. His reputation for tolerance was completely established by the kind, good-natured way in which he advocated the admission of Guillaume Porquier, who had now renewed his application.

'I have seen the young man,' he said; 'he came to me to make a general confession, and I ended by giving him absolution. There is forgiveness for every sin. We must not treat him as a leper just because he pulled down a few signboards in Plassans, and ran into debt at Paris.'

When Guillaume was elected, he said to the young Maffres, with a grin:

'Well, you owe me a couple of bottles of champagne now. You see that the Curé does all that I want. I have a little machine to tickle him with in a sensitive place, and then he begins to laugh, my boys, and he can't refuse me anything.'

'Well, it doesn't seem as though he were very fond of you, anyhow,' said Alphonse; 'he looks very sourly at you.'

'Pooh! that's because I tickled him too hard. You will see that we shall soon be the best friends in the world.'

Abbé Faujas did, indeed, seem to have an affection for the doctor's son. He declared that this young man wanted guiding with a very gentle hand. In a short time Guillaume became the moving spirit of the club. He invented amusements, showed them how to make kirsch-water punch, and led young fellows fresh from college into all sorts of dissipation. His pleasant vices gave him enormous influence. While the organ was pealing above the billiard-room, he drank away, and gathered round him the sons of the most respectable people in Plassans, making them almost choke with laughter at his broad stories. The club now got into a very fast way, indulging in doubtful topics of conversation in all the corners. Abbé Faujas, however, appeared quite unconscious of it. Guillaume said that he had a splendid noddle, teeming with the greatest thoughts.

'The Abbé may be a bishop whenever he likes,' he remarked. 'He has already refused a living in Paris. He wants to stay at Plassans;

he has taken a liking to the place. I should like to nominate him as deputy. He's the sort of man we want in the Chamber! But he would never consent; he is too modest. Still it would be a good thing to take his advice when the elections are at hand. We may trust anything that he tells us. He wouldn't deceive anybody.'

Meantime, Lucien Delangre remained the serious man of the club. He showed great deference to Abbé Faujas, and won the group of studious young men over to the priest's side. He frequently walked with him to the club, talking to him with much animation, but subsiding into silence as soon as they entered the general room.

On leaving the café established beneath the Church of the Minims, the Abbé regularly went to the Home of the Virgin. He arrived there during play-time, and made his appearance with a smiling face upon the steps of the playground.

Thereupon the girls surrounded him, and disputed with each other for the possession of his pockets, in which some sacred pictures or chaplets or medals that had been blessed were always to be found. Those big girls quite worshipped him as he tapped them gently on their cheeks and told them to be good, at which they broke into sly smiles. The Sisters often complained to him that the children confided to their care were utterly unmanageable, that they fought, tore each other's hair, and did even worse things. The Abbé, however, regarded their offences as mere peccadilloes, and as a rule simply reproved the more turbulent girls in the chapel, whence they emerged in a more submissive frame of mind. Occasionally he made some rather graver piece of misconduct a pretext for sending for the parents, whom he sent away again quite touched by his kindness and good-nature. In this wise the young scapegraces of the Home of the Virgin gained him the hearts of the poor families of Plassans. When they went home in the evening, they told the most wonderful things about his reverence the Curé. It was no uncommon occurrence to find a couple of them in some secluded corner of the ramparts on the point of coming to blows to decide which of them his reverence liked the better.

'Those young hussies represent from two to three thousand votes,' Trouche thought to himself, as from the window he watched Abbé Faujas showing himself so amiable.

Trouche himself had tried to win over 'the little dears,' as he called the girls; but the priest, distrusting him, had forbidden him to set foot in the playground; and so he now confined himself to throwing sugar-plums there, when the Sisters' backs were turned.

The Abbé's day's work did not end at the Home of the Virgin. From there he started on a series of short visits to the fashionable ladies of Plassans. Madame Rastoil and Madame Delangre welcomed him with delight, and repeated his slightest words everywhere. But his great friend was Madame de Condamin. She maintained an air of easy familiarity towards him betokening the superiority of a beautiful woman who is conscious that she is all-powerful. She spoke now and again in low tones, and with meaning smiles and glances, which seemed to indicate that there was some secret understanding between them. When the priest came to see her, she dismissed her husband. 'The government was going to hold a cabinet-council,' so the conservator of rivers and forests playfully said, as he philosophically went off to mount his horse.

It was Madame Rougon who had brought Madame de Condamin to the priest's notice.

'She has not yet absolutely established her position here,' the old lady explained to Abbé Faujas. 'But there is a good deal of cleverness under those pretty, coquettish airs of hers. You can take her into your confidence, and she will see in your triumph a means of making her own success and power more complete. She will be of great use to you if you should find it necessary to give away places or crosses. She has retained an influential friend in Paris, who sends her as many red ribbons as she asks for.'

As Madame Rougon kept herself aloof from reasons of diplomacy, the fair Octavie thus became Abbé Faujas's most active ally. She won over to his side both her friends and her friends' friends. She resumed her campaign afresh every morning and exerted an astonishing amount of influence merely by the pleasant little waves of her delicately gloved fingers. She had particular success with the *bourgeoises,* and increased tenfold that feminine influence of which the priest had felt the absolute necessity as soon as he began to thread the narrow world of Plassans. She succeeded, too, in closing the mouths of the Paloques—who were growing very rabid about the state of affairs at the Mourets' house—by throwing a honied cake to the two monsters.

'What! do you still bear us a grudge, my dear lady?' she said one day, as she met the judge's wife. 'It is very wrong of you. Your friends have not forgotten you; they are thinking about you and are preparing a surprise for you.'

'A fine surprise, I'll be bound!' cried Madame Paloque, bitterly.

'No, we are not going to allow ourselves to be laughed at again. I have firmly made up my mind to keep to my own affairs.'

Madame de Condamin smiled.

'What would you say,' she asked, 'if Monsieur Paloque were to be decorated?'

The judge's wife stared in silence. A rush of blood to her face turned it quite blue, and made her terrible to behold.

'You are joking,' she stammered. 'This is only another plot against us—if it isn't true, I'll never forgive you.'

The fair Octavie swore that she had spoken nothing but the truth. The distinction would certainly be conferred upon Monsieur Paloque, but it would not be officially notified in the 'Moniteur' until after the elections, as the government did not wish it to appear as if it were buying the support of the magistracy. She also hinted that Abbé Faujas was not unconcerned in the bestowal of this long-desired reward, and said that he had talked about it to the sub-prefect.

'My husband was right, then,' exclaimed Madame Paloque, in great surprise. 'For a long time past he has been worrying me dreadfully to go and apologise to the Abbé. But I am very obstinate, and I would have let myself be killed sooner. But since the Abbé makes the first move—well, we ask nothing more than to live at peace with everyone. We will go to the Sub-Prefecture to-morrow.'

The next day the Paloques were very humble. Madame Paloque accused Abbé Fenil of the blackest conduct; and related with consummate impudence how she had gone to see him one day, and how he had spoken in her presence of turning 'the whole of Abbé Faujas's clique' neck-and-crop out of Plassans.

'If you like,' she said to the priest, taking him aside, 'I will give you a note written at the vicar-general's dictation. It concerns you. He tried, I believe, to get several discreditable stories inserted in the "Plassans Gazette."'

'How did this note come into your hands?' asked Faujas.

'Well, it's sufficient that it is there,' she replied, without any sign of embarrassment.

And, with a smile, she continued:

'I found it. I recollect, by the way, that there are two or three words written in the vicar-general's own hand. I may trust to your honour in all this, may I not? We are upright, honest people, and we don't want to compromise ourselves.'

She pretended to be affected by scruples for three days before bringing him the note; and Madame de Condamin was obliged to assure her privately that an application to have Monsieur Rastoil pensioned off would shortly be made, so that her husband could succeed to his post. Then she gave up the paper. Abbé Faujas did not wish to keep it himself, but took it to Madame Rougon, and charged her to make use of it—keeping herself, however, strictly in the background—if the vicar-general showed the slightest sign of interfering in the elections.

Madame de Condamin also dropped a hint to Monsieur Maffre that the Emperor was thinking about decorating him, and she made a formal promise to Doctor Porquier to find a suitable post for his good-for-nothing son. She showed the most obliging kindliness at the friendly afternoon meetings in the gardens. The summer was now drawing to a close, but she still arrived in light toilettes, shivering slightly and risking a cold, in order to show her arms and overcome the last scruples of the Rastoil party. It was really under the Mourets' arbour that the election was decided.

'Well, my dear sub-prefect,' said Abbé Faujas one day with a smile, when the two sets of guests were mingling together; 'the great battle is drawing near.'

They had now arrived at discussing the political struggle in a quiet friendly way. In the gardens at the back of the houses they cordially grasped each other's hands, while in front of them they still feigned an appearance of hostility. On hearing Abbé Faujas, Madame de Condamin cast a quick glance at Monsieur Péqueur des Saulaies, who bent forward with his habitual elegance and said all in a breath:

'I shall remain in my tent, Monsieur le Curé. I have been fortunate enough to make his excellency understand that it is the duty of the government, in the immediate interests of Plassans, to hold itself aloof. There will be no official candidate.'

Monsieur de Bourdeu turned pale. His eyelids quivered and his hands trembled with delight.

'There will be no official candidate?' cried Monsieur Rastoil, greatly moved by this unexpected news, and departing from the reserve which he generally maintained.

'No,' replied Monsieur Péqueur des Saulaies: 'the town contains a sufficient number of honourable men to make its own choice of a representative.'

He bowed slightly towards Monsieur de Bourdeu, who rose from his seat, and stammered:

'Undoubtedly, undoubtedly.'

While these remarks were being exchanged Abbé Surin had got up a game of 'hot and cold;' and Monsieur Rastoil's daughters and Monsieur Maffre's sons and Séverin were busy hunting for the Abbé's handkerchief, which he had rolled into a ball and hidden. All the young people were flitting about their elders, while the priest called in his falsetto voice:

'Hot! Hot!'

Angélique at length found the handkerchief in Doctor Porquier's gaping pocket, where Abbé Surin had adroitly slipped it. They all laughed and considered the selection of the hiding-place a very ingenious joke.

'Bourdeu has a chance now,' said Monsieur Rastoil, taking Abbé Faujas aside. 'It is very annoying. I can't tell him so, but we shan't vote for him: he has compromised himself too much as an Orleanist.'

'Just look at your son Séverin!' cried Madame de Condamin, interrupting the conversation. 'What a big baby he is! He put the handkerchief under Abbé Bourrette's hat.'

Then she lowered her voice as she continued:

'By the way, I have to congratulate you, Monsieur Rastoil. I have received a letter from Paris, from a correspondent who tells me that he has seen your son's name on an official list. He will be nominated assessor to the public prosecutor at Faverolles, I believe.'

The presiding judge bowed with a flushed face. The minister had never forgiven the election of the Marquis de Lagrifoul. Since then a kind of fatality had seemed to prevent him from finding either a place for his son or husbands for his daughters. He had never uttered any complaints, but his compressed lips had often borne witness to his feelings on the matter.

'I was remarking to you,' he resumed, to conceal his emotion, 'that Bourdeu is dangerous. But he isn't a Plassans man, and he doesn't know our requirements. We might just as well re-elect the Marquis.'

'If Monsieur de Bourdeu persists in his candidature,' rejoined Abbé Faujas, 'the Republicans will poll an imposing minority, which will have a very bad effect.'

Madame de Condamin smiled. She pretended to understand nothing about politics, and slipped away while the Abbé drew the presiding judge aside to the end of the arbour, where they continued the conversation in subdued tones. As they slowly strolled back again, Monsieur Rastoil remarked:

'You are quite right. He would be a very suitable candidate. He belongs to no party, and we could all unite in supporting him. I am no fonder of the Empire than you are, but it would be childish to go on sending deputies to the Chamber for no other purpose than to obstruct and rail at the government. Plassans is suffering from such tactics. What we want is a man with a good head for business, a local man who can look after the interests of the place.'

'Hot! Hot!' now cried Aurélie in her fluty voice.

Abbé Surin passed through the arbour at the head of the searchers, hunting for the handkerchief.

'Cold! Cold!' exclaimed the girl, laughing at their lack of success. One of the young Maffres, however, lifted up a flower-pot and there discovered the handkerchief folded in four.

'That big stick Aurélie might have very well crammed it into her mouth,' said Madame Paloque, 'There is plenty of room for it, and no one would ever have thought of looking for it there.'

Her husband reduced her to silence with an angry look. He would no longer allow her to indulge in bitter language. Fearing that Monsieur de Condamin might have overheard her, he exclaimed:

'What a handsome lot of young people!'

'Your success is certain, my dear sir,' the conservator of rivers and forests was saying to Monsieur de Bourdeu. 'But be careful what you do when you get to Paris. I hear from a very trustworthy source that the government has resolved upon taking strong measures if the opposition shows itself too provoking.'

The ex-prefect looked at Monsieur de Condamin very uneasily, wondering if he was making fun of him. Monsieur Péqueur des Saulaies merely smiled, and stroked his moustaches. Then the conversation became general again, and Monsieur de Bourdeu thought he could detect that everyone was congratulating him upon his approaching triumph, with a discretion that was full of tact. He enjoyed the sweets of an hour's imaginary popularity.

'It is surprising how much more quickly the grapes ripen in the sun,' remarked Abbé Bourrette, who had never moved from his chair, but now raised his eyes to the arbour.

'In the north,' Doctor Porquier explained, 'grapes can often only be got to ripen by freeing them from the surrounding leaves.'

They were beginning to discuss this point, when Séverin in his turn cried out: 'Hot! Hot!'

But he had hung the handkerchief with such little concealment upon the garden door that Abbé Surin found it at once. When the Abbé hid it again, the whole troop vainly scoured the garden for nearly half an hour, and at last gave it up. Then the Abbé showed it to them lying in the centre of a flowerbed, rolled up so artistically that it looked like a white stone. This was the most effective stratagem of the afternoon.

The news that the government had determined to run no candidate of its own quickly spread through the town, where it gave rise to great excitement. This abstention had the natural effect of disquieting the various political sections, who had each counted upon the diversion of a certain number of votes in favour of the official candidate to enable their own man to win. The Marquis de Lagrifoul, Monsieur de Bourdeu and hatter Maurin appeared to divide the support of the voters pretty equally amongst them. There would certainly be a second ballot, and heaven only could tell what name would then appear at the top of the list. However, there was certainly some talk of a fourth candidate, whose name nobody quite knew, some moderate equable man who would possibly bring the different parties into concord and harmony. The Plassans electors, who had grown a little alarmed since they had felt the imperial bridle about their necks, would have been only too glad to come to an understanding, and choose one of their fellow-citizens who would be acceptable to all parties.

'The government is wrong to treat us like refractory children,' said the politicians of the Commercial Club, in tones of annoyance. 'Anybody would suppose that the town was a hot-bed of revolution. If the authorities had been tactful enough to bring forward the right sort of candidate, we should all have voted for him. The sub-prefect has talked about a lesson. Well, we shan't receive the lesson. We shall be able to find a candidate for ourselves, and we will show that Plassans is a town of sound sense and true liberty.'

They then began to look about for a candidate. But the names which were proposed by friends or interested parties only served to increase the confusion. In a week's time there were twenty candidates before Plassans. Madame Rougon, who had become very uneasy, and quite unable to understand the position, went to see Abbé Faujas, full of indignation with the sub-prefect. That Péqueur was an ass, she cried, a fop, a dummy, of no use except as a pretty ornament to the official drawing-room. He had already allowed the government to be defeated, and now he was going to compromise it by an attitude of ridiculous indifference.

'Make yourself easy,' said the priest, with a smile; 'this time Monsieur Péqueur des Saulaies is confining himself to obeying orders. Victory is certain.'

'But you've got no candidate!' cried Madame Rougon, 'Where is your candidate?'

Then the priest unfolded his plans to her. She expressed her approval of them; but she received the name which he confided to her with the greatest surprise.

'What!' she exclaimed,' you have chosen him! No one has ever thought of him, I assure you.'

'I trust that they haven't,' replied the priest, again smiling. 'We want a candidate of whom nobody has ever thought, so that all parties may accept him without fancying that they are compromising themselves.'

Then with the perfect frankness of a shrewd man who has made up his mind to explain his designs, he continued:

'I have very much to thank you for. You have prevented me from making many mistakes. I was looking straight towards the goal, and I did not see the strings that were stretched across the path, and which might, perhaps, have tripped me up and brought me to grief. Thank heaven! all this petty childish struggle is over, and I shall soon be able to move at my ease. As for the choice I have made, it is a good one; you may feel quite assured of that. Ever since my arrival at Plassans, I have been looking about for a man, and he is the only one I have found. He is flexible, very capable, and very energetic. He has been clever enough not to embroil himself with a single person in the place, which is no common accomplishment. I know that you are not a very great friend of his, and that is the reason that I did not confide my plan to you sooner. But you will see that you are mistaken, and that he will make his way rapidly as soon as he gets his foot into the stirrup. What finally determined me in his favour is what I heard about his means. It is said that he has taken his wife back again three separate times, after she had been detected in actual unfaithfulness, and after he had made his good-natured father-in-law pay him a hundred thousand francs on each occasion. If he has really coined money in that way, he will be very useful in Paris in certain matters. You may look about as much as you like; but, putting him aside, there is only a pack of imbeciles in Plassans.'

'Then it is a present you are making to the government?' said Félicité, with a laugh.

She allowed herself to be convinced. The next day the name of Delangre was in everybody's mouth. His friends declared that it was only after the strongest pressure had been brought to bear upon him that he had accepted the nomination. He had refused it for a long time, considering himself unworthy of the position, insisting that he was not a politician, and that the Marquis de Lagrifoul and Monsieur de Bourdeu had, on the other hand, had long experience of public affairs. Then, when it had been impressed upon him that what Plassans urgently needed was a representative who was unconnected with the political parties, he had allowed himself to be prevailed upon. He explicitly declared the principles upon which he should act if he were returned. It must be thoroughly understood, he said, that he would not go to the Chamber either to oppose or support the government under all circumstances; he should look upon himself solely as the representative of the interests of the town; he would always vote for liberty with order, and order with liberty, and would still remain mayor of Plassans, so that he might show what a conciliatory and purely administrative task he had charged himself with. These views struck people as being singularly sensible. The knowing politicians of the Commercial Club vied with each other that same evening in lauding Delangre.

'I told you so; he is the very man we want. I shall be curious to see what the sub-prefect will say when the mayor's name heads the list. The authorities can scarcely accuse us of having voted like a lot of sulking school-boys, any more than they can reproach us with having gone down on our knees before the government. If the Empire could only receive a few lessons like this, things would go much better.'

The whole thing was like a train of gunpowder. The mine was laid, and a spark was sufficient to set it off. In every part of Plassans simultaneously, in all the three quarters of the town, in every house, and in every family, Monsieur Delangre's name was pronounced amidst unanimous eulogies. He had become the expected Messiah, the saviour, unknown the previous day, revealed in the morning, and worshipped ere night.

Even in the sacristies and confessionals of Plassans, his name was buzzed about; it mingled with the echoes in the naves, sounded from pulpits in the suburbs, was passed on from ear to ear like a sacrament, and made its way into the most distant homes of the pious. The priests carried it about with them in the folds of their cassocks; Abbé Bourrette bestowed on it the respectable cheeriness of his corporation, Abbé Surin the grace of his smile, and Monseigneur Rousselot the charm of his pastoral blessing. The fashionable ladies were never tired of talking of Monsieur Delangre. He had such a kind disposition, they said, and such a fine sensible face. Madame Rastoil learned to blush again at mention of him; Madame Paloque grew almost pretty in her enthusiasm, while as for Madame de Condamin, she was ready to fight for him, and won all hearts to his side by the tender way in which she pressed the hands of the electors who promised to vote for him. The Young Men's Club, too, grew passionately enthusiastic on his behalf. Séverin made quite a hero of him, and Guillaume and the young Maffres went canvassing for him through all the disreputable parts of the town.

On the day of the election his majority was overwhelming. The whole town seemed to have conspired together to return him. The Marquis de Lagrifoul and Monsieur de Bourdeu, bursting with indignation and crying that they had been betrayed, had retired from the contest, and thus Monsieur Delangre's only opponent was the hatter Maurin. The latter received the votes of some fifteen hundred intractable Republicans of the outskirts of the town; while the mayor had the support of the country districts, the fervent Bonapartists, the townsmen of the new quarter who were amenable to clerical influence, the timid shopkeepers of the old town, and even certain simple-minded Royalists of the district of Saint-Marc, whose aristocratic denizens chiefly abstained from voting. Monsieur Delangre thus obtained thirty-three thousand votes. The business was managed so promptly, the victory was won with such a dash, that Plassans felt quite amazed, on the evening of the election, to find itself so unanimous. The town half fancied that it had just had a wonderful dream, that some powerful hand must have struck the soil and drawn from it those thirty-three thousand electors, that army, almost alarming in its numbers, whose strength no one had ever before suspected. The politicians of the Commercial Club looked at one another in perplexity, like men dazed with victory.

In the evening, Monsieur Rastoil's friends joined those of Monsieur Péqueur des Saulaies, to congratulate each other, in a little drawing-room at the Sub-Prefecture, overlooking the gardens, Tea was served to them. The great victory of the day ended by a coalition of the two parties. All the usual guests were present.

'I have never systematically opposed any government,' said Monsieur Rastoil, after a time, as he accepted some little cakes which

Monsieur Péqueur des Saulaies offered him. 'The judicial bench ought to take no part in political struggles. I willingly admit that the Empire has already accomplished some great things, and that it has a still nobler future before it, if it continues to advance in the paths of justice and liberty.'

The sub-prefect bowed, as though this eulogy was addressed to himself personally. The previous evening, Monsieur Rastoil had read in the 'Moniteur' a decree appointing his son assistant public prosecutor at Faverolles. There was also a good deal of talk about a marriage between his eldest daughter and Lucien Delangre.

'Oh, yes! it is quite settled,' Monsieur de Condamin said in low tones to Madame Paloque, who had just been questioning him upon the subject. 'He has chosen Angéline. I believe that he would rather have had Aurélie, but it has probably been hinted to him that it would not be seemly for the younger sister to be married before the elder one.'

'Angéline! Are you quite sure?' Madame Paloque murmured maliciously. 'I fancy that Angéline has a likeness—'

The conservator of rivers and forests put his finger to his lips, with a smile.

'Well, it's just a toss-up, isn't it?' she continued. 'It will strengthen the ties between the two families. We are all good friends now. Paloque is expecting his cross, and I am quite satisfied with everything.'

Monsieur Delangre did not arrive till late. He received, as newspaper writers say, a perfect ovation. Madame de Condamin had just informed Doctor Porquier that his son Guillaume had been nominated chief clerk at the post-office. She was circulating good news through the room, declaring that Abbé Bourrette would be vicar-general the following year; that Abbé Surin would be a bishop before he was forty, and that Monsieur Maffre was to have a cross.

'Poor Bourdeu!' exclaimed Monsieur Rastoil, with a last sigh of regret.

'Oh, there's no occasion to pity him!' cried Madame de Condamin, gaily. 'I will undertake to console him. He is not cut out for the Chamber. What he wants is a prefecture. Tell him that he shall have one before long.'

The merriment increased. The fair Octavie's high spirits, and the desire which she showed to please everybody, delighted the company. It was really she who was doing the honours of the Sub-Prefecture. She was the queen of the place. And, while she seemed to be speaking quite playfully, she gave Monsieur Delangre the most practical advice in the world about the part he ought to play in the Corps Législatif. She took him aside and offered to introduce him to several influential people, an offer which he gratefully accepted. About eleven o'clock, Monsieur de Condamin suggested that the garden should be illuminated, but his wife calmed the enthusiasm of the gentlemen, and said that such a course would be inadvisable, for it would not do to appear to be exulting over the town.

'Well, what about Abbé Fenil?' she suddenly asked Abbé Faujas, as she took him aside into one of the window recesses. 'He has not made any movement, has he?'

'Abbé Fenil is a man of sense,' the priest replied. 'It has been hinted to him that he would do well not to interfere in political matters for the future.'

In the midst of all the triumphant joy, Abbé Faujas remained grave. He had won after a hard fight. Madame de Condamin's chatter wearied him; and the satisfaction of these people, with their poor vulgar ambitions, filled him with disdain. As he stood leaning against the mantel-piece, with a far-off look in his eyes, he seemed to be buried in thought. He was master now, and no longer compelled to veil and suppress his real feelings. He could reach out his hand and seize the town, and make it tremble in his grasp. His tall, black figure seemed to fill the room. The guests gradually drew their chairs closer to him, and formed a circle round him. The men awaited some expression of satisfaction from his lips, the women besought him with their eyes, like submissive slaves. But he bluntly broke through the circle and went away the first, saying but a brief word or two as he took his leave.

When he returned to the Mourets' house, going thither by way of the Impasse des Chevillottes and the garden, he found Marthe alone in the dining-room, sitting listlessly on a chair against the wall, looking very pale, and gazing with a blank expression at the lamp, the wick of which was beginning to char. Upstairs, Trouche was having a party, and could be heard singing a broad comic song, which Olympe and his guests accompanied by striking their glasses with the handles of their knives.

XX

Abbé Faujas laid his hand on Marthe's shoulder. 'What are you doing here?' he asked.' Why haven't you gone to bed? I told you that you were not to wait for me.'

She started up and stammered:

'I thought you would be back much earlier than this. I fell asleep. I dare say Rose will have got some tea ready.'

The priest called for the cook and rated her for not having made her mistress go to bed. He spoke in authoritative tones that admitted of no reply.

'Bring the tea for his reverence, Rose,' said Marthe.

'No, I don't want any tea,' the priest said with a show of vexation. 'Go to bed immediately. It is absurd. I can scarcely control myself. Show me a light, Rose.'

The cook went with him as far as the foot of the staircase.

'Your reverence knows that I am not to blame,' she said. 'Madame is very strange. Ill as she is, she can't stop for a single hour in her room. She can't keep from coming and going up and down, and fidgetting about merely for the sake of being on the move. She puts me out quite as much as anyone else; she is always in my way, preventing me from getting on with anything. Then she drops down on a chair and sits staring in front of her with a terrified look, as though she could see something horrible. I told her half a score of times at least, to-night, that you would be very angry with her for not going to bed; but she didn't even seem to hear what I said.'

The priest went upstairs without replying. As he passed the Trouches' room he stretched out his arm as though he was going to bang his fist on the door. But the singing had stopped, and he could tell from the sounds within that the visitors were about to take their departure, so he quickly stepped into his own room. Almost immediately afterwards Trouche went downstairs with a couple of men whom he had picked up in some low café, crying out on the staircase that he knew how to behave himself and was going to see them home. Olympe leant over the banisters.

'You can fasten the doors,' she said to Rose. 'He won't be back before to-morrow morning.'

Rose, from whom she had not been able to conceal her husband's misconduct, expressed much pity for her, and growled as she fastened the doors:

'What fools women are to get married! Their husbands either beat them or go off after hussies. For my part, I'd very much rather keep as I am.'

When she went back into the dining-room she found her mistress again in a sort of melancholy stupor, with her eyes fixed upon the lamp. She shook her and made her go upstairs to bed. Marthe had become very timid. She said she saw great patches of light on the walls of her room at nighttime, and heard violent blows at the head of her bed. Rose now slept near her, in a little dressing-room whence she hastened to calm her at the slightest uneasiness. That night she had not finished undressing herself before she heard Marthe groaning, and, on rushing into her room, she found her lying amidst the disordered bed-clothes, her eyes staring widely in mute horror, and her clenched fists pressed closely against her mouth to keep herself from shrieking. Rose was obliged to talk to her and soothe her as though she were a mere child, and even had to look behind the curtains and under the furniture, and assure her that she was mistaken, for there was really no one there. These attacks of terror ended in cataleptic seizures, when the unhappy woman lay back on her pillow, with her eyelids rigidly opened as though she were dead.

'It is the thought of the master that torments her,' Rose muttered, as she at last got into bed.

The next day was one of those when Doctor Porquier called. He came regularly twice a week to see Madame Mouret. He patted her hands and said to her with his amiable optimism:

'Oh! nothing serious will come of this, my dear lady. You still cough a little, don't you? Ah! it's a mere cold which has been neglected, but which we will cure with some syrups.'

But Marthe complained to him of intolerable pains in her back and chest, and kept her eyes upon him, as if trying to discover from his face and manner what he would not say in words.

'I am afraid of going mad!' she suddenly cried, breaking into a sob.

The doctor smilingly reassured her. The sight of him always caused her keen anxiety, she felt a sort of alarm of this gentle and agreeable man. She often told Rose not to admit him, saying that she was not ill, and had no need to have a doctor constantly to see her. Rose shrugged her shoulders, however, and ushered the doctor into the room. However, he had almost ceased speaking to Marthe about her ailments, and seemed to be merely making friendly calls upon her.

As he was going away, he met Abbé Faujas, who was returning from Saint-Saturnin's. The priest questioned him respecting Madame Mouret's condition.

'Science is sometimes quite powerless,' said the doctor gravely, 'but the goodness of Providence is inexhaustible. The poor lady has been sorely shaken, but I don't altogether give her up. Her chest is only slightly attacked as yet, and the climate here is favourable.'

Then he started a dissertation upon the treatment of pulmonary diseases in the neighbourhood of Plassans. He was preparing a pamphlet on the subject, not for publication, for he was too shrewd to wish to seem a *savant,* but for the perusal of a few intimate friends.

'I have weighty reasons,' he said in conclusion, 'for believing that the equable temperature, the aromatic flora, and the salubrious springs of our hills, are extremely effective for the cure of pulmonary complaints.'

The priest had listened to him with his usual stern expression.

'You are mistaken,' he said slowly, 'Plassans does not agree with Madame Mouret. Why not send her to pass the winter at Nice?'

'At Nice?' repeated the doctor, uneasily.

He looked at the priest for a moment, and then continued in his complacent way:

'Nice certainly would be very suitable for her. In her present condition of nervous excitement, a change of surroundings would probably have very beneficial results. I must advise her to make the journey. It is an excellent idea of yours, Monsieur le Curé.'

He bowed, parted from the Abbé, and made his way to Madame de Condamin, whose slightest headaches caused him endless trouble and anxiety. At dinner, the next day, Marthe spoke of the doctor in almost violent terms. She swore that she would never allow him to visit her again.

'It is he who is making me ill,' she exclaimed. 'This very afternoon he has been advising me to go off on a journey.'

'And I entirely agree with him in that,' declared Abbé Faujas, folding his napkin.

She fixed her eyes upon him, and turned very pale as she murmured in a low voice:

'What! Do you also want to send me away from Plassans? Oh! I should die in a strange land far away from all my old associations, and far away from those I love.'

The priest had risen from his seat, and was about to leave the dining-room. He stepped towards her, and said with a smile:

'Your friends only think of what is good for your health. Why are you so rebellious?'

'Oh! I don't want to go! I don't want to go!' she cried, stepping back from him.

There was a short contest between them. The blood rushed to the Abbé's cheeks, and he crossed his arms, as though to withstand a temptation to strike Marthe. She was leaning against the wall, in despair at her weakness. Then, quite vanquished, she stretched out her hands, and stammered:

'I beseech you to allow me to remain here. I will do whatever you tell me.'

Then, as she burst into sobs, the Abbé shrugged his shoulders and left the room, like a husband fearing an outbreak of tears. Madame Faujas, who was tranquilly finishing her dinner, had witnessed the scene and continued eating. She let Marthe cry on undisturbed.

'You are extremely unreasonable, my dear child,' she said after a time, helping herself to some more sweetmeats. 'You will end by making Ovide quite detest you. You don't know how to treat him. Why do you refuse to go away from home, if it is necessary for your health? We should look after the house for you, and you would find everything all right and in its place when you came back.'

Marthe was still sobbing, and did not seem to hear what Madame Faujas said.

'Ovide has so much to think about,' the old lady continued. 'Do you know that he often works till four o'clock in the morning? When you cough all through the night, it disturbs him very much, and distracts his thoughts. He can't work any longer, and he suffers more than you do. Do this for Ovide's sake, my dear child; go away, and come back to us in good health.'

Then Marthe raised her face, red with weeping, and throwing all her anguish into one cry, she wailed: 'Oh! Heaven lies!'

During the next few days no further pressure was brought to bear upon Madame Mouret to induce her to make the journey to Nice. She grew terribly excited at the least reference to it. She refused to leave Plassans with such a show of determination that the priest himself recognised the danger of insisting upon the scheme. In the midst of his triumph she was beginning to cause him terrible anxiety and embarrassment. Trouche declared, with his snigger, that it was she who ought to have been sent the first to Les Tulettes. Ever since Mouret had been taken off, she had secluded herself in the most rigid religious practices, and refrained from ever mentioning her husband's name, praying indeed that she might be rendered altogether oblivious of the past. But she still remained restless, and returned from Saint-Saturnin's with even a keener longing for forgetfulness than she had had when she went thither.

'Our landlady is going it finely,' Olympe said to her husband when she came home one evening. 'I went with her to church to-day, and I had to pick her up from the flagstones. You would laugh if I told you all the things that she vomited out against Ovide. She is quite furious with him; she says that he has no heart, and that he has deceived her in promising her a heap of consolations. And you should hear her rail, too, against the Divinity. Ah! it's only your pious people who talk so badly of religion! Anyone would think, to hear her, that God had cheated her of a large sum of money. Do you know, I really believe that her husband comes and haunts her at night.'

Trouche was much amused by this gossip.

'Well, she has herself to blame for that,' he said. 'If that old joker Mouret was put away, it was her own doing. If I were Faujas, I should know how to arrange matters, and I would make her as gentle and content as a sheep. But Faujas is an ass, and you will see that he will make a mess of the business. Your brother, my dear, hasn't shown himself sufficiently pleasant to us for me to help him out of the bother. I shall have a rare laugh the day our landlady makes him take the plunge.'

'Ovide certainly looks down upon women too much,' declared Olympe.

Then Trouche continued in a lower tone:

'I say, you know, if our landlady were to throw herself down some well with your noodle of a brother, we should be the masters, and the house would be ours. We should be able to feather our nest nicely then. It would be a splendid ending to it all, that!'

Since Mouret's departure, the Trouches also had invaded the ground-floor of the house. Olympe had begun by complaining that the chimneys upstairs smoked, and she had ended by persuading Marthe that the drawing-room, which had hitherto been unoccupied, was the healthiest room in the house. Rose was ordered to light a big fire there, and the two women spent their days in endless talk, before the huge blazing logs. It was one of Olympe's dreams to be able to live like this, handsomely dressed and lolling on a couch in the midst of an elegantly furnished room. She even persuaded Marthe to have the drawing-room re-papered, to buy some new furniture and a fresh carpet for it. Then she felt that she was a lady. She came downstairs in her slippers and dressing-gown, and talked as though she were the mistress of the house.

'That poor Madame Mouret,' she would say,' has so much worry that she has asked me to help her, and so I devote a little of my time to assisting her. It is really a kindness to do so.'

She had, indeed, quite succeeded in winning the confidence of Marthe, who, from sheer lassitude, handed over to her the petty details of the household management. It was Olympe who kept the keys of the cellar and the cupboards, and paid the tradesmen's bills as well. She had been deliberating for a long time as to how she should manage to make herself equally free in the dining-room. Trouche, however, dissuaded her from attempting to carry out that design. They would no longer be able to eat and drink as they liked, he said; they would not even dare to drink their wine unwatered, or to ask a friend to come and have coffee. Then Olympe declared that at any rate she would bring their share of the dessert upstairs. She crammed her pockets with sugar, and she even carried off candle-ends. For this purpose, she made some big canvas pockets, which she fastened under her skirt, and which it took her a good quarter of an hour to empty every evening.

'There! there's something for a rainy day,' she said, as she bundled a stock of provisions into a box, which she then pushed under the bed. 'If we happen to fall out with our landlady, we shall have something to keep us going for a time. I must bring up some pots of preserves and some salt pork.'

'There is no need to make a secret of it,' said Trouche. 'If I were you, I should make Rose bring them up, as you are the mistress.'

Trouche had made himself master of the garden. For a long time past he had envied Mouret as he had watched him pruning his trees, gravelling his walks, and watering his lettuces; and he had indulged in a dream of one day having a plot of ground of his own, where he might dig and plant as he liked. So, now that Mouret was no longer there, he took possession of the garden, planning all kinds of alterations in it. He began by condemning the vegetables. He had a delicate soul, he said, and he loved flowers. But the labour of digging tired him out on the second day, and a gardener was called in, who dug up the beds under his directions, threw the vegetables on to the dung-heap, and prepared the soil for the reception of pæonies, roses and lilies, larkspurs and convolvuli, and cuttings of geraniums and carnations. Then an idea occurred to Trouche. It struck him that the tall sombre box plants, which bordered the beds, had a mournful appearance, and he meditated for a long time about pulling them up.

'You are quite right,' said Olympe, whom he consulted on the matter. 'They make the place look like a cemetery. For my part, I should much prefer an edging of cast-iron made to resemble rough wood. I will persuade the landlady to have it done. Anyhow, pull up the box.'

The box was accordingly pulled up. A week later the gardener came and laid down the cast-iron edging. Trouche also removed several fruit-trees which interfered with the view, had the arbour painted afresh a bright green, and ornamented the fountain with rock-work. Monsieur Rastoil's cascade greatly excited his envy, but he contented himself for the time by choosing a place where he would construct a similar one, 'if everything should go on all right.'

'This will make our neighbours open their eyes,' he said in the evening to his wife. 'They will see that there is a man of taste here now. In the summer, when we sit at the window, we shall have a delightful view, and the garden will smell deliciously.'

Marthe let him have his own way and gave her consent to all the plans that were submitted to her, and in the end he gave over even consulting her. It was solely Madame Faujas that the Trouches had to contend against, and she continued to dispute possession of the house with them very obstinately. It was only after a battle royal with her mother that Olympe had been able to take possession of the drawing-room. Madame Faujas had all but won the day on that occasion. It was the priest's fault if she had not proved victorious.

'That hussy of a sister of yours says everything that is bad of us to the landlady,' Madame Faujas perpetually complained. 'I can see through her game. She wants to supplant us and to get everything for herself. She is trying to settle herself down in the drawing-room like a fine lady, the slut!'

The priest however paid no attention to what his mother said; he only broke out into sharp gestures of impatience at her complaints. One day he got quite angry and exclaimed:

'I beg of you, mother, do leave me in peace. Don't talk to me any more about Olympe or Trouche. Let them go and hang themselves, if they like.'

'But they are seizing the whole house, Ovide. They are perfect rats. When you want your share, you will find that they have gnawed it all away. You are the only one who can keep them in check.'

He looked at his mother with a faint smile.

'You love me very much, mother,' said he, 'and I forgive you. Make your mind easy; I want something very different from the house. It isn't mine, and I only keep what I gain. You will be very proud when you see my share. Trouche has been useful to me, and we must shut our eyes a little.'

Madame Faujas was then obliged to beat a retreat; but she did so with very bad grace. The absolute disinterestedness of her son made her, with her material baser desires and careful economical nature, quite desperate. She would have liked to lock the house up so that Ovide might find it ready in perfect order for his occupation whenever he might want it. The Trouches, with their grasping ways, caused her all the torment and despair felt by a miser who is being preyed upon by strangers. It was exactly as though they were wasting her own substance, fattening upon her own flesh, and reducing herself and her beloved son to penury and wretchedness. When the Abbé forbade her to oppose the gradual invasion of the Trouches, she made up her mind that she would at any rate save all she could from the hands of the spoilers, and so she began pilfering from the cupboards, just as Olympe did. She also fastened big pockets underneath her skirts, and had a chest which she filled with all the things she collected together—provisions, linen, and miscellaneous articles.

'What is that you are stowing away there, mother?' the Abbé asked one evening as he went into her room, attracted by the noise which she made in moving the chest.

She began to stammer out a reply, but the priest understood it all at a glance, and flew into a violent rage.

'It is too shameful!' he said. 'You have turned yourself into a thief, now! What would the consequences be if you were to be detected? I should be the talk of the whole town!'

'It is all for your sake, Ovide,' she murmured.

'A thief! My mother a thief! Perhaps you think that I thieve, too, that I have come here to plunder, and that my only ambition is to lay my hands upon whatever I can! Good heavens! what sort of an opinion have you formed of me? We shall have to separate, mother, if we do not understand each other better than this.'

This speech quite crushed the old woman. She had remained on her knees in front of the chest, and she sank into a crouching position upon the floor, very pale and almost choking, and stretching out her hands beseechingly. When she was able to speak, she wailed out:

'It is for your benefit, my child, for yours only, I swear. I have told you before that they are taking everything; your sister crams everything into her pockets. There will be nothing left for you, not even a lump of sugar. But I won't take anything more, since it makes you angry, and you will let me stay with you, won't you? You will keep me with you, won't you?'

Abbé Faujas refused to make any promises until she had restored everything she had taken to its place. For nearly a week he himself, superintended the secret restoration of the contents of the chest. He watched his mother fill her pockets, and waited till she came back upstairs again to take a fresh load. For prudential reasons he allowed her to make only two journeys backwards and forwards every evening. The old woman felt as though her heart was breaking as she restored each article to its former place. She did not dare to cry, but her eyelids were swollen with tears of regret, and her hands trembled even more than they had done when they were ransacking the cupboards. However, what afflicted her more than anything else was to see that as soon as she had restored each article to its rightful position, Olympe followed in her wake and took possession of it. The linen, the provisions, and the candle-ends, merely passed from one pocket to another.

'I won't take anything more downstairs,' she exclaimed to her son, growing rebellious at this unforeseen result of her restorations. 'It isn't the least good, for your sister only walks off with everything directly I put it back. The hussy! I might just as well give her the chest at once! She must have got a nice little hoard together! I beseech you, Ovide, let me keep what still remains. Our landlady will be none the worse off for it, because she will lose it anyhow.'

'My sister is what she is,' the priest replied tranquilly; 'but I wish my mother to be an honest woman. You will help me much more by not committing such actions.'

She was forced to restore everything, and from that time forward she harboured fierce hatred against the Trouches, Marthe, and the whole establishment. She often said that the day would come when she should have to defend Ovide against everybody.

The Trouches were now reigning in all sovereignty. They completed the conquest of the house, and made their way into every corner of it. The Abbé's own rooms were the only ones they respected. It was only before him that they trembled. But even his presence in the house did not prevent them from inviting their friends, and indulging in debauches till two o'clock in the morning. Guillaume Porquier came with parties of mere youths. Olympe, notwithstanding her thirty-seven years, then simpered and put on girlish airs; and flirted with more than one of the college lads. The house was becoming a perfect paradise to her. Trouche sniggered and joked about it when they were alone together.

'Well,' she said, quite tranquilly, 'you do as you like, don't you? We are both free to do as we please, you know.'

Trouche had, as a matter of fact, all but brought his pleasant life to an abrupt conclusion. There had been an unpleasant affair at the Home of the Virgin in connection with one of the girls there. One of the Sisters of St. Joseph had complained of Trouche to Abbé Faujas. He had thanked her for telling him, and had impressed upon her that the cause of religion would suffer by such a scandal. So the affair was hushed up, and the lady patronesses never had the faintest suspicion of it. Abbé Faujas, however, had a terrible scene with his brother-in-law, whom he assailed in Olympe's presence, so that his wife might have a weapon against him, and be able to keep him in check.

The Trouches had been troubled for a long time past by another matter. Notwithstanding their life of clover, although they were provided with so many things out of Marthe's cupboards, they had got terribly into debt in the neighbourhood. Trouche squandered his salary away in cafés, and Olympe wasted the money which she drew out of Marthe's pockets by indulging in all sorts of silly fancies. As for the necessaries of life, they made a point of getting these upon credit. There was one account which made them particularly uneasy, that of a pastrycook in the Rue de la Banne, which amounted to more than a hundred francs, for the pastrycook was a rough, blunt sort of man, who had threatened to lay the whole matter before Abbé Faujas. The Trouches thus long lived in a state of alarm, but when the bill was actually presented to him Abbé Faujas paid it without a word, and even forgot to address any reproaches to them on the subject. The priest seemed to be above all those sordid little matters, and went on living a gloomy and rigid life in this house that was given up to pillage, without appearing conscious of the gradual ruin which was falling upon it. Everything, indeed, was crumbling away around him, while he continued to advance straight towards the goal of his ambition. He still camped like a soldier in his big bare room, indulging in no comforts, and showing annoyance when any were pressed upon him. Since he had become the master of Plassans, he had dropped back into complete carelessness as to his appearance. His hat became rusty, his stockings muddy; his cassock, which his mother mended every morning, looked just like the pitiful, worn-out rag which he had worn when he first came to Plassans.

'Pooh! it is very good yet,' he used to say, when anyone hazarded a timid remark about it.

He made a display of it, walked about the streets in it, carrying his head loftily, and altogether unheeding the curious glances which were cast at him. There was no bravado in the matter; he was simply following his natural inclinations. Now that he believed that he need no longer lay himself out to please, he fell back into all his old disdain for mere appearance. It was his triumph to sit down just as he was, with his tall, clumsy body, rough, blunt manner and torn clothes, in the midst of conquered Plassans.

Madame de Condamin, distressed by the strong smell which emanated from his cassock, one day gently took him to task about his appearance.

'Do you know,' she said to him, laughing, 'that the ladies are beginning to detest you? They say that you now never take the least trouble over your toilet. Once upon a time, when you took your handkerchief out of your pocket, it was just as though there were a choir-boy swinging a thurible behind you.'

The priest looked greatly astonished. He was quite unaware of any change in himself. Then Madame de Condamin, drawing a little nearer to him, said in a friendly tone:

'Will you let me speak quite frankly to you, my dear Curé? It is really a mistake on your part to be so negligent of your appearance. You scarcely shave, and you never comb your hair; it is as rough and tumbled as though you had been fighting. I can assure you that all this has a very bad effect. Madame Rastoil and Madame Delangre told me yesterday that they could scarcely recognise you. You are really compromising your success.'

The priest gave a laugh of defiance, as he shook his powerful unkempt head.

'Now that the battle is won,' he merely replied, 'they must put up with my hair being uncombed.'

Plassans had, indeed, to put up with him with his hair uncombed. The once seemingly flexible priest was now transformed into a stern, despotic master who bent all wills to his own. His face, which had again become cadaverous in hue, shone with eyes like an eagle's, and he raised his big hands as though they were filled with threats and chastisements. The town was positively terrified on beholding the master it had imposed upon itself, with his shabby, dirty clothing and unkempt hair. The covert alarm of the women only tended, however, to strengthen his power. He was stern and harsh to his penitents, but not one of them dared to leave him. They came to him in fear and trembling, in which they found some touch of painful pleasure.

'I was wrong, my dear,' Madame de Condamin confessed to Marthe, 'in wanting him to perfume himself. I am growing accustomed to him, and even prefer him as he is. He is indeed a man!'

Abbé Faujas was supreme at the Bishop's. Since the elections he had left Monseigneur Rousselot only a show of authority. The Bishop lived amidst his beloved books in his study, where the Abbé, who administered the diocese from an adjoining room, virtually kept him prisoner, only allowing him to see those persons whom he could fully trust. The clergy trembled before this absolute master. The old white-headed priests bent before him with all humility and surrender of personal will. Monseigneur Rousselot, when he was alone with Abbé Surin, often wept silent tears. He regretted the impetuous mastery of Abbé Fenil, who had, at any rate, intervals of affectionate softness, whereas now, under Abbé Faujas's rule, he felt a relentless, ceaseless pressure. However, he would smile again and resign himself, saying with a sort of pleasant self-satisfaction:

'Come, my child, let us get to work. I must not complain, for I am now leading the life which I always dreamed of—a life of perfect solitude amongst my books.'

Then he sighed, and continued in a lower tone:

'I should be quite happy if I were not afraid of losing you, my dear Surin. He will end by not tolerating your presence here any longer. I thought that he looked at you very suspiciously yesterday. Always agree with him, I beseech you; take his side and don't spare me. Ah me! I have only you left now.'

Two months after the elections Abbé Vial, one of the Bishop's grand-vicars, went to settle at Rome. Abbé Faujas stepped into his place as a matter of course, although it had been promised long ago to Abbé Bourrette. He did not even promote the latter to the living of Saint-Saturnin's which he vacated, but preferred to it a young ambitious priest whom he had made a tool of his own.

'His lordship would not hear of you,' he said curtly to Abbé Bourrette when he met him.

When the poor old priest stammered out that he would go and see the Bishop, and ask for an explanation, Abbé Faujas added more gently:

'His lordship is too unwell to see you. Trust yourself in my hands; I will plead your cause for you.'

From his first appearance in the Chamber in Paris Monsieur Delangre had voted with the majority. Plassans was conquered for the Empire. Abbé Faujas almost seemed actuated by a feeling of revenge in the rough way in which he treated the prudent townspeople. He again closed the little doors that led into the Impasse des Chevillottes, and compelled Monsieur Rastoil and his friends to enter the Sub-Prefecture by the official door facing the Place. When he appeared at the sub-prefect's friendly gatherings, the guests showed themselves very humble in his presence. So great was the fascination he exercised, and so great the fear he inspired, that even when he was not present nobody dared to make the slightest equivocal remark concerning him.

'He is a man of the greatest merit,' declared Monsieur Péqueur des Saulaies, who now counted on being promoted to a prefecture.

'A very remarkable man, indeed,' chimed in Doctor Porquier.

All the company nodded their heads approvingly till Monsieur de Condamin, who began to feel irritated by this eulogistic unanimity, amused himself by putting them into embarrassment.

'Well, he hasn't a pleasant temper, anyway,' said he.

This remark had a chilling effect upon the company. Each was afraid that his neighbour might be in the terrible Abbé's pay.

'The grand vicar has an excellent heart,' Monsieur Rastoil prudently remarked; 'but, like all great minds, he appears at first sight to be a little stern.'

'It is just so with me; I am very easy to get on with, but I have always had the reputation of being a hard, stern man,' exclaimed Monsieur de Bourdeu, who had become reconciled with the party again after a long private interview which he had had with Abbé Faujas.

Then, wishing to put everyone at ease again, the presiding judge exclaimed:

'Have you heard that there is a probability of a bishopric for the grand vicar?'

At this they brightened up. Monsieur Maffre expressed the opinion that it would be of Plassans itself that Abbé Faujas would become bishop, after the retirement of Monseigneur Rousselot, whose health was very feeble.

'Everyone would gain by it,' said Abbé Bourrette guilelessly. 'Illness has embittered his lordship; I know that our excellent Faujas has made the greatest efforts to persuade him out of certain unjust prejudices which he entertains.'

'He is very fond of you,' asserted Judge Paloque, who had just received his decoration; 'my wife has heard him complain of the way in which you are neglected.'

When Abbé Surin was present, he, too, joined in the general chorus; but, although he had a mitre in his pocket, to use the expression of the priests of the diocese, the success of Abbé Faujas made him uneasy. He looked at him in his pretty way, and, calling to mind the Bishop's prediction, tried to discover the weak point which would bring that colossus toppling in the dust.

The gentlemen of the party, it should be said, had had their desires satisfied; that is, excepting Monsieur de Bourdeu and Monsieur Péqueur des Saulaies, who were still waiting for the marks of the government's favour. These two were, consequently, the warmest partisans of Abbé Faujas. The others, to tell the truth, would have been glad to rebel, if they had dared. They were growing secretly weary of the continual gratitude which was exacted from them by their master, and they ardently wished that some strong, bold hand would effect their deliverance. One day Madame Paloque, with an affectation of indifference inquired:

'What has become of Abbé Fenil? I haven't seen or heard of him for an age.'

There was profound silence. Monsieur de Condamin was the only one present capable of venturing upon such dangerous ground. They all looked at him.

'Oh!' he said quietly, 'I believe he shuts himself up at his place at Les Tulettes.'

Madame de Condamin added with an ironical smile:

'He can sleep quietly now. His career is over; he will take no part again in the affairs of Plassans.'

There was only Marthe who remained a real obstacle in Abbé Faujas's path. He felt that she was escaping him more and more each day. He stiffened his will and called up all his forces as priest and man to bend her, without succeeding in moderating the flame which he had fanned into life. She was striving to reach the logical end of her passionate longings, and insisted upon forcing her way further and further into the peace and ecstasy and perfect self-forgetfulness of divine happiness. It was bitter pain and anguish to her to be, as it were, walled in and prevented from reaching that threshold of light, of which she fancied she caught a glimpse, though it seemed to be ever receding from her reach. She shivered and trembled now at Saint-Saturnin's in the coldness and the gloom amidst which she had once felt such thrills of delight. The peals of the organ no longer stirred her with a tremor of voluptuous joy; the white clouds of incense no longer lulled her into sweet mystic dreams; the gleaming chapels and the sacred pyxes that flashed like stars, the chasubles with their sheen of gold and silver, all now seemed pale and wan to her eyes that were dull and dim with tears. Like a damned soul yearning after Paradise, she threw up her arms in bitter desperation and besought the love that denied itself to her, sobbing and wailing:

'My God, my God! why hast Thou forsaken me?'

Bowed down with shame, hurt, as it were, by the cold silence of the vaulted roof, Marthe left the church, burning with the anger of a scorned woman. She had wild dreams of pouring out her blood, and she writhed madly at her impotence to do more than to pray, at being unable to spring at a single bound into the arms of God. And when she returned home, she felt that her only hope was in Abbé Faujas. It was he alone that could make her God's. He had revealed to her the initiatory joys; he must now tear aside the whole veil. But the priest fell into a passion with her and treated her roughly, refusing to hear her so long as she was not on her knees before him, humble and unresisting like a corpse. She listened to him, standing upright, sustained by an impulse of revolt that thrilled her whole being, as she vented upon him the bitterness that came of her deceived yearnings, and accused him of the base treachery which was torturing her.

Old Madame Rougon often thought it was her duty to intervene between the Abbé and her daughter, as she had formerly done between the latter and Mouret. Marthe having told her of her troubles, she spoke to the priest like a mother-in-law desiring the happiness of her children and doing her best to restore peace in their home.

'Well,' she said to him with a smile, 'can't you manage to live in peace? Marthe is constantly complaining and you seem to be perpetually grieving her. I know very well that women are exacting, but you must confess that you are a little wanting in consideration. I am extremely distressed by what occurs; it would be so easy for you to arrange matters pleasantly! Do, I beg of you, my dear Abbé, be a little more gentle with her.'

She also scolded him in a friendly fashion for his slovenly appearance. She could see, with her shrewd feminine intelligence, that he was abusing his victory. Then she began to make excuses for her daughter. The dear child, she said, had suffered a great deal, and her nervous sensitiveness required most careful treatment; but she had an excellent disposition and an affectionate nature which a clever man might mould after his own wishes. One day, however, when she was thus showing him how he might make Marthe what he liked, Abbé Faujas grew weary of her perpetual advice.

'No, no!' he cried, 'your daughter is mad; she bores me to death. I won't have anything more to do with her. I would pay the fellow well who would free me of her.'

Madame Rougon looked him keenly in the face and tightly pressed her lips.

'Listen to me, my friend,' she said after a short silence; 'you are wanting in tact, and that will prove your ruin. Overthrow yourself, if you like; I wash my hands of you. I assisted you, not for your own sake, but to please our friends in Paris. They wrote to me and asked me to pilot you, and I did so. But understand this, I will never allow you to come the master over me. It's all very well for little Péqueur, and simple Rastoil, but we are not at all afraid of you, and we mean to remain the masters. My husband conquered Plassans before you did, and I warn you that we shall keep our conquest.'

From that day forward there was great coldness between the Rougons and Abbé Faujas. When Marthe again came to complain to her mother, the latter said to her very plainly:

'Your Abbé is only making a fool of you. If I were in your place I shouldn't hesitate to tell him a few plain truths. To begin with, he has been disgustingly dirty for a long time past, and I can't understand how you can bear to take your meals at the same table with him.'

Madame Rougon had, in truth, hinted at a very ingenious plan to her husband, by which the Abbé should be ousted, and they themselves should reap the reward of his success. Now that the town voted properly, Rougon, who had not cared to risk the conduct of the campaign, was quite able to keep it in the proper path. The green drawing-room would become all the more influential, and Félicité began to await developments with that crafty patience to which she owed her fortune.

On the day when her mother told her that the Abbé was only making a fool of her, Marthe again repaired to Saint-Saturnin's resolved upon a last supreme appeal. She remained in the deserted church for two hours, pouring out her soul in prayer, waiting longingly for the ecstasy that came not, and torturing herself with her search for consolation. Impulses of deep humility stretched her prostrate upon the flag-stones, momentary thrills of rebellion made her start up again with her teeth clenched, while her whole being, wildly racked and strained, broke down at not being able to grasp or kiss aught save the aching void of her own passion. When she rose and left the church the sky seemed black to her; she was not conscious of the pavement beneath her feet; the narrow streets left upon her the impression of some immense lonely wilderness. She threw her hat and shawl upon the dining-room table and went straight upstairs to Abbé Faujas's room.

The Abbé sat buried in thought, at his little table. His pen had fallen from his fingers. He opened the door, still full of his thoughts, but when he saw Marthe standing before him, very pale, and with the light of deep resolution burning in her eyes, he made a gesture of anger.

'What do you want?' he asked. 'Why have you come upstairs? Go down again and wait for me, if you have anything to say to me.'

She pushed him aside and entered the room without speaking a word.

The priest hesitated for a moment, struggling against the influence which was prompting him to raise his hand against her. He remained standing in front of her, without closing the door that was wide open.

'What do you want?' he repeated. 'I am busy.'

Then Marthe closed the door, and having done so, drew nearer to the Abbé and said to him:

'I want to speak to you.'

She sat down and looked about the room, at the narrow bed, the shabby chest of drawers, and at the big black wooden crucifix, the sight of which, as it stood out conspicuously on the bare wall, gave her a passing thrill. A freezing silence seemed to fall from the ceiling. The grate was quite empty; there was not even a pinch of ashes in it.

'You will take cold,' said the priest in a calmer voice. 'Let us go downstairs, I beg you.'

'No; I want to speak to you,' said Marthe again.

Then, clasping her hands together like a penitent making her confession, she continued:

'I owe you much. Before you came, I was without a soul. It was you who willed that I should be saved. It is through you that I have known the only joys of my life. You are my saviour and my father. For these last five years I have only lived through you and for you.'

Her voice broke down and she almost slipped upon her knees. The priest stopped her with a gesture.

'And now, to-day,' she cried, 'I am suffering and have need of your help. Listen to me, father. Do not withdraw from me. You cannot abandon me thus. I tell you that God does not listen to me any longer. I do not feel His presence any longer. Have pity upon me, I beseech you. Advise me, lead me to those divine graces whose first joys you made me know; teach me what I should do to cure myself, and ever advance in the love of God.'

'You must pray,' said the priest gravely.

'I have prayed; I have prayed for hours with my head buried in my hands, trying to lose myself in every word of adoration, and yet I have not received consolation. I have not felt the presence of God.'

'You must pray and pray again, pray continually, pray until God is moved by your prayers and descends to you.'

She looked at him in anguish.

'Then there is nothing but prayer?' she asked. 'You cannot give me any help?'

'No; none at all,' he replied roughly.

She threw up her trembling hands in a burst of desperation, her breast heaving with anger. But she restrained herself, and she stammered:

'Your heaven is fast closed. You have led me on so far only to crush me against a wall. I was very peaceful, you will remember, when you came. I was living quietly at home here, without a single desire or curiosity. It was you who awoke me with words that stirred and roused my heart. It was you who made me enter upon a fresh youth. Oh! you cannot tell what joys you brought me at first! It was like sweet soft warmth thrilling my whole being. My heart woke up within me. I was filled with mighty hopes. Sometimes, when I reflected that I was forty years old, it all seemed foolish to me, and I smiled, and then I defended myself, for I felt so happy in it all. Now I want the promised happiness. I am growing weary of the desire for it, a desire that burns me and tortures me. I have no time to lose, now that my health has broken down, and I don't want to find myself deceived and duped. There must be something more; tell me that there is something more.'

Abbé Faujas stood quite impassive, letting this flood of words pass without reply.

'Ah! So there is nothing else! there is nothing else!' she continued, in a burst of indignation; 'then you have deceived me! Down there on the terrace, on those star-lit evenings, you promised me heaven, and

I believed your promises. I sold myself, and gave myself up. I was quite mad during those first transports of prayer. To-day the bargain holds no longer. I shall return to my old ways, and resume my old peaceful quiet. I will turn everybody out of the house, and make it as it used to be; I will again sit in my old corner on the terrace, and mend the linen. Needlework never wearies me. And I will have Désirée back to sit beside me on her little stool. She used to sit there, the dear innocent, and laugh and make dolls—'

Then she burst into a fit of sobbing:

'I want my children! They were my safeguard. Since they left I have lost my head, I have done things that I ought not to have done. Why did you take them from me? They went away from me one by one, and the house became like a strange house to me. My heart was no longer wrapped up in it, I was glad when I left it for an afternoon; and when I came back in the evening, I seemed to have fallen amongst strangers. The very furniture seemed cold and unfriendly. I quite hated the house. But I will go and fetch them again, the poor darlings. Everything will become as it used to be directly they return. Oh! if I could only sink down again into my old sleepy quiet!'

She was growing more and more excited. The priest tried to calm her by a method which he had often before found efficacious.

'Be calm, my dear lady, be calm,' he said, trying to take her hands, and hold them between his own.

'Don't touch me!' she cried, recoiling from him. 'I don't want you to do so. When you hold me I am as weak as a child. The warmth of your hands takes all my resolution and strength away. The trouble would only begin again to-morrow; for I cannot go on living like this, and you only assuage me for an hour.'

A deep shadow passed over her face as she continued:

'No! I am damned now! I shall never love my home again. And if the children come, they would ask for their father—Oh! it is that which is killing me! I shall never be forgiven till I have confessed my crime to a priest.'

Then she fell upon her knees.

'I am a guilty woman. That is why God turns His face from me.'

Abbé Faujas tried to make her rise from her knees.

'Be silent!' he cried loudly. 'I cannot hear your confession here. Come to Saint-Saturnin's to-morrow.'

'Father,' she said entreatingly, 'have pity upon me. To-morrow I shall not have the strength for it.'

'I forbid you to speak,' he cried more violently than before. 'I won't listen to anything; I shall turn my head away and close my ears.'

He stepped backward and crossed his arms, trying to check the confession that was on Marthe's lips. They looked at each other for a moment in silence, with the lurking anger that came from their conscious complicity.

'It is not a priest who listens to you,' said the Abbé in a huskier voice. 'Here there is only a man to judge and condemn you.'

At this she rose from her knees, and continued feverishly: 'A man! I prefer it, for I am not confessing; I am simply telling you of my wrong-doing. After the children had gone, I allowed their father to be put away too. He had never struck me, the unhappy man. It was I myself who was mad.... Oh, you cannot guess what frightful nightmares overwhelmed me and made me hurl myself upon the floor.

All hell seemed to be racking my brain with its torments. He, poor man, with his chattering teeth, excited my pity. It was he who was afraid of me. When you had left the room he dared not venture near me; he passed the night on a chair.'

Again did Abbé Faujas try to stop her.

'You are killing yourself,' he exclaimed. 'Don't stir up these recollections. God will take count of your sufferings.'

'It was I who sent him to Les Tulettes,' she continued, silencing the priest with an energetic gesture. 'You all told me that he was mad. Oh, the unendurable life I have led! I have always been terrified by the thought of madness. When I was quite young, I used to feel as though my skull were being opened and my head were being emptied. I seemed to have a block of ice within my brow. Ah! I felt that awful coldness again, and I was perpetually in fear of going mad. They took my husband away. I let them take him. I didn't know what I was doing. But, ever since that day, I have been unable to close my eyes without seeing him over yonder. It is that which makes me behave so strangely, which roots me for hours to the same spot, with my eyes wide open. I know the place; I can see it. My uncle Macquart showed it to me. It is as gloomy as a prison, with its black windows.'

She seemed to be choking. She raised her handkerchief to her lips, and when she took it away again it was spotted with blood. The priest, with his arms rigidly crossed in front of him, waited till the attack was over.

'You know it all, don't you?' she resumed, in stammering accents. 'I am a miserable guilty woman, I sinned for you. But give me life, give me happiness, I entreat you!'

'You lie,' said the priest slowly. 'I know nothing; I was ignorant that you were guilty of that wickedness.'

She recoiled, clasping her hands, stammering, and gazing at him with a look of terror. And at last, utterly unable to restrain herself, she broke out wildly and recklessly:

'Hear me, Ovide, I love you, and you know that I do, do you not? I have loved you, Ovide, since the first day you came here. I refrained from telling you so, for I saw it displeased you; but I knew quite well that you were gaining my whole heart. Then it was that I emptied the house for your sake. I dragged myself on my knees, and became your slave. You surely cannot go on being cruel for ever. Now that I am ill and abandoned, and my heart is broken and my head seems empty, you surely cannot reject me. It is true that we have said nothing openly before; but surely my love spoke to you, and your silence made answer. Oh! I love you, Ovide, I love you, and it is killing me.'

She burst into another fit of sobbing. Abbé Faujas had braced himself up to his full height. He stepped towards Marthe and poured out upon her all his scorn of woman.

'Oh, miserable creature!' he said. 'I hoped that you would be reasonable, and that you would never lower yourself to the shame of uttering all that vileness. Ah! it is the eternal struggle of evil against will. You are the temptation from below that leads men to base backsliding and final overthrow. The priest has no worse enemy than such as you; you ought to be driven from the churches as impure and accursed!'

'I love you, Ovide,' she again stammered; 'I love you; help me.'

'I have already come too near you,' the priest continued. 'Go away and depart from me; you are Satan! I will beat you if it be necessary to force the evil spirit from your body.'

She sank into a crouching posture against the wall, silent with terror at the priest's threatening fist. Her hair became unloosened, and a long white lock fell over her brow. As she looked about the room for a refuge, she espied the big black crucifix, and she still had strength left to stretch her hands towards it with a passionate gesture.

'Do not implore the Cross!' cried the priest in wild anger. 'Jesus lived chastely, and it was that which enabled Him to die.'

At that same moment Madame Faujas came into the room, carrying on her arm a big provision basket. She put it down at once on seeing her son so wrathful, and threw her arms around him.

'Ovide, my child, calm yourself,' she said, as she caressed him.

Then, turning upon the cowering Marthe an annihilating glance, she cried:

'Can you never leave him at peace? Are you not ashamed of yourself? Go downstairs; it is quite impossible for you to remain here. This is no place for such as you!'

Marthe did not move. Madame Faujas had to lift her up and push her towards the door. The old woman stormed at her, charging her with having waited till she had gone out, and making her promise that she would never again come upstairs to make such scenes. And finally she banged the door violently behind her.

Marthe went on, reeling down the stairs. She had ceased sobbing, and kept repeating to herself:

'François will come back again; François will turn them all out into the street.'

XXI

The Toulon coach, which passed through Les Tulettes, where it changed horses, left Plassans at three o'clock. Marthe, goaded on by a fixed, unswerving resolve, was anxious not to lose a moment. She put on her shawl and hat, and ordered Rose to dress immediately.

'I can't tell what madame's after,' said the cook to Olympe: 'but I fancy we're going away for some days.'

Marthe left the keys in the cupboard doors; she was in a hurry to be off. Olympe, who went with her to the front door, vainly tried to ascertain where she was going and how long she would be away.

'Well, make yourself quite easy,' she said to her in her pleasant way, as they parted; 'I will look after everything, you will find things all right when you come back. Don't hurry yourself, take the time to do all you want. If you go to Marseilles, bring us back some fresh shell-fish.'

Before Marthe had turned the corner of the Rue Taravelle, Olympe had taken possession of the whole house. When Trouche came home he found his wife banging the doors and examining the contents of the drawers and closets, as she hummed and sang and rushed about the rooms.

'She's gone off and taken that beast of a cook with her,' she cried to him as she lolled into an easy-chair. 'What luck it would be if they should both get upset into a ditch and stop there! Well, we must enjoy ourselves for as long as we have the chance. It's very nice being alone, isn't it, Honoré? Come and give me a kiss! We are quite by ourselves now, and we can do just as we like.'

Marthe and Rose reached the Cours Sauvaire only just in time to catch the Toulon coach. The coupé was disengaged. When the cook heard her mistress tell the conductor to set them down at Les Tulettes, she took her place with an expression of vexation, and before the coach had got out of the town she had begun grumbling in her cross-grained fashion.

'Well, I did think that you were at last going to behave sensibly! I felt sure that we were going to Marseilles to see Monsieur Octave. We could have brought back a lobster and some oysters. Ah! I shouldn't have hurried myself so if I had known. But it's just like you. You are always hunting after troubles, and always doing things that upset you.'

Marthe was lying back in her corner in a semi-conscious condition. Now that she was no longer stiffening herself against the pains which oppressed her heart, a death-like faintness was creeping over her. But the cook did not even look towards her.

'Did anyone ever hear of such an absurd idea as going to see the master?' she continued. 'A cheerful sort of sight it will be for us. We shan't be able to sleep for a week after it. You may be as frightened as you like at nights, now; you won't get me to come and look under the furniture for you. It isn't as though your going to see him could do the master any good. He's just as likely to fly at your face as not! I hope to goodness that they won't let you see him. It's against the rules, I know. I ought not to have got into the coach when I heard you mention Les Tulettes, for I don't think you would have ventured to go on such a foolish errand all by yourself.'

A deep sigh from Marthe checked her flow of words. She turned round to her mistress, saw her pale and suffocating, and grew still angrier than before as she opened the window to let in some fresh air.

'There now, you'll have to come and lie in my arms! Don't you think you'd have been ever so much better in bed, taking care of yourself? To think that you have had the good fortune to be surrounded by pious, holy people without being the least bit grateful to God Almighty for it! You know it's only the truth I'm saying. His reverence the Curé and his mother and sister, and even Monsieur Trouche himself, are all attention towards you. They would throw themselves into the fire for you; they are ready to do anything at any hour of the day or night. I saw Madame Olympe crying—yes, crying—the last time you were ill. And what sort of gratitude do you show them for all their kindness and attention? Why, you do all you can to distress them, and set off on the sly to see the master, although you know quite well that you will grieve them dreadfully by doing so, for it's impossible that they should be fond of the master, who treated you so cruelly. I'll tell you what, madame—marriage has done you no good; you've got infected with all the master's bad nature. There are times when you are every bit as bad as he is.'

All the way to Les Tulettes she continued in this strain, eulogising the Faujases and the Trouches, and accusing her mistress of every kind of wrongdoing. And she concluded by saying:

'Ah, they are the sort of people who would make excellent masters if they could only afford to keep servants. But fortune merely comes in the way of bad-hearted folks!'

Marthe, who was now calmer, made no reply. She gazed out of the window, watching the scraggy trees and the wide-stretching fields which spread out like great lengths of brown cloth. Rose's growlings were lost amidst the noisy jolting of the coach.

When they reached Les Tulettes, Marthe hastened towards the house of her uncle Macquart, followed by the cook, who had now subsided into silence, contenting herself by shrugging her shoulders and biting her lips.

'Hallo! is that you?' cried the uncle in great surprise. 'I thought you were in your bed. I heard that you were very ill. Well, my little dear, you really don't look very strong. Have you come to ask me for some dinner?'

'I should like to see François, uncle,' said Marthe.

'François?' repeated Macquart, looking her in the face. 'You would like to see François? It is a very kind thought of yours. The poor fellow has been crying for you a great deal. I have seen him from the end of my garden knocking his fist against the walls while he called for you to come to him. And so it is to see him that you have come, eh? I really thought that you had forgotten all about him over yonder.'

Big tears welled into Marthe's eyes.

'It will not be very easy to see him to-day,' Macquart continued. 'It is getting on for four o'clock, and I'm not at all sure that the manager will give you leave. Mouret hasn't been very quiet lately. He smashes everything that he can lay his hands on, and talks about burning the place down. Those madmen are not in a pleasant humour every day.'

Marthe trembled as she listened to her uncle; she was going to question him, but instead of doing so she merely stretched out her hands supplicatingly.

'I beseech you to help me,' said she. 'I have come on purpose. It is absolutely necessary that I should speak to François to-day, at once. You have friends in the asylum, and you can obtain me admission.'

'No doubt, no doubt,' he replied, without committing himself further.

He appeared to be in a state of great perplexity, unable to divine the real cause of Marthe's sudden journey, and revolving the matter in his own mind from a point of view known only to himself. He glanced inquisitively at the cook, who turned her back upon him. At last a slight smile began to play about his lips.

'Well,' he said, 'since you wish it, I will see what I can do for you. Only, remember, that if your mother is displeased about it, you must tell her that I was not able to dissuade you. I am afraid that you may do yourself harm; it isn't a pleasant place to visit.'

Rose absolutely declined to accompany them to the asylum. She had seated herself in front of a fire of vine-stocks, which was blazing on the great hearth.

'I don't want to have my eyes torn out,' she said snappishly. 'The master isn't over fond of me. I would rather stop here and warm myself.'

'It would be very good of you if you were to get us some mulled wine ready,' Macquart whispered in her ear. 'The wine and sugar are in the cupboard yonder. We shall want it when we come back.'

Macquart did not take his niece to the principal gate of the asylum. He went round to the left and inquired at a little door for warder Alexandre, with whom, on his appearance, he exchanged a few words in a low voice. Then they all three silently entered the seemingly interminable corridors. The warder walked in front.

'I will wait for you here,' said Macquart, coming to a halt in a little courtyard. 'Alexandre will remain with you.'

'I would rather be left alone,' said Marthe.

'Madame would very quickly have enough of it, if she were,' Alexandre replied, with a tranquil smile. 'I'm running a good deal of risk as it is.'

He took Marthe through another court, and stopped in front of a little door. As he softly turned the key, he said in a low voice:

'Don't be afraid. He has been quieter to-day, and they have been able to take the strait-waistcoat off. If he shows any violence you must step out backwards, and leave me alone with him.'

Marthe trembled as she passed through the narrow doorway. At first she could only see something lying in a heap against the wall in one of the corners. The daylight was waning, and the cell was merely lighted by a pale glimmer which fell from a grated window.

'Well, my fine fellow!' Alexandre exclaimed familiarly, as he stepped up to Mouret and tapped him on the shoulder; 'I am bringing you a visitor. I hope you will behave properly.'

Then he returned and leant against the door, keeping his eyes fixed upon the madman. Mouret slowly rose to his feet. He did not show the slightest sign of surprise.

'Is it you, my dear?' he said in his quiet voice. 'I was expecting you; I was getting uneasy about the children.'

Marthe's knees trembled under her, and she looked at him anxiously, rendered quite speechless by his affectionate reception. He did not appear changed at all. If anything, he looked better than he had done before. He was sleek and plump, and cleanly shaved. His eyes, too, were bright; all his former little mannerisms had reappeared, and he rubbed his hands and winked, and stalked about with his old bantering air.

'I am very well indeed, my dear. We can go back home together. You have come for me, haven't you? I hope the garden has been well looked after. The slugs were dreadfully fond of the lettuces, and the beds were quite eaten up with them, but I know a way of destroying them. I have some splendid ideas in my head that I'll tell you of. We are very comfortably off, and we can afford to pay for our fancies. By the way, have you seen old Gautier of Saint-Eutrope while I've been absent? I bought thirty hogsheads of common wine from him for blending. I must go and see him tomorrow. You never recollect anything.'

He spoke in a jesting way, and shook his finger at her playfully.

'I'll be bound that I shall find everything in dreadful disorder,' he continued. 'You never look after anything. The tools will be all lying about, the cupboard doors will be open, and Rose will be dirtying the rooms with her broom. Why hasn't Rose come with you? Ah, what a strange creature she is! Do you know, she actually wanted to turn me out of the house one day? Really, she seems to think that the whole place belongs to her. She goes on in the most amusing way possible. But you don't tell me anything about the children. Désirée is still with her nurse, I suppose. We will go and kiss her and see if she is tired of staying there. And I want to go to Marseilles as well, for I am a little uneasy about Octave. The last time I was there I found him leading a wild life. As for Serge, I have no anxiety about him; he is almost too quiet and steady. He will sanctify the whole family. Ah! I quite enjoy talking about the house and the children.'

He rattled along at great length, inquiring about every tree in his garden, going into the minutest details of the household arrangements, and showing an extraordinary memory of a host of insignificant matters. Marthe was deeply touched by the gentle affection which he manifested for her. She thought she could detect a loving delicacy in the care which he took to say nothing that savoured of reproach, to make no allusion, however slight, to all that had passed. She felt, indeed, that she was forgiven, and she vowed that she would atone for her crime by becoming the submissive servant of this man who was so sublime in his good nature. Big silent tears rolled down her cheeks, and her knees bent under her in her gratitude.

'Take care!' the warder whispered in her ear. 'I don't like the look of his eyes.'

'But he isn't mad!' she stammered; 'I swear to you that he isn't mad! I must speak to the manager. I want to take him away with me at once.'

'Take care!' the warder repeated sharply, pulling her by her arm.

Mouret had suddenly stopped short in the midst of his chatter, and was now crouching upon the floor. Then, all at once, he began to crawl along beside the wall, on his hands and knees.

'Wow! wow!' he barked in hoarse, prolonged notes.

He gave a spring into the air and fell upon his side.

Then a dreadful scene ensued. He began to writhe like a worm, beat his face with his fist, and tore his flesh with his nails. In a short time he was half naked, his clothes in rags, and himself bruised and lacerated and groaning.

'Come away, madame, come away!' cried the warder. Marthe stood rooted to the floor. She recognised in the scene before her her own writhings at home. It was in that way that she had thrown herself upon the floor of her bedroom; it was in that way that she had beaten and torn herself. She even recognised the very tones of her voice. Mouret vented the same rattling groan. It was she who had brought the poor man into this miserable state.

'He is not mad!' she stammered; 'he cannot be mad, it would be too horrible! I would rather die!'

The warder put his arm round her and pushed her out of the cell, but she remained leaning against the door on the other side. She could hear a terrible struggle going on within, screams like those of a pig being slaughtered; then a dull fall like that of a bundle of damp linen, and afterwards death-like silence. When the warder came out of the cell, the night had nearly fallen. Through the partially open doorway, Marthe could see nothing.

'Well, upon my word, madame,' cried the warder, 'you are a very queer person to say that he is not mad. I nearly left my thumb behind me; he got firmly hold of it between his teeth. However, he's quieted now for a few hours.'

And as he took her back to her uncle, he continued: 'You've no idea how cunning they all are. They are as quiet as can be for hours together, and talk to you in quite a sensible manner; and then, without the least warning, they fly at your throat. I could see very well that he was up to some mischief or other just now when he was talking to you about the children, for there was such a strange look in his eyes.'

When Marthe got back to Macquart, in the small courtyard, she exclaimed feverishly in a weak, broken voice: 'He is mad! he is mad!'

'There's no doubt he's mad,' said her uncle with a snigger. 'Why, what did you expect to find? People are not brought here for nothing. And the place isn't healthy either. If I were to be shut up there for a couple of hours, I should go mad myself.'

He was watching her askance, and he noted her nervous start and shudder. Then, in his good-natured way, he said:

'Perhaps you would like to go and see the grandmother?'

Marthe made a gesture of terror, and hid her face in her hands.

'It would be no trouble to anyone,' he said. 'Alexandre would be glad to take us. She is over yonder, on that side, and there is nothing to be afraid of with her. She is perfectly quiet. She never gives any trouble, does she, Alexandre? She always remains seated and gazing in front of her. She hasn't moved for the last dozen years. However, if you'd rather not see her, we won't go.' [1]

As the warder was taking his leave of them, Macquart invited him to come and drink a glass of mulled wine, winking the while in a certain fashion which seemed to induce Alexandre to accept the invita-

[1] 'Aunt Dide's life and death at Les Tulettes are described in 'Dr. Pascal.'—Ed.

tion. They were obliged to support Marthe, whose legs sank beneath her at each step. When they reached the house, they were actually carrying her. Her face was convulsed, her eyes were staring widely, and her whole body was rigidly stiffened by one of those nervous seizures which kept her like a dead woman for hours at a time.

'There! what did I tell you?' cried Rose, when she saw them. 'A nice state she's in! How are we to get home, I should like to know? Good heavens! how can people take such absurd fancies into their heads? The master ought to have given her neck a twist, and it would have taught her a lesson, perhaps.'

'Pooh!' said Macquart; 'I'll lay her down on my bed. It won't kill us if we have to sit up round the fire all night.'

He drew aside a calico curtain which hung in front of a recess. Rose proceeded to undress her mistress, growling as she did so. The only thing they could do, she said, was to put a hot brick at her feet.

'Now that she's all snug, we'll have a drop to drink,' resumed Macquart, with his wolfish snigger. 'That wine of yours smells awfully nice, old lady!'

'I found a lemon on the mantel-piece,' Rose said, 'and I used it.'

'You did quite right. There is everything here that is wanted. When I make a brew, there's nothing missing that ought to be in the place, I assure you.'

He pulled the table in front of the fire, and then he sat down between Rose and Alexandre, and poured the hot wine into some big yellow cups. When he had swallowed a couple of mouthfuls with great gusto, he smacked his lips and cried:

'Ah! that's first-rate. You understand how to make it. It's really better than what I make myself. You must leave me your recipe.'

Rose, greatly mollified by these compliments, began to laugh. The vine-wood fire was now a great mass of glowing embers. The cups were filled again.

'And so,' said Macquart, leaning on his elbows and looking Rose in the face, 'it was a sudden whim of my niece to come here?'

'Oh, don't talk about it,' replied the cook; 'it will make me angry again. Madame is getting as mad as the master. She can no longer tell who are her friends and who are not. I believe she had a quarrel with his reverence the Curé before she set off; I heard them shouting.'

Macquart laughed noisily.

'They used, however, to get on very well together,' said he.

'Yes, indeed; but nothing lasts long with such a brain as madame has got. I'll be bound that she's now regretting the thrashings the master used to give her at nights. We found his stick in the garden.'

Macquart looked at her more keenly, and, as he drank his hot wine, he said:

'Perhaps she came to take François back with her.'

'Oh, Heaven forbid!' cried Rose, with an expression of horror. 'The master would go on finely in the house; he would kill us all. The idea of his return is one of my greatest dreads; I'm in a constant worry lest he should make his escape and get back some night and murder us all. When I think about it when I'm in bed, I can't go to sleep. I fancy I can see him stealing in through the window with his hair bristling and his eyes flaming like matches.'

This made Macquart very merry, and he rapped his cup on the table.

'It would be very unpleasant,' he said, 'very unpleasant. I don't suppose he feels very kindly towards you, least of all towards the Curé who has stepped into his place. The Curé would only make a mouthful for him, big as he is, for madmen, they say, are awfully strong. I say, Alexandre, just imagine poor François suddenly making his appearance at home! He would make a pretty clean sweep there, wouldn't he? It would be a fine sight, eh?'

He cast glances at the warder, who went on quietly drinking his mulled wine and made no reply beyond nodding his head assentingly.

'Oh! it's only a fancy; it's all nonsense,' added Macquart, as he observed Rose's terrified looks.

Just at that moment, Marthe began to struggle violently behind the calico curtain; and she had to be held for some minutes in order that she might not fall upon the floor. When she was again stretched out in corpse-like rigidity, her uncle came and warmed his legs before the fire, reflecting and murmuring as if without paying heed to what he said:

'The little woman isn't very easy to manage, indeed.'

Then he suddenly exclaimed:

'The Rougons, now, what do they say about all this business? They take the Curé's side, don't they?'

'The master didn't make himself pleasant enough for them to regret him,' replied Rose. 'There was nothing too bad for him to say against them.'

'Well, he wasn't far wrong there,' said Macquart. 'The Rougons are wretched skinflints. Just think that they refused to buy that cornfield over yonder, a magnificent speculation which I undertook to manage. Félicité would pull a queer face if she saw François come back!'

He began to snigger again, and took a turn round the table. Then, with an expression of determination, he lighted his pipe.

'We mustn't forget the time, my boy,' he said to Alexandre, with another wink. 'I will go back with you; Marthe seems quiet now. Rose will get the table laid by the time I return. You must be hungry, Rose, eh? As you are obliged to stay the night here, you shall have a mouthful with me.'

He went off with the warder, and fully half an hour elapsed. Rose, who began to tire of being alone, at last opened the door and went out to the terrace, where she stood watching the deserted road in the clear night air. As she was going back into the house, she fancied she could see two dark shadows in the middle of a path behind a hedge.

'It looks just like the uncle,' thought she; 'he seems to be talking to a priest.'

A few minutes later Macquart returned. That blessed Alexandre, said he, had been chattering to him interminably.

'Wasn't it you who were over there just now with a priest?' asked Rose.

'I, with a priest!' he cried. 'Why, you must have been dreaming; there isn't a priest in the neighbourhood.'

He rolled his little glistening eyes. Then, as if rather uneasy about the lie he had told, he added:

'Well, there is Abbé Fenil, but it's just the same as if he wasn't here, for he never goes out.'

'Abbé Fenil isn't up to much,' remarked the cook. This seemed to annoy Macquart.

'Why do you say that? Not up to much, eh? He does a great deal of good here, and he's a very worthy sort of fellow. He's worth a whole heap of priests who make a lot of fuss.'

His irritation, however, promptly disappeared, and he began to laugh upon observing that Rose was looking at him in surprise.

'I was only joking, you know,' he said. 'You are quite right; he's like all the other priests, they are all a set of hypocrites. I know now who it was that you saw me with. I met our grocer's wife. She was wearing a black dress, and you must have mistaken that for a cassock.'

Rose made an omelet, and Macquart placed some cheese upon the table. They had not finished eating when Marthe sat up in bed with the astonished look of a person awaking in a strange place. When she had brushed aside her hair and recollected where she was, she sprang to the floor and said she must be off at once. Macquart appeared very much vexed at her awaking.

'It's quite impossible,' said he, 'for you to go back to Plassans to-night. You are shivering with fever, and you would fall ill on the road. Rest here, and we will see about it tomorrow. To begin with, there is no conveyance.'

'But you can drive me in your trap,' said Marthe.

'No, no; I can't.'

Marthe, who was dressing with feverish haste, thereupon declared that she would walk to Plassans rather than stay the night at Les Tulettes. Her uncle seemed to be thinking. He had locked the door and slipped the key into his pocket. He entreated his niece, threatened her, and invented all kinds of stories to induce her to remain. But she paid no attention to what he said, and finished by putting on her bonnet.

'You are very much mistaken if you imagine you can persuade her to give in,' exclaimed Rose, who was quietly finishing her cheese. 'She would get out through the window first. You had better put your horse to the trap.'

After a short interval of silence, Macquart, shrugging his shoulders, angrily exclaimed:

'Well, it makes no difference to me! Let her lay herself up if she likes! I was only thinking about her own good. Come along; what will happen will happen. I'll drive you over.'

Marthe had to be carried to the gig; she was trembling violently with fever. Her uncle threw an old cloak over her shoulders. Then he gave a cluck with his tongue and set off.

'It's no trouble to me,' he said, 'to go over to Plassans this evening; on the contrary, indeed, there's always some amusement to be had there.'

It was about ten o'clock. In the sky, heavy with rain clouds, there was a ruddy glimmer that cast a feeble light upon the road. All the way as they drove along Macquart kept bending forward and glancing at the ditches and the hedges. When Rose asked him what he was looking for, he replied that some wolves had come down from the ravines of La Seille. He had quite recovered his good humour. However, when they were between two and three miles from Plassans the rain began to fall. It poured down, cold and pelting. Then Macquart began to swear, and Rose would have liked to beat her mistress, who was moaning underneath the cloak. When at last they reached Plassans the rain had ceased, and the sky was blue again.

'Are you going to the Rue Balande?' asked Macquart.

'Why, of course,' replied Rose in astonishment.

Macquart thereupon began to explain that as Marthe seemed to him to be very ill, he had thought it might perhaps be better to take her to her mother's. After much hesitation, however, he consented to stop his horse at the Mourets' house. Marthe had not even thought of bringing a latchkey with her. Rose, however, fortunately had her own in her pocket, but when she tried to open the door it would not move. The Trouches had shot the bolts inside. She rapped upon it with her fist, but without rousing any other answer than a dull echo in the hall.

'It's of no use your giving yourself any further trouble,' said Macquart with a laugh. 'They won't disturb themselves to come down. Well, here you are shut out of your own home. Don't you think now that my first idea was a good one? We must take the poor child to the Rougons'. She will be better there than in her own room; I assure you she will.'

Félicité was overwhelmed with alarm when she saw her daughter arrive at such a late hour, drenched with rain and apparently half dead. She put her to bed on the second floor, set the house in great commotion, and called up all the servants. When she grew a little calmer, as she sat by Marthe's bedside, she asked for an explanation.

'What has happened? How is it that you have brought her to me in such a state as this?'

Then Macquart, with a great show of kindness, told her about 'the dear child's' expedition. He defended himself, declared that he had done all that be could to dissuade her from going to see François, and ended by calling upon Rose to confirm him, for he saw that Félicité was scanning him narrowly with her suspicious eyes. Madame Rougon, however, continued to shake her head.

'It is a very strange story!' she said; 'there is something more in it than I can understand.'

She knew Macquart, and she guessed that there must be some rascality in it all from the expression of delight which she could detect in his eyes.

'You are a strange person,' said he, pretending to get vexed in order to bring Madame Rougon's scrutiny to an end; 'you are always imagining something extraordinary. I can only tell you what I know.

I love Marthe more than you do, and I have never done anything that wasn't for her good. Shall I go for the doctor? I will at once, if you like.'

Madame Rougon watched him closely. She even questioned Rose at great length, without succeeding, however, in learning anything further. After all, she seemed glad to have her daughter with her, and spoke with great bitterness of people who would leave you to die on your own doorstep without even taking the trouble to open the door. And meantime Marthe, with her head thrown back upon her pillow, was indeed dying.

XXII

It was perfectly dark in the cell at Les Tulettes. A draught of cold air awoke Mouret from the cataleptic stupor into which his violence earlier in the evening had thrown him. He remained lying against the wall in perfect stillness for a few moments, his eyes staring widely; then he began to roll his head gently on the cold stone, wailing like a child just awakened from sleep. But the current of chill damp air swept against his legs, and he rose and looked around him to see whence it came. In front of him he saw the door of his cell wide open.

'She has left the door open,' said he aloud; 'she will be expecting me. I must be off.'

He went out, and then came back and felt his clothes after the manner of a methodical man who is afraid of forgetting something, and finally he carefully closed the door behind him. He passed through the first court with an easy unconcerned gait as though he were merely taking a stroll. As he was entering the second one, he caught sight of a warder who seemed to be on the watch. He stopped and deliberated for a moment. But, the warder having disappeared, he crossed the court and reached another door, which led to the open country. He closed it behind him without any appearance of astonishment or haste.

'She is a good woman all the same,' he murmured. 'She must have heard me calling her. It must be getting late. I will go home at once for fear they should feel uneasy.'

He struck out along a path. It seemed quite natural to him to find himself among the open fields. When he had gone a hundred yards he had altogether forgotten that Les Tulettes was behind him, and imagined that he had just left a vine-grower from whom he had purchased fifty hogsheads of wine. When he reached a spot where five roads met, he recognised where he was, and began to laugh as he said to himself:

'What a goose I am! I was going up the hill towards Saint-Eutrope; it is to the left I must turn. I shall be at Plassans in a good hour and a half.'

Then he went merrily along the high-road, looking at each of the mile-stones as at an old acquaintance. He stopped for a moment before certain fields and country-houses with an air of interest. The sky was of an ashy hue, streaked with broad rosy bands that lighted up the night like dying embers. Heavy drops of rain began to fall; the wind was blowing from the east and was full of moisture.

'Hallo!' said Mouret, looking up at the sky uneasily, 'I mustn't stop loitering. The wind is in the east, and there's going to be a pretty downpour. I shall never be able to reach Plassans before it begins; and I'm not well wrapped up either.'

He gathered round his breast the thick grey woollen waistcoat which he had torn at Les Tulettes. He had a bad bruise on his jaw to which he raised his hand without heeding the sharp pain which it caused him. The high-road was quite deserted, and he only met a cart going down a hill at a leisurely pace. The driver was dozing, and made no response to his friendly good-night. The rain did not overtake him till he reached the bridge across the Viorne. It distressed him very much, and he went to take shelter under the bridge, grumbling that it was quite impossible to go on through such weather, that nothing ruined clothes so much as rain, and that if he had known what was coming he would have brought an umbrella. He waited patiently for a long half-hour, amusing himself by listening to the streaming of the downpour; then, when it was over, he returned to the highroad, and at last reached Plassans, ever taking the greatest care to keep himself from getting splashed with mud.

It was nearly midnight, though Mouret calculated that it could scarcely yet be eight o'clock. He passed through the deserted streets, feeling quite distressed that he had kept his wife waiting such a long time.

'She won't be able to understand it,' he thought. 'The dinner will be quite cold. Ah! I shall get a nice reception from Rose.'

At last he reached the Rue Balande and stood before his own door.

'Ah!' he said, 'I have not got my latchkey.'

He did not knock at the door, however. The kitchen window was quite dark, and the other windows in the front were equally void of all sign of life. A sense of deep suspicion then took possession of the madman; with an instinct that was quite animal-like, he scented danger. He stepped back into the shadow of the neighbouring houses, and again examined the house-front; then he seemed to come to a decision, and went round into the Impasse des Chevillottes. But the little door that led into the garden was bolted. At this, impelled by sudden rage, he threw himself against it with tremendous force, and the door, rotted by damp, broke into two pieces. For a moment the violence of the shock almost stunned Mouret, and rendered him unconscious of why he had broken down the door, which he tried to mend again by joining the broken pieces.

'That's a nice thing to have done, when I might so easily have knocked,' he said with a sudden pang of regret. 'It will cost me at least thirty francs to get a new door.'

He was now in the garden. As he raised his head and saw the bedroom on the first floor brightly lighted, he came to the conclusion that his wife was going to bed. This caused him great astonishment, and he muttered that he must certainly have dropped off to sleep under the bridge while he was waiting for the rain to stop. It must be very late, he thought. The windows of the neighbouring houses, Monsieur Rastoil's as well as those of the Sub-Prefecture, were in darkness. Then he again fixed his eyes upon his own house as he caught sight of the glow of a lamp on the second floor behind Abbé Faujas's thick curtains. That glow was like a flaming eye, and seemed to scorch him. He pressed his brow with his burning hands, and his head grew dizzy, racked by some horrible recollection like a vague nightmare, in which nothing was clearly defined, but which seemed to apply to some long-standing danger to himself and his family—a danger which grew and increased in horror, and threatened to swallow up the house unless he could do something to save it.

'Marthe, Marthe, where are you?' he stammered in an undertone. 'Come and bring away the children.'

He looked about him for Marthe. He could no longer recognise the garden. It seemed to him to be larger; to be empty and grey and like a cemetery. The big box-plants had vanished, the lettuces were no longer there, the fruit-trees had disappeared. He turned round again, came back, and knelt down to see if the slugs had eaten everything up. The disappearance of the box-plants, the death of their lofty greenery, caused him an especial pang, as though some of the actual life of the house had departed. Who was it that had killed them? What villain had been there uprooting everything and tearing away even the tufts of violets which he had planted at the foot of the terrace? Indignation arose in him as he contemplated all this ruin.

'Marthe, Marthe, where are you?' he called again.

He looked for her in the little conservatory to the right of the terrace. It was littered with the dead dry corpses of the box-plants. They were piled up in bundles amidst the stumps of the fruit-trees. In one corner was Désirée's bird-cage, hanging from a nail, with the door broken off and the wire-work sadly torn. The madman stepped back, overwhelmed with fear as though he had opened the door of a vault. Stammering, his throat on fire, he went back to the terrace and paced up and down before the door and the shuttered windows. His increasing rage gave his limbs the suppleness of a wild beast's. He braced himself up and stepped along noiselessly, trying to find some opening. An air-hole into the cellar was sufficient for him. He squeezed himself together and glided inside with the nimbleness of a cat, scraping the wall with his nails as he went. At last he was in the house.

The cellar door was only latched. He made his way through the darkness of the hall, groping past the walls with his hands, and pushing the kitchen door open. Some matches were on a shelf at the left. He went straight to this shelf, and struck a light to enable him to get a lamp which stood upon the mantelpiece without breaking anything. Then he looked about him. There appeared to have been a big meal there that evening. The kitchen was in a state of festive disorder. The table was strewn with dirty plates and dishes and glasses. There was a litter of pans, still warm, on the sink and the chairs and the very floor. A coffee-pot that had been forgotten was also boiling away beside the stove, slightly tilted like a tipsy man. Mouret put it straight and then tidily arranged the pans. He smelt them, sniffed at the drops of liquor that remained in the glasses, and counted the dishes and plates with growing irritation. This was no longer his quiet orderly kitchen; it seemed as if a hotelful of food had been wasted there. All this guzzling disorder reeked of indigestion.

'Marthe! Marthe!' he again repeated as he returned into the passage, carrying the lamp as he went; 'answer me, tell me where they have shut you up. We must be off, we must be off at once.'

He searched for her in the dining-room. The two cupboards to the right and left of the stove were open. From a burst bag of grey paper on the edge of a shelf some lumps of sugar had fallen upon the floor. Higher up Mouret could see a bottle of brandy with the neck broken and plugged with a piece of rag. Then he got upon a chair to examine the cupboards. They were half empty. The jars of preserved fruits had been attacked, the jam-pots had been opened and the jam tasted, the fruit had been nibbled, the provisions of all kinds had been gnawed and fouled as though a whole army of rats had been there. Not being able to find Marthe in the closets, Mouret searched all over the room, looking behind the curtains and even underneath the furniture. Fragments of bone and pieces of broken bread lay about the floor; there were marks on the table that had been left by sticky glasses. Then he crossed the hall and went to look for Marthe in the drawing-room. But, as soon as he opened the door, he stopped short. This could not really be his own drawing-room. The bright mauve paper, the red-flowered carpet, the new easy-chairs covered with cerise damask, filled him with amazement. He was afraid to enter a room that did not belong to him, and he closed the door.

'Marthe! Marthe!' he stammered again in accents of despair.

He went back to the middle of the hall, unable to quiet the hoarse panting which was swelling in his throat. Where had he got to, that he could not recognise a single spot? Who had been transforming his house in such a way? His recollections were quite confused. He could only recall some shadows gliding along the hall; two shadows, at first poverty-stricken, soft-spoken, self-suppressing, then tipsy and disreputable-looking; two shadows that leered and sniggered. He raised his lamp, the wick of which was burning smokily, and thereupon the shadows grew bigger, lengthened upon the walls, mounted aloft beside the staircase and filled and preyed upon the whole house. Some horrid filth, some fermenting putrescence had found its way into the place and had rotted the woodwork, rusted the iron and split the walls. Then he seemed to hear the house crumbling like a ceiling from dampness, and to see it melting like a handful of salt thrown into a basin of hot water.

But up above there sounded peals of ringing laughter which made his hair stand on end. He put the lamp down and went upstairs to look for Marthe. He crept up noiselessly on his hands and knees with all the nimbleness and stealth of a wolf. When he reached the landing of the first floor, he knelt down in front of the door of the bedroom. A ray of light streamed from underneath it. Marthe must be going to bed.

'What a jolly bed this is of theirs!' Olympe was just exclaiming;'

you can quite bury yourself in it, Honoré; I am right up to my eyes in feathers.'

She laughed and stretched herself and sprang about amidst the bed-clothes.

'Ever since I've been here,' she continued, 'I've been longing to sleep in this bed. It made me almost ill wishing for it. I could never see that lath of a landlady of ours get into it without feeling a furious desire to throw her on to the floor and put myself in her place. One gets quite warm directly. It's just as though I were wrapped in cotton-wool.'

Trouche, who had not yet gone to bed, was examining the bottles on the dressing-table.

'She has got all kinds of scents,' he said.

'Well, as she isn't here, we may just as well treat ourselves to the best room!' continued Olympe. 'There's no danger of her coming back and disturbing us. I have fastened the doors up. You will be getting cold, Honoré.'

But Trouche now opened the drawers and began groping about amongst the linen.

'Put this on, it's smothered with lace,' he said, tossing a night-dress to Olympe. 'I shall wear this red handkerchief myself.'

Then, as Trouche was at last getting into bed, Olympe said to him:

'Put the grog on the night-table. We need not get up and go to the other end of the room for it. There, my dear, we are like real householders now!'

They lay down side by side, with the eider-down quilt drawn up to their chins.

'I ate a deuced lot this evening,' said Trouche after a short pause.

'And drank a lot, too!' added Olympe with a laugh. 'I feel very cosy and snug. But the tiresome part is that my mother is always interfering with us. She has been quite awful to-day. I can't take a single step about the house without her being at me. There's really no advantage in our landlady going off if mother means to play the policeman. She has quite spoilt my day's enjoyment.'

'Hasn't the Abbé some idea of going away?' asked Trouche after another short interval of silence. 'If he is made a bishop, he will be obliged to leave the house to us.'

'One can't be sure of that,' Olympe petulantly replied. 'I dare say mother means to keep it. But how jolly we should be here, all by ourselves! I would make our landlady sleep upstairs in my brother's room; I'd persuade her that it was healthier than this. Pass me the glass, Honoré.'

They both took a drink and then covered themselves up afresh.

'Ah!' said Trouche, 'I'm afraid it won't be so easy to get rid of them, but we can try, at any rate. I believe the Abbé would have changed his quarters before if he had not been afraid that the landlady would have considered herself deserted and have made a rumpus. I think I'll try to talk the landlady over. I'll tell her a lot of tales to persuade her to turn them out.'

He took another drink.

'Oh! leave the matter to me,' replied Olympe; 'I'll get mother and Ovide turned out, as they've treated us so badly.'

'Well, if you don't succeed,' said Trouche, 'I can easily concoct some scandal about the Abbé and Madame Mouret; and then he will be absolutely obliged to shift his quarters.'

Olympe sat up in bed.

'That's a splendid idea,' she said, 'that is! We must set about it tomorrow. Before a month is over, this room will be ours. I must really give you a kiss for the idea.'

They then both grew very merry, and began to plan how they would arrange the room. They would change the place of the chest of drawers, they said; and they would bring up a couple of easy-chairs from the drawing-room. However, their speech was gradually growing huskier, and at last they became silent.

'There! you're off now!' murmured Olympe, after a time. 'You're snoring with your eyes open! Well, let me come to the other side, so that, at any rate, I can finish my novel. I'm not sleepy, if you are.'

She got up and rolled him like a mere lump towards the wall, and then began to read. But, before she had finished a page, she turned her head uneasily towards the door. She fancied she could hear a strange noise on the landing. At this she cried petulantly to her husband, giving him a dig in the ribs with her elbow:

'You know very well that I don't like that sort of joke. Don't play the wolf; anyone would fancy that there was somebody at the door. Well, go on if it pleases you; you are very irritating.'

Then she angrily absorbed herself in her book again, after sucking a slice of lemon left in her glass.

With the same stealthy movements as before, Mouret now quitted the door of the bedroom, where he had remained crouching. He climbed to the second floor and knelt before Abbé Faujas's door, squeezing himself close to the keyhole. He choked down Marthe's name, that again rose in his throat, and examined with glistening eye the corners of the priest's room, to satisfy himself that nobody was shut up there. The big bare room was in deep shadow; a small lamp which stood upon the table cast just a circular patch of light upon the floor, and the Abbé himself, who was writing, seemed like a big black stain in the midst of that yellow glare. After he had scrutinised the curtains and the chest of drawers, Mouret's gaze fell upon the iron bedstead, upon which lay the priest's hat, looking like the locks of a woman's hair. There was no doubt that Marthe was there, thought Mouret. Hadn't the Trouches said that she was to have that room? But as he continued gazing he saw that the bed was undisturbed, and looked, with its cold, white coverings, like a tombstone. His eyes were getting accustomed to the gloom. However, Abbé Faujas appeared to hear some sound, for he glanced at the door. When the maniac saw the priest's calm face his eyes reddened, a slight foam appeared at the corner of his lips, and it was with difficulty that he suppressed a shout. At last he went away on his hands and knees again, down the stairs and along the passages, still repeating in low tones:

'Marthe! Marthe!'

He searched for her through the whole house; in Rose's room, which he found empty; in the Trouches' apartments, which were filled with the spoils of the other rooms; in the children's old rooms, where he burst into tears as his hands came across a pair of worn-out boots which had belonged to Désirée. He went up and down the stairs, clinging on to the banisters, and gliding along the walls, stealthily exploring every apartment with the extraordinary dexterity of a scheming maniac. Soon there was not a single corner of the place from the cellar to the attic which he had not investigated. Marthe was nowhere in the house; nor were the children there, nor Rose. The house was empty; the house might crumble to pieces.

Mouret sat down upon the stairs. He choked down the panting which, in spite of himself, continued to distend his throat. With his back against the banisters, and his eyes wide open in the darkness, he sat waiting, absorbed in a scheme which he was patiently thinking out. His senses became so acute that he could hear the slightest sounds that arose in the house. Down below him snored Trouche, while Olympe turned over the pages of her book with a slight rubbing of her fingers against the paper. On the second floor Abbé Faujas's pen made a scratching sound like the crawling of an insect, while, in the adjoining room, Madame Faujas's heavy breathing seemed like an accompaniment to that shrill music. Mouret sat for an hour with his ears sharply strained. Olympe was the first of the wakeful ones to succumb to sleep. He could hear her novel fall upon the floor. Then Abbé Faujas laid down his pen and undressed himself, quietly gliding about his room in his slippers. He slipped off his clothes in silence, and did not even make the bed creak as he got into it. Ah! the house had gone to rest at last. But the madman could tell from the sound of the Abbé's breathing that he was yet awake. Gradually that breathing grew fuller, and at last the whole house slept.

Mouret waited on for another half-hour. He still listened with strained ears, as though he could hear the four sleepers descending into deeper and deeper slumber. The house lay wrapped in darkness and unconsciousness. Then the maniac rose up and slowly made his way into the passage.

'Marthe isn't here any longer; the house isn't here; nothing is here,' he murmured.

He opened the door that led into the garden, and went down to the little conservatory. When he got there he methodically removed the big dry box-plants, and carried them upstairs in enormous armfuls, piling them in front of the doors of the Trouches and the Faujases. He felt, too, a craving for a bright light, and he went into the kitchen and lighted all the lamps, which he placed upon the tables in the various rooms and on the landings, and along the passages. Then he brought up the rest of the box-plants. They were soon piled higher than the doors. As he was making his last journey with them he raised his eyes and noticed the windows. Next he went out into the garden again, took the trunks of the fruit-trees and stacked them up under the windows, skillfully arranging for little currents of air which should make them blazc freely. The stack, seemed to him but a small one, however.

'There is nothing left,' he murmured: 'there must be nothing left.'

Then, as a thought struck him, he went down into the cellar, and recommenced his journeying backwards and forwards. He was now carrying up the supply of fuel for the winter, the coal, the vine-branches, and the wood. The pile under the windows gradually grew bigger. As he carefully arranged each bundle of vine-branches, he was thrilled with livelier satisfaction. He next proceeded to distribute the fuel through the rooms on the ground-floor, and left a heap of it in the entrance-hall, and another heap in the kitchen. Then he piled the furniture atop of the different heaps. An hour sufficed him to get his work finished. He had taken his boots off, and had glided about all over the house, with heavily laden arms, so dexterously that he had not let a single piece of wood fall roughly to the floor. He seemed endowed with new life, with extraordinary nimbleness of motion. As far as this one firmly fixed idea of his went, he was perfectly in possession of his senses.

When all was ready, he lingered for a moment to enjoy the sight of his work. He went from pile to pile, took pleasure in viewing the square-set pyres, and gently rubbed his hands together with an appearance of extreme satisfaction. As a few fragments of coal had fallen on the stairs, he ran off to get a brush, and carefully swept the black dust from the steps. Then he completed his inspection with the careful precision of a man who means to do things as they ought to be done. He gradually became quite excited with satisfaction, and dropped on to his hands and knees again, and began to hop about, panting more heavily in his savage joy.

At last he took a vine-branch and set fire to the heaps. First of all he lighted the pile on the terrace underneath the windows. Then he leapt back into the house and set fire to the heaps in the drawing-room and dining-room, and then to those in the kitchen and the hall. Next he sprang up the stairs and flung the remains of his blazing brand upon the piles that lay against the doors of the Trouches and Faujases. An ever-increasing rage was thrilling him, and the lurid blaze of the fire brought his madness to a climax. He twice came down the stairs with terrific leaps, bounded about through the thick smoke, fanning the flames with his breath, and casting handfuls of coal upon them. At the sight of the flames, already mounting to the ceilings of the rooms, he sat down every now and then and laughed and clapped his hands with all his strength.

The house was now roaring like an over-crammed stove. The flames burst out at all points, at once, with a violence that split the floors. But the maniac made his way upstairs again through the sheets of fire, singeing his hair and blackening his clothes as he went. And he posted himself on the second-floor, crouching down on his hands and knees with his growling, beast-like head thrown forward. He was keeping guard over the landing, and his eyes never quitted the priest's door.

'Ovide! Ovide!' shrieked a panic-stricken voice.

Madame Faujas's door at the end of the landing was suddenly

opened and the flames swept into her room with the roar of a tempest. The old woman appeared in the midst of the fire. Stretching out her arms, she hurled aside the blazing brands and sprang on to the landing, pulling and pushing away with her hands and feet the burning heap that blocked up her son's door, and calling all the while to the priest despairingly. The maniac crouched still lower down, his eyes gleaming while he continued to growl.

'Wait for me! Don't get out of the window!' cried Madame Faujas, striking at her son's door.

She threw her weight against it, and the charred door yielded easily. She reappeared holding her son in her arms. He had taken time to put on his cassock, and was choking, half suffocated by the smoke.

'I am going to carry you, Ovide,' she cried, with energetic determination. 'Hold well on to my shoulders, and clutch hold of my hair if you feel you are slipping. Don't trouble, I'll carry you through it all.'

She hoisted him upon her shoulders as though he were a child, and this sublime mother, this old peasant woman, carrying her devotion to death itself, did not so much as totter beneath the crushing weight of that big swooning, unresisting body. She extinguished the burning brands with her naked feet and made a free passage through the flames by brushing them aside with her open hand so that her son might not even be touched by them. But just as she was about to go downstairs, the maniac, whom she had not observed, sprang upon the Abbé Faujas and tore him from off her shoulders. His muttered growl turned into a wild shriek, while he writhed in a fit at the head of the stairs. He belaboured the priest, tore him with his nails and strangled him.

'Marthe! Marthe!' he bellowed.

Then he rolled down the blazing stairs, still with the priest in his grasp; while Madame Faujas, who had driven her teeth into his throat, drained his blood. The Trouches perished in their drunken stupor without a groan; and the house, gutted and undermined, collapsed in the midst of a cloud of sparks.

XXIII

Macquart did not find Porquier at home, and so the doctor only reached Madame Rougon's at nearly half-past twelve. The whole house was still in commotion. Rougon himself was the only one who had not got out of bed. Emotion had a killing effect upon him, said he. Félicité, who was still seated in the same armchair by Marthe's bedside, rose to meet the doctor.

'Oh, my dear doctor, we are so very anxious!' she murmured. 'The poor child has never stirred since we put her to bed there. Her hands are already quite cold. I have kept them in my own, but it has done no good.'

Doctor Porquier scanned Marthe's face, and then, without making any further examination, he compressed his lips and made a vague gesture with his hands.

'My dear Madame Rougon,' he said, 'you must summon up your courage.'

Félicité burst into sobs.

'The end is at hand,' the doctor continued in a lower voice. 'I have been expecting this sad termination for a long time past; I must confess so much now. Both of poor Madame Mouret's lungs are diseased, and in her case phthisis has been complicated by nervous derangement.'

He took a seat, and a smile played about his lips, the smile of the polished doctor who thinks that even in the presence of death itself suave politeness is demanded of him.

'Don't give way and make yourself ill, my dear lady. The catastrophe was inevitable and any little accident might have hastened it. I should imagine that poor Madame Mouret must have been subject to coughing when she was very young; wasn't she? I should say that the germs of the disease have been spreading within her for a good many years past. Latterly, and especially within the last three years, phthisis has been making frightful strides in her. How pious and devotional she was! I have been quite touched to see her passing away in such sanctity. Well, well, the decrees of Providence are inscrutable; science is very often quite powerless.'

Seeing that Madame Rougon still continued to weep, he poured out upon her the tenderest consolations, and pressed her to take a cup of lime-flower water to calm herself.

'Don't distress yourself, I beg you,' he continued. 'I assure you that she has lost all sense of pain. She will continue sleeping as tranquilly as she is doing at present, and will only regain consciousness just before death. I won't leave you; I will remain here, though my services are quite unavailing. I shall stay, however, as a friend, my dear lady, as a friend.'

He settled himself comfortably for the night in an easy chair.

Félicité grew a little calmer. When Doctor Porquier gave her to understand that Marthe had only a few more hours to live, she thought of sending for Serge from the Seminary, which was near at hand. She asked Rose to go there for him, but the cook at first refused.

'Do you want to kill the poor little fellow as well?' she exclaimed. 'It would be too great a shock for him to be called up in the middle of the night to come to see a dead woman. I won't be his murderer!'

Rose still retained bitter feelings against her mistress. Ever since the latter had been lying there dying she had paced round the bed, angrily knocking about the cups and the hot-water bottles.

'Was there any sense in doing such a thing as madame did?' she cried. 'She has only herself to blame if she has got her death by going to see the master. And now everything is turned topsy-turvy and we are all distracted. No no; I don't approve at all of the little fellow being startled out of his sleep in such a way.'

In the end, however, she consented to go to the Seminary. Doctor Porquier had stretched himself out in front of the fire, and with half-closed eyes continued to address consolatory words to Madame Rougon. A slight rattling sound began to be heard in Marthe's chest. Uncle Macquart, who had not appeared again since he had gone away two good hours previously, now gently pushed the door open.

'Where have you been?' Félicité asked him, taking him into a corner of the room.

He told her that he had been to put his horse and trap up at The Three Pigeons. But his eyes sparkled so vividly, and there was such a look of diabolical cunning about him, that she was filled with a thousand suspicions. She forgot her dying daughter for the moment, for she scented some trickery which it was imperative for her to get to the bottom of.

'Anyone would imagine that you had been following and playing the spy upon somebody,' she said, looking at his muddy trousers. 'You are hiding something from me, Macquart. It is not right of you. We have always treated you very well.'

'Oh, very well, indeed!' sniggered Macquart. 'I'm glad you've told me so. Rougon is a skinflint. He treated me like the lowest of the low in the matter of that cornfield. Where is Rougon? Snoozing comfortably in his bed, eh? It's little he cares for all the trouble one takes about the family.'

The smile which accompanied these last words greatly disquieted Félicité. She looked him keenly in the face.

'What trouble have you taken for the family?' she asked. 'Do you grudge having brought poor Marthe back from Les Tulettes? I tell you again that all that business has a very suspicious look. I have been questioning Rose, and it seems to me that you wanted to come straight here. It surprises me that you did not knock more loudly in the Rue Balande; they would have come and opened the door. I'm not saying this because I don't want my dear child to be here; I am glad to think, on the contrary, that she will, at any rate, die among her own people, and will have only loving faces about her.'

Macquart seemed greatly surprised at this speech, and interrupted her by saying with an uneasy manner:

'I thought that you and Abbé Faujas were the best of friends.'

She made no reply, but stepped up to Marthe, whose breathing was now becoming more difficult. When she left the bedside again, she saw Macquart pulling one of the curtains aside and peering out into the dark night, while rubbing the moist window-pane with his hand.

'Don't go away to-morrow without coming and talking to me,' she said to him. 'I want to have all this cleared up.'

'Just as you like,' he replied. 'You are very difficult to please. First you like people, and then you don't like them. I always keep on in the same regular easy-going way.'

He was evidently very much vexed to find that the Rougons no longer made common cause with Abbé Faujas. He tapped the window with the tips of his fingers, and still kept his eyes on the black night. Just at that moment the sky was reddened by a sudden glow.

'What is that?' asked Félicité. Macquart opened the window and looked out. 'It looks like a fire,' he said unconcernedly. 'There is something burning behind the Sub-Prefecture.'

There were sounds of commotion on the Place. A servant came into the room with a scared look and told them that the house of madame's daughter was on fire. It was believed, he continued, that madame's son-in-law, he whom they had been obliged to shut up, had been seen walking about the garden carrying a burning vine-branch. The most unfortunate part of the matter was that there seemed no hope of saving the lodgers. Félicité turned sharply round, and pondered for a minute, keeping her eyes fixed on Macquart. Then she clearly understood everything.

'You promised me solemnly,' she said in a low voice, 'that you would conduct yourself quietly and decently when we set you up in your little house at Les Tulettes. You have everything that you want, and are quite independent. This is abominable, disgraceful, I tell you! How much did Abbé Fenil give you to let François escape?'

Macquart was going to break out angrily, but Madame Rougon made him keep silent. She seemed much more uneasy about the consequences of the matter than indignant at the crime itself.

'And what a terrible scandal there will be, if it all comes out,' she continued. 'Have we ever refused you anything? We will talk together to-morrow, and we will speak again of that cornfield about which you are so bitter against us. If Rougon were to hear of such a thing as this, he would die of grief.'

Macquart could not help smiling. Still he defended himself energetically, and swore that he knew nothing about the matter, and had had no hand in it. Then, as the sky grew redder, and Doctor Porquier had already gone downstairs he left the room, saying, as if he were anxiously curious about the matter:

'I am going to see what is happening.'

It was Monsieur Péqueur des Saulaies who had given the alarm. There had been an evening party at the Sub-Prefecture, and he was just going to bed at a few minutes before one o'clock when he perceived a strange red reflection upon the ceiling of his bedroom. Going to the window, he was struck with astonishment at seeing a great fire burning in the Mourets' garden, while a shadowy form, which he did not at first recognise, danced about in the midst of the smoke, brandishing a blazing vine-branch. Almost immediately afterwards flames burst out from all the openings on the ground-floor. The sub-prefect hurriedly put on his trousers again, called his valet, and sent the porter off to summon the fire-brigade and the authorities. Then, before going to the scene of the disaster, he finished dressing himself and consulted his mirror to make sure that his moustache was quite as it should be. He was the first to arrive in the Rue Balande. The street was absolutely deserted, save for a couple of cats which were rushing across it.

'They will let themselves be broiled like cutlets in there!' thought Monsieur Péqueur des Saulaies, astonished at the quiet, sleepy appearance of the house on the street side, where as yet there was no sign of the conflagration.

He knocked loudly at the door, but could hear nothing except the roaring of the fire in the well of the staircase. Then he knocked at Monsieur Rastoil's door. There piercing screams were heard, hurried rustlings to and fro, banging of doors and stifled calls.

'Aurélie, cover up your shoulders!' cried the presiding judge, who rushed out on to the pathway, followed by Madame Rastoil and her younger daughter, the one who was still unmarried. In her hurry, Aurélie had thrown over her shoulders a cloak of her father's, which left her arms bare. She turned very red as she caught sight of Monsieur Péqueur des Saulaies.

'What a terrible disaster!' stammered the presiding judge. 'Everything will be burnt down. The wall of my bedroom is quite hot already. The two houses almost join. Ah! my dear sub-prefect, I haven't even stopped to remove the timepieces. We must organise assistance. We can't stand by and let all our belongings be destroyed in an hour or two.'

Madame Rastoil, scantily clothed in a dressing-gown, was bewailing her drawing-room furniture, which she had only just had newly covered. By this time, however, several neighbours had appeared at their windows. The presiding judge summoned them to his assistance, and commenced to remove his effects from his house. He made the time-pieces his own particular charge, and brought them out and deposited them on the pathway opposite. When the easy-chairs from the drawing-room were carried out, he made his wife and daughter sit down in them, and the sub-prefect remained by their side to reassure them.

'Make yourselves easy, ladies,' he said. 'The engine will be here directly, and then a vigorous attack will be made upon the fire. I think I may undertake to promise that your house will be saved.'

All at once the window-panes of the Mourets' house burst, and the flames broke out from the first floor. The street was illumined by a bright glow; it was as light as at midday. A drummer could be heard passing across the Place of the Sub-Prefecture, some distance off, sounding the alarm. A number of men ran up, and a chain was formed to pass on the buckets of water; but there were no buckets; and still the engine did not arrive. In the midst of the general consternation Monsieur Péqueur des Saulaies, without leaving the two ladies, shouted out orders in a loud voice.

'Leave a free passage! The chain is too closely formed down there! Keep yourselves two feet apart!'

Then he turned to Aurélie and said in a low voice:

'I am very much surprised that the engine has not arrived yet. It is a new engine. This will be the first time it has been used. I sent the porter off immediately, and I told him also to call at the police-station.'

However, the gendarmes arrived before the end. They kept back the inquisitive spectators, whose numbers increased, notwithstanding the lateness of the hour. The sub-prefect himself went to put the chain in a better order, as it was bulging out in the middle, through the pushing of some rough fellows who had run up from the outskirts of the town. The little bell of Saint-Saturnin's was sounding the alarm with cracked notes, and a second drum beat faintly at the bottom of the street near the Mall. At last the engine arrived with a noisy clatter. The crowd made way for it, and the fifteen panting firemen of Plassans came up at a run. However, in spite of Monsieur Péqueur des Saulaies's intervention, a quarter of an hour elapsed before the engine was in working order.

'I tell you that it is the piston that won't work!' cried the captain angrily to the sub-prefect, who asserted that the nuts were too tightly screwed.

At last a jet of water shot up, and the crowd gave a sigh of satisfaction. The house was now blazing from the ground-floor to the second-floor like a huge torch. The water hissed as it fell into the burning mass, and the flames, separating into yellow tongues, seemed to shoot up still higher than before. Some of the firemen had mounted on to the roof of the presiding judge's house, and were breaking open the tiles with their picks to limit the progress of the fire.

'It's all up with the place!' muttered Macquart, who stood quietly on the pathway with his hands in his pockets, watching the conflagration with lively interest.

Out in the street a perfect open-air drawing-room had now been established. The easy-chairs were arranged in a semicircle, as though to allow their occupants to view the spectacle at their ease. Madame de Condamin and her husband had just arrived. They had scarcely got back home from the Sub-Prefecture, they said, when they had heard the drum beating the alarm. Monsieur de Bourdeu, Monsieur Maffre, Doctor Porquier, and Monsieur Delangre, accompanied by several members of the municipal council, had also lost no time in hastening to the scene. They all clustered round poor Madame Rastoil and her daughter, trying to comfort and console them with sympathetic remarks. After a time most of them sat down in the easy-chairs, and a general conversation took place, while the engine snorted away half a score yards off and the blazing beams crackled.

'Have you got my watch, my dear?' Madame Rastoil inquired. 'It was on the mantelpiece with the chain.'

'Yes, yes, I have it in my pocket,' replied the president, trembling with emotion. 'I have got the silver as well. I wanted to bring everything away, but the firemen wouldn't let me; they said it was ridiculous.'

Monsieur Péqueur des Saulaies still showed the greatest calmness and kindly attention.

'I assure you that your house is in no danger at all,' he remarked. 'The force of the fire is spent now. You may go and put your silver back in your dining-room.'

But Monsieur Rastoil would not consent to part with his plate, which he was carrying under his arm, wrapped up in a newspaper.

'All the doors are open,' he stammered, 'and the house is full of people that I know nothing about. They have made a hole in my roof that will cost me a pretty penny to put right again.'

Madame de Condamin now questioned the sub-prefect.

'Oh! how terrible!' she cried. 'I thought that the lodgers had had time to escape. Has nothing been seen of Abbé Faujas?'

'I knocked at the door myself,' said Monsieur Péqueur des Saulaies, 'but I couldn't make anyone hear. When the firemen arrived I had the door broken open, and I ordered them to place the ladders against the windows. But nothing was of any use. One of our brave gendarmes who ventured into the hall narrowly escaped being suffocated by the smoke.'

'As Abbé Faujas has been, I suppose! What a horrible death!' said the fair Octavie, with a shudder.

The ladies and gentlemen looked into one another's faces, which showed pale in the flickering light of the conflagration. Doctor Porquier explained to them, however, that death by fire was probably not so painful as they imagined.

'When the fire once reaches one,' he said in conclusion, 'it can only be a matter of few seconds. Of course, it depends, to some extent, upon the violence of the conflagration.'

Monsieur de Condamin was counting upon his fingers.

'Even if Madame Mouret is with her parents, as is asserted, that still leaves four—Abbé Faujas, his mother, his sister, and his brother-in-law. It's a pretty bad business!'

Just then Madame Rastoil inclined her head towards her husband's ear. 'Give me my watch,' she whispered. 'I don't feel easy about it. You are always fidgetting, and you may sit on it.'

Someone now called out that the wind was carrying the sparks towards the Sub-Prefecture, and Monsieur Péqueur des Saulaies immediately sprang up, and, apologising for his departure, hastened off to guard against this new danger.

Monsieur Delangre was anxious that a last attempt should be made to rescue the victims. But the captain of the fire brigade roughly told him to go up the ladder himself if he thought such a thing possible; he had never seen such a fire before, he declared. The devil himself must have lighted it, for the house was burning like a bundle of chips, at all points at once. The mayor, followed by some kindly disposed persons, then went round into the Impasse des Chevillottes. Perhaps, he said, it would be possible to get to the windows from the garden side.

'It would be very magnificent if it were not so sad,' remarked Madame de Condamin, who was now calmer.

The fire was certainly becoming a superb spectacle. Showers of sparks rushed up in the midst of huge blue flames; chasms of glowing red showed themselves behind each of the gaping windows, while the smoke rolled gently away in a huge purplish cloud, like the smoke from Bengal lights set burning at some display of fireworks. The ladies and gentlemen were comfortably seated in their chairs, leaning on their elbows and stretching out their legs as they watched the spectacle before them; and whenever there was a more violent burst of flames than usual, there came an interval of silence, broken by exclamations. At some distance off, in the midst of the flickering brilliance which every now and then lighted up masses of serried heads, there rose the murmur of the crowd, the sound of gushing water, a general confused uproar. Ten paces away the engine, with its regular, snorting breath, continued vomiting streams of water from its metal throat.

'Look at the third window on the second floor!' suddenly cried Monsieur Maffre. 'You can see a bed burning quite distinctly on the left hand. It has yellow curtains, and they are blazing like so much paper.'

Monsieur Péqueur des Saulaies now returned at a gentle trot to reassure the ladies and gentlemen. It had been a false alarm.

'The sparks,' he said, 'are certainly being carried by the wind towards the Sub-Prefecture, but they are extinguished in the air before they reach it. There is no further danger. They have got the fire well in hand now.'

'But is it known how the fire originated?' asked Madame de Condamin.

Monsieur de Bourdeu asserted that he had first of all seen a dense smoke issuing from the kitchen. Monsieur Maffre alleged, on the other hand, that the flames had first appeared in a room on the first floor. But the sub-prefect shook his head with an air of official prudence, and said in a low voice:

'I am much afraid that malice has had something to do with the disaster. I have ordered an inquiry to be made.'

Then he went on to tell them that he had seen a man lighting the fire with a vine-branch.

'Yes, I saw him too,' interrupted Aurélie Rastoil. 'It was Monsieur Mouret.'

This statement created the greatest astonishment. The thing seemed impossible. Monsieur Mouret escaping and burning down his house—what a frightful story! They overwhelmed Aurélie with questions. She blushed, and her mother looked at her severely. It was scarcely proper for a young girl to be constantly looking out of her window at night-time.

'I assure you that I distinctly recognised Monsieur Mouret,' she continued. 'I had not gone to sleep, and I got up when I saw a bright light. Monsieur Mouret was dancing about in the midst of the fire.'

Then the sub-prefect spoke out:

'Mademoiselle is quite correct. I recognise the unhappy man now. He looked so terrible that I was in doubt as to who it might be, although his face seemed familiar. Excuse me; this is a very serious matter, and I must go and give some orders.'

He went away again, while the company began to discuss this terrible affair of a landlord burning his lodgers to death. Monsieur de Bourdeu inveighed hotly against lunatic asylums. The surveillance exercised in them, he said, was most imperfect. The truth was that Monsieur de Bourdeu was greatly afraid lest the prefecture which Abbé Faujas had promised him should be burnt away in the fire before his eyes.

'Maniacs are extremely revengeful,' said Monsieur de Condamin, in all simplicity.

This remark seemed to embarrass everyone, and the conversation dropped. The ladies shuddered slightly, while the men exchanged peculiar glances. The burning house had become an object of still greater interest now that they knew whose hand had set it on fire. They blinked with a thrill of delicious terror as they gazed upon the glowing pile, and thought of the drama that had been enacted there.

'If old Mouret is in there, that makes five,' said Monsieur de Condamin. Then the ladies hushed him and told him that he was a cold-blooded, unfeeling man.

The Paloques, meanwhile, had been watching the fire since its commencement from the window of their dining-room. They were just above the drawing-room that had been improvised upon the pathway. The judge's wife at last went out, and graciously offered shelter and hospitality to the Rastoil ladies and the friends surrounding them.

'We can see very well from our windows, I assure you,' she said.

And, as the ladies declined her invitation, she added:

'You will certainly take cold; it is a very sharp night.'

But Madame de Condamin smiled and stretched out her little feet, which showed from beneath her skirts.

'Oh dear no! we're not at all cold,' she said. 'My feet are quite toasted. I am very comfortable indeed. Are you cold, mademoiselle?'

'I am really too warm,' Aurélie replied. 'One could imagine that it was a summer night. This fire keeps one quite warm and cosy.'

Everyone declared that it was very pleasant, and so Madame Paloque determined to remain there with them and to take a seat in one of the easy-chairs. Monsieur Maffre had just gone off. He had caught sight, in the midst of the crowd, of his two sons, accompanied by Guillaume Porquier, who had all three run up from a house near the ramparts to see the fire. The magistrate, who was certain that he had locked his lads up in their bedroom, dragged Alphonse and Ambroise away by the ears.

'I think we might go off to bed now,' said Monsieur de Bourdeu, who was gradually growing more cross-grained.

However, Monsieur Péqueur des Saulaies had reappeared again, and showed himself quite indefatigable, though he never neglected the ladies, in spite of the duties and anxieties of all kinds with which he was overwhelmed. He sprang hastily forward to meet Monsieur Delangre, who was just coming back from the Impasse des Chevillottes. They talked together in low tones. The mayor had apparently witnessed some terrible sight, for he kept passing his hand over his face, as though trying to drive away some awful vision that was pursuing him. The ladies could only hear him murmuring, 'We arrived too late! It was horrible!' He would not answer any questions.

'Only Bourdeu and Delangre will regret Abbé Faujas,' Monsieur de Condamin whispered in Madame Paloque's ear.

'They had business on hand with him,' the latter replied quietly. 'Ah! here is Abbé Bourrette. He is weeping from genuine sorrow.'

Abbé Bourrette, who had formed part of the chain of men who passed the buckets on, was sobbing bitterly. The poor man refused all consolation. He would not sit down, but remained standing, with anxious, troubled eyes, watching the last beams burn away. Abbé Surin had also been seen; but he had disappeared after picking up in the crowd all the information he could.

'Come along; let us be off to bed,' exclaimed Monsieur de Bourdeu. 'It is foolish of us to stop here.'

The whole party rose. It was settled that Monsieur Rastoil and his wife and daughter should spend the night at the Paloques'. Madame de Condamin gently tapped her dress, which had got slightly creased, in order to straighten it. The easy-chairs were pushed out of the way, and the company lingered yet a few more moments while bidding each other good-night. The engine was still snorting, and the fire was dying down amidst dense black smoke. Nothing was to be heard but the tramping of the diminishing crowd and the last blows of a fireman's axe striking down a beam.

'It is all over!' thought Macquart, who still kept his position on the opposite pathway.

He remained there a few moments longer, listening to the last words which Monsieur de Condamin exchanged in low tones with Madame Paloque.

'Bah!' said the judge's wife, 'no one will cry for him, unless it's that big gander Bourrette. He had grown quite unendurable, and we were nothing but his slaves. His lordship the Bishop, I dare say, has got a smiling face just now. Plassans is at last delivered!'

'And the Rougons!' exclaimed Monsieur de Condamin. 'They must be quite delighted.'

'I should think so, indeed. The Rougons must be up in the heavens. They will inherit the Abbé's conquest. Ah! they would have paid anyone well who would have run the risk of setting the house on fire.'

Macquart went away feeling extremely dissatisfied. He was beginning to fear that he had been duped. The joy of the Rougons filled him with consternation. The Rougons were crafty folks who always played a double game, and whose opponents were quite certain to end by getting the worst of the struggle. As Macquart crossed the Place of the Sub-Prefecture he swore to himself that he would never set to work in this blind way again.

As he went up to the room where Marthe lay dying he found Rose sitting on one of the stairs. She was in a fuming rage.

'No, indeed, I will certainly not stop in the room!' she cried. 'I won't look on and see such things. Let her die without me; let her die like a dog! I no longer have any love for her; I have no love for anyone. To send for the poor little fellow to kill him! And I consented to go for him! I shall hate myself for it all my life! He was as white as his nightshirt, the angel! I was obliged to carry him here from the Seminary. I thought he was going to give up the ghost on the way, he cried so. Oh! it's a cruel shame! And there he has gone into the room now to kiss her! It quite makes my flesh creep. I wish the whole house would topple down on our heads and finish us all off at one stroke! I will shut myself up in some hole somewhere, and live quite alone, and never see anyone again—never, never! One's whole life seems made up of things that make one weep and make one angry!'

Macquart entered the room. Madame Rougon was on her knees, burying her face in her hands, and Serge, with tears streaming down his cheeks, was standing by the bedside supporting the head of the dying woman. She had not yet regained consciousness. The last flickering flames of the conflagration cast a ruddy reflection upon the ceiling of the room.

At last a convulsive tremor shook Marthe's body. She opened her eyes with an expression of surprise, and sat up in bed to glance around her. Then she clasped her hands together with a look of unutterable terror, and died even as she caught sight of Serge's cassock in the crimson glow.

THE END